W9-BZO-911

CAT MAN

BOOKS BY EDWARD HOAGLAND

Cat Man

The Circle Home

The Peacock's Tail

Notes from the Century Before: A Journal from British Columbia

The Courage of Turtles

Walking the Dead Diamond River

The Moose on the Wall

Red Wolves and Black Bears

African Calliope: A Journey to the Sudan

The Edward Hoagland Reader

The Tugman's Passage

City Tales

Seven Rivers West

Heart's Desire

The Final Fate of the Alligators

Balancing Acts

Tigers & Ice

Compass Points

Hoagland on Nature

qaji 1/21/17

CAT MAN

A novel

Edward Hoagland

THE LYONS PRESS
Guilford, Connecticut
An imprint of The Globe Pequot Press

Copyright © 1955 by Edward Hoagland

ALL RIGHTS RESERVED. No part of this book may be reproduced or
transmitted in any form by any means, electronic or mechanical, including
photocopying and recording, or by any information storage and retrieval
system, except as may be expressly permitted in writing from the publisher.
Requests for permission should be addressed to The Lyons Press, Attn:
Rights and Permissions Department, P.O. Box 480, Guilford, CT 06437.

The Lyons Press is an imprint of The Globe Pequot Press.

10 9 8 7 6 5 4 3 2 1

Printed in the United States of America

First published by Riverside Press, 1955

ISBN 1-58574-861-7

Library of Congress Cataloging-in-Publication data is available on file.

● FOR MARY

CON

Eby

Eby

TENTS

CAT MAN

Eby

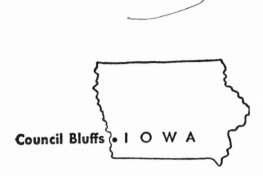

Council Bluffs • I O W A

BLOOD WAS SMEARED on the floor and on the door of 127 car. The print of a hand was outlined on the doorknob in a coating of blood. Blood stained the blankets on some of the beds in the front. The vestibule of the railroad sleeping car looked as though someone had come through with an enormous brush and lots of globby, thick brown paint. That was where they'd beaten Heavy, the porter, with the handle broken off his own broom.

Fiddler woke up because the niggers on the other side of the partition which divided the car were raising a hullabaloo about something. The worst thing about niggers was their noisiness. If they'd been more quiet about it, Fiddler wouldn't have minded so much when they reached their black hands through cracks and stole if you turned your back.

The niggers were jabbering about a "killin'," and Fiddler gathered from what they said that the killin' was not in their own section of the car, but in the Animal Department's. The information snapped him from his sleep like a fire alarm. Usually he shared his bunk with somebody else, but the department was so short-handed right now that he had the whole space to himself. It scared him, being alone in the bunk. He rolled over to the edge and looked up and down the aisle, seeing very little because it was still dark. He could see nobody in the aisle. The train wasn't moving, which meant it must be standing in the yards of today's town. He tried to think what town the route card listed for today — a couple of weeks west of Chicago. Today was Sunday, he finally calculated, but that didn't help him remember the town. He gave up. It didn't matter anyhow.

Voices went past outside, probably the Train crew going to get the work started. The car stank of wine and piss as always after a payday night. Fiddler put on his clothes, swung down from his bunk in the second tier, the middle tier. He started checking to make sure his friends were all right. The bear man and the lion man slept together, and Fiddler could see them both. Red was in his bunk. Brownie's bed was empty. Brownie was the Animal Department boss. Nobody would kill a boss; but Brownie wouldn't have gotten out of bed if there hadn't been some kind of trouble. In the bunk opposite Fiddler's, Chief lay deeply asleep. But the niggers kept saying "Chief." Fiddler could pick that word from their yammering and it made him stop breathing to listen — to nothing. The white section of 127 car was quiet; people had scarcely begun to wake up. Chief was snoring, a little restlessly now. He looked drunk, but his face held all its dark, rich color. He wasn't hurt.

Fiddler had made the mistake of leaving his shoes on the floor for the night, payday night. A shallow yellow pool surrounded them. He got his fingers stinking wet when he picked them up, and the soles reeked. He'd have to wear them and he deserved it. The rummies didn't even bother to aim, getting rid of the beer they drank, and he'd known it; he'd seen it a million times — the first trickle under the can door becoming a multitude of trickles by midnight. And when there were too many winos trying to get into the can at once he'd seen them go right on the floor, hoping nobody was awake to notice, if they were alive enough to "hope" anything. Fiddler was disgusted with himself for forgetting how it was on a payday night, as if he didn't care. He sat on Red's bunk to put on his shoes. At least they'd be stone-broke by Monday and quit messing up the place for a few days. Even in spots where the piss hadn't got, there was an itchy grime on the floor.

Red slept like a little boy, but he had more freckles than ten little boys.

Fiddler walked up toward the front of the car, past the Elephant Department. Further still, the Ringstock men were sleeping peacefully. The horses were the ring stock, and the men who had charge of them were smaller than the Elephant or Animal men — a tough, scrappy bunch of cowboys and ex-racetrack grooms, plus the usual winos every department had.

Little Chief, the young Indian on Horses, was up. He always got up early. He grinned at Fiddler and with a sweep of his right arm indicated all the spilled blood. It looked like a gang of kids had been playing with paint. "Who —" Fiddler started to ask. Little Chief shushed him and led him over to the porter's bunk, which was fitted with a purple curtain, as if for some fancy Extra Special Guy. Little Chief tore aside the curtain and pulled back the sheet to show the welts and red slashes and the sprawling fresh black scabs that covered the man's back and rear end. Between the scabs the flesh sagged and gleamed the limp, watery white of a frog's belly. Little Chief pinched several spots to prove that the blood would still flow. The porter, Heavy, groaned but did nothing, said nothing.

Little Chief answered the groan — "Son of a bitch!"

"So who did it for Christ sake?"

"Chief; your big Chief and me. We got him. He tried to cut him and I got the knife — that great big butcher knife he had — and I held it till Chief could get him. He came for Chief with the knife, and I got it. I couldn't get it away, but I kept onto it till Chief could reach him. I had it by the blade." Little Chief raised his left hand, jerked it forward in a grabbing motion. The muscles under his cheekbones stood out like stretched strings. His forehead clenched to hold the eyes in. Most of a sheet was wrapped around his hand. "I got it by the blade and we took care of him then. We beat the piss out of him then!" Little Chief grinned his quick, handsome grin and struck the air with his good hand. He spoke fast. He let a lot of words come out at once, and a lot more, and a lot more, in a rhythm. He always spoke that way. Fiddler told himself that Little Chief must be okay.

"You go see Brownie. He'll get you to a hospital." Fiddler started back to where Chief slept. He was afraid Chief was hurt. He was really frightened.

"They've got a car coming. I just wait an' it comes."

"Yeah, Brownie will fix it," Fiddler said, mostly to himself. How long had that kid been up? Did he stay up all night? Grabbing a knife by the blade!

A few people were beginning to hump around in their beds and cough — prepare to get up. Chief was lying on his side, facing the aisle, trying to light a cigarette, being very deliberate and patient, emotionless. He looked at Fiddler without a sign of recognition. Neither of them said anything. Chief's eyes were a charred black, dull as ashes. The cigarette caught the fire and Chief's wide, husky face sucked powerfully. He was trying to remember something; he looked blankly at Fiddler. He smoked and smoked, inhaling everything. Wrinkles in his forehead signified a headache, and a bad one. The cigarette glowed to a fierce burn at each draw. Gradually Chief's eyes lighted; embers in them lighted, flickered, and sparkled and danced like candle flames. His eyes no longer hung ponderously in a stare, but darted and thrust at Fiddler's, up and down the aisle, into the bunk below, through the ventilation grating — outside. "Where's that crazy kid?" Chief asked suddenly.

"He's okay. He's up front."

"WHERE'S THAT CRAZY KID?"

"Hey you Wampus, Fat Gut!" shouted Little Chief, jogging down the aisle with a handsome grin smoothly spreading on his face, not showing the pain in any way that Fiddler could make out.

Chief had kept all his clothes on in bed, so it didn't take him long to get up. The aisle was filling with men now, and the hoarse burble of talking, the first staccato coughs. Chief was still partly drunk — rocky on his feet like a bear, with the strength to pull out a four-year-old tree by the roots. "What is this here!" he roared, seeing the floor. The talking stopped, but not the coughing. The coughing only increased as more old winos woke up and straggled into the aisle with sour, hung-over expressions hardly flinching when the whisper of Chief's fight was passed along. Coughing echoed in the car and drowned all other sounds — rat-tat-tatting, gasping, gargling, coughs which in a second ran from bullfrog chug to teapot whistle, which skidded from low to high pitch like a yodel — snorts, wheezes, sneezes through the throat, coughs that eased forth cautiously and coughs that must have clawed out flesh and blood. But the old men kept the clams in their mouths; they didn't spit them on the floor. — They were sobering up.

Chief and Little Chief kidded each other, pretended to cough. They were in good humor. They ignored the injured hand and greeted the winos — "WHY DON'T THEY GO OUTSIDE TO DIE?" Nobody answered or made a move, so Chief himself started outside after "FRESH AIR!" Elephant men on one foot trying to pull on shoes hobbled out of the way. Ringstock men lighting cigarettes humbly let their matches get blown out as the two Chiefs, rowdy as miniature cyclones, plunged by. Fiddler trailed behind, practically biting his nails, worrying. There were places at the front of the car, in corners, where it seemed Heavy had crouched while they were beating him. Blood had coagulated in ugly splotches the size of frying pans. Heavy had so many enemies in the car, he must have been scared to cry for help.

Outside, Little Chief stopped and took a leak between the cars. His hand hampered him, unbuttoning and buttoning his pants, but he didn't joke about it. He tried to pretend nothing was wrong until he lost his temper — "*God*dam!" His hand — his arm to the elbow — looked grisly, looked really bad. Chief scowled. The mood of both Chiefs became somber. Fiddler felt more confident of being able to keep them under control.

"We better wait right here. If Brownie's getting an ambulance he'll come here," Fiddler said.

"He's getting a car." Little Chief wanted it understood.

Red jumped down the steps of the train. "Car — schmar, it better get here quick!" He was flailing his arms in the air, trying to force them into a shirt, and ready to talk a blue streak. "Did the bastard cut you that bad? Jesus, we were all asleep. We would have killed him for you." Red smiled. He loved excitement. He was Fiddler's age; they were friends because of that, but not close friends. — "Where's the road, Fiddler?"

"Jesus, where is it? I don't know." No car or ambulance would drive across a mile of cornfields to reach them. There had to be a road. A house would be a clue, but they couldn't discover a single house in sight or even a trace of a farmer's dumping road. The flatcars had to be unloaded at a crossing, and they couldn't even see the flats. It was too dark. Dawn was on the horizon still, and high in the sky.

Chief cursed briefly. "Son of a bitching — they stick us out here!" But it was an unusual morning when they didn't have to walk half, three-quarters of a mile down the tracks to the crossing. Stranding the cars which had people in them on the siding furthest from where the people needed to be was a regular practice — so long as no big shot was involved. The big shots all traveled on the second train, which had hardly left yesterday's town yet.

"Did anybody see where Brownie went?" Fiddler asked, not expecting an answer.

A mob of Ringstock and Elephant men came out, but they had no more idea where the crossing was than Chief or Fiddler. They eyed Little Chief's crusted swathe of sheets and mumbled, "Where are we?" None of them had enough clothes. They were all winos. It was chilly so early in the morning, a Sunday morning. They shivered. Early morning was like a soured pear in their mouths. They pushed sluggish fingers through their hair and left it as waxy and flattened as ever. The pointlessness of having to be up before five when very little would be done before seven wasn't worth laughing at, spitting at. And this was just the beginning. They were beyond Detroit, Chicago, and the states full of cities now. There'd be one-day stands clear to Seattle, and pretty soon the jumps each night would start getting so long the circus would madly set up and tear down for a single show — two meals a day and a grueling rush, rush.

The men separated on a departmental basis. The Elephant men set off in one direction and Ringstock chose the opposite way. They were too cold and old and sick to enjoy the gamble or make bets. Most of them would rather have found a beer joint than the crossing anyway.

"Come on, there it comes," said Chief.

Little Chief nodded. "Yeah, she's comin'." Two lights were floating in the distance, swinging. They weren't car headlights, and they made the tracks shine under them. Steadily they came nearer, suspended in the air. A bell dinged warningly. It was a string of flats with two brakemen with lanterns on the front because it was being pushed. All along the track the departments ranged themselves to catch a ride — Animals, Elephants, Ringstock, Lay-out, Cookhouse, Sideshow, Wardrobe, Big Top, Seats, Props, Lights. The last, oldest, sickest winos clambered out of the sleeping cars and ran to try and save themselves a hike of God knows how far. The train was coming fast. The first wagons were the Cookhouse wagons, but before Fiddler could recognize all of them in the half-light, the Sideshow wagons came in view, rattling along. In no time the train was abreast of Fiddler, with men already clinging precariously to the sides of the flatcars, struggling to get on. The bell ding-ding-ding-ding-dinged. These hick engineers weren't used to having a swarm of men pile on a train while it was moving.

Suddenly Fiddler worried about Little Chief — the train was going so fast — he dashed beside it and just began to drop behind when Little Chief nimbly pounced like a one-armed monkey against the train, Chief next to him matching stride for stride. Little Chief's legs and body went up in a ball, pivoted on his good hand, and tumbled down lightly like a wad of cotton on the boards of the flatcar under a wagon. Fiddler and Chief both leapt then and landed safely.

The three of them were together. Fiddler smiled, tried to conceal his breathlessness. Sometimes there was no way of telling Chief was a middle-aged man. He grinned like a kid — a wild, runaway kid. His eyes pierced into Fiddler, dancing with tiny lights. Fiddler was going to warn him not to start jumping off and on the train just because it was fun to do it once. But Little Chief burst in, "*God*dam, the sonofabitch is bleeding again! I hit it. Lookit the thing!"

Chief scowled with a dull, drunken face.

The blood was finding channels between the layers of sheet, soaking the sheet, softening and sliding between the old scabs. It leaked out, on Little Chief's pants. He held the hand away from him and the blood ran between the rivets on the flatcar's steel, dripping faster and faster. Small drops clumped together, forming long cylindrical blobs that hardly broke from one another, they came so fast.

BETWEEN LUNCH and the start of the come-in, when the crowd nosing around was as big as it ever got, two niggers standing near the highway had had a fight. It happened not far from the Animal Department's top and Fiddler saw most of it. One smashed a wine bottle across the other's face. The jig who had been hit, and evidently blinded, stumbled out on the road screaming and was killed by a car which couldn't possibly have avoided him. The jig killer, if you could call him that, ran in a frenzy in the opposite direction until he was cornered by the cops and clubbed like a rat in a feedbin.

Everybody in the Animal Department thought the whole thing hilarious. And when news arrived that during the pursuit the cops had blundered onto the great perennial crap game which included almost every Negro in the show — that the entire Big Top crew was under arrest — it began to sound as though the Lord had Come Down in the Animal top. People went nuts. They howled, got down on the ground and couldn't get up, they thought it was so funny.

Fiddler didn't say a word, but he made up his mind to quit. He felt ashamed to be living with guys who were so cruel, who had no more respect for law and order. And he'd been disgusted by the filthy, ragged way they lived for a long time. Fiddler didn't tell anybody about his plan because he had no real friends and, after all, he didn't want to lose the circus job before being sure of something better. During the come-in he stood watch as usual in front of the cages, but he left as soon as he got off duty, when the show started. He hurried and changed his clothes — changed his shirt and socks. He didn't have very many clothes. No extra pair of pants, no decent shoes, nothing to put on his hair, no comb. Fiddler had been with the circus three weeks, taking care of the gnu and then being shifted to cats as the department lost men. Not owning anything for the rain, he'd prayed for dry weather. Except for the first night or so his luck had held.

"I met a girl who wants somebody to sit next to her in the show. So I'm obliging her!" He told the quickest story he could think of, but nobody would lend him a clean pair of pants. Joining way back in Albany, he still hadn't made any friends. He needed a haircut too. Everybody was calling him Fiddler because of his hair, and fairies mistook him for one of them. But he couldn't borrow so much as a quarter from these bums.

Detroit proper was a high-priced six-mile bus ride, too high-priced. He didn't want a skid row job anyway. He wanted to be out of the city, away from bars. Near the lot there was a choice of the trackless trolley yards or a big De Soto factory. He headed for the factory — work with a future in it and a "ladder" to climb. With his training Fiddler deserved a whitecollar job. He felt very, very happy to be quitting. He walked with a lilt, phrasing a line: "I'm an accountant and I can work harder than any old fogey you've got now. I'm young. I'm all set to go." The music for the lion act tingled in the air. When he crossed the highway he was fast on his feet, dodging cars like Fanta, the cat trainer, in the center ring.

Trim white signs pointed the way to the employment office. The buildings were as large as big-city railroad stations, bustling, whistling and smoking. Glassed-in bridges connected them, and wide roads. Such a conglomeration of clinking, chain-rattling, buzz-sawing and bebopping came out, it was easy to visualize the whole history of car manufacture going on at once inside. Stanley Steamers spluttering. Lincoln Continentals whining to Florida at well over a mile a minute. The office was painted a delicate green, and the girls were primped and manicured pretty as dreams. He filled out a form and went in to see an Assistant Personnel Manager.

The manager read through Fiddler's form, clutching it close to his face and craning his head out of the chair like a turtle half turned on its back. He was a queer, nearsighted old bird.

"You graduated from high school and were in the Navy and went to accounting school, David, but then what did you do?" In spite of the way he looked he asked his first question quick as a fox.

"Oh, I was home. And I stayed around New York awhile. — I've been traveling around a little."

"Yes, what did you do?"

"Well, I went out west — "

"Did you work?"

Fiddler fidgeted. "Well, just a few jobs here and there; various jobs. I haven't worked much. I wanted to see a few places. I mean I wanted to see just a little of the world while I was young and single, before I settled down for good. It's educational. I saw New York and a few places out west — "

"You had an opportunity to 'see the world' in the Navy. — Do you like the circus? You've only been with them for three weeks according to what you've written here. And you don't give us any other information about the last six months, and you don't even have a certificate from your accounting school — do you? You've been what they call 'on the bum.' You wouldn't stay with us two weeks, I expect. You wouldn't be paid until the end of your second week here, and I expect you'd starve before the first week was over — if you had any money you'd get your hair cut! Or else you'd wander off."

"I wash! I keep myself decent! I don't go round knifing people! I'm not a bum! The circus isn't right — I've read books — I was fourth in my class in school! and we weren't poor. These clothes — "

"And you're an alcoholic. It's written all over your face as plain as it can be. And that's why you don't have any money, and that's why you can't remember what you've done for the last six months."

Fiddler didn't feel like interrupting again, or stirring in his seat. There was a short, excruciating silence.

"I wish you would tell your friends not to come over here, David. We talked to half the circus over here this morning. You stay with

the one job at least long enough — at least stay with the circus! —
what's going to become of you if you're too restless to even hold
a job with a *circus!* And get your hair cut, David. You'd be a
good-looking boy if you didn't look like a drunk. And tell your
friends not to come over here. We aren't a sanitorium. We hire
Detroit people who are sound of mind and body and intend to live
here permanently." The Assistant Personnel Manager tossed Fiddler's form sheet in the wastebasket and finished his speech. "Don't
let anybody else come over here, because I'm simply not going to
have the patience to lecture many more of you men. I'd like to
help you, but I'm running out of patience."

He still resembled a turtle, slumping in his chair, round, flat-
chested, with small goggle-eyes. By some quirk Fiddler remembered
when he was a child putting his finger up to the beak of a pet turtle
to see how tame it was. The turtle had bit — pinched his finger
white. After holding on for a suitable length of time the turtle
let go just as abruptly as it had bit and then serenely went about its
business, forgetting the incident. The man was like that, softly
dumdeedumming, preoccupied with things in his desk drawer.

Fiddler's spirits were in his toes when he left the office. The
lawns surrounding the buildings had been clipped as close as golf
greens. The buildings were gigantic whitewashed blocks of stone
whose windows glinted hard as quartz. Fiddler kept on the grass
instead of on the paved walk and kicked the grass.

The circus remained where it had been, with music and flags
waving and the whole blue-green immensity of canvas in the big
top undulating because of only a slight, fresh breeze. All of
Detroit had assembled on the lot if not inside the top. Traffic was
bottlenecked. Innumerable balloons were escaping and innumerable children were crying for more, and chameleons-peanuts-pink-
candy-beanies. The sideshow barkers were keyed up to their best,
summoning every footsore, ancient wisecrack, pulling every verbal
gimmick to draw and ream the suckers. Fiddler had to show his
mealticket as identification before the big top guards would let him
go under the sidewall.

Behind the cage line Chief was watering the cats. The tigers were drinking. Chief watched them, brooding and so intent it seemed that he was in the cage, waiting for them to finish and attack.

"Can you work, Fiddler? Can you stand up and work?" Chief was scornful.

"Sure; why shouldn't I be able to?"

"You do the rest of this. I've got an *appointment*. There's no work in this."

Appointment meant that Chief was going drinking with some of his Indian friends. "Okay," Fiddler told him. There had been several mornings when Fiddler had not been worth much as a helper. He owed Chief a lot of work. Chief could always work in the morning. He could bulldoze through the worst hangover on earth.

The band was blaring, fake rockets were being shot off, and all the rest of the hogwash. Still it was peaceful being alone behind the cages and nobody watching, the noise in the background and all the fools braying and jigging to it. Fiddler picked at his scalp nervously. He had dandruff. The hairs were falling out at his temples — he could pull them out without the slightest twinge of pain. And yet his hair strayed shamefully down the nape of his neck and dangerously hung on the tops of his ears, so that people were calling him "Fiddler."

It was true. There was no work to watering. Just watch them drink. But watching them destroyed the feeling of being alone. One tiger was through. A barred door had been closed between her cage and her mate's, and she lay uneasily against the wall, her face turned toward Fiddler. She stared at him with eyes liquid and urgent, wide. The tiger eyes couldn't plead, but they poured around his head the insistence of a frantic queen. Fiddler had seen what Chief did. He tried it — an old-fashioned Bronx cheer, but soft and incredibly slow, the lips loose, like the daintiest snuffle. The tiger lurched up, paced fast, her eyes like floodlights on him. She ruffled her breath with the sound he had made and he answered. The thought that he could talk with her was very pleasing. She paced back and forth, back and forth, exactly twice, as if it were a formality or a rhythm. Then she sat down. Her haunches almost touched the bars. Her head and shoulders pointed away, but nervously she looked around every few seconds. Fiddler gingerly placed his hand on the base of her tail, began scratching. At the first contact she started and trembled. Her seven-foot body shook at the touch of his fingertips. He took a stance so that only a part of his arm would be within clawing range, so that he could in an instant jump backwards if she were playing a trick. But the tiger had set no trap. She stayed sitting, wriggling the muscles up her back and stirring with each tickle. Fiddler relaxed somewhat, let his fingers creep higher on her body; the fur was so soft and the smaller muscles felt round and vaguely like a girl's fingers when he pressed them. His hand was a baby's, patting its mother's back, stroking her fuzzy bathrobe.

The tiger rose and padded straight at him — he got out of the way. First she gazed vacantly through him like a wistful girl, and then she plastered on Fiddler her hot wide eyes which could have gulped him up and crackled the bars to tinfoil.

She paced back and forth, back and forth, exactly twice, seated herself and mildly began rubbing the bunches of fur around her cheek and neck on the bars. She made the soft fluffing sound and Fiddler answered. She rubbed and rubbed — the edge of her chin, behind her ears, her eyebrows. It didn't take Fiddler long to get up nerve. The tiger sat broadside to the bars. He stood even with her ribs, where the forepaw nearest the bars would be out of position to reach for him and the other would have to be awkwardly poked backward under her stomach. He scratched her shoulder as if he were scratching a cow. By the time he'd managed to picture the tiger merely flipping on her side and making an easy catch — tearing him to shreds — by that time he was too immersed in doing a good job of scratching to be frightened. Industriously he burrowed into her white stomach-fur to find the itchy places. She cooed the Bronx cheer and he tried to figure out where in her nose or throat it was produced. She kept massaging the side of her face against the bars. Fiddler longed to rub it for her and only with effort compelled his hands to stick low, on her shoulder, where at least she couldn't get him with her teeth. Not for weeks had Fiddler felt so pleased with himself and happy. The shoulder was bigger than his whole chest; he could lay his fingers in the rug-deep fur between the ribs and count the heart beats. With teeny ticklings he stirred the tiger into ecstasy, forced her thick paws to work against the floor and froze her giant body still as ice in luscious pleasure; wrung a sigh from her belly. Fiddler made the tiger's head nod up and down as if she were a trained horse. For a long while he kept it up, staying behind her shoulder.

Council Bluffs • 11

THE FLATCAR creaked and banged, jerking and slamming against the ones in front and behind. A loose bolt on a big red water truck clacked. The truck's springs were bad; they squeaked. Poorly packed objects shifted in wagons and thumped. The rocking motion of the train and the noise caused the monkeys to caper and screech in their cages. The frisky bears wrestled, wuffed when they were knocked against the bars. The herds of horses in the stockcars munched hay, shuffled and tromped on the floor like herds of centipedes. Male lions roared at intervals, which started the females growling in sympathy — the cubs bawled goose-squawks out of high-flown baby pride.

Tickatickatickaticka Tickatickatickaticka Tickatickatickaticka sounded the wheels over the stretches of track.

Little Chief's hand kept bleeding. Fiddler gripped his own two hands together. He couldn't just sit there watching the bandages give off blood. It welled out of the bandages, melting and by-passing the old clots.

"You know about stopping it?" Chief asked angrily. He glared at Fiddler and Little Chief.

Little Chief had withdrawn into his thoughts. He seemed unaware that he was bleeding. "I know they use tourniquets," Fiddler said. "I've forgotten how. They taught us in the Navy."

"They taught you crap in the Navy! Here's what you do." Chief took hold of the arm and probed at the underside with his thumbs. When he found the right spot to press the blood-flow slowed considerably. "See?" he demanded of Fiddler.

"Yep."

Little Chief paid no attention. He masked his face as if he were listening to something in the distance, as if he were stalking something. He bent over, the pupils of his eyes expanding, like an animal hunting. The slant at the corners of his eyes made him look like a wolf. He was lithe and proud and wild as a wolf. He was Fiddler's age — a kid — but always an Indian kid, acting like one. Usually at this time in the morning he'd be riding his horses from the train to the lot, mounted bareback on one and leading the others by rope halters. They were stocky, cream-white performers' horses and he looked strange on them — limber-bodied, slant-eyed, poised to whoop and kill a buffalo. The people in the streets of any town knew that he was an Indian. He made them know it. Fiddler had seen them drive cars onto the sidewalk to get out of his way. Sometimes Little Chief would boast that "in his country" the whites were afraid even yet of his tribe. He was a Blackfoot. And then he'd taunt Chief for being a Mohawk — they had been beaten so soon. And then the two of them would catch each other by the hair, when they were partly drunk, laughing like chuckling bears, and threaten to take each other's scalp. Chief was darker-colored, burly and not so slant-eyed. Chief was much older, stronger; his wildness lay deeper, in his chocolate-black eyes, waiting like a bomb. Little Chief was a yearling cub compared to Fiddler's Chief. And Fiddler's Chief, in the right mood, could be a father. In a rough, stormy way he'd treat Fiddler like a son. At those times Fiddler felt invincible, peacock-sure, as if he himself were an Indian.

Still there were people struggling onto the train to save themselves some exercise. Now they belonged to the Cookhouse or one of the other departments which started its work earlier than the Animal men. They'd woken up earlier and walked farther. For several of them riding the flats was a new experience, and they strutted a little before settling down. They searched for prize positions "to see to California." They climbed into the cabs of trucks and roosted on the seats of tractors. One newcomer had a

loud, bitter laugh which he used regularly every few seconds. Another man, as soon as houses began to appear, boasted about what
he was planning to steal before it got fully light.

Chief shrugged his shoulders impatiently. The laugh was getting
on his nerves.

Fiddler couldn't see very far ahead but he knew they were nearing the crossing. Most of the circus men along the tracks weren't
bothering to grab a ride any more. Only a few show-off kids took
the trouble, and they had an easy time because the train was snorting and grating its wheels, preparing to stop.

"Get out!" Chief shouted. "GET OUT!" He kept his hands
steady on Little Chief's arm and turned the rest of his body —
"You better get OUT!" The man with the loud laugh stared at
him scared stiff. For a moment he didn't seem certain if Chief was
speaking to him or somebody else. So Chief made it clear. "YOU!"
he said with a fist and pointed finger blunt as a gun.

The man didn't jump off the train himself. But his laugh did.
He lost his laugh right away.

Chief carefully readjusted his hands on Little Chief's arm and
surveyed the scenery calmly. When he was drunk his moods
shifted suddenly. He turned on Fiddler with a gruff smile. "What
are you going to do, Fiddler?" Chief liked to catch his friends by
surprise, see if he could stump them.

"I'm going to sober you up."

"Yeah."

"I am!"

Chief grinned. "I bet you would, Fiddle."

They were on good terms, which made Fiddler very happy. Riding the flats in the open air was fun. Even being up so early wasn't
too bad because of what you could see — the white dawn rising
from the horizon like a cloudbank blowing upward. The day was
going to be nice and it would be fun spending it sobering somebody
up, especially Chief, working with him and making him quiet and
reasonable. Every shade of blue could be seen in the sky, from the
white-blue horizon to the pockets of night remaining straight
overhead. The sky was limitless. Low, knotty brush grew beside

the tracks. Fiddler couldn't tell where the good farmland began because the ground rolled. Dew or a light night rain had wet the brush so that it glistened in points. It was beautiful — a hazy gray with star-points glistening — but this was not good land. The train squealed, the wheels or brakes squealed high like a pig, as it slowed down. Fiddler was constantly looking for a place to quit the circus, and he would have liked to get a farm job.

When the train had come to a halt they helped Little Chief down. "I can get off," he said, but they didn't take him seriously. His skin had paled to a yellow; his eyes were drowsy. The three of them walked together and then Red ran up and made a fourth. The injured hand hung down by itself. Everybody avoided touching it. The blood was the color of shellac; nothing else could be seen. The sheet was painted over with blood.

The flatcars had been parked at the crossing on a track off the main line, where they could be kept all day and where the second train's flats could be fitted in beside them. The switch engine unhooked and went back, probably to bring the sleeping cars closer now that nobody was in them.

The Train crew had already started work. They were pulling the runs from underneath the lead flatcar. They yanked with bent arms, straining in unison. In jolts the long steel planks slid out and were lowered to make an incline down which the trucks and wagons could roll to the road. It was like pulling fifty-foot swords out of rusty sheaths; it was rough work. The men were panting when they finished. Next they had to lay iron plates as bridges between all the flatcars, knock the chocks from under countless tires, wrench a hundred heavy wagonpoles into position to be hooked on to trucks and caterpillars. They had to unload the entire train in a couple of hours and then when the second train came they'd have that to unload too. The most unpleasant work in the circus was Train crew — the hardest, the worst hours, plenty of missed meals. Only winos took it, and Little Chief, crippled and dizzy as he was, could have accomplished more than most of them. At least Little Chief had one whole hand. A job on the trains was as hazardous to fingers as taming snapping turtles.

But the mangled hands weren't what shocked you. The Train crew made way for Little Chief and his escort, and there were a lot of young guys Fiddler's age — stumbling and crouched over and sick, feeling the way — they couldn't seem to see the ground, some of them. Blistered faces, bloodshot eyes, wrists jiggling out of control, clothes that looked like rat skins sewed together. Ministers in missions had sent them out to get a job. Someone at the lot had told them, "They won't hire you up here. You go down to the train. Go to the crossing. They won't hire you up here." Fiddler had said that to people himself — black-and-blue, toothless winos who would start hoofing it, four or five miles sometimes, because they couldn't afford to take a bus.

Fiddler's expression hardened. He remembered his own befuddled face in gas station mirrors six or seven weeks ago. Not toothless or blue-black, but traced with tiny, swelling arteries, his nose a sharpening, hungry line. And when he looked away from the Train crew faces the pants were there or the shoes, duplicates of what he'd worn his first weeks on the show.

Brownie, the Animal Department boss, was waiting in the no-man's land between the townies and the Train crew. A hundred-fifty or two hundred townies had assembled to watch the circus unload. Brownie stood in front of them as ill at ease as if they'd been a Sunday school. Brownie's pants were olive-green; his shirt flared red. Picking him out of a crowd was not difficult. He was old, tanned, and strong in a wiry way, like an overseer of slaves, Fiddler liked to say, and blind in one eye. A busy Red Cross or Gray Lady in a uniform waited beside Brownie, scratching her hands together, ogling Little Chief, wondering if "that" was "*him.*" Brownie couldn't answer her, not politely. He was a funny man. All his life with carnies and circuses and he still couldn't stand and pass the time of day courteously with a townie. Sarcasm was as much a part of his speech as the Florida accent he had. He could no more control one than the other. He wasn't looking at the woman. She was confronted with that sunken sore of a left eye and in an added flurry because of it. Brownie's good eye was fixed on Chief and Fiddler. He listened to the lady, obviously not trusting himself to speak, and grinned as though she were a Talking Frog.

"I goddam well couldn't call for a cop car, could I?" he muttered to Fiddler.

She fluttered like a moth and led them to a station wagon with some benevolent name lettered on its door. "Are you going to be all right?" she asked Little Chief. She fingered her bosom to straighten it or feel if it was still there. "My, we had no idea it was going to be this serious."

"Ma'am, it's not very serious. It's just his hand," Brownie told her.

Chief watched phlegmatically. Little Chief got in the car without help and was driven away, the lady, at the wheel, waving goodby.

"Why didn't the Horse boss do it, Brownie? Why did he make you do the dirty work?" Fiddler wanted to know.

"He didn't make me do anything. That bastard couldn't make me blow my nose! His man was out of it, that's why. He didn't care what happened to Chief, so he was going to call the cops. His man is off the show. He can't work with that hand. So he was going to get the cops because it was the least trouble. He didn't give a damn."

"Yep, but they couldn't bother Chief, when the guy tried to kill him. If Heavy tries to kill you, they can't bother you then! It was self-defense!"

Red interrupted, "Let's get coffee, Judge." He was like a finicky old man, having to have his coffee promptly the first thing every morning.

"They don't use the same laws for showpeople, you know. They want to leave them alone. If the trouble doesn't involve people in the town they won't worry about it — you're out in a day and the next town, or the next state, can take care of it — *unless* you go and rub their noses in it. And if you make it so they have to *'investigate'* " — Brownie could pack a pile of contempt into a word — "why you can't tell what the sonofabitches'll do. — They'll quarantine your leopards for having chickenpox!"

"Do you suppose it would be too much to ask if we went and got coffee now, Judge?" Once Red figured out some little joke, like calling Fiddler "Judge," he never knew when to stop.

"Okay, I'll go with you. Is Chief coming?"

"He's gone."

"God, we'd better stay with him. He may get in a fight. He's still drunk."

"That son of a bitch better get with it today," Brownie warned. "I won't take any crap. I got up at four A.M., and he better make it worth it."

"Yeah, well the joint's up the street here. We've got to walk quite a ways. The lot's up here and the joint's on the way." Red's mind was single-track. Fiddler would rather not have gone with him at all.

Most of the circus men except the Train crew were heading in the same direction. Brownie was one of those who stayed behind. He went to find his truck on the flatcars. It was a stubby blue pickup squeezed between the blacksmith wagon and the cages, and until he'd seen it safely off the train he wouldn't leave it. He'd get a paper, second-hand if necessary, and sit in the truck and read every article twice over, sure that some idiot would squash the blacksmith wagon into his precious, darling truck unless he stayed on the spot to supervise.

Fiddler and Red joined the throng on the road. The twenty-four-hour man had given directions about where coffee could be bought at this hour in the morning. Fiddler didn't especially want coffee. Since he hadn't been drinking his mouth tasted okay. He wasn't sleepy or cold. But for Chief and Red coffee was a ritual, and this morning Fiddler had to stick with Chief.

As usual there was a battle. The townies had massed themselves across the road to watch the operations, as they said. Like chickens they risked suffocation, flocking together at the spectacle. The circus men pushed into the townies, oaring with their arms to get through. The townies, thinking that something exciting must be happening, got up on their tiptoes — which only made it easier to push them aside. Temporary openings were forced. But the trucks and cats were being started up. The engines made a racket. The lions were grunting on the flatcars. The Train crew boss began tweedling directions with his whistle. And very soon the townies became convinced that something they must not miss seeing was being done. They pressed forward, closing the passages which the circus men had made. Eagerly they chattered questions at each other and vigorously they blocked the road.

Fiddler's technique for wiggling through was to assume a pleasant, affable expression and gaze straight at the townies as though he was about to answer all their questions. Then when they relented and made room for him to speak, he said, "Excuse me," and gained as much ground as he possibly could. Red worked on a parallel path, treading on people's toes and rubbing up against the women so that they would either give him a thrill, or get out of his way, or both. Some of the older circus men circled the crowd and some, with patience, simply waited on the outskirts for the first tractor to come ramming down the runs from the train and scatter the townies like so many grasshoppers in a field.

Of the methods Red's proved to be the fastest. It seemed to be the most fun also — "One little woman did a burlie house routine right close against me!"

Chief was in a gang of men, outwalking them with big strides, when Red and Fiddler caught up with him. "I'm gonna see that fella!" Chief said very forcefully. Little Chief still occupied his mind, and probably drinking and the fight. He might go on a bat and get lost, arrested.

"We have to clean those cages today some time," Fiddler reminded, wanting to be subtle.

Chief glowered.

Red broke in, "This is swank." He nodded at the houses along the street, the hammocks, lace curtains, screened porches, the flower gardens in the back. Children had crept outdoors to sit on doorsteps and under windows on the grass. They were soundless, unsmiling. Chief was soundless and unsmiling too. He chose the center of the street for his path and overtook group after group of circus men, who parted for him, eying him.

As soon as they could hear the trucks Chief led Red and Fiddler onto the sidewalk. "Want to get killed?" he demanded, and he was laughing, then relapsed into silence. Fiddler didn't like to have to walk so close to the houses. It made him uneasy. He imagined men's and women's faces sneering at him from behind the frilled curtains, passing judgment on him — "a bum." Suddenly the cavalcade of trucks with long gaudy wagon strings in tow monopolized the street, loud as fleets of fire engines, hosing the whole neighborhood with torrents of noise. Racket-banners flew that slapped from house to house to house along the rows. The pandemonium must have made the snottiest grandmother blink and duck. The trucks and trailing wagons swept out of sight.

"I'm goin' to chew somebody up today," said Red, chewing on a stalk of grass. "Jesus-Jehosophat! Today's goin' to be a good day for me. The first copper I meet I'm goin' to spit on his badge. I'm goin' to take off today. Where shall I go, Fid? Arizona's the place, none of this cold all the time, rain — no rain in Arizona. The stinkin' monkeys, they'll have to get somebody else to take care of the monkeys. And you can come with me, Fid."

"Don't get your balls in an uproar," Fiddler told him.

Whoever was leading turned left on a backlot dirt road. The new road was much narrower, hemmed in by cornfields, without houses. The corn was chest high. There was no room to spread out, and Chief was surrounded by clusters of people and not so conspicuous; but still he was the object of attention. The Seat men and some of the men on Props, Lights and Wardrobe looked him over, not saying much. Obviously they all knew about the fight. Chief ignored everybody. The flimsy circus cap perched on top of his bushy, black hair like a toy. Chief was not tall but he was husky as a bear, and he sort of ambled, fast, like a bear. His teeth showed, and the missing teeth; he was poking his tongue in and out through the holes as he often did when thinking.

Chief heard the bus before anyone else. "Want to get killed?" he challenged Fiddler again. The circus bus plowed into their midst honking, its door open. Several bosses stuck their heads out the windows shouting at people in their departments that if they thought they'd have time for coffee before work they were wrong.

The men whose names were called pulled themselves into the moving bus and were carried away. Another swift squadron of trucks passed, hauling stakedrivers and Cookhouse wagons and caterpillars on carriages, raising eddies of dust. It made Fiddler impatient to get to the lot and skip the coffee.

"God, you people make me go a long ways to get you your coffee."

Chief snorted. "What the hell is that? Get the hell outa here then!"

Red had a broad, insolent grin on his puss, growing bigger and bigger. Fiddler's temper started heating up — but Red was looking up the road, not at him. Somebody familiar was standing there at the side of the road — the pale, fleshless face, the unmistakable jerking of the jaw. Fiddler quickly clamped a grip on the muscles around his own mouth; but Red didn't make the effort. Red grinned and laughed outright. Taylor was standing there talking to himself at a great rate, his lips gibbering up and down, his eyes boring at Chief. "Look at that guy!" Red crowed. Red positively leered with anticipation. They couldn't hear Taylor yet — only watch his mouth race. Drawing nearer and nearer Red cocked his head, sprained his ears to catch the snatches of phrases. Taylor took care of the hipp and the rhino. "Taylor's my penitentiary name," he had said his first day on the show and repeated every day since, mixed with the drivel he spewed. "Oh, baby, baby, baby, baby, baby, baby, baby!" Red bubbled delightedly.

Abreast of Taylor they heard, "Did ya kill him? Heavy was a ringer to die. I coulda told ya in Des Moines. He told me to make him a coat. He thought he oughta split a gut, making out it was funny. Ya'll get yours. I ain't no tailor. Screw ya, I said" — scarcely audible.

They were out of hearing almost immediately. Taylor remained at the side of the road, talking, turning his head to hold his eyes pinned on them. He didn't come after them. Fiddler kept a straight face, but Red was in hysterics, bouncing on his feet. Red dodged around, shadowboxed, gloated back over his shoulder as they got farther and farther away. "The son of a bitch is still at it! He's still chewing the fat all right. Look at him! By God that guy

should be in the show! He's a clown. He's a riot! Beatin' the gums
— beatin' the gums — beatin' the gums — beat the gums! — hey,
nutty! nutty! telling us all about Heavy and him, nutty as a fruit-
cake! nutty, nuts! Look at him, Fiddler!"

It was contagious. Fiddler glanced back just once and felt like
doing something crazy too, like sprinting at top speed and kicking
his heels and biting at leaves. The diner's dull neon glow was
visible now on a highway at the end of the dirt road. "I'll beat
you to the diner!" Fiddler snapped, already grabbing a head start,
but Red was beside him instantly. They burst between the old
stodgy Prop men or whatever they were — winos who couldn't
run — and broke free into the clear. They ran together and didn't
try to beat each other, although they set a ruthless pace. The
running put stitches in Fiddler's ribs and prickled his back with
sweat. Red and he left Chief behind and Taylor far behind.

The dawn was giving way to morning. The sun itself had not
appeared, but the sky was bright — everywhere a rich blue. Light
shot high off the horizon to pinnacles of clouds and made them
radiant. The moon sat low over the far green corn like a dab of
mist, white and insignificant. Running was perfect, with the sky
so wide, blue and vast and gorgeous it dwarfed the archipelagos
of puffy clouds. The sky a world in its own right plumped on top
of the Earth-world and higher than all the ranging rocketships,
bluer than oceans, swallowing vision and boundless. A Canadian
chill on the wind and the sun not up — they ran; they couldn't
smile for fear their lips would tear loose, they ran with such force.
The giddy heat jarred up in their bodies, they gasped to breathe.
Blood beat in the drums of their ears.

Amazingly soon the diner confronted them — whitewashed wood,
silver chrome, suddenly steps to be met two at a time clump-clump-
clump — a silver sliding door which opened, stubbornly slow,
closed and shut out the sky, the wind, the running and left a boxed,
shadowy interior stale-smelling of coffee and sugared dough.

The counterman was alone in the diner when Fiddler and Red
rushed hurtling into the room and seized every table and chair
in reach to keep from flying flat on their faces. "Wow! Oh Jesus-
God!" Red panted. "Wow! We ran!"

Fiddler could hardly breathe, he needed so much air at once —
he gulped and gulped as if he were laughing, choking with laughter, and he used half the furniture in the place to support himself.
Red leaned on the other half in convulsions. It was funny. And
then Fiddler realized he was staring crazily at the counterman,
so that the guy was flushed and fussing with the coffee urn, twirling dials, and must think Fiddler was laughing at him. And Fiddler
really laughed then, lost all control and laughed and laughed, still
watching the counterman, until his stomach muscles hurt. Red
laughed too. They both just stood there in the middle of the
diner laughing to split a gut, sometimes holding on to chairs and
sometimes clutching their bellies to lessen the ache of laughing,
when they knew very well that nothing they could do with their
hands could stop their bellies from aching until they had finished
laughing — they went right on laughing, partly at the fat, woman-
ish counterman with his double chin but mostly at nothing at all.

The whacking laughter echoed off the walls. The counterman
didn't know what to do. He kept looking up pleasantly and trying
to start a conversation — Fiddler couldn't begin to hear what he
said — and then he'd go to manipulating the coffee urn dials
again, and stop and put his hands over his ears, smiling as if it
was a joke, at the same time squinting toward his phone.

"Okay, hell, let's take it easy," Fiddler puffed. Gradually he
got control of himself. He came to the counter, rubbing his stomach
muscles and groaning, "Ooooooh. . . . Have you got some coffee
and a couple of doughnuts?"

"Sure. Sure. Gladly. You boys have a pretty hard night?" The
counterman was cheery as a bird, quick to forgive everything.

Red had recovered himself. "No sir, mister, we slept; and I'll
take a cup of coffee an' four sugar doughnuts, an' it's black coffee."

"Sure. She's on the way. Glad to have company. All night by
yourself's lonely. Don't ever work an all-night job. You boys going
on into Omaha?" The counterman paused with the empty cups
in his hand. Red impatiently waggled his fingers.

"Omaha? Where in hell is Omaha? Are we showing Omaha,
Fiddler?" He looked at Fiddler, and the counterman, bringing the
coffee, also looked to Fiddler, as though Fiddler were an authority.

"It's across the river," said the counterman. He didn't add "Isn't it?" in so many words, but the question was in his voice.

Fiddler snickered, "I don't know."

"What I say is, across the river is Nebraska — it's Nebraska. You get across the bridge and you're 'cross the Missouri River and you're in Nebraska." He practically pleaded for agreement.

"Christ, I don't know," Red said in disgust, flipping out a coin and paying and ignoring the guy. Red stirred sugar into his coffee.

The circus water trucks zipped past the diner on the return trip from the lot. "What are them?" With a pimply arm the counterman opened a window and peered at the trucks until they disappeared. "Huh? Them aren't regular rigs. What are they, do you think?" Fiddler was supposed to answer.

"Trucks."

"I wonder what kind of trucks, though. That's what I want to know. Well I guess there's plenty of kinds of trucks in the world we hardly never see."

The next thing to provoke the counterman's curiosity was Fiddler's hands. Scars and scratches marked them up like the scrawlings of a pen, shiny white and reddish and livid blue. Townies always noticed. He'd gotten most of them the last few weeks, but he was used to them. They were part of his hand, like the veins; they were sunken in as deep as veins. Circus people didn't notice, just townies.

"Did you cut your hands? That's *something*. You probably don't like to talk about it, huh? The Japs did it to you in the war probably."

"Yeah," Fiddler said.

Red grinned. "Put 'em away, Fid."

"Abracadabra!" The counterman's eyes bugged. The fingers flexed like spider legs and, striped with shiny white and red and livid blue, the hands slid out of sight.

"I read about what they did. Them Japs!"

The door rattled open. People barged in shaking the floor with their stamping — shivering and blustering because of the cold — a man couldn't afford to buy a coat, the show was as cheap as the

day after Christmas and if a man found time to get way into town
the stores would tell him their clientele was millionaires. Joyfully
the counterman pumped the spigot of the coffee urn.

"You boys want coffee?"

Coffee, yes. This cold was worth pneumonia to a man. Shorty
was sick with it already, after that rainstorm in Mason City, and
Heavy was sicker, but not from pneumonia — practically mur-
dered. Mousy slunk into the seat next to Fiddler — "Hey save
a seat for Chief, Red" — and bit into a jellyroll with wee, sharp
teeth. He was small and his face was dingy gray with pinched,
thin lips. The story went that he was no mouse in fight, but a
biting rabid fury. You buyin' or cryin'? I'm not kidding you
that sucking lot was the worst we ever had, *nothing* could go. It
was sand, see, all sand, and the goddam wagons went up to the
axles in it. Three cats on a wagon! the tail end'ud go down in
the sand and the front'ud rear up — Close that goddam window!
Why do they leave the goddam window open? Couple o' cupcakes,
five coffees — four blacks. So who's Chief agoin' to bump off now?
The son of a bitch ain't agoin' to touch me, I can tell you that,
he ain't touching me! The window slammed shut.

"That seat's saved, mister," Red informed somebody. You ever
done that? Ride on the front of the cat? You don't want to fall
off! It'ud make hash out of you, all the ants'ud eat you up. The
son of a bitching advance man — I'm not kidding you, that was
the worst. And Chief had killed the best man that ever lived.
Chairs scraped in high, crying tones. Dime, quarters and wadded,
greasy bills lay on the counter, guarded by dozens of frowzy eyes.
The day after payday everybody had money and everybody was
buying coffee, reaching for napkins, sugar, besieging the counterman.

"What a crowd! What is this? What is it?" he whispered to
Fiddler, almost panicky, and he jangled the tin trays of doughnuts,
put cream in the coffee when nobody wanted cream. — Goddam
it I didn't want it brown! Can you give me black, mac, like I asked
for? The door couldn't be closed; people milled and shoved
through, old mealy mushhead winos whose hair grew long enough
to braid and kids trying to cultivate mustaches, people with glass

eyes, cross eyes, wall eyes, clubfeet, gangling long-nosed men like herons, harelips, stringbeans, butterballs, ex-fishermen-sheepherders-orange-pickers, squat tough guys with smoked jailbird complexions, morons, Portuguese, Swedes, Texans, little pipsqueak drunks — mostly fly-by-night new faces, but some were old, that had been with the show a month or more, and they'd known Heavy, they said, and Chief had better watch his step. One of them guys just come from there three weeks ago and he told everybody there was lots of three-dollar houses and a five and a eight there close around and all them guys started blabbing "Do they have peep holes? Do they have peep holes?" And the fat-assed pimp told 'em all, sure, sure. "How much?" "A quarter" he said "and you get to see the sights."

"I ought to call the boss," the counterman was mumbling. "Somebody, I ought to call somebody."

"That seat's saved, mister!" Red insisted, anger slicing through his voice. Pig wanted it. Pig's mustache was all smeared with drying coffee and sugar from doughnuts and frosting from cupcakes he'd been stuffing down his throat. Like all winos, long ago he'd lost his last tooth; he pretended to chew. His lips had shrunk into his mouth and his lower lip pressed against his mustache. Pig didn't have the sense to shave off the mustache, so it wouldn't get smeared with sugar and brown frosting and coffee the color of tobacco juice. Pig was so stinking drunk he almost didn't have the wits to leave the stool alone when Red told him to. Red was ready to kill him. And Pig's buddies began heckling Red. They'd been served; they didn't need the seat. They thought they owned the place because they'd bought coffee. They thought they were Popeyes and coffee was spinach, that now the coffee was in their systems they could go around picking fights. Yipes! you can't kill a man! The cops'ill fix him — somebody'll fix him. Chief'ill get his ass hung in a sling! "That's the way to get yo' poontang an' steee-ill have money lef' fo' beeeeaa!" — That's what one of them southern sonofabitches said. I should have creamed the son of a bitch.

The diner had not been built to contain so many people. It bulged. The doughnuts were all gone. "Don't have none!" the harried counterman was bleating to the crops of new customers. Pig had found a place to sit, but Pig's buddies were still congregated around Red. They weren't worried about the stool at the counter any more. Heavy must have worked on Props at one time because he'd somehow weaseled a lot of friends from that department — they were Prop men, all the ones Fiddler recognized — nearly the whole Prop department crystallizing into a mob. Heavy this, Heavy that, as though it was any of their business.

"Hell, like hell, like hell," Red was saying over and over like a stuck record. And the crowd ranted at him, What did Heavy ever do? Chief gets tanked to the gills and kills a guy; what kind of a country is this? There's electric chairs. Where is the son of a bitch? Fiddler's mind wouldn't function right. He saw individual warts on faces and rotten teeth in mouths shouting; he wasn't frightened but his mind worked slow as a sloth, fumbling, picking out stupid purple warts on faces, not able to focus. Red was on the very verge of a fight. "Your goddam Heavy was drunk! He pulled his goddam *butcher* knife! Who was drunk! He cut a guy's hand off, for Jesus Christ sake!"

The pack of fifteen, twenty Prop men raved, yapped "Where's Chief? We'll kill the sonofabitch!" The coffee had cleared their heads and woke up the liquor in them at the same time. They were crazed, nuts; they thought they could eat fire.

"I'm with you Red," said Fiddler, numbly moving to get beside him. But something scratched at Fiddler's shoulder.

Mousy grimaced, eyes slits in the skin, no eyelids. "If *he* don't come — "

"Hold it, boys! Please let's hold it, boys!" quavered the counterman. Half the Seat Department was lined up behind Mousy, and they were as bad as the Prop men. Loud mouths gaped open, tongues lolling — Where's Chief? — the filthy harelipped Seat men with noses missing, halves of ears, cheeks seamed from knife fights, dirty bruised grizzled gang fighters. We'll get Chief. We'll cut his you-know-whats off! Fiddler waved his hands in front of Mousy's nose, wanting to pinch it. Chief came in the door with another Indian. Neutral Light and Wardrobe men had clustered around the door. They let him through; he was laughing at some joke with his friend without a care in the world, and pretty soon everyone had let him through, as if in slow motion; nobody attempted to stop him, he just walked through to the counter laughing at some joke. Silence fell.

"Give me black coffee and a jellyroll." Chief took the stool which Red had saved.

The Seat and Prop men grumbled in undertones and some went back and slyly sipped the half-drunk coffees on the counter to gain strength and rouse the liquor in themselves once more.

"You boys need any directions about where you want to get?" pleaded the counterman.

"Black coffee and a jellyroll I said!" Chief felt elated. He clapped Fiddler on the back. His eyes glittered. "You run off, did you?" The other Indian didn't order anything. He worked on Lights and he was a Sioux, Fiddler had heard. He was not a big man but he wore a shirt banded like the rainbow with great brilliant swipes of red, green, orange, yellow, and the shirt made him appear imposing if not big. Lo and behold he was sober — a sober Indian! — and his eyes were blue, not dark, very piercing, tingling sky-blue eyes that he set probing through the mob. He seemed formidable — keen and lynx-fierce and not the least drunk, with perhaps the whole Light Department on his side. Chief laughed irrepressibly at some joke and the Sioux laughed with him, standing beside him, holding the crowd at bay.

When the pale and quaking counterman, who would probably never be the same, brought Chief his coffee, "What's the matter?" Chief demanded and then buried the answer in laughter. Chief, drunk, could terrify an elephant if he chose to, but right now he was jovial and gay. Only the Sioux was preventing what might go into a full-scale riot.

At the height of the uproar Pig had been peacefully licking crumbs off the counter. Now for no reason except maybe that a quiet had settled among his friends, Pig hoisted his bleary head and bawled, "Where's Heavy?" — trying to make it a taunt — "Heavy's killed. Where's Heavy?"

Nobody said a word. The winos listened, waited brittle as tinderwood. Fiddler's mouth tasted of hot straw.

Chief's gust of laughter cracked the tension. "He's in bed."

That floored the winos. "Where's Heavy?" Pig said again, with his mouth full of coffee so that it dribbled down his chin. He baaaed like a sick goat and his voice died out and left a kind of vacuum, a discouraged hush among the winos.

They probably would have stayed discouraged if Red hadn't had to drill in his two-cents' worth. "Why don't you keep your goddam noses clean — "

"Cut it out now, boys," begged the counterman aimlessly.

" — You bums come queerin' around this show. You'd drink your own piss if somebody put it in a bottle!"

"Listen Buster — " Mousy hissed; he couldn't be heard in the din. The counterman held fast to the coffee urn with both petrified hands. Fiddler hurriedly backed off his stool to get room to move. Red thumbed his nose at the Prop men.

"You stink like a pig! That's a good name for you, you dead stinking wino!" Fiddler shouted and couldn't even hear himself. The counterman spilled a quart of coffee on the floor, kicked at the puddles in a daze. Pig grinned imbecilically. The Light and Wardrobe men were slipping out the door and the counterman looked toward his phone, paralyzed, yearning to reach the phone.

Mousy led the Seat Department. They steamrollered into Fiddler throwing punches, scrabbling, clawing, trying to knee him, old jaundiced brutal men with sewage reeking on their breaths. Red and the Sioux came to Fiddler's aid. Pepperpot Red brandished a spoon. "Dig out their eyes!" cheered the Sioux — his own burned like blue flames, his arms fanned a gale — he laughed as if it was a sport and stopped the ratty little winos cold. In his screaming shirt he withered them and made them scamper.

Chief handled the other mob alone. "COME HERE THEN!" he boomed and they did just the opposite. They gave out a couple of broken-off squeals and scattered. And when he lumbered after them they wheeled to and fro in the cramped space of the diner, upsetting furniture and china. He herded them like cattle. He buffaloed them. Fiddler, Red and the gaudy-shirted Sioux relaxed as spectators.

"What's he doing?" Fiddler wondered.

"I guess he busts their fingers if they grab for him." The Sioux thought it was a great joke.

Chief returned to the counter, wolfed down his jellyroll and coffee and paid. "Let's go, Fiddle." They left. The Sioux stayed behind because he hadn't eaten yet.

The sun was biting the horizon, sending harsh straight shafts of light that hurt the eyes. "Now we'll get warmed up!" Chief felt good. He clapped his hands mischievously and poked Fiddler. "*Them* fellas are gonna get warmed up too! They were sleepy. They don't wake up as quick as me and you. And they didn't have nothing with them. Wait till they get to their wagons — they got a *arsenal* in their wagons!" Chief prattled about it like a kid and chuckled. He hardly seemed drunk, he was so lively and exuberant. "You want to trip, Fiddle? Tie your shoes! What d'you want to be, a ragamuffin?" And Red, who could never be fazed, began waltzing around as he usually did when he was pleased and excited and ready to burble out some plan. When Fiddler obediently stopped to tie his shoelaces both Chief and Red waited for him, which was amazing.

"We'll catch girls today, Fid. Today's the day. We'll catch 'em an' we'll cootchie-cootchie-coo 'em till they jus' beg an' beg an' beg an' beg for more!"

Fiddler couldn't help but get in the mood. "How about you, Chief, are you going to stand on the sidelines?"

"Sidelines! What the hell is that you say? I'll be at *home plate!*"

They went along the highway, Red waltzing and fitting a fancy fandango into the waltz, and pretty soon the bus came rolling up behind, honking, with its door open. The driver wouldn't slow down. He grinned through the windshield at them and Fiddler and Chief leapt, one pell-mell after the other, through the door as it came past, landing like a one-two punch almost in the wiseguy's lap. Red with a princely self-assurance refused to leap or plunge — Red *waltzed* into the speeding bus, never varying his footwork, like a charm. He made it.

RED COULD GRIN the craziest, lopsidedest grins in the world, and he'd scrunch up his nose and circle a girl with a bouncy, wide-stepping, I-got-my-pants-soaked strut. He'd wear some rakish, crumbling hat. He'd pretend to have gum on his shoe, hop around pitifully like an old man, trying to pick it off, until out of the goodness of her heart she might consent to let him lean on her shoulder. Then Red would lean real close and whisper some uproarious joke in her ear with blue eyes fixed out of focus and a roguish, lopsided grin. She'd laugh; if she was young she'd laugh, and sometimes Red would have himself a girl from then on, all day. He'd pull stunt after stunt, do the weirdest, most freakish tricks to flabbergast the little townie girl. She'd hang around on pins and needles to see what he'd do next. Only Wing Ding on the midway could rival Red at picking up girls, and Wing Ding was successful mostly because he'd lost an arm and knew how to make girls mother him. Red was rugged competition. If there were two, Red always got the best and Fiddler the worst girl, Fiddler admitted to himself, smiling.

Red misunderstood the smile. "They still there, Fid? What're they doing?" Red was in the wagon and couldn't see.

"They're curious. One's combing her hair. They're young kids and they're making themselves available, I would say." Trees grew few and far between along the road. The girls were in the shade of one, alone and restless, bored, very conscious of Fiddler's glance. He laughed. "They wish they could find out what's in here."

Behind the girls was the road, behind that a big, dry, sparsely grown field and, beyond, the channel of the Mississippi.

"Like hell, mister. They wish we was *showin'* 'em what's in here."

"I hope so." Fiddler lifted the rest of the bale of straw into the wagon and then sat straddling the wagonpole in the shade of the wagon. Red crawled around shaking straw evenly over the floor. The barred door opened inward so the girls couldn't see it and had no way of knowing the wagon was a cage. All they could see was the outer door, which looked like any other red wagon door. And the sides were boarded up, so the whole cage seemed like a regular wagon. Fiddler rested his chin on his arms in the doorway and comfortably straddled the wagonpole. The flood-plain of the river stretched three miles, where a range of high, hot, carved hills rose, baked and sandy, as a massive backdrop to the circus. Fiddler was sick of the sight. The sun glared power-fully; his eyes were watering. The wagon was dark, cool and cozy like a tiny cave. Dark, jungle-green ferns and vines had been painted on the walls. He would just as soon have crawled inside and gone to sleep.

"Are they cherry?"

He'd almost forgotten about the girls. "I don't know, but they're awful young, Red. I told you, but they really are."

"Never too young. — You quit your racket, Buddy." Buddy was the fly in the soup, spoiling the peace of the wagon, making trou-ble. He was still locked in his sleeping box in the corner and growing increasingly mad about it. He was heaving the whole box back and forth on the floor by jumping in it. "You be patient!" Red told him. Red had arranged the milk and fruit artistically in the opposite corner from Buddy. Buddy's big, luminescent, baby eyes were on them and his slender ape fingers pinched the lock futilely. He made no sound; the box did the talking for him, slamming up and down. Buddy was a muscular four years old.

"Not thirsty, is he?" Buddy wasn't Fiddler's animal. He had to be tactful.

"No, I gave him water early. — You got to wait, you Buddy, and you'll get your milk from them an' your banana, an' we'll get our foolin', an' we'll all be happy."

Buddy wasn't satisfied.

The girls under the tree wore ten-cent-store kerchiefs and sateen jackets with their names in white script on the back — Patty and Jean. In their restlessness they turned round and round like models on a pedestal. Patty had taken off her kerchief to comb her hair. She held it flapping from her hand like a silk streamer. Her blouse was silky too and white. The bob of yellow hair flounced in the breeze. Above the girls the tree blew with a whirling blur of branches and leaves. The hot white sun shone on the leaves and on the ground nearly everywhere. The girls were careful to stay under the tree. Fiddler lolled watching them with one eye lazily closed, his head on his arms, in the cool of the shade.

Red had finished spreading the straw. He lay in it now, fluffing and tossing it until the straw almost floated, airy and luxurious, and the inside of the wagon looked like a soft sexy hayloft. Buddy ruined the picture, whamming his box up and down, prying his lanky, red, orangutang arms between the bars on the little window. The box slammed against the wall. Fiddler was afraid Buddy's fingers would get crushed. He was blindly groping with his fingers, trying to open the box. He couldn't see where he was putting his hands.

"Why can't we let him out?" The box teetered on edge and crashed down, wavered indomitably up again — two disembodied arms thrashing from the window — and slammed down finally like a rock.

"Buddy! Quit, sonofabitch!" Red charged to the box, rapped on it. Buddy's worn, tapering hands reached from the black inside, unclasping, extended loose and pleading. The gray fingertips drew designs in the air, circles the size of pennies and V's upside down and X's. The wagon was still.

"They wouldn't come in here, the trouble is," Red suddenly explained. "They'd be scared of him. This has got to be done cautious, Fid. They wouldn't come in *with* him, but after they're in they'll want to let him out, when they see how little he is an'

how much he wants out. They'll wanta feed him like a baby."
Red began to roll in the straw like a happy baby himself at the
foot of the box. Gaily he put up his hands toward Buddy's and
smiled at something in his head, some plot. Buddy whimpered
high and quick and paddled the air.

Red rattled on, "We play it slow an' easy and let them do everything. — Wow! That's it! Wow! That is it — let *them* do everything! — Buddy's in his box, so they can't see him unless they
come in the wagon, so they do, an' hold his hand and feel sorry for
him an' want to let him out and feed him. 'You can't do that! How
can you do that? He'll run away!' Hah, hah, hah, hah, hah. See,
Fid? An' they get mad and say we're being selfish an' cruel, Buddy's
hungry an' not even as big as their littlest kid brother an' it's like
a prison in there an' Buddy wants to play with them — they'll be
petting his fingers — 'Just the same as a person's 'cept for the
pretty hair, such cute baby nails. Shut the door, silly; lock it if
you have to, stupid!' is what they'll say. Hah, hah, hah, hah, hah,
hah, they'll get a teeny-weeny mad on, kissing Buddy's fingers and
beggin' us to let him out." Red tumbled and somersaulted in the
straw, beat his fists on his knees, completely enthralled. Buddy's
arms had stopped waving. Buddy was hidden inside the box again,
rocking again, bumping the box back and forth, and his muted cry
was like an angry jay. He was Red's animal. Fiddler could do
nothing.

"So we shut the door like they say!" — the heavy barred door
whirred, clanged shut *pow!* an inch from Fiddler's nose.

"Watch it, goddam you!"

" — So we shut the door: They don't hardly even notice, except
they can let him out now. But they get to the padlock, the padlock
stops 'em, they have to persuade us to let 'em use the key. Buddy's
crying, an' it's dark as night in here with the doors locked — it's
goddam dark, you know, nobody can see, they'll never see you
again, you leave town, so they don't worry. There ain't much space
in here — " Red spoke so fast he panted. He crept and threw his
arms around imaginary girls. He flung himself backward, stretched
and kicked one side of the cage and shoved the opposite side with

the flat of his hands — "ain't much space at all. I got all the keys. Buddy comes swingin' out of the box. You know how he comes, rarin' out. That would scare 'em; it wouldn't be the same as petting his fingers and pokin' his nose when he's locked up. They'll *retreat* then, they'll get behind us for protection an' hold on to our shoulders — kneel down behind us gigglin' and put their white little honey cherry hands up here." Red skittered his hands around his own neck, hair and shoulders, rolling, tumbling in the straw. In the dark at the back of the cage Buddy rhythmically battered his box on the floor with an eerie gull cry. The box itself seemed grotesquely alive.

"But once we catch Buddy they won't be so scared. We'll have him in our lap feedin' him and lettin' him drink his milk — gettin' it on his mouth so he looks cute as a baby, fat tummy and staring around with his big eyes and wanting to be petted, loved up, cuter than anything in the world, playin' with his baby toes an' white all over his lips. We'll be fixing his hair an' cleanin' his ears. Them girls — they're behind us, 'member, part scared and part faking, holding on" (Red acted it out, rapidly tipping his fingers along his ribs as a girl would have done from behind and bundling straw in his lap) " — they're goin' to reach right down over us an' try to hug him, cuddle their little cherry heads in here an' a-hug-hug." He stroked his cheek and under his chin and tumbled on the mounds of straw, squalling with pleasure.

Tantalized, Fiddler straddled the wagonpole. "Well, are we going to do it or not?"

"What you mean?"

"Those girls are still waiting. They're there under the tree."

"Yeah? What're they like?" Red lay quiet on his back in the straw, showed no inclination to move.

"I told you they're too young, fourteen or fifteen, but we can mess with them anyway."

"Too young? What the shit did you do in the Service?" Red said as if he was trying to start an argument instead of setting about to make the thing come true. But after a moment he stood up looking like a man of straw and whaled hell out of his pants and shirt and all but tore his hair out by the roots. He got rid of the straw. He grinned. "Got to pretty up nice, Fid." He jokingly primped at his sandy-red hair and left a few curlicue frizzes sticking out in the short part above the ears. — It was no joke. Any girl would want to brush those frizzes flat. Just one skim of a hand and he'd be the "cutest boy in town." Fiddler had watched girls itch to do it, squirm and not be able to fight their eyes away from Red until it had been done.

Red took command, shining melodrama in his eyes. "Okay. We bring 'em to your cats. That'll give 'em a thrill. You do your stuff, and they'll think we're great. Then — to Buddy."

Buddy's box tilted and bammed down and tilted, slammed down, tilted, crashed desperately, careening. "Can't you let him out?"

Agile as a cat, Red jumped from the wagon. The girls turned the other way, elaborately nonchalant. Red snatched up a stone, skipped it hard along the ground past them. Both startled faces darted around, beginning to pout and huff. Anxious, concerned, Red raced to the girls. The strong sun lit his hair and tanned arms as if he were a movie star. "Hey, I didn't hit *you*, did I?" He dropped on his knees to see that no harm had been done to their feet. Fiddler followed quickly but didn't go down on his knees.

"I'm sorry," Red murmured like a chastened child.

"You're sorry, I bet. It's kind of too late now." Patty scowled down at Red reprovingly. He remained on his knees. Patty lifted her foot to raise her skirt, hopped closer, feeling the injury. The stone had missed by about three yards. Patty was a young kid, but sexy, that was the thing. She flaunted herself in a cellophane blouse. It was sexiness scrappy, brassy, tomboy. Overnight she'd grown a figure and didn't know quite what to do, but anyway the world was going to hurry and wake up and howl and court her.

Red held out his hands like a supplicant toward the foot. "Let me see. I'm sorry. — Please."

"No you don't." Patty managed a few ungainly hops away; but she tottered. Red sprang up, ran to embrace her and nestle her like a lamb in his arms and prevent her from falling.

Patty wiggled free. "What do you think you can do?" She was

shocked. "I don't know what right you think you can take!"

"I got a right to think you're pretty."

"You got a right to mind your own business." Her tone of voice belied her words. She let Red put his hands on her arms and gently swing her so she faced the hills and he was behind her. Gently Red swayed her from side to side as if they were dancing drowsy late at night.

"We ought to go out tonight, honey. You can show me the town." His voice whisked like a feather. He could have kissed her without any trouble. Fiddler was amused and somewhat envious.

"Beautiful girls, beautiful hills and old Lady Mississippi just across the road — this must be a nice town," Fiddler said to the girl who was supposed to be his. "Do you live by the river?"

"Patty does." She nodded toward the other girl. "I live in town. It's a stupid town." She was shy. He felt how much taller and older he must seem. She wouldn't meet his eyes but kept tucking her blouse into her skirt and tinkling the charms on a bracelet she wore. Jean was very young — hardly in high school — and had put on a blouse too big for her and painted her fingernails inaccurately. She stood close to Fiddler, watching his shoes and hands. Jean was meek and passive.

"It is a dummy town," Patty agreed. "It ain't like the places you've been to."

"Screw the places I've been to! I'm here an' you're here an' we'll go swimming then tonight if you don't want to go to town, an' we'll show you the sights now." Red possessively flicked a bug off her blouse front and wrapped his arms around Patty.

Languorous as a movie star, she slipped loose, said "No," smiling the reverse.

"Sights hithertofore never revealed to human ears! The trumpet of the elephant, the snarling of the striped tiger!" Fiddler spieled, trying to coax a laugh out of his girl. He couldn't do it. She smiled at him submissively and dropped her eyes. As a sort of test he undid her kerchief, running his hands along her shoulders, up her throat and under her chin to the knot. Jean didn't stir. He tied it around her neck like a bandanna. "Now you're beautiful."

She glanced up apologetically as if she should have had it that way before, and then lowered her eyes to his hands. He could have had her using yellow lipstick or snipped off her eyelashes! This was going to be too easy.

"Well, the thing we can show you best is the animals because that's what we take care of," Fiddler said, very businesslike. He didn't put his arm around her. "Red, what first? — By the way, he's Red Rooney and I'm David Cipato."

"You're Fiddler an' you're good; don't be ashamed. He can play as good as Harry James. You tour 'em the cats and then we'll take 'em to see Buddy."

"Who's Buddy?" Patty asked, pertly clinging to Red. But she was like a kid sister and she hadn't even fixed the frizzes in his hair yet and she wasn't even looking at him but was goggling around for people to see she was out with a boy in his twenties. When you robbed the cradle this was what you got — a couple of little kid sisters who had crushes on their Science teacher probably and were all aflitter with the do's and don't's of Frenchkissing the boys next door.

"He's darling, that's what you'll say," Red teased. All Red wanted was one thing. He had no sense of decency; he didn't care where he got it. Fiddler began to hope the scheme with Buddy wouldn't come off.

The sunlight fell mottled through the leaves, golden and green, but out of the tree's shade it was white like off sheet metal and filled the air, strong, white and warm. The four of them walked toward the cat cages. Fiddler had expected it to be hot in the sun, but, no, the heat was mostly in the distance on the hills, sifting and shimmering like blown sand. The hills had smooth, rounded tops like eastern hills and dry, sharply gashed western sides.

"Do you go in the circus always? Where are the places you've gone to?" Fiddler's girl asked. She didn't raise her eyes from his hands or hips or crotch or whatever she was looking at down there.

"We just came from Milwaukee. You've been there, haven't you?" Jean shook her head. "No? Well, there and Chicago,

Detroit, Cleveland, Toledo. I joined in Albany, New York. We mostly stay out of big cities because you don't make money there. You can rest up in a big city but you don't make money, the bosses say." Fiddler was formal. "— Here they are. These are the cat cages. What shall I show you, leopards?" He struck the latches up. Part of the cage wall swung down, hinged at the bottom, leaving only the bars. Both girls oohed. Sweetheart flashed past and past and past in a glorious pattern of bright yellow and black. Sweetheart was in heat and the cage hummed with her growling purr. Fiddler stuck his hand in —

"EEEaaaaa! that's what's wrong with your hands!" his girl sobbed; she grabbed his other one. She'd been looking at his scars all the time! The purr hiccupped, shifted gears and went on at an hysterical rate, buzzing, zooming from the cage. Sweetheart rammed her body sideways against the bars, scraping hard against them. Fiddler tickled down her back. Sweetheart revved and fumed and stormed like a motor warming up. She crashed against the bars, against Rajah, the male, and came back at Fiddler for more. She mashed her face into his hand and rubbed it there fiercely. She drove her claws at the metal flooring of the cage. She strained her body violently against the bars; the tail slipped through, stretched straight out, stiff as a steel spring. Fiddler held the tail so his girl could feel it. — She squealed, just barely touched it — then suddenly she bent and kissed the tip, frantic, clutching Fiddler round the waist. The sunlight flashed on her bracelet. Cupping her fingers, Fiddler's girl stroked the tail and kissed it with tiny mouse squeaks. He held the leopard still by massaging the fur along her ribs. Sweetheart purred hoarsely, grabbing for breath.

Red went to the other end of the cage to try and show off for his girl, but Rajah reached out tentatively. Red had to back away. Rajah's tail switched to and fro in spurts. His gray eyes were very round and wide. He gazed at Fiddler, stalked toward his mate. Then Fiddler knew playtime was up. He fingered Sweetheart's legs. — That was the trigger, that set her off, noise raging from her throat, like a child with a vicious attack of croup. She dashed in a circle in the cage, while Fiddler's girl hugged him and he kissed her and she scarcely knew it. The male, Rajah, stood in the center of the circle, tensed, powerful, with lustrous fur, waiting like a tough, champion wrestler, slightly crouching. Sweetheart stumbled and weakened, narrowed her circuit, swung round him nearer and nearer and slower, and crept down, flattened herself at his feet. She drew her muscles tight and straight, in parallel lines, and lay in position, her head low over her forepaws. Rajah licked the short, dense fur between his female's ears with stabbing tongue. Sweetheart impetuously lapped at her own feet and squinted her eyes. Suddenly Rajah let out a strangled scream-growl which started and was throttled somewhere in his throat, tried to get out again and was throttled. He chewed and tore at her ear. She screamed, snarled, spun under him and knocked him away with a hard, swiping paw. Then, lying apart on their bellies, the two leopards growled sporadically and gradually fell silent.

Fiddler had his back to the cage. Both arms were squeezed around his girl. He was kissing her neck and her ear, the lobe of her ear, and the kerchief on her neck as she quivered, staring over her shoulder at the leopards.

"Hey! you Fiddler! What are you doing there?" Chief banged onto the scene and he was mad. "What are you doing around here?" His voice pounded at Red like a sledge hammer. "You ain't got no BUSINESS round this cage! You don't do this cage! You ain't got no business round this cage!"

Chief turned on Fiddler again with that "Fiddle" and the scorn. "Fiddle — you can take this *slut!* you can take her out in the field — that grass, see? And you can break her backbone!"

"Now you," he told the girl Jean. — Patty had already scrammed. "You want to be fixed. Rajah will fix you! — Rajah! Rajah!" The leopard rose in one motion, came to the bars. "Here, Rajah. Here." Chief grasped the girl by both shoulders and "walked" her on her toes toward the cage. She wriggled helplessly. The charms on her bracelet tinkled.

"No, please; no, please!" she whispered, not daring to scream. But a shriek was forcing up her throat — Fiddler could see it. Chief let go. She practically flew, she went so fast. She ran.

Chief was naked except for shoes and a pair of jeans streaked purple with dirt. On his arm was the single tattoo of an Indian girl with braids. He helped Fiddler close the cage. The leopards seemed calm and serene. "You don't open up your cage for anybody! You hear? You fool around all you want out there" — Chief waved at the field beyond the road. "But when you're here you work. You don't open up your cage for anybody! You understand me? Nobody messes with these animals. You don't open up your cage for anybody. You know that, boy."

Council Bluffs • III

FIDDLER'S BUS pulled onto the lot, jouncing over the rough ground. A bonfire blazed at the far end. The bus curved toward the fire, releasing a steady trickle of men who were needed at various points. The sideshow wagons were half unloaded. The cookhouse poles were up and the stakes in; the canvas sections were being laced together. The giant oval outline of the big top had been marked with long pins, and two mechanical stakedrivers were tracing out the course, one clockwise, the other counterclockwise. At each pin they stopped, drove two stakes, and snailed ahead to the next. The clattering structure on the back end seemed about to tip them over, it was so tall, noisy, the hammers clanged up and down inside so hard. The job would take better than three hours. The stakedrivers moved on caterpillar treads, as slow as caterpillars.

The lot was suitably large and level where it counted and bounded on one side by the highway which ran to a bridge over the river. Only a stretch of brush separated the lot from the river. Across the highway was an amusement park. The lot had not been used for much. The grass hadn't even been grazed on. Through the bus window the breeze was chilly. The dew would be cold. Fiddler didn't see any place to sit down, no rock on the field or an old crate and no shelter of any kind, just the fire. It wasn't a "lot" yet, it was a field. The sleepy men working on scarcely a ghost of the circus didn't look like they were accomplishing much. Fiddler wouldn't even be able to work. He'd have to just stand around until the cages came. It made him feel almost homeless.

The driver jockeyed the bus to a total standstill. Red, Chief and Fiddler stepped out, thankful they didn't have to jump for their lives, for once. "So long," grinned the driver.

"Yeah, the wiseacre," Red muttered. Red wasn't in a very good mood any more. As soon as something happened — if somebody tried to start another fight with Chief — he'd pep up all right. But now he was silent, suffering from a letdown. That was Red, all or nothing. Now it was nothing.

The cold grass wet Fiddler's feet. The fire was the obvious place to go, the only place. Woolly-haired jigs squatted around it as if they were still in Africa. It was their fire. Across the highway the amusement park with its Ferris wheel, carrousel, loop-the-loop, and funhouse buildings seemed substantial and permanent; all wood and steel. The guys who worked there didn't have to huddle around fires with niggers every morning. They stayed in bed with their wives. And probably they didn't drink. They raised families and owned houses. The circus would have to hustle not to look ragbag next to that outfit.

Magee, the boss of the circus till noon or so, accompanied Chief and Fiddler and Red to the fire. Magee was the earliest man on the lot. He was strolling around, checking the blueprint he'd had in his mind as he'd laid out the big top with a tape measure and his marker pins. He knew where everything would be; on the train last night he could have drawn plans for this particular town, where each wagon would be spotted. Over the years Magee had memorized the lots right across the country. Everything until lunch would be done according to his orders. Magee was one of Fiddler's heroes, and Fiddler was excited to be close to him.

Chief had tensed up, though. All of a sudden Fiddler did too — realizing Magee could blacklist Chief, over Brownie the Department boss's head, or even have him arrested! Maybe that was why he was going with them to the fire! Magee was gauging Chief, soberly judging him. Chief held himself straight and stern and marshaled all his dignity. His strides were as measured as Magee's. Chief did not try to act tough. Magee could be equally tough. Magee was Chief's size. He had a square, bulky build and square, careful hands and flat gray eyes like a wall to look at. Magee was dressed impeccably in high galoshes for the grass and a topcoat, sportjacket, handpainted tie, monogrammed shirt and tiepin. He groomed his hair like a big shot and carried his heavy hands ready and out from his body in a way that showed he could use them. The stony gaze at Chief became approving.

"Take it easy, Chief." The voice was hoarse from years of shouting: a great big man with a slender stick in his hands for pointing at what he wanted done.

The jigs had full possession of the fire. Most of the white men on the lot belonged to departments which worked the first thing in the morning. Departments with time to kill, like Wardrobe and Ringstock, hadn't arrived yet. The miscellaneous white men at the fire didn't get on well with each other or anybody else. They had no friends to have coffee with.

The jigs were afraid of what Magee was going to say or do. Magee terrified them. A moldering, cracked-in chickencoop near the fire was furnishing the fuel. Magee kicked a new hole in the side.

"No wood but that, huh?"

The jigs shook their heads and pitifully hugged themselves and shivered. Then their very heartbeats seemed suspended for his verdict.

"It isn't worth a damn, but if he sues it's your ass. — And get it all. Don't leave any. Maybe he's forgotten about it." Magee walked off.

The jigs breathed again.

Chief despised the jigs and they knew it. They were afraid of Chief. He received a place of honor at the fire, and Red and Fiddler squeezed in beside him. The heat kindled the blood in Chief's face. He was a wonderful strong brown-red to the chunks of his cheekbones; the flames crimsoned his chin. The jigs must envy Chief's color, Fiddler thought.

Ordinarily the jigs couldn't have coffee in the morning because there were seldom more than one or two spots open and if they'd tried to go where everybody else was getting it they would have been slaughtered, they wouldn't have stood a chance. So they had to wake up some other way, without coffee. Toasting themselves around as big a fire as possible was their method — they didn't have the clothes to stay warm otherwise. Toasting themselves to normal liveliness.

The roof of the chickencoop still would hold a few men at a time, so when the jigs got tired of ripping the walls apart they climbed up there; or else they went to shooting crap. They made a lot of noise. The largest, roundest jigs had bass voices, but most of them were not especially large or round. They were under six feet, built like powerhouse halfbacks, young, slim — almost wasp-waisted — until their backs went up like fans to shoulders thick and big. Their shirts were part stripped off, smeared with dirt like tar. One guy was ashen-colored and his hair in kinks and curls entirely hid his ears. He flirted around the others, climbed on and off the coop, following the powerhouses.

Jigs moseyed from splitting wood to squatting in the firelight, shooting crap. If a guy rolled a seven — "Huzzee! Dem four-pick-a-trey did come!" — he'd whup the ground and duckwalk round and round, dodging two-by-fours when he got between the fire and the coop. A tall jig with a shirt in tatters bent double from the waist to clap him on the keester. Even though they'd just been paid the day before, their dough was gone. The jigs had pennies left, handfuls of pennies which stuck like taffy to their fingers. They wahooed, talked with their hands, and chewed up the air, and the pennies never fell off.

A short, gabby white man without much sense had joined the game. He had dimes — nickels and dimes — in his left hand and clutched the pennies he won in his right. The system was okay, so long as his right hand did everything, rolled and paid off and raked in, and he snuggled the left in the folds of his shirt. The lazy Negroes pondered the trees and the fire. But they watched and weren't so lazy. Boxcars was rolled when it was needed and in the triumph forgetfully the *left* hand reached — Up! they batted it. Silver flew. Peck, peck, peck flashed the fingers. Peck, peck, scoop! Nowhere was the silver to be seen. The ground was clean.

"Hey," the white man protested.

"Play!" laughed Chief.

The jigs started playing again without a word. The silver wasn't used as stakes, but you could see it clinging to their fingers. The white man kept his mouth shut. Furiously he whittled a board.

"They ought to be in jail. You oughtn't to do that, Chief," Fiddler complained.

Chief laughed, "Fiddlesticks!" He was drunk.

Whole pieces of the chickencoop's walls were in the fire. Flames forked and scrambled up to cover them. The sagged roof rumbled. All the jigs got off but one, and he was a jitterbug. He called for a partner! Everybody saw the roof was going to cave in. No one wanted to go up there with him.

"Scaredy, scaredy!" the jitterbug hooted into a general hush. None of the other jigs answered back. The mechanical stake-drivers' clattering was loud across the lot. The goof shuffled into a dance routine. The creaking roof sustained him. His clothes were shapeless as pajamas.

Looming in front of the fire stood the King, a mountainous seven-foot jig, a Goliath, who looked to Fiddler like he'd eaten cannibal pots and pots full of other jigs and grown bigger and Bigger and BIGGER—HUGE AS A BARN. The King was counting his money (including some dimes). The ash-colored guy had singled him out— "He's my man, King is." Nothing could distract the King.

The jitterbug put a foot through the roof. He couldn't get it out. "Haayulp!" Boards broke and the other foot went through also. "Haayulp!" Ominously the roof supported him by the knees; by the thighs. The walls inched outward. "Haaaaayulp!"

The King ignored the fairy's pokes while he was counting his money. But when the King stopped he turned, plucked him up like a kernel of popcorn and dangled him over his mouth— "Yum! Yum! Yum!" —jolted him, dropped him a foot and caught him like lightning— "You ain't cooked!" —thrust him over the fire. The little guy spidered with six legs and six lungs and twenty voice boxes:

"My Lord! My Loardeee!"

The great King solemnly closed his eyes and intoned like a

tuba: "Deea Lawd, we all hope to pray dat you accept dis man into Youa Heaven despite of his sins, many as dey be, and dat you don't burn him any mowa, because we is gonna do a good fricassee job right down heea." The fairy spluttered in the smoke and coughed, slapped himself where the heat stung. Fiddler smelled his singeing hair.

The chickencoop roof collapsed; the walls heeled over and fell, mushrooming choking clouds of the powdery dung-feed dust that carpets chickencoops. Fiddler sneezed.

"Hot damn!" Red whispered joyfully.

The King set the fairy down and went to fish the jitterbug out of the wreckage. He was okay except for some scratches from nails. The King cuffed him a little for being so stupid.

More white men were arriving — a new busload, and the trucks brought some — all headed for the fire.

The jigs were going full blast again, getting wood to the fire. There was lots of wood. They formed a bucket brigade, each guy trying to inundate the next one down the line, clunk him on the head while he was trying to clunk the *next* guy's head. Soon they were throwing instead of passing. The people at the end of the brigade found themselves targets and beat a retreat, and the fire was practically smothered. But then the flames rallied and kept the pace, mounting higher and higher on a stack of half-burned boards. The jigs hollered with glee. Everything, the splinters, the dust of the coop, was hurled in the fire, and uprooted grass, a hat or two; and the jigs stood back, loafing, hands on their hips, enjoying it.

"Dat's bigger dan Hell. You see dat, you seen Hell, real Hell. I ain't funnin'. Dat's Hell."

They discovered they'd forgotten the dice. They'd heaped wood on the fire and left the dice on the ground in the middle of it.

"You gotta get dem bones out, Charlie, you gotta go after dem bones. You lef' 'em. How we gonna play? Huh? How we gonna play wi'out de ivory?"

"*Me! Wha'?* I need a *suit,* assbestose; I ain't goin' after nothin' hot! — Man, no! N–O, No! man! No, N–O!" He was emphatic, but he was the smallest. He couldn't do a thing. They all herded close to Charlie, teasing.

But when they took their eyes off him, there was the fire surrounded by white men, ringed clear around with white men, and more coming. The jigs' mouths opened in a dull surprise that tightened into anger. They weren't the southern jigs who'd ridden the show train up from winter quarters and would have done what they were told automatically; and they weren't the old New York and Boston jigs with half the season to get used to it — it happened every morning. These were new, Chicago jigs mostly. They weren't resigned to having their fire taken away even yet, after two weeks, and they didn't like it.

Nobody said much, except the short white man whose dimes had been stolen. "You boogs better get out of here," he told them. Fiddler was embarrassed.

Chief stared at the jigs with icy contempt. White men shoved between them and the fire, and the jigs grudgingly backed out of the way. — It wasn't that a few at a time wouldn't have been allowed around the fire. But not a whole horde. Fiddler wished they would just go. They had their toes tromped on; they were elbowed, shouldered, kneed; and the jigs backed off further and further until they were shivering and rubbing their arms and no heat reached them. Chief stared and glared at the brawny King, the proportions of his body. The King was literally half again as broad as Chief. The King took nobody's side. He looked unhappy and stood out of the way. Finally and sadly he led all the jigs off into the brush towards the river. Fiddler felt relieved. Chief stared at the whopping back of the King as if at a maggot.

"Them fellas could fight."

Bulging from tears in the shirts of the young halfback powerhouses was an awful lot of muscle. Even Charlie, the guy they'd picked on, and the fairy jig had more than the average wino-white man at the fire. "Maybe they learned at home they'd get lynched," Fiddler suggested.

"D'they lynch Indians? — If they ever do, they don't when there's more than him around."

One wino puked, barked his cookies in front of everybody. A mixture of liquor and coffee came out. He moaned. Chief spat restlessly. Everybody acted neutral to Chief. The men had heard about the row with Heavy but they weren't going to make a fuss because of it. They weren't on Seats or Props. The cold was their big problem. Some of them needed their noses wiped, and everyone in the bunch coughed and hacked. They were sick. — "Guddam arctic's as bad's this. Wonder it don't snow with that guddam pokey sun. *B'rrrrr!*" The sun hadn't warmed the air sufficiently for winos. The sun hadn't done a very good job — for winos who drank up the money they should have spent on clothes and then sold what clothes they did have for more wine. The sun was a fresh, cheerful yellow now, putting colors on the fields, in the leaves, toning the white-dark dawn extremes to a placid blue in the sky. But for wino-invalids it wasn't enough of a radiator.

"Let's go, Chief. We can find a better place," Fiddler said at last. "The cages ought to be here any time."

"Fart on the cages! I'm stayin' here, be comfortable," Red put in. Fiddler didn't care whether he came or not. He threw his money away. If he couldn't save enough for proper clothes, then Fiddler didn't want him.

"Come on," said Chief. The two of them left together. "I'm gonna visit the kid today, in the hospital. I'm going to town to the hospital." Fiddler's spirits sank. That again.

They went out in the middle of where the big top would be and idly looked for a place to sit down. So much empty space made Fiddler, standing, feel lonely and exposed. He was not Magee surveying a domain. They might go watch the niggers build another fire — Fiddler laughed to himself. Already they had one started on the riverbank, of brush and small stuff which burned in darts and crackles. Fiddler was hungry. All he lacked was a frying pan, a dozen eggs, and a couple of pounds of pig.

The highway teemed with people and cars. More and more the town was waking up to the terrific fact it had a circus in its lap. Cars were stopping. Cars were pulling off the highway. Hardly any went by, unless to turn around at the gate of the amusement park. The convoys of circus trucks had to thread their wagon trains through a bottleneck of cars, something they were expert at. But every once in a while a big interstate diesel truck hove in sight cruising along on a schedule. The old electric horn would blaaaat, blaaaat and the air brakes f'ch-sssssssssss-f'ch! The driver'd be cursing, knowing if it wasn't a million-dollar fire it must be a circus to jam up things at this hour of the morning.

The cars were from both directions, the fathers bending to the windshields as they drove and the rest of the family almost out the windows watching for the lot. The cookhouse they sighted first, since nothing else was up. Arms pointed — "There it is! there it is!" The cars eased cautiously onto the grass. The families piled out and clustered with neighbors from home to chat about how exciting it was, all the funny-shaped, colorful wagons, and how much land it took, and was that tent there (the cookhouse) the big top? was this the whole circus? — the parents joking about how long it had been since they were up so early and agreeing they should have brought rubbers and this was an experience children mustn't miss. The kids tugged. "We'll be late! They're *doing* it all!" The parents lagged stodgily, still overcome with their virtue and accomplishment in getting even this far, and worrying about wet feet. . . . Chief and Fiddler luckily were out of earshot. Just looking at a mass of townies, Fiddler could hear the chatter in his ears, from so many, many towns, always the same chat. It was better when the sun wasn't up and they were mere silhouettes — a whole horizon dark sometimes with townies — or on a foggy morning when you'd have to figure out where voices came from, if you wanted to. These were precious minutes while the townies lingered near the highway. Soon they'd be everywhere, like gnats.

The Seat men and their buddies appeared on the edge of the lot by the highway. They must have walked from the diner. A single figure separated from them and strode to a parked jeep, jumped in and barreled toward Chief and Fiddler.

Chief chuckled, "Boss! It's the Boss, boy!" — which meant it was the Boss Chief, the Head Canvasman. The jeep was equipped with stakedriving apparatus. The Boss Chief would put in the little clumps of stakes that anchored the big top's centerpoles. White people called him "Chief" like any other Indian, but the Indians had named him "Boss" because he was the only one of them to reach a boss status and get paid like a boss. The Boss Chief was minus an ear. As a kid he'd bet somebody his ear against theirs, the story went, and lost. Then he'd turned more serious — become a boss.

"They must have been telling him their troubles," Fiddler said. Candle flames flickered in the depths of Chief's eyes. He didn't reply. He hurried to meet his friend, Fiddler after him, kicking through the grass. The grass grew shin high. The cats and elephants and ponderous seat wagons hadn't stomped over it yet. It wasn't as lush or as Irish green in the sun as grass on the eastern lots, but brown and nice still. The show would take the ginger out of it. The grass would grow after the show left, but not like before.

The Boss Chief skidded his jeep to a halt. The pair of bright-eyed Indians punched each other mockingly.

"I see you got it all laid out, Mr. Menagerie Chief."

"Yeah, I got it fixed. Where's your tent? Where's your poles? Where's your blasted tent?"

"We're waiting on you! You ain't spotted all your wagons yet. You ain't even got your train unloaded." Then the Boss Chief quit fooling: "Was your boy with you?"

"Him? He was sleeping, weren't you, Fiddle? He was in bed." The tone of voice was not so much scornful as matter of fact. — Is he of age? — Not yet. Fiddler flushed.

"Maybe it'ud been better if you'd both been in bed," said the Boss. He was speaking as a Boss. In spite of his grave expression, his eyes glittered in sympathy with Chief.

"But he did pretty good this morning."

"Yeah?"

The circus water trucks hauled a whole slew of wagons onto the lot — the runner raced in front, beckoning directions — cut them loose and powered away, just as quick as that. "There are the cages!" shouted Fiddler. The big lay-out cat clacked and clanked toward the wagons as fast as it could, the little pinman hanging on behind like a monkey. The cat seemed certain to bulldoze right into the wagons but at the last instant spun in its tracks, hooked on to a string. It was cages, but the wrong ones — the act cages and the dog wagon. Fiddler had to be patient. The lay-out cat maneuvered, snorting and starting and stopping, and the pinman bobbed on and off, unhooking the wagons one by one. Then the cat returned to the lot entrance and pulled Fiddler's entire line of cages into the deep grass behind the cookhouse, where he wanted them. They rolled prim and well-kept-looking behind the big cat. He was proud of them.

"He's got to see his babies," Chief laughed as Fiddler rushed off.

The cages were behind Number 4 Wagon, the Ice Box, in two-foot grass where the manure could be raked out and left as it fell. The pinman scarcely had a chance to chock the wheels before the townies were on the spot to find out what was up. The lay-out cat steamed at them as it went and scattered them momentarily. Fiddler opened his tiger cage just to look at "his girl," say good morning. The townies scurried and swirled in his wake. She came to the bars with a flat, blank, murderous sheen in her eyes for the townies. He stood within easy range of her paws; his face nearly brushed against hers at the bars. Past his ear she roared her tiger's roar — more abrupt than a lion's, bristling with the actual sound of breath, like a gasp, titanic. Fiddler could hear the townies trip over themselves as they fled back.

But then they were coming again — "What in the world have you got there?"

"Yes, ma'am," he said, and shut the cage. The lady had folds in her neck like a chicken's wattles.

The lay-out cat returned with more cages and put them behind the first string. Frank, the rhino, had pried the boards off the bars of his cage; the fastenings weren't right. He was exposed to the public when he shouldn't have been, bumping his horn on the bars, boisterously swinging his head as if he was aiming a home run.

Like a conscientious soul, the pinman suggested, "You better tell the guy who takes care of him, that batty guy that talks to himself."

"I can do it," Fiddler replied. He petted Frank, reached between the bars and took hold of Frank's head, laid his arms along both sides of Frank's face. The head remained still. The eyes closed blissfully.

"He'll break your arms to bits, kid!" the pinman warned. "I've seen you do the stupidest — " The cat lurched and carried him off clasped on for dear life, the nosy son of a bitch. What business was it of his? What a sucker's job he had.

Frank's head was formed like a turtle's, even to the hooked lip and dull turtle eyes; but his ears flared out like the bells of trumpets and his horn was wedge-shaped, high. His body was big as a bus, long, made for ramming. Frank closed his eyes, let out a deep breath and propped himself on his elbows to be petted. Fiddler scratched behind the huge ears, over the eyes and in the itchy areas at the base of the horn.

"What's his name, mister?" a kid asked.

"Frank."

"Can I touch him?"

The people were crowded around. They'd blow cigarette smoke in Frank's eyes and get their fingers crushed — more than their fingers if you gave them time. Fiddler started boarding up the cage. He was trying to make the fastenings stick when — "Number 12, hey, Fiddler!" Red sang out in the distance. Fiddler glanced between the cages. Yes, the wagon was there. He had to leave Frank's cage no better than he'd found it. Kids were climbing on all the wagons, peeking in the air vents.

"Get off there! They'll scratch out your eyes!" Fiddler yelled. He didn't wait to see the results because they were always discouraging. The day's work had begun.

The lay-out cat driver set Number 12 Wagon precisely where Brownie wanted it, next to his truck, and Brownie gave him a salute. The Animal Department in full, impressive muster moved forward to help unload the wagon. There was Taylor, the madman, Brownie, the boss, and Coca Cola — the wagon ladder almost came down on Coca Cola's head when they opened the door; he didn't have the co-ordination to get out of the way; Chief caught

it and saved him — there was Coca Cola who'd graduated to Coca
Cola and aspirin from wine, and Chief, Fiddler, Red.

After the ladder, the next thing out of the wagon was Nigas,
the Department's dog. His real master was serving a life sentence
for murder, so he belonged to everybody. He was fox-red, small,
spunky, with eyes black and hard as two beads. He was in ecstasy
to be free in the sun and grass with Chief, Fiddler and Brownie,
his favorites. After Nigas, the wheelbarrow came out and the
stakes, hammers, the water barrels for humans and animals, the
top, the poles from the wall racks, the butchering board and sawhorses, the axe, shovel, cage tools — brushes and scrapers — the
crum boxes and the stray tiger cub in its cage. Everything was
painted red except the tiger cub and the top. The Animal Department's color was red.

Fiddler went up on the wagon and caught the ropes that were
thrown to him and lashed one end of the top to the wagon. Mean-
while Chief drove five stakes, shocking them into the earth a foot
at a blow with his big sixteen-pound sledge. The canvas went
up, the poles were set, the lines were noosed to the stakes and guyed
out, and the flaps of the top tied out for ventilation. Next door
the horse tops were going up, although the horses hadn't come up
from the crossing yet, and Murphy, the Ringstock dog, was running
and barking like Nigas. The Animal men were lucky in not
having to put up much canvas. Their cages were exhibited in
the big top, so they only needed a shelter large enough for themselves. The crum boxes were placed in a square inside the top.
Coca Cola had to open his right up and burrow after aspirin and
Coke amongst his crummy stuff to send him into Happyland.
"Crum" box was the word for his.

Chief grabbed a scraper, stakes and his hammer. Fiddler took
the broom and a coil of rope. The scraper and broom were each
iron rods about ten feet long, the scraper having a small iron bar
at one end instead of a brush. They were toted on the shoulder.
They see-sawed when you walked, and all the townies wondered
what they were for and followed to find out.

The lot was still bare and open. The four ticket wagons and the silver office wagon were spotted at the front of what would be the big top — the sideshow would be catty-corner to them — and the commissary wagon marked the middle of the backyard, with the cookhouse on one side and the Wardrobe and Band wagons in the process of being spotted beside the half-raised horse tops at the other. The cookhouse was up; the sideshow poles were up; the horse top canvas was stretched out on the ground, billowing a little wherever a breeze could get under it. But in the center of it all the grass grew undisturbed. There wasn't a pole or a bundle of canvas. The stakedrivers had hardly gotten a fourth of the way around.

Passing the cookhouse, Fiddler and Chief could smell the ham cooking, the biscuits, the cream of wheat. Fiddler was hungry as hell. When they reached the cages there were the same kids climbing to peer in the upper vents. "Get off there; they'll claw your eyes out!" Fiddler ordered.

"GET DOWN OFF THERE!" said Chief.

They did.

Chief drove the row of stakes faster than Fiddler could tie the rope between them. The people ranked themselves along the rope, holding on to it. You had to give them something to hold on to or they'd simply press closer and closer to the cage until they were pushed up against the bars and you were pushed against the bars and they could hold on to the bars. Mothers would lift up babies to kiss the lion's nose. It was unbelievable. Even using the rope, when the first wagon was opened, the leopards' wagon, some kid got carried away and ran under the rope and nearly escaped Chief's arm. The leopards were crazy to get him, lunging with their paws — he was almost close enough. Chief chased the kid back. The mother wagged her finger at the naughty child to play such a prank when the man didn't want him in there.

Chief worked fast. There was never a chance to fool with the animals when Chief was there because he worked fast. He put the pressure on Fiddler and deliberately kept him from playing with the cats. Earlier, Fiddler's petting the animals had been a point of argument with them, but now Chief just stopped him whenever he could. "Get your hands outa there!" he'd say. Chief would give each cage a rough once-over with the scraper, pulling out the dung. Then he'd go back and cut the meat, fill the wheelbarrow and come with it — and Fiddler had better be through. It was Fiddler's job to brush the residue of straw out of the cages so the floors would be clean for the cats to eat off of — "Clean as your plate," Chief said.

"Are they tame?" a voice asked, presumably referring to the leopards.

"Nope," said Fiddler. Chief didn't answer questions, which was the best policy if you could block your ears and not hear them repeated and repeated and repeated. Of course the questions were repeated and repeated and repeated even when you answered them, because new people came.

"Across the wide Missouri!" Chief boomed out tunelessly for no reason and turned to Fiddler with a toothy grin, a missing-toothy grin.

"Missouri?"

"Sure!"

"Missouri? Oh, yeah, that's where we are, isn't it? That's the river, the guy in the diner said."

"Sure, Missouri River! Big River! You had schooling, boy. You should know that stuff!"

The only other sign of drink in Chief besides this sudden outburst was the headache wrinkles over his eyes, and he'd had those all morning.

"You should keep track where you are! I didn't have much school, but I know," Chief concluded.

There were five leopards: Rajah, Sweetheart, Taboo, who was black, and Minny, the fat one, and Rita, who was wilder than the day she'd been caught. They lived together harmoniously except when one of the females would get in heat and go stir-crazy. Rajah, being the only male, enjoyed himself. He had a large, square build and was supercilious when you petted him, demanding to inspect your hands, then stalking back and forth indifferently. Sweetheart was the gentle one. You could put your arms between her paws or stroke her lips or *kiss* her lips — Fiddler had done that once, as an experiment. Taboo was glossy black and slender, pretty, quite trustworthy. Minny was the old one, a fat, quiet, well-adjusted cat. Minny had a policy — not to try particularly to hurt someone she knew would not hurt her — an easy, lazy policy. You could pet her back and flanks and neck. She'd curl her upper lip but not really mind. Rita was the nuisance, lightning Rita always flattened in a corner, watching her chance. Her eyes were deep gray-blue and her spots were navy blue, not black. What should be white on a leopard was gray on Rita, so that sometimes she looked dingy. But now and then the blue would mingle with the gray and make her very beautiful, misty blue, loose-muscled, small and slim and gray. Fiddler would ache to touch her.

Chief worked like an automaton, it seemed to Fiddler. He was patient. He didn't hit the leopards. He let them get out of the way of the scraper. But he didn't pet them or treat them like friends. He just raked out their cage and went to the next; and Fiddler took over with the broom.

Fiddler avoided hitting the cats almost as well as Chief. Rajah, Sweetheart and the panther, Taboo, were on their feet, prowling and sniffing. Minny was lying down but she'd get up when the broom nudged her and lie down somewhere else. Rita dashed at the bars if she felt threatened, and when she saw she couldn't reach Fiddler she'd get out of the way. Sweetheart and Taboo stayed beside the bars, pacing fast in flowing, perpetual motions, one black, the other golden-yellow spotted black. They moved in opposite directions and never looked at each other, slipping by effortlessly. Rajah was master of the cage, so he wouldn't exercise in any one line. He marched obliquely from front to back and along the walls and across his females' paths. Rajah was unpredictable. Fiddler had to go slow to keep from hitting him with the broom.

How'd you like to have one 'uv them for a fur coat, Gin? —I'm sure I'd love it, dear, if you could ever buy it for me. I wonder if that bud ever gets in the cage with them damn'd things. When do they feed 'em? How dangerous are they in captivity? Those

*are what, panthers? — Leopards, silly. — One of them's a panther.
He's black. — They've just painted him black — you can see his
spots; look — you have to look carefully. Mister, when do they
have the big tent up? Mister? I'd like to see him stick his hand
in there. — Benny, you've seen more than enough. There are other
things, Benny; come.*

"They're beauties, aren't they?" a kid said to his girl, and he
put his hand on her shoulder, twined his fingers in her hair and
tickled her so she giggled and wriggled. "But not like *you*. You're
prettier. You're much better." The lucky bastard!

From the highway drifted a funnel of dust and in the middle,
in the clear space, pranced the horses, ready to perform, proud and
prancing, white and palamino, brown, black and calico.

"The horses! The horses! Here comes the horses!" Fiddler
shrieked sarcastically to watch the townies scuttle. He pointed and
some of them did go, particularly the girls. They skipped away.

"Mommy, the horses! The horses!"

The leopards gyrated. The horse scent threaded in to them and
they could catch a crack of a glimpse at the corner of the cage.
They lay aquiver on their bellies, gorging on the sight. Their
gulping eyes were brilliant. They shifted their feet to center the
weight over the muscles — sprang! on-off the ledge above the door
and caromed round and around and around the *top* of the cage
eternally, never coming down. The leopards loop-the-looped, did
edgewise figure-eights across the cage from floor to ceiling. Fiddler
snuck the broom in and out so cleverly it didn't interfere. But
when he grasped the handle tight his hands hurt him; the scars
were stiff and painful, turning reddish.

Some of the men on the horses were old, battered winos, who
clung on through the kindness of the horses and who would have
been much healthier not wearing clothes, their clothes were so
filthy. Some were cowboys, who sat lackadaisically like burrs. And
some were the ordinary stalwart, rough little half-pints who are
always found around horses. — The horses weren't bothered. The
horses didn't care who or what was on them. They spraddled
their legs or pussyfooted, clicked hooves, did tricks. They didn't

wear saddles. They ignored their riders and came preened and prancing, nodding, nipping each other in a drove like spangled gypsy horses, like low-slow-frisky-flying flashy-painted tropic birds, like no horses Iowa ever could have seen before.

The crowd grew behind Fiddler. Newcomers more than replaced the horse enthusiasts and it would have required a staff of twenty expert Sightseeing guides to answer all the questions. Fortunately one question drowned out another; all Fiddler heard was a babble. Most people seemed to get the idea that the big top was put up early in the morning. They would arrive far too soon for that great event. Others, intending to beat the first wagon to the lot and watch the first stake driven, would arrive much too late. In any case, flocks of townies appeared just when Fiddler was working and, whatever they had planned to see, they all hurried over to watch dirty straw being raked out of cages so dark the animals were sometimes mere shadows in them unless you were as close as Fiddler. The townies gathered and they yapped. *Which is the most fierce? Are these animals used in the ring? I wish he'd show us his claws; I wish he'd make him show us his claws. Could you explain — keeper, oh keeper, could you explain. . . .*

The wagon next to the leopards' contained three separate cages. Three lion cubs were cramped into one, a cheetah was in another, and a barrel of a jaguar in the third.

Round as a lapdog and nearly the weight of a tiger, the jaguar was strange. Nobody understood him. He'd been with the show, in that same cage narrower than the length of his body, for many years. But his face looked young, unformed, like the face of an overgrown, lowering boy — a school bully's. Piggy eyes, eyebrows contracted. He was a riddle. He dreamed and dreamed all the time. — He'd wake, whack the scraper, roar and chew the ornamentation on the bars, snap at somebody's hand. Then he'd doze off again and be safe as a rug for a day, sprawled out with his eyes rolling in dreams, rising only to drink water prodigiously whenever it was offered. The jaguar rubbed his chin on the bars. The musty, pleasant, early sunlight made him blink. His head was square, his coat as short as the fur of a lion and a deeper yellow than a leopard's coat — the bulls-eye spotted pattern more pronounced and striking. The most versatile of cats, with burly, wrestler lines, the bowed legs of a climber, the dense hair of a swimmer, and grizzly bear-sized teeth to fight an anaconda or a crocodile. The jaguar didn't give any trouble while Fiddler worked. He kept out of the way.

Beside the jaguar lived the cheetah. She was like a woman, nervous, light and slim. When she came in heat they would try to make love through the partition screening. It was ridiculous. She was shaped just the opposite from him. Her bones were long, quick, and the graceful muscles on her legs were for running, not clawing. She was dainty and co-operative, with nails and fur and flat flanks like a dog's and only the small cat face to remind you what she was.

The cheetah's cage was as easy as the jaguar's and Fiddler was well started on it when there was a commotion between the wagons. A family straggled through. The mother had trouble getting over the wagonpole because of her skirts. "What's this, the animals?" she wondered.

"Do you see the rope, ma'am?"

"Where?" piped up the little girl, peering into the jaguar cage for a rope.

"Geez, he's big, I'll say, ain't he?" said the son, shoving close to the bars beside his sister. The collars of their sailor suits were at the level of the cage floor.

"Don't get hurt!" the mother warned.

"You see, ma'am, if you'd just stand behind the rope they wouldn't get killed," Fiddler explained with superhuman self-control. "The rest of the people are behind the rope and their children are safe." The jaguar's pudgy paws flexed unbelievingly. He edged forward. Fiddler decided not to let the lady "learn a lesson." He yanked the two kids back and sleepily the jaguar half struck at him instead.

"Oh! Help! Thank you very much!" the lady said.

"See, if you'd stand behind the rope — "

"Yes, we will, thank you; we were exploring. Come here, Joanie."

Fiddler's anger was a sodden lump in his chest. It didn't come out. He thrust his hand in the cheetah's cage and up to her face. She hissed like steam with pink, wide-open mouth. Her eyes stared away until they forgot, and she forgot, still staring away at nothing. Fiddler petted her slowly, gently tugging her ears. The townies oohed as if he were a hero. He pushed the cheetah aside and continued working. Fiddler used the broom methodically and well. Chief and he were proud of their cages.

Wasn't that lucky! Doesn't that man know his stuff, though, honey? What would happen if one of them things got loose! Huh? What would it do? — I can tell you what I'd do!

The lion cubs were seven months old and the general size of springer spaniels, with forelegs thick as Fiddler's arm and hard as blocks of wood. Their paws were swollen, immensely muscle-packed. The cubs had seen the horses briefly when the wagon was first opened. They'd bulled into each other scrambling for ways to get out and they'd kept it up because of the fresh air, the sudden flood of sunlight and moving, talking figures. Probably also the horse scent trailed across the lot from the Ringstock tops and kept them excited. But the moment the broom was in the cage they forgot everything else. The cubs were murder on the broom, piled on — 40 — 80 — 120 pounds — took fat, chopping bites, clawed and hung on. Fiddler sweated, even in the morning chill, and he was hungry and the cuts on his hands hurt from dragging the goddam broom out, jamming it in with them fighting it, pulling it out.

"Look out how you're doing, fool!" Something laid hold of the broom violently behind him. Trouble with the townies came in bunches.

Fiddler exploded. "Leggo of that!" A man had clamped on to the end of the broom with both hands. "Leggo, you stupid sonofabitch! What in hell do you think you're trying to do?"

"Can you see the child? You almost hit the child!" There was a kid inside the rope, a girl around six.

"Hit her! Can't you keep your goddam kids out of our way? We've got to clean these cages. We've got to watch these cats. We can't be watching what's behind us all the time!"

Chief was at the last cage in the line. He walked down, carrying his scraper high like a spear. "Listen, you mister, you keep your kids outa there! We ain't got eyes in the back of our heads! You keep your kids outa there!" Chief was drunk and grim. He was as tall as the townie and about three times as broad — chunky. His hair bushed up wild and black. The eyes were wedged in his iron-red face like two stones.

Ostentatiously the townie examined the kid's head for injuries. "All right," he said. Fiddler turned back to his work, making sure to be no more careful about what was getting in the way behind him than he'd been before.

"I didn't *misbehave* in a long time, Fiddle! When was the last time? Not for a long time till last night."

Always play along with a drunken Indian.

— "In Chicago you went to every cathouse on Eighteenth Street and scared the wits out of all the nigger girls, and then in Milwaukee you went and told the giant his mother was a giraffe. He was a 'sonofagiraffe.' "

"Hah, hah, hah, hah, hah, hah, hah, hah! Yep! *He* wouldn't get down off that stage. I told him, 'Get down off there, you' — hah, hah, hah, hah — 'sonofagiraffe! We'll see who's bigger!' *He* wouldn't do it. 'Sober up, Chief! Sober up, Chief!' he said — he *squeaked!* That guy, he wouldn't get down. But that was in Wisconsin. Long time ago. I didn't do anything wrong since Wisconsin, boy. That's a long time."

"Yep."

Chief went back to the wagon he'd been working on, closed it and left to fix the meat.

The best method of cleaning the cubs' cage seemed to be to pinch their tails and get them next to the bars and keep them frantic after one hand, pinching and snatching, while with the other you swept all the straw as near as possible — then really latch on to the broom and *pull*. Fiddler did. He finished with the cubs.

It's like a grab-bag! What's next? — I remember from the first man! This is better than the circus. I'm glad we didn't sleep. Oh! beautiful, tigers!

Ajax was so tall that, sitting down, the whole top half of his body was out of sight in the upper recesses of the cage. Even Fiddler at the bars had to stoop to look at him. *Let's see you touch him, mister! — Naah, he don't dare.*

The lay-out cat spotted the elephant wagon, Number 31, just beyond the cages.

"You're late! Goddam to hell you're late!" Bull men popped out of the grass and went to work like crazy because the bulls would be along any minute now.

"*I'm* late!" the driver gave it back. "The sonofabitchin' truck was late! You bastards'ud — " The cat spun so sharp it hurled dirt clods in the bull men's faces and took off.

Snippy, Ajax's mate, watched, tentatively crouched down on her paws, her head cocked quizzically. She paced a quick circle in the cage and resumed her crouch.

"You Snippy. What did you do?" said Fiddler, feeling warm with affection. She looked at him. Her eyes had just a glint of pink in the usual tiger gray. She didn't look at him for long. Her gaze streamed into the crowd and at the rhino, whose cage faced hers, and beyond. Her big body drew compact and then, instead of doing anything, she relaxed and looked at Fiddler idly. The gaze blurred; she looked past him. *Ooooh, it's scary! Lift me up! They could sure tear through a place, couldn't they? Now is that a male and her a female? They must know him. He certainly isn't afraid of them, is he? Henry, we need something like that to catch our mouse.*

Snippy got up and hurried in a tight circle and crouched lightly down again with the pink glint in her eyes that was not a color but a trick of light. But she was in the path of the broom. Fiddler tapped his fingers on her paw. Absent-mindedly she rose, circled the cage, came back, looked at him. The pupils of her eyes adjusted to the light. The black shrank and the gray replaced it, perfectly concentrically, as it transformed from black. Snippy looked over Fiddler's shoulder, scanning the crowd. Her ears twitched back. Somehow, somewhere she'd developed such a hatred for certain people in the show — the sideshow impresarios with their tuxedos and sharpie, grease-slicked hair, for instance — that she'd pick them out of multitudes of people and keep a bead on them, roar and rage if they got near. "It's too early, Snippy," Fiddler told her. "They're not here." She padded in a circle, crouched softly and started past him, not searching for anybody now, just staring.

"Johnny — say, Johnny! Johnny — Johnny!"

From experience Fiddler had learned "Johnny" or Jimmy-Mike-Bob-Harry meant him and that if he didn't want to be shouted at for the rest of the morning he'd better answer this particular type of guy.

"Yep?"

"How do they catch a thing like that?"

"I don't know," Fiddler said to cut the conversation off.

"They dig a hole in the jungle, don't they? And cover it with stuff so's something'll fall in?"

"If you know, why do you ask?"

" 'Cause that's how I caught my wife!"

"George!" squawked a woman. People snickered.

Ajax sat peacefully while the cage was being cleaned. When Fiddler told him to change sides he did, pausing only to bend and look out at a dog which was barking. The dog yipped and ran. Ajax was so enormous the bars were actually no bigger than some of his stripes. When he sat down, again the upper half of his body was hidden from sight. *Whew! Jesus Christ, I'd give a year's pay to shoot something like that! Would he eat me? Poke him so he'll get down so we can look at him. How much would that big feller weigh? How much do you feed him in a week?*

Frank, the rhino across the way, raised a rumpus when he saw Ajax. He aimed his horn and plunged at the bars. Some of the people were afraid he'd bust loose; they pushed back. Taylor was raking out the cage and he kept right on. When Frank calmed down the people began to throng in toward the cage again but then they stopped as if they'd come up against a brick wall. Taylor didn't use bricks to make room to work in. He didn't even need a rope.

Taylor talked: "My penitentiary name, yaah, Taylor. I'm ex-con." Fiddler could hear a smattering of words and he could read the lips; he knew the words from hours of listening to them. Naturally today Taylor was discussing The Downfall of Heavy, the Porter: "He's here some place, the guy wha' killed 'um. He killed by beatin' — two did. They beat 'um — Heavy — he tol' me ta make him a suit, he used ta tell me that. 'I ain't no tailor! Screw ya! That's my penitentiary name! I ain't no tailor! Lissen!' I told 'um. He was askin' for it. I coulda told 'um in Des Moines. He was a boob! He was booby! He oughta huv' been in the hatch! They oughta huv' got 'um with the striped suits! 'I'll make ya a *striped* suit,' I told 'um once time, '*Striped!*' — hah, hah, hah, hah, hah, hah, hah, yaah! 'Ya're a boob!' I told 'um."

People couldn't stand to have that kind of thing spewed in their ear. The townies wavered back, gawking at Taylor as much as at the rhino. But every once in a while some new person would barge into the vacant space, dragging and lecturing children and not paying any attention. — He'd get a load of Taylor in his ear, a real blast from behind, from ambush, and jump like a shot deer — "The guy wha' killed 'um. He's here some place." — and peep around for Heavy's murderers, for penitentiary guards, and wilt out of hearing. When one young man made the error of *laughing!* "Tee-hee, tee-hee all ya want!" Taylor gabbled, foaming. "Tee-hee, yaah, tee-hee! Tee-hee! Tee-hee! But they beat 'um. An' oh they took 'um and beat 'um so the blood came out 'uv his sides and in his ears. I saw it. They had 'um down. They took him and beat 'um. You c'n tee-hee!" Taylor threw himself on the ground, shielded his head with his arms, thrashed and struggled, made gushing motions in front of his mouth and ears. The people cleared out. They came to watch Fiddler. Taylor got up, continued working and talking to "'umself," and Fiddler had double the crowd to cope with.

The second tiger wagon was harder to clean. The male was almost as large as Ajax and he wasn't sitting quietly. He pawed the female and she laced him with her pretty orange paws. He was panting. Saliva bubbles showed on his chin and the ruff of fur on the back of his neck was mussed. He couldn't stay away —

traipsing back and forth, every which way, all heated up, much
too big for the cage, as big as four men in a bathroom. Beautifully
she snarled with ivory teeth white as the fur on her face and lips
as black as the blackest stripe. Her face was round like a prize
pussycat's — the fur stuck out in a collar. She was gorgeous. When
the broom blundered too near she sprang, grabbed it seemed like
a yard out of the cage at Fiddler, dropped a roar like a piledriver
on him. She jumped back then and bounded across the broom,
turned, snapped it up but let go instantly before Fiddler could
even brace for a fight. And the male kept beside her step by step,
sometimes with his tongue out to lick and sometimes with that
hot mouth yawned and the four tusks like thumbs ready to catch
her head and hold her still. The head bobbed and the jaws that
could have enclosed it glided over, flexing. She boxed his ears.
She stung his nose. With her starched, prim frills of creamy fur,
her orange paws and black paint-stroked, yolk-yellow body, she
boxed his ears.

The trucks towed the first series of floats, each neatly draped with
canvas, onto the lot. The flags went up the cookhouse poles, Old
Glory and the "Hotel" flag which meant it was time to eat. A
hundred bums and winos began pulling themselves out of hiberna-
tion in the grass. Fiddler could see at least a hundred. It was
amazing how huge a personnel the circus had at mealtimes. Chief
appeared down at the leopard cage with the meat. The winos
were making cracks about "breakfast" as they passed the wheelbarrow on their way to eat. Fiddler finished with the tigers in a
hurry. He did very well, considering what was going on in the
wagon. *What's the scoop? Is the big tiger trying to eat the little
one? Do these animals become tame for you when you take care
of them? Is it true that a lion is the king of beasts? We've made a
bet.*

The coarse sand-and-turpentine lion smell gave the last wagon
away. It smelled as good as any perfume to Fiddler. He loved it.
Big Joe was lying right by the bars and Fiddler sunk his hands in
the handsome red mane, hiding even his wrists in it. "You Joe!"
he said. Joe grimaced and bit the air irritably but couldn't turn

for Fiddler without some effort because Fiddler had caught him sideways to the bars. Before Joe decided to make the effort Fiddler had him enjoying it, squinting, rubbing his ear on Fiddler's arm and groaning with the pleasure of being scratched deep under his mane.

Far across the lot the elephants came gallumphing, bugling split-off noises. The bull men rode, some on the necks and some on the heads, holding on to a corner of an ear and letting their boots dangle down between the eyes. The best bulls briskly wore their men like hats and gallumphed so rhythmically the men went up and down like sailors and could sit with no hands and their eyes closed. Bingo, in fact, rode with no hands. He only had one and he probably had fleas; his hand was busy. The lead bull, Ruth, the queen bull, carried Bingo. She pretended she was going to toss him off. She trumpeted and flapped her ears in preparation. Bingo wasn't a bit disturbed. He called her bluff.

The elephant boss rode a gray horse which kept the bulls in line by butting and bullying them — a real swashbuckling horse. On the highway that horse not only bullied the bulls but also the townspeople's cars, cleared them out of the way, and on the lot its job was forcing paths through the mobs of people. It was the toughest, cockiest horse in the world.

The bulls had been traveling fast from the crossing — the horse had made them — but now they eased up and shouldered through the clustered wagons. Their trunks swept above the grass and wrenched out clumps as people flick a finger. They held their heads steady so the bull men wouldn't be thrown off but let their snake trunks play and curve and snuffle up Black-eyed Susans in the grass, empty Crackerjack boxes. Today the bulls were brown. Elephants were supposed to be gray — everyone knew that; zoo elephants were gray. Even the bull boss's horse was a pachydermous gray. But the bulls themselves only looked gray when the town they happened to be in had gray dust. They were covered with dust. They blew it on themselves, they collected it, they prided themselves on it, grew bristles on their backs especially to catch it. Like chameleons, they changed color as they moved from place to place. If a freak town had red dust or white dust the bulls were red or white that day. Iowa's dust made them brown and they chugged along, swaying from foot to foot. The horse lined them up in the high grass where they would be out of the way of the rest of the circus and the bull boss dismounted, uncoiled his black whip, laid the lash on the ground. The men grabbed hold of an ear and slid off or clung to a trunk and were lifted down.

There was an Indian on bulls. Daisy, his elephant, was the tallest of the herd and he took advantage of her height by standing on the crest of her head and shouting, "Chief! Hey Wampus!" Daisy cradled him with her trunk and set him down.

The bull boss cracked and slithered his whip, holding the bulls in a row and not minding at all if an occasional backlash kept the townies out of his hair. More than half Fiddler's audience had left to see the elephants. From every part of the lot the townies were running — kids and fathers and older sisters and mothers, strung out in that order. The poor bull men, trundling bales of hay, were having a hell of a time in the traffic.

"Rope them off!" Fiddler laughed, secure behind his stakes, when three kids tumbled under the lion wagon screeching "El'- phants" and just about rollblocked his legs from under him. People dashed for the elephants as if for the end of a rainbow — Hallelu- jah! But the bull boss kept an incompressible zone of fifty-one feet between the bulls and the townies. He was in the center. His whip was twenty-five feet long.

The bulls rocked backward and forward like pitchers winding up, tossed their trunks up and down. Finally the hay was brought. The bulls broke the wire binding of the bales for themselves. They stepped on the bales and let their weight crush down, all the time solemnly waving their trunks like massive wands. Then the trunks plunked down, furled mouthfuls of hay. The elephants ate.

In the lion wagon Bessie growled, sounding like gears stripping. Joe would get up for the broom but not Bessie. She made a terrible, crinkled-up face and glared like a child in the quiet stage of a temper tantrum. Fiddler aimed the broom to hit her in the soft spot behind the elbow on the side. Bessie blocked it, jerking her elbow back with a grinding, crotchety growl. The tigers would have been hopping and roaring, they were so nervous, but Bessie chewed the broom lazily, lying down. Something on it must have tasted very bad, because her lips drew up; she let go and acted as if she were going to sneeze. Her lips scrunched up so high Fiddler could see every one of her teeth, even the molars. She got up; she gave up; and stood out of the way. She scraped her tongue between her teeth and growled to herself a scratchy, feathery growl.

Chief-on-Bulls came under the rope to escape the crowd. He was going to see Chief. "How's your Chief, kid?"

"He'll be fine if we can get him sober."

"Where was you last night, Bullfrog?" Chief demanded loud as a bull from where he was feeding the jaguar. The three of them, Little Chief, Chief-on-Bulls, and Fiddler's own Chief, had traveled together in 127 car and been buddies since Chicago; but Chief-on-Bulls hadn't been there last night.

"Nooky! Nooky, you cat-taming sonofabitch! We had a girl on the flats! We took a girl out'uv Sioux City. They must'uv had the alarms ringin' last night. We had her in the Columbus Discovers America float, with the canvas over — cozy — dark — plenty of space."

"What is this story?" blurted a shocked matron.

"You got a daughter, lady? You keep her home tonight, unless you want her Discovering America!"

Chief made the animals work to get their meat. He made them pull it through the bars. The jaguar's arm was far out of the cage, fastened on to a piece. "Git it! Git it!" shouted Chief-on-Bulls, punching one hand into the other and strolling down toward Chief. He was tall and raw-boned, with a Roman nose. He was Alaskan. He'd sailed south on a fishing boat to Seattle and started bumming east to see "the States." But by the time he'd reached Chicago he was ready to turn right around, join the show and head west again to go back home.

"You brave?" Chief challenged, loud so everyone could hear.

"I can tar the daylights out of *you!*"

"You see them cubs? You feed them baby cubs, let's see you. Fiddle'll teach you how. Come here, Fiddler!"

Fiddler came.

The bull man took a couple of chunks of meat and the lion cubs struck at them so fast reflexes saved him from a scratching, nothing else. He jumped. "Wow, Devils!"

Chief grinned and bent next to the cheetah's cage with a tongue-shaped, bloody piece of liver. "Whatcha gonna do, Cheet?" Cheetah crept to the bars with mouth stretched full-open, dribbling, hissing, eyes insane. Chief, delighted, hissed back, dangled the meat close to the bars, where Cheetah jabbed at it with helpless dog-feet. She stamped on his hands as they snuck in the cage and teased her feet. Chief laughed and hissed. Cheetah dripped saliva on the floor and hunched in desperation — mewed. Chief mimicked the mew and finally let her snatch away the meat.

Fiddler didn't know whether he thought that kind of thing was right to do. He went back to the big lions' wagon.

Chief fed the cubs and moved to the tigers. Chief held the meat on the end of a prong and the orange paws swiped at it, making a wind that ruffled his hair.

The lion, Joe, nosed the bars. He was hungry. Dots seethed in the brown of his eyes and the colorless drool from his mouth wet his paws. He stared at the ground, the people, Fiddler — through everything as through air. He grunted once with gruff impatience and then once at Bessie, turning his head, to keep her back. In his eyes the pupils were perfectly round and fixed, like celluloid disks, but the brown seethed with floating lines and dots.

"Here's this fella's!" said Chief, bringing Joe a dripping hunk of meat and bone. It wouldn't go under the bars. It got stuck. Joe tugged with his claws dug like fingers into the bone and his teeth grappling, growls rumbling out of him like breakers. Chief drove the prongs at the meat again and again. It took both Joe and Chief to get the meat into the cage, there was so much of it. Joe's mouth was smeared with blood and he was excited, swishing his tail.

"You ain't got none of them fellas in Alaska!"

"No," the bull man admitted, "but we've got bears that 'ud make them circus bears piss in their britches!"

Chief told Fiddler, "You eat. I'll take the crap back."

"That's all right. I'll help you."

"Eat! You eat, boy!"

"Okay."

Fiddler felt just as hungry as Joe or the cheetah. At three-thirty the previous afternoon the circus had given him supper. If anybody had tried to stop him now as he walked to the cookhouse, there would have been blood on the Iowa grass.

THE RAIN SHEETED down so loud it was hard to think and harder still to hear what anyone said, impossible to hear the show going on. Performers in skimpy costumes made shivery exits a few yards away, wrapping themselves in towels and bathrobes as they ran. David got a side view of several rows of people watching the show muffled in raincoats, reluctant even to bring out their hands to clap. Most of the ground was muck. David's first official job had been to help spread straw on the runway where people would be coming out when the show was over.

It was a pretty bleak beginning. David had been thrown out of his room in the city at five o'clock in the afternoon for not paying his rent and for being a "rummy," his landlady said, who was herself the fattest, whiniest rumdum on Green Street. She'd known he was hungry and didn't have money to eat on and she'd led him into her room on purpose so he could smell all the food she had, see the boxes of candy and the leftovers still on her lunch dishes. She'd shaken a paper under his nose. She'd told him he'd have to find a job if he didn't want to starve, and then, instead of letting him look through the ads himself, she'd caught his finger and brought it to one of them, twisting his finger and smelling so strongly of perfume he thought it would ooze on his head as she bent over him. Scraggling hair, fat, shovy breasts. "I had a boy-friend in the circus," David's landlady had trilled as though she were still young enough to have a boyfriend. She'd pinched his shoulder and arm and bent over him, smelling of perfume, as if she owned him. David remembered feeling crawly, wondering if she

really was going to throw him out and wishing he had a drink —
she'd give him a drink; if not something to eat, then a drink. But
no, she'd stood him on his feet, led him out of the room. "You
rummy, you're going to be in the circus like my boyfriend, and you
c'n come back and see me when you c'n pay for your room, 'cause
I'm a respectable lady. I don't have no men who can't pay for
their room."

She'd taken David to a bus stop, flagged a bus and climbed right
in with him and paid for him, slapped him on the rear end as if
she owned him. "Honey," she told the driver, "take him to the
circus and don't let him out before — And *you* come back and see
me some time when you've got something in your pocket besides
your pool stick. Hee-hee-hee!" That was the last David saw of her
— pulpy, purple-red lips laughing at the big joke.

So David had gotten a job, which was one relief. And so far he
hadn't had to do much of anything except keep out of the rain.
It had started raining soon after he'd been assigned to the Animal
Department and found his way there. He'd helped a couple of the
men he'd be working with put canvas over the hay and bags of
feed and take some washing off the ropes that held their little top
up and "guy out" the ropes to withstand the storm. From then on
it had rained, rained and rained. Brownie, the boss, hadn't given
David anything to do except scatter straw on the runways for a
few minutes. Didn't even sign him up. "You'll quit before we tear
down tomorrow if it keeps on raining," Brownie had said.

It kept on raining. It got so that water blanketed the whole
ground, every patch of grass. There was no dirt, only mud. But
that was okay. If David could have eaten something he wouldn't
have minded any amount of rain. If he could have had some milk
and eggs and meat and peas and bread. David thought he was
reaching the stage of hunger where he could think of nothing but
food. He hadn't eaten for forty-eight hours. That wasn't so long
really, he knew, but what he knew didn't seem to help the feeling
in his belly. It had been too late to get supper when he'd reached
the circus — the first show over and the people gone. "Mealtime!
Mealtime! You gotta wait till the next mealtime!" the cookhouse
boss had shouted. Brownie had gotten mad at being asked for a

loan. The other men in the Animal Department's top said they didn't have any money. And they probably didn't — they looked broke — but they'd eaten.

The evening show had started. David had wandered into the big top to watch, but it wasn't worth it in the rain. He'd been sidetracked to what seemed the dryest spot, next to the elephants and behind a big cage-wagon that was humming away like a refrigerator. A group of men were there sitting on gunnysacks and empty peanut packing boxes. It turned out they were Animal men too. But they didn't have any money or food. The one called Robinson seemed to be the leader. He answered all of David's questions in an authoritative voice. David kept asking lots of questions because he couldn't just sit and feel his stomach eating itself, churning and almost climbing up to gnaw his throat.

"What do we have to do?"

"Nothing till the suckers leave," Robinson said.

"Then what?"

"Shut the cages up. Then that's all."

"Then where do we sleep?"

"Wherever you can. We'll be here tomorrow so you stay anywhere you can."

Robinson had the openest, pleasantest face David had seen in the circus yet. He was easy to talk to. The others hadn't deigned to notice David. There was a boy David's age who limped from polio or the war or something. Hopalong was what they called him. He sat facing the wagon, not saying a word. And opposite him a man had hunched himself into the machinery that made the wagon hum. This man didn't once open his mouth either. From cap to shoes he was dressed in black — not rain clothes, black work clothes. And he looked sad enough to be in mourning. Between Hopalong and the man in black Robinson and David sat, and in front of them, in the center limelight, were "Dry Wash" and "Daff."

"He's the creep who *really* hates the rain. He don't like to get wet — do you, Dry Wash?" Daff demanded. " — He ain't had soap or water on him since he quit wearing diapers." Daff's laughter flapped out of him, harsh as burlap on the ears. He was a board-thin, lank-faced individual with hair dry and long as a clown's wig combed in one direction over the side of his head and a long, Pinnochio nose. He'd been teasing Dry Wash steadily.

"Hitler thought he was smart!" Dry Wash replied. He stuck his little finger in his ear and dug and dug and pulled it out, cleaned it off.

The man in black was chewing his lip and absently watching a woman run toward the cage licking the rain from her lips. She was carrying some fruit, so David immediately became very intent. He could see bananas, grapes and round fruit of some kind, apples, oranges or maybe plums. She was a stumpy gnome of a woman with a crop of dense monkey hair and a wizened, leathery face. An oldtimer obviously. There were all three — apples, oranges and plums, as well as the bananas and green grapes. She had a tattered square of quilt drawn over her shoulders instead of a raincoat. David was not alone in lacking a coat. Nobody had one. But they all had eaten; and she held probably fifteen pounds of fruit heaped in her arms.

"Can you spare an apple, do you think?" David asked, but she was in the wagon. She triggered the latch with one finger and slipped into the wagon without even answering. David caught a glimpse of two baby gorillas or chimps fawning and scrambling up the woman's legs in the lighted cage before the door slammed shut.

"She don't know you," Robinson explained. "But she loves them monks so, you might not have got any if you were her own husband. They're her babies."

"What are they?"

"Gorilla monks. They're valuable. They have to eat right and they're air-conditioned even. It's glassed. They don't hardly breathe the same air we do."

"You ought to see him when he takes a bath," Daff went on.

Dry Wash interrupted, "Listen now, Hitler thought he was smart as hell too" — wringing his little finger in his ear again.

" — First he picks up a couple of rolls of toilet paper somewhere, from a can, in a gas station or some place, a can. And then he goes into the giraffe wagon, just like anybody else — that's where we clean up. So he strips like anybody else. So, so then he takes the paper an' *wipes* himself with it! you know, hard, all over his body, all over, everywhere, with a handful of can paper! I spied on him once. Hah, hah, hah!"

"Listen now, some people think they can get away with anything, but they're not so smart as what they suppose!" Dry Wash interrupted again. That ear-rubbing seemed to be something he did every time he spoke.

"And the poor giraffe man" — Daff pointed at Hopalong — "he's got to clean it up. It's like after a spitball fight. Kids roll up little balls. The paper does that; all filthy balls from being rubbed on him, all over him."

Dry Wash *did* seem to be unusually miserable in the rain, and the water *had* washed white streaks on his face. He was under a particularly bad leak, although anywhere you sat (except scrunched into machinery like the man in black) you were bound to get wet. The rope ribbing of the big top stood out gaunt and skeletal between huge hanging pouches of trapped water. Water dripped from most of the pouches; some places it poured. Just outside, an unbroken sheet clattered off the big top into the lake that was the ground. Even if you could keep your clothes dry, by having eyes on top of your head and jumping-jack legs, you couldn't keep your shoes from getting wet. There was no possibility of that. David tried to remind himself how uncomfortable the rain was — as in his mind he stared through that boarded-up back side of the gorilla cage.

"What time do they have breakfast?"

"Food, food, food. The first thing you said was about food. What's the matter, you miss a few meals?" Robinson laughed jokingly.

"He looks like it," jeered Daff. "I'll make your mouth water. I'll tell you what we had. We had liver-and-onions and roast-beef-and-brown-gravy. We could choose."

"Why don't you keep your mind on little girls?" Robinson told him. " — He always has to be starting fights with somebody. — You've missed a few yourself, Daff. And there's one now." Robinson pointed.

Daff strained forward, stretched flat in the mud to leer at the legs of a little girl who was crossing the runway with 'her father, to look up her skirts.

Robinson warned him. "Some day some kid's going to have a paratrooper for a father, and he's going to stomp the eyes right out of your head and bust up your hands like a sonofabitch!" He turned to David. "He's awful! He'll give us all a bad name — if he don't get us all arrested! 'Molesting children.' These town cops will kill you for that!"

The gorilla woman emerged, with three apples left! David didn't say anything. He knew she'd saved them for him. And when she kept right on going, he waited to catch her eye. She was almost out of hearing before he really realized the apples were not for him. She went to where the elephants were chained. She walked along the row until she came to one sprawled sick on the ground, its trunk a grotesque fifth leg and its bloated side heaved up like a hill. Feebly the trunk reached, took the apples and flopped back down in the mud before groping its way to deposit them in the mouth. David envied the elephant. The others trumpeted forlornly.

"Here's Brownie." Robinson was on his feet.

Brownie shouted, "We're gonna close these cages. It's wet; it's leaking. Nobody'll look at 'em anyhow." David, not knowing what to do, stood up and started toward the boss immediately, then stopped and waited for the others and went with them. He stepped in mud ankle-deep. He had a pair of cracked, cast-off shoes that were about like cardboard for keeping out water. "Close 'em up! What a sonofabitching night this is going to be! Close 'em up! They ought to tear down and blow the town." Brownie had a terrible-looking left eye. He slogged away, muttering. He wore rubber boots which covered him to his knees and a long black fireman's coat and even a hat. He shouldn't complain.

"Get up top, kid, will you?" said Robinson.

"Where?"

"Behind the cages. There's things to climb up. Here's Chief. He's got the pole."

Obediently David went around behind a wagon that said GNU

— *Africa* and contained a strange, horned, striped cross between a zebra and a cow. He looked in vain for a ladder behind the cage, under the cage. At last on the end of the wagon he saw rungs going up and he climbed. They were very slippery, as if coated with ice. The roof of the wagon had nothing to hold on to except a flap which David was made to understand he should unhook and let down in "Just a minute for Jesus Christ sake! Wait! We gotta close the bottom!" David waited, kneeling, spacing out the weight of his body to keep his balance and avoid sliding off. It was slick as ice up there. Water had leaked in buckets onto the metal roof. Daff and Hopalong slammed up the bottom flap and the third guy, Chief, a big, dark, Indian-looking guy, stuck a pole against the flap David was holding and David let it go down. Then Daff and Hopalong slammed the two side flaps shut with a bang that shook the wagon. Robinson stood off to the side as if he were a sort of supervisor who didn't have to work.

Robinson shouted, "Jump, kid, jump!" Daff and Hopalong had closed the bottom flap of the next cage in line.

David hesitated. "What do you mean?"

"You're s'posed to be up there!" Chief roared at Robinson. "Why ain't you up there?"

"Hurry up. They're waiting on you. Jump!" Robinson repeated. It was only seven feet or so to the next wagon, but both surfaces gleamed treacherous with rain, with a ten-foot drop in between and the wagonpole to land across. David jumped, skidding, beating his arms. Then there was another wagon to jump to, and another; ten more. The arc lights swung high off the quarterpoles and made the wagon tops gleam silver. Great sinister pockets of canvas bellied down overhead, incessantly trickling water and making the footing even more slippery. People in nearby seats turned around to watch David instead of the show. And he put on an exhibition with his leaps, sliding all over the place, clutching at air, juggling himself on the balls of his feet. He certainly couldn't get drunk on this job!

When he got on the ground again, unhurt, Brownie beckoned and said, "None of these bums can do anything. Here," and gave him the pole Chief had used to lower the flaps.

"What do I do?"

"Chase those bastards in. Get up on the cage."

It was the giraffe pen Brownie was talking about. It was open and two wagons were parked in the entrance. The giraffes were supposed to go in the wagons. David shinnied up the fence and brandished the pole like a wild westerner. The giraffes bucked and protested, but not very vigorously because they were getting rained on through holes in the canvas. They seemed to know that being shut up for the night would be comfortable. Hind legs gangling like rudders and necks bold stalks out in front, they vaulted into the wagons.

Brownie was already gone. David had intended asking him where to sleep.

"Where does he sleep?"

"Huh?" said Daff.

"Where does the boss sleep?"

"In the wagon."

"In the wagon with the giraffes?"

"No! Hah, hah, hah, hah! No, our wagon, Number 12, the department wagon. He's got a cot he uses."

"Would there be room for me in there?"

"In the wagon with Brownie? Hell, no! He don't let nobody in there." Daff had to share the joke with the others. — "This kid wanted to know if Brownie slept with the giraffes and he wanted to sleep with him! Hah, hah, hah!"

Hopalong laughed. Robinson smiled. "There's tons of flops around here," Robinson explained. "Don't worry about it. You'll have ten thousand seats in there when the suckers get out." Hopalong, Daff and Robinson went under the sidewall and outside. David tagged along.

"Where do you sleep?"

"Kid, I sleep in the orang cage, me and Hopalong and Robinson and the orang," said Daff, although David hadn't been talking to him. "There ain't no room for nobody else."

The rain had softened. David could almost feel it letting up.

The wind seemed to be blowing the very drops away. And the circus was going strong. The music not only was audible; it oompahed in the grandest fashion. The midway lights blasted up at the smothering cushions of sopping clouds, staining them orange and yellow and red. Wind sissed on a row of trees somewhere and water plopped instead of spilling off the big top. The little wagon and top the department used looked exceedingly small. They entered the top, to be greeted with — "Don't nobody touch that bed. That's my bed!" — and a jabbing arm and a very grumpy Indian face. A canvas laid over a bale of hay was Chief's "bed."

"It'll be pouring again in five minutes, you'll see," Brownie was saying as he poked a flashlight around trying to find something. When the beam happened to hit David Brownie exclaimed, "Goddam, what'uve we got, another queer? Your hair's as long as a goddam — as a goddam violinist!"

"I don't have any money," David said angrily.

Hopalong, Daff and Robinson opened their boxes and picked out an assortment of torn pants and scraps of quilt and army blanket which they could wrap themselves in for the night. They cursed because their belongings had gotten wet — the boxes like everything else were sitting in puddles of water. That was one thing David didn't have to worry about, belongings. Then the three of them headed back to the big top. David followed, not knowing what else to do. They went to a cage, opened a barred door in the front and crawled inside. This time David couldn't come along, because Hopalong closed the door in his face and clicked the padlock.

"See, we don't wanna get rolled. We lock it."

Behind Hopalong an ape was cavorting, trying to entertain and postpone being caught. Daff and Robinson were after it and there wasn't much room. The chase was short. Once caught, the thing buttered up to them, hugging and whimpering and sentimental. But Robinson worked it over to a box in the corner and stuffed it in. Its arms were long, grabbing in all directions to escape from the box. Robinson rammed in the door and fixed the padlock. Daff and Hopalong were smoothing the straw in the cage to sleep on.

"Now he's locked in and we're locked in and you're the only one that's free!" Robinson said to David, laughing. "But you want to sleep with us, do you?"

— "There ain't no space!" Daff broke in.

Robinson's pleasant brown eyes looked very deeply into David's. A smile crept over his lips persuasively. "Look, when they clear those suckers out of here you'll have ten thousand seats to sleep on." Robinson's hair was awfully long too. It was a wavy type that didn't look as bad long as David's straight hair. But David wondered what Robinson would do if Brownie ever said he looked like a queer and a violinist. David looked at the hair again and began to see that actually it was freshly cut, cut long around the ears deliberately.

"Not tonight, honey," whispered Robinson with eyes moistening and a mincing smile.

Chilled with disgust, David left.

There was still the problem of getting a bed of some kind. He might have to forget he was hungry until tomorrow, but sleep he was determined to find. And he didn't want to sit in one of those folding show chairs all night.

The man in black was squeezed into the compartment of the gorilla wagon with the machinery like before. But now he was asleep. It looked dangerous. David noticed that, although on three sides the guy didn't have an inch to spare, he wasn't quite touching any of the apparatus. He seemed to be in precisely the same position as when he'd been awake. He hadn't slumped a bit. So maybe he always slept there, without getting burned or caught in the gears! Maybe there wasn't any place else to sleep!

A family of performers was gathered in a corner jabbering to itself in some foreign language and trying to wipe dry the springboard and seesaw contraptions it used in its act.

David went back out to the department's top.

"What do you want, boy?" Chief demanded grumpily.

"I'm looking for a place to sleep and I'm looking for something to eat. I haven't eaten for two days."

Chief was seated on his canvas-covered bale of hay with water trickling all around him, sewing what looked like a string of beads on to what appeared to be a belt. David couldn't imagine how he could see in the slight glimmering of light which penetrated the tent.

"What am I s'posed to do about it?"

"I thought you could give me some help." David felt willing to grasp at any straw.

"Jesus Christ! Help? Jesus Christ, boy! What d'ya mean, help? Everybody wants help. Who the hell doesn't want help when they come on this show. When I come on this show I had my head beat open so you could see the brains! What d'ja say, you're hungry? Everybody's hungry when they come on this show! If I helped *one-hundredth* the people who come on this department in a year, I wouldn't have a STITCH! Two days you haven't eaten? I've seen men go without eatin' eight, ten days! Didja tell the boss you was hungry? He'd have given you some of the animals' food. Carrots, apples. Didja? No, you was ashamed. 'Can you lend me a dollar?' — I heardja. That's all you said. I don't know where he is now. What have you got to be ashamed of? You're as good as anybody — anybody *watchin'* that show!"

Chief got up blustering and beefing and loud. David followed him toward the big top. "When I come on this show I had my head beat open so bad you could see my brains! Hah, hah, hah, hah, I had to comb my hair specially to hide them when I was gettin' a job! They don't want to see your brains on this show. Hah, hah, hah, hah!" He put his hand in his pocket. "You see how much money I got, all together?" It was eighty or ninety cents. "That's all I got. That's all. And that's more than anybody else in this department has to his name! Everybody's hungry when they come on this show."

Chief stood in the entryway to the seats, surveying the eager-beaver butchers who bustled up and down the aisles waving their wares.

"Doggie, doggie. Hey, red hot! Hey, doggie, doggie. Red hot! Hey, doggie, doggie. Hey, red hot!"

Chief called to the kid selling hot dogs, "C'mere."

"How many?" asked the kid.

"One."

"Mustard?"

Chief turned to David. "Mustard?"

"Yes, thanks."

"That's fifteen."

"It's a dime. I'm with the show," Chief told the kid.

"We charge fifteen for a frank. I don't care who you're with."

"Come on. You pay ten if you're in the show. Come on!" Chief's voice menaced and he reached out, extracted the hot dog from the kid's hand and put two nickels in its place. "Come on!" he had to say again, even though the transaction had been completed. The kid was holding his tray with one hand and seemed to be debating whether to put it down and try to take the hot dog back by force. It took still one more "Come on!" before the kid gave up and walked sneeringly away.

"Those guys, they make a nickel profit, see? They're rich. But they shouldn't make no profit off of people in the show!" Chief explained. Then he called over one of the Coca-Cola butchers and worked the same deal, getting less of a protest this time because the guy was older and more cynical.

"Okay, okay," he said sarcastically, accepting Chief's dime.

"Now you want a place to sleep." Chief sloshed off through the mud with his heavy work boots, expecting David to keep up in cardboard shoes. Chief took him to the giraffe pen. "Them giraffes are gone and they've got straw. You sleep there. Find a place where it don't leak and pile it up there and sleep there. — You got a friend!" Somebody was already sleeping in the pen. "He's Rabbit. He's got big ears. Hah, hah, hah, hah, he loves the fat lady. You know what she says? 'You're only in the creases,' she says to him. She kicked him out. Hah, hah, hah, hah, didja ever hear of a thing like that!"

David smiled. "Okay. Thanks a hell of a lot, Chief, a real lot. Soon as I can get some money I'll pay you back."

"You'll be warm. Get a lot of straw and get in it." Chief went under the sidewall and out of sight.

First David ate his supper slowly, religiously. Then, pretending to himself that he was full, he tramped over every part of the pen with his hands and eyes raised as if he were praying, looking for the largest space between leaks. When he found it he was very disappointed to see giraffe manure in the straw underneath. He had to separate all the dirty straw from the clean and crawl around feeling for dry straw to add to what little he had. It didn't really seem to matter, though, whether he slept in dry straw or not, since his clothes were wringing wet. And he could hear it beginning to rain harder. David's penmate, Rabbit, hadn't picked much of a place to bed down. He was being dripped on; and he lay so still that David wondered if the guy was alive, when he didn't forget about him. Finally, as David was ready to stretch out and sleep, a shirt landed on his head.

"You'll be warm," said Chief decisively. The sidewall slammed down. He was gone again.

David snuggled into the straw, using the shirt as a pillow to keep the straw from scratching against his face. The band played and played; people clapped, cheered. The tempo of the rain increased. The storm began to renew. David couldn't get to sleep because the sound was not steady. A hard rain might have been lulling, so long as its noise stayed the same. But the rain drummed harder, faster, louder. By degrees the wind grew until it flayed the canvas. The whole big top shivered and pliantly gave with the wind; quarterpoles creaked, and every fourth or fifth sidepole was lifted bodily by the canvas and swung like a stick from its mooring. David sat up uneasily to watch.

The elephants couldn't stand to have the sidepoles swinging loose behind them, cracking them on the rump. They whistled, caterwauled, growled like lions, bawled like bears. They were chained by the legs to stakes, and the chains went taut as piano wire, heaved and went taut again. Men came running with hooks and clubs — David lay down again — he was in the circus, after all, and should be used to such things, and he was tired, hungry; the whole night was a mess. By the time curiosity had got the better of him and he sat up for another look the chains were being stripped from the elephants' feet. They were being rushed in single file out through a lift in the sidewall, protesting with growls and whistles and bawls. Dimly David saw the water pouring off the big top splash on the elephants' backs as if they were going under a waterfall. The men got doused too. Even yet David could taste mud spatters on his own lips and remember the mud outside. Mud the consistency of cereal, mud you could skate through, then in places mud that would try to suck off your shoes — your socks! — your *toes!*

The gap between the bleachers and grandstand gave David a view of one of the rings. When he saw the elephants again they were standing on their heads, streaming mud and water, and partly climbing on each other's backs, desperately being driven through all their repertoire of tricks. It looked like a finale. The big top resounded to the spanking of the storm. The wind whooped and punished the canvas. Rain drummed; lashes of it sounded like cloth tearing and ran down straining into a thousand holes or swashing over the sidepoles onto the ground. Some of the spectators had drawn their raincoats over their heads so that they looked like turtles. The men who handled the elephants had got so soaking wet they were sleek and shone like seals in the spotlights. And they barked like seals. Light glared off the wet ring curbing and the steel sides of the bleachers and silver quarterpoles.

David squirmed into the straw as far as he could, wrapping his face in Chief's shirt. Circus noises were deadened, but not the rain's lambasting. That kept him awake. It wasn't like rain on a roof. It was Niagara, the sky falling in. It was the kind of roar that made you feel like an ant. Water was flooding the straw; David knew he was going to be wet. Pretty soon he heard voices, high-pitched and quavering. The show was over. The people were coming out. He poked his head from under the shirt. The straw they had spread on the runways had vanished in mud, and people had no choice of routes but had to wade right through it. The ones in front wouldn't go until they were pushed by the ones behind, who couldn't see. And by the time the ones behind had sighted the bogs of mud they could scarcely even hesitate because *they* were being shoved forward.

"They've got their troubles too!" David laughed out loud. He turned to see if Rabbit was awake. But no, the guy still lay motionless on his stomach, his face pressed so deep in the straw David wondered if he was breathing. At least one of his ears was certainly very big.

Ushers shepherded the people out. The elephants returned to their chains and stakes and shrieked only once in a while. The elephant men piled hay in strategic spots, bedded down in front of their animals. The lights went off. The wind quit walloping quite so hard and the rain gentled. But Rabbit didn't stir. He didn't even seem to shiver, while the lights were on and David could see. David shivered, though — so strenuously he couldn't get to sleep. The rain became only a soothing patter, but everything he touched was cold and drenched. He didn't worry about covering his face any more; he wrappd the shirt around his belly. Then, just as exhaustion was slipping him to sleep, Rabbit started coughing. They were horrible, sob-sounding coughs. David was afraid now he'd never be able to sleep.

"Did you ever taste blood in your spit? It ain't like a goober. It don't hold together," Rabbit said. He sounded frightened.

David did manage to fall asleep. Only once he woke, and found his legs and arms coated in congealed mud. Behind the elephants, under the loop in the sidewall, moonlight was fingered on pools left outside. Rabbit lay clutching straw in both hands, again silent and prone.

Council Bluffs • IV

HAM-CREAM-GRAVY-AND-BISCUITS was the main dish. The ham tasted lively like unsmoked meat gnawed off a pig, and Fiddler had fourths. He also drank three cups of coffee and several bowls of cream of wheat — the cream of wheat was very watery. Chico and Chiclet sat opposite Fiddler at the long board-and-sawhorse table. They were good company. They didn't talk much, but flashed their shiny Mexican smiles whenever Fiddler chose to speak. Chico took care of the act bears and claimed Chiclet helped him, twelve-year-old Chiclet. Anyway, he got Chiclet mealtickets and let him travel and sleep on top of the bear cage at night.

Besides Chico and Chiclet, Fiddler didn't know many men at the table except by sight. He recognized lots of people but had never spoken to most of them. Also there were plenty of brand new faces. Fiddler had been with the show longer than almost anyone he recognized; he felt like an old hand. The Seat and Prop men's jobs didn't start until the big top was up, and they ate when the cookhouse first opened, so nobody was giving Fiddler any trouble. Eating was awful serious business for just about everybody — not because they worked so hard, but because any hour they might get canned and be walking the road again. The gist of the talk about the fight seemed to be that the man who kept his mouth shut wouldn't get it bashed in. No one knew whether the two Chiefs had killed Heavy or not (Fiddler himself wasn't sure that Heavy hadn't died eventually, when he came to think about it), but the wise thing to do was not to go nosing, or even to wonder, but just keep one's teeth in one's food — and there would be a momentary silence on the subject.

Something you could say for the circus was that it gave people tans. They might be as blackened around the eyes as raccoons and not change their shirts in a month and not be able to close their lips on a mouthful of food, so that it dribbled out, but they all had their tans. And the wind had chapped their skin tough. The life sat well on a kid under twenty, except for the boozing. The weakest faces in certain ways became strong.

Breakfast was quick. Fiddler had gotten into the habit of eating fast because often instead of somebody nice like Chico he'd have a gumming wino opposite him or guy with the dents of a billy club plain on his head. When he stepped outside Fiddler stood for a moment, seeing how things were progressing. The sideshow centerpoles were up and the sidepoles set and a bunch of sideshow men and townie boys were kneeling under the shrouds of canvas, ready to wrestle up the quarterpoles. Most of the midway trucks and wagons had arrived but hadn't even been opened. Those concession people were always slow to start to work. The generator wagon for the midway was at the end of the sideshow, right by the big top Front Door. The light wagons for the rest of the show had been spotted near the Animal Department. The two mechanical stakedrivers still were plugging around the great oval which would be the big top. The stake wagon, carrying the reserve supply, was near the elephant men. — Ah, there it was! The green outhouse truck was parked by the elephant men, and that must be where the jigs who went around setting up toilets were at work. Fiddler smiled, pleased with himself. He looked around for some lost newcomer to feel superior to.

But nevertheless he had to wait in line, use newspaper, and sit on an ashcan seething with flies.

Both the Elephant Department's tents were up, the one for the men and the splendid, separate one for the arch-necked horse who led the file to and from the train, preserving order. Fiddler got along fine with the bull department. They had to be strong and work all day; there weren't so many winos. He stopped to see the bulls being watered since that was always fun.

"How's it going, kid?" said One-arm Bingo, coming over. He liked anybody Fiddler's age and looked out for them.

Fiddler made a circle of his thumb and finger. Bingo watched intently. Everything he watched he watched intently. "Okay," Fiddler went on and said, smiling. Bingo was one of his favorite guys. Bingo was almost always serious. Once in a very long time he was joking behind his concentration, but so seldom there was no use suspecting.

Bingo appraised Fiddler with eyes like a bird's — black and bright — and angry and gay and approving and fierce. He was thin as a weasel and burned up energy so fast he had to spend his pay on food between-meals — *couldn't* drink. "Let 'em squall. Don't worry about a goddam bunch of lushes. We're all on your side." And taut on his toes he rose, staring at something, and down, with the shrewd aplomb of a kid whose dog has just had pups his parents have said he can keep. Now it was like individual muscles were leaping, and his eyes hard-driving at Fiddler, away, at Fiddler. "Let 'em squall!" And he spat arms-length through a V of his fingers. What a friend to have!

The elephants were grouped in fours like chatty ladies around barrels. Hoses from several trucks were pumping water in as the bulls' own hoses sucked it out. The bulls mouthed their trunks like lollipops, drank leisurely, and plunked them back in the barrels for more. During the hotter part of the day they'd shoot water on their backs and up between their legs, but now they were content with wetting just the eyes. They squirted circles which extended to their ears and met between their eyes and made it look like they were masked for Halloween. Slow–humpedy–dumpedy–dump they moved, like elephants, like nothing else.

The fact the bulls were being watered meant most everything was off the train and up on the lot. Otherwise the trucks wouldn't have time to start tanking water around. Fiddler ambled back towards Number 12 Wagon. He'd have nothing to do until the water came for his department, which might be a while. Different drivers brought water to different departments. The guy assigned to the Animal men stopped off for a few beers. Brownie didn't have suck enough to get a better guy.

The punk boss stood in the midst of a plague of kids trying to explain that, yes, he would have jobs for them when the second train came in and the big top was going up and he did want them to hang around till then, but, please, not to hang around *him* — give him some peace, please! Fiddler hurried past so as not to draw the crowd.

A flap in the Animal top was tied up for an opening. Fiddler dragged one of the crum boxes into the space and sat there. Brownie was in the wagon but soon came out and grunted, seeing Fiddler where he usually sat.

"Where do you want me to sit?"

"On your ass."

"I reckon so." Brownie pulled a folding chair out of the wagon and tipped back against the wheel beside Fiddler. Nigas, the department's dog, ran down the wagon ladder steps and lay at Brownie's feet. The other feet, protruding from between the tires, belonged presumably to Coca Cola. He liked to lie under wagons, which was fine except when the wagons were going to be moved and you had to remember to roll him out of the way in time. Beyond Coca Cola's feet was a small crate covered by a canvas, which should contain a very mischievous tiger cub. Fiddler hoped it still contained the cub. Nigas kept glancing at the crate, and that was encouraging.

"Chief has to kill some meat today. We're out," Brownie mentioned wearily. His sunken, blind eye was on the side toward Fiddler.

"You found a horse?"

"Yeah. The guy at the gas station — I got some gas — said he knew a couple of guys who might have horses, and one guy said he had a couple it didn't pay to feed and he wanted a couple of passes and thirty bucks, and I said a couple of passes and fifteen bucks. He took it. And I'll get the fifteen back when I sell the hides. Tell Chief when you see him."

"He never came to breakfast. Where did he go?"

"Sure he did. Him and the bulls' Chief, when they brought your stuff back."

"I didn't see him in the cookhouse."

"He better be around. Twenty or thirty of these guys you was fighting with — I heard — was over here making believe to stand around, the sonofabitches. I chased 'em. He causes that much trouble — I'll can him — he better be around to work."

Townie sightseeing families in unending succession were passing, and Fiddler watched them unhappily. If Chief *had* gone AWOL Fiddler wanted to take Brownie's mind off it. "Everybody's dressed so fine, why's that?"

"Early mass, early something. It's Sunday."

If you did look at the people you had to be careful not to give them any reason to suspect you would be willing to talk to them. Some jerk who'd watched you clean cages would rush over — "Remember me?" — and a mob behind him. You had to look into space past their heads or keep your eyes on their legs. The best thing was not to let your eyes go anywhere near them.

Coca Cola with a groan shifted the position of his feet. From the crate a yellow paw turkey-tracked with black cuffed a corner of the canvas up and stretched to tap-tap-tap his shoes. Moaning, Coca Cola moved his feet again. The paw vanished; the canvas hung undisturbed.

Brownie was respectfully watching Magee, who seemed headed for the Animal Department. Magee was no taller than Chief, but he strolled like a modest giant who refrained from crushing holes into the ground. He didn't hurry and didn't get mad and you often couldn't tell if he was going to speak to you or somebody else because he didn't throw his weight around long-distance. He still wore galoshes, open so as not to muss his pants, but had left his topcoat somewhere as the sun had hit its stride. Sunday or not, out in a hick place like Iowa Magee was the best-dressed man on any lot, at least until the silver wagon bosses came.

"I fired Heavy," Magee said carefully.

"He didn't die?" asked Fiddler.

"No." — Magee was looking at Brownie, not Fiddler. "He can hardly move now, but by the time we get to Wyoming or Denver you can probably kick him out. He can't walk, so I'm letting him stay in the car a few days." He stopped for a moment as if that was all. Everything he said was grammatical. It took an effort and he didn't like to make the effort long. "I don't want any more trouble. He was a bad customer, but he won't be starting anything more." He looked at Brownie until Brownie wryly had to drop his eye and then he looked at Fiddler like a tommygun until Fiddler also couldn't stand it. Magee had the same bleak perfect circles to his eyes as the cats, only in human proportions. "I'll even fire your Chief," he said and laughed gently.

"I may fire the sonofabitch myself." — Brownie thought of something. "Who's going to feed him, lying down there!" he shouted. "I'm not having a goddam thing to do — "

"I don't know. Let him feed himself." Magee tapped the little stick he always carried on his palm. He put his foot on the wagon ladder and smoothed the crease in his pants and smoothed his hair with a puffy, boxer hand, his arm that could throw a log of a punch moving no more than a watchmaker's. He took his foot down and rubbed Nigas' stomach with his toe, stooped to flick away a piece of dirt he'd left on Nigas. Fiddler got a gander at that fat hip pocket of Magee's. Five thousand dollars anyway, his roll. He kept it like that, and everybody in the show, from the newest escaped-con-desperado on down, knew, and would sooner have shot FBI men than try for.

Magee stood companionably by the wagon, and Brownie was pleased. Brownie stared at the edge of his tipped-back chair with a happy, wry twist to his mouth. Magee surveyed the lot. Once in a while he raised his stick and gave an order with it, sending a truck somewhere, pointing out things to a boss that the boss had forgotten. His eyes seemed to grow a tiny bit smaller until what he wanted was done. Usually Magee didn't speak. The little stick nodded and nodded until it was done. Sometimes the lot was a small-town airport, sometimes a fairground, sometimes the midst of a soybean field or the middle of Cleveland, Ohio. But Magee was the same; so the lot was the same.

"Hi," said a man, smiling smugly. He carried a satchel. "Want to see sompmm?"

Fiddler laughed, because there were not in the United States two men who more obviously did not want to see "sompmm" than Brownie and Magee.

"Get away! Get out!" Brownie shouted. It was too late. The man was unzipping his bag. Brownie brought his chair down on all its four legs in a hurry, loosened himself and got his feet under him. You never could tell what they might have, a rattler, a Czechoslovakian hand grenade.

Brownie didn't relax until he saw it was mice. They were white and having a nervous breakdown. Magee walked away. "He's gone," Brownie told the townie. "I don't want to see them. I can't go because this is my wagon, so why don't *you* go and make it easier?"

"Don't make me feel bad. Sarah, Margo, Pam and Lu, and Tony — Tony's the male. They can dance. I thought you fellas might like to see, bein' in the business of puttnn on entertainment and all. I've done entertainnn myself — course nothin' to yours — and I picked them up all the way over in New Sharon from a guy that had two hundred! Can you imagine it? Two hundred, in a kids' sand box. It was like a camp meetnn; oooh they were stirrnn around! He charged me a dollar apiece, which is pretty good, considernn you don't have to train them. I did a little trainn, but I didn't have to, I just like to have things extra good. The man I was goinn show it to said you were in charge of animals so you'd be more interested than him, an' I notice you have a dog so you like animals. I like dogs too. Mice is only my hobby."

A checkerboard, folded twice, was strapped under his satchel. He opened it on the ground and poured the mice out on it. They were chewing their feet and chasing their tails and, once they'd got used to being in the sun, started catapulting themselves in the air. They scurried in circles and pinwheeled and rolled and up on their hind feet danced. — "Camp meetnn, see? 'O Lord! Lord! O Lord!' Hah-hah-hah. Actually it's not all trainn. There's sompmm wrong with them up here." He tapped his head. "They don't live as long as other mice."

"I shouldn't think they'd want to," Fiddler said. Brownie had heard too many, many crackpots over the years to enjoy the guy. He was twisting different directions in his chair, getting desperate.

"Sarah's the strongest and Margo's the longest, and Lu is the thin one and Pamela's none. That's how I keep them straight, with the rhyme. 'Pamela's none' means she's not the strongest or the longest or the thin one. People can't figure that out right off. Tony's the male, so he's easy. It's quite sompmm, they're a panic, but they take it out of you, always jumpmm like that."

Nigas was trained to leave animals alone unless he was told otherwise, and Brownie didn't call on Nigas. Brownie leaned sideways. There was a click, as of a latch. The mice continued to jive it up like frogs on a stove. "And the funny thing is, they never stop," the man went on. "Only to eat and sleep. They eat and sleep lots; you can see why. They're fun. They're a regular *circus!* Hah-hah!"

The tiger cub took steps too long and stumbled and swayed like a drunk. It was a ball of fur half head and half paws — a big belly also, but harder to see. The mice didn't jump any higher. They couldn't. The cub killed two, mostly with its weight. Brownie picked the cub up, in case the man might try to hurt it.

"Oh, bad kitten!" Brownie moaned, calming it with his hands. "How did it get out? Oh, bad kitten! *Bad* kitten!" He stopped and looked at the man, his face a picture of grief. Then in a flash, "Get out of here, you stupid goop!" he yelled, reaching into the wagon. "Where'sat gun? Where is it? That shotgun!" He rattled some tools. The man and his satchel scrammed. Brownie returned the cub to its box.

Peace for a time blessed 12 Wagon.

The next visitor was a man who had a tie to sell, and then a man who wanted to discuss arthritis, and some kids Nigas nearly bit, and some older kids wanting to know how much Brownie would charge to pimp them up two circus broads, and a man who didn't want to talk at all — just palishly stand and act like he was in the show.

"Sundown's here!" Brownie exclaimed suddenly, checking his watch. Sundown was the twenty-four-hour man, and he was on time. Usually he came very late, which was why Brownie called him Sundown. He was strutting in front of a townie feed truck, flourishing a carven cane. He wore metal-rimmed glasses and looked soft, like a dentist. He wouldn't ride on the running board. He had to strut in

front of the truck. Of the three twenty-four-hour men Sundown
was worst; things went off worst in his towns. But today he was
early!

"That's fine," Sundown said loudly, pointing his cane where he
wanted the feed truck to stop. "Here at the Animal Department we
want five bales of hay, one alfalfa, and five straw. — Brownie, is
that going to be fine?" He swelled proud as Punch and looked
straight at Brownie (something he was usually scared to do), waiting like a happy dog for praise. His mouth was even slightly open.

"Fine, Sundown." Brownie grimaced.

It didn't deflate the guy. He strode away in a sputtering fettle of
anger, snappishly shaking his cane in the air like a dentist waving
an unpaid bill.

"He don't belong in a circus. He ain't like showpeople. He don't
belong in a circus, the sonofabitch," Brownie muttered.

Fiddler went to where the feed men were stacking the bales and
lay down as soon as they were through. He liked to lie by the corn-
colored straw and the hay, smelling it. He was always glad when the
hay was delivered on time because he'd take a nap beside it before
the water came. The sun was mellower there and you weren't
so liable to get run over by something, or stepped on by townies, as
out in the open. Now, though, most of the things that might run
a person over were down at the crossing waiting for the second train.
The second was behind schedule. Even the midway stands were going up now, with their bunting and flimsy, decorative canvas. The
sideshow men had almost finished putting up the billboards, the
final job for their outfit.

Secretly Fiddler hoped the driver on 3 truck, or whichever it
was, would take plenty of time getting out of the beer joint and
bringing the water. He clasped his hands contentedly on his chest.
The sunlight closed his eyes for him and swirled patterns of sand
on the lids. Reds, yellows, starfish, snakes. He was so comfortable
he didn't once open his eyes when Brownie kicked Coca Cola awake
and, despite the groans about deathly sickness, made him take hay
to his animals. Or when Red came after straw and bragged of his
long-shot gambles at catching a girl, called Fiddler a loafer and

threatened to drop a bale on his head. Or when the first townies wanted to sit on the hay. — "You can't, that's why! You break the bales when you sit on them and then my men'll be toting handfuls of hay all day, that's why. Soncfabitching lot lice!" The sun made Fiddler pleasantly leaden and sipped out his strength. More townies begged to sit on the bales; and, again, others; and, again, others; and, again, different ones; and, again, new ones; and, again, still another batch, asking particularly to sit on the straw because of hay fever. Poor Brownie's tirades became just a droning. Fiddler was drowsing off, when, out of the flickerings of images, memories, he thought of the baby tiger. He swore at himself and his conscience and finally sat up.

"That cat can't stay in that box with the canvas, Brownie. It's getting too hot. Without any air. That sun's getting hot."

"Yeah, take it off and we'll have a crowd big enough for a carny. Sure, take it off. I know he's hot. But what're you goin' to do with the lot lice?"

It was the first time they'd had this trouble. Brownie has schleazed the cub in some deal only the other day and there wasn't a cage for it. Always before when they'd carried stock outside the regular cages it had been a new monkey or a freak midget sheep — something Fiddler didn't feel so responsible for. It was funny how guys like Brownie could pick up an animal like a tiger, worth a thousand bucks or more, for probably five hundred dollars every time — and then, with the care he'd have to give it, it would be twice as likely to die as if some zoo man had bought it instead. The show guy *had* to be twice as shrewd a sharp.

Fiddler got a brainstorm. "I know what I'll do." He put the bales in a triangle. Since eight were left, one side was two bales high and the others three. Even the two-bale side was tall enough to hide the tiger pretty well. He went to the wagon for a piece of rope and then to the box.

"Oh no! Hey! Please! You can't sit there!" At Brownie's note of anguish Fiddler looked around. — Oh no! She was fit to be a fat lady! Her rear end was so big, so broad, so weighted — "Please, miss!" Brownie was rising from his chair. — It was bigger than an elephant's foot, and Fiddler could picture it bursting, not a mere one bale, as the elephants did with their feet, but two at once! She was panting and plucking up her skirts, getting on tiptoe to sit on the low side of the triangle.

"What?" asked the lady in a high, gentle voice. A little girl of normal proportions was with her.

"Don't sit there, please. I'm trying to save my hay in bales so that my men can carry it." Brownie's voice was returning to its usual sarcastic tones, after the surprise.

"I can't sit here?"

"No, ma'am."

"Oh, you should let people sit there," she said, waddling away, obviously very tired.

Brownie blew out a breath. "I'm going to read." He climbed in the wagon and closed the door until just his head stuck out. Then he hollered, "Paper boy! Paper boy!" as loud as if he were calling pigs. "Do you see one?" he asked Fiddler, and then he shouted the same thing again. Both of them looked out over the wide-circling expanse of the circus, all the tents, grass, all the showpeople and separate hives of activity and teeming townie tourist parties. The bull department's hay was a formless mound being fought and slid on by kids.

"There," Fiddler said. A boy with a bicycle basket of Sunday papers was pedaling erratically toward Number 12, getting directed by the boss of every department he passed. Brownie disappeared in the wagon. He left the wagon open enough for the paper to be handed in and a bar of reading light to enter.

Fiddler let out the tiger cub again, catching it by the collar as it bounced into the sunlight. The collar fitted well, considering they'd taken it off the first townie dog they'd seen in Sioux City yesterday. Fiddler tied the rope he'd gotten on to the collar and carried the cub — it wouldn't be led — to the pen he'd fixed. He lay on the ground at one end of the triangle with his head and shoulders inside. The cub was as big as a jackrabbit and could do plenty. For safety's sake Fiddler hid his face in the crook of his arm and held the rope short so he kept his free hand always touching the tiger.

He didn't want it pouncing on his head. Unfortunately, if the hand was always on the cub, the cub was always conscious of the hand and chewing on it. This was okay until the little cat's imagination went wild. Fiddler had to bat the cub around to remind it that the hand was a friend, not prey or dead meat. And the rope jerked. The scars and cuts on his hand hurt from being chewed. He couldn't begin to relax, much less sleep.

"Whewee!" said the fat woman's voice, hushed. "Dear, I have to rest. That man isn't here, is he?" She didn't notice Fiddler. Her eyes were on the wagon. The little girl was tiptoeing to peer under it and see if Brownie was on the other side. Fiddler didn't speak up because he felt sorry for the lady. After a glance he put his face in the crook of his arm again. She sighed with relief, creaking her weight down, snapping wires and crushing one bale into the other. Let her sit down, Fiddler thought. He heard her take off her shoes, rub her feet and sigh several times. The cub had gotten away from Fiddler's hand. He felt for it.

"EEYAAAAAAAA!" The rope yanked taut. The claws were in her behind. Fiddler tried to stop laughing; it wasn't funny. Nigas leapt into the lady's lap and under her struggling arms barked at the tiger. She was trying to stand up. Fiddler got the cat loose. It was mad and he had to grab the scruff of its neck and hold it out in the air. She was hopping in stocking feet, slapping her hind end. Brownie came blundering out of the wagon, hearing the horrible scream. Sheets of his paper sailed after him.

Fiddler conquered his laughter. "Sit down," he told the lady. He carried the cub out of the critical area. Brownie didn't say anything. The woman was fat enough so he didn't. The damage was done, and, being in the circus, he only made fun of normal people. Since it was impossible for him to talk politely to a townie, he didn't say anything.

The woman acted amazingly sensible. She saw that nothing more was going to happen and that she might as well take a rest now that she could. "My goodness, what a morning!" She massaged her rear end. The motion of her arms joggled her breasts and the lumps of fat in front of her shoulders. She was wonderful to watch; the dress was so full. "Do you have any iodine?" She blushed. "I guess not. Where would I go?" The dress had some rips which she worriedly felt while massaging. One place pink underpants showed; in another, white skin.

"Don't worry. Nobody's goin' to look at your tail!" Brownie snorted, turning away — like Fiddler he'd been doing just that. The lady reseated herself, wincing a little. She put on her shoes. And then she laughed at what had happened!

"What is that animal?" she wanted to know. And she laughed at the whole thing.

Brownie picked together his paper and sat in his chair and wreaked his revenge on everyone else who tried to sit on the hay or gawk at the cat. . . . "You can't see the big tiger because we charge and you're too cheap to pay a dime. Aren't you? And if you hang around here, ma'am, we'll step all over your corns because you're in our way, ma'am! You're trespassing. — And give you lice and fleas because we're all lousy, all of us. Woops! Got one!" (pinching his arm) . . . . "And what do *you* want, you stupid bastard? Get out of here!"

Sometimes he was subtler. An old man began lifting off one of the top bales. He wanted to sit with his "feet on the ground."

"Whoa!" Brownie told him. "How are the planes goin' to know?"

"What?" said the man. "What?"

"I said how are the planes goin' to know? That's the signal. They've got to see that." He formed his hands in a V like the two sides left of the pen and pointed them straight in the air. The townie looked up gullibly for planes. Brownie laughed, called him a fool and sent him off in a daze. Brownie could choose his victims unfailingly. They never raised a stink; he didn't try stuff on the wrong guy. But he was sometimes kind of cruel, Fiddler thought. The fat woman sat very still in her immunity, like a dog being hunted over. She seemed to know that Brownie wouldn't hurt her.

Nigas and the tiger soon got used to each other. For Nigas this meant ignoring the cub. But, to ignore it, he had to be out of its reach. The cub wanted to wrestle. Neither of them was afraid of the other, or really of anything else in the world. Nigas had been born in a vacated lions' cage and smelled tigers and tigers galore. He'd crisscrossed the country with shows all his life and been fed from the hands of a thousand men, including some lulus, been through innumerable crises. Fires, riots, wrecks, blowdowns. Along with his masters, he'd bummed under freights and jungled by rivers and sweated out thirty-day stretches in jail. When no townie dog could have lived, Nigas had flourished. More elephants had tried to clobber him than dogcatchers. He'd acquired that quality, which only the best dogs got, of being a different size each time you looked at him. And now that his eyes were bluing a little and his joints beginning to stiffen, Nigas acted all the readier for trouble — he was sensitive about his age. As a watchdog he knew enough to bark at people, not dogs, but when there were plenty of Animal men at Number 12 and Nigas was on his own time, he focused on dogs. And he wasn't so old. He'd case a town with a practised leer and casually pick up the snazziest, smoochiest, frilly-furred, candy-tongued, silvery-curly-haired nooky in town — two or three stylish numbers — and, say, he'd parade! Great Danes? They'd run for the hills. Dobermans, Airedales? They'd root up the manholes, getting away. And suave Nigas, as big as a pail, he'd blitzkrieg the hydrants like lightning had hit, he'd saunter, he'd romp, and show that terror-struck, quaking tank town just what the hell a dog was like that had been everywhere — from Oregon to New Orleans to Hollywood and Vine.

The cub had stayed in a cage the three months of its life and experienced almost nothing. But it wasn't like a puppy in its ignorance; the cub wasn't humble. Tearstains ran down both sides of its nose. Its fur was too fuzzy. Its personality had hardly begun to jell. *Ow-Wow-Wow* was the loudest thing it could say, and, when it drank, water got into its nose and made it sneeze. When life became very thrilling it might forget all about its little rat teeth and its claws, forget to use them. — But try pushing that cub around. Try putting it on the defensive, even. The snarl would spread smooth and bright and white as a jungle tiger's — wobbling at you on oversized feet without a qualm.

The cub wasn't good company for a child, and Nigas was no better. Fiddler made the fat woman's girl stay back with her mother.

"Sssssst!" Brownie went, eyebrows lifting crookedly. He raised a finger and with the other hand reached in the wagon for a stake. Nigas stood bristled for battle. Brownie got the stake and drifted, quiet as fog, from his chair, along the side of the wagon. Nigas stalked beside him, and the little tiger, sensing the excitement, crept after them with feathery stealth.

Somebody was messing around in the front of the wagon.

"All right, you can come out now!" Brownie commanded, melodramatic as hell. He was chopping a pit in the ground.

The guy was bent over the vegetable bin. He turned, not fazed at all. "I'm lookin' for carrots." Fiddler knew his face.

Brownie was mad because the guy had sneaked into the wagon without asking. "When I was on Ringstock," he shouted, "my horses got carrots too! Just as goddam many as yours ever get."
— The cub crouched, bobbed forward twice on its paws, gauging the distance, and rushed, reared almost upright and hit Brownie's shin with perfect form like a great Bengal bringing down a buffalo. "But I bought 'em! I bought 'em!" Brownie roared, trying to ignore the cub. "I didn't steal 'em, you sonofabitch! I bought 'em! Now get outa there!"

Nigas was disgusted by the stupid cub's mistake. He was trying to bark at the robber and growl imprecations over his shoulder at the same time. The Ringstock man was laughing at the spectacle of the cub, but his face darkened. "You call me a — "

"Get outa there!"

A squad car was approaching, Fiddler saw. They always cruised around the lot in the morning, staggered by this terrible overnight influx of criminal elements into their town and trying to memorize faces so as to get them to jail as quickly as possible if they didn't leave with the show by tomorrow. Brownie hadn't spotted the car. He'd turned sarcastically to the inevitable gathering of townies. "I oughta bean the sonofabitch, don't you think? Goddam Ringstock. What do you say, should I bean him?"

The Ringstock man had his eye on the two cops, and they were

watching Brownie vigorously demonstrating How To Finish Somebody Off With An Iron Stake.

"What's your trouble?" the cop asked, who was driving. He rested
his arm on the window in a confident, cop way.

Brownie saw who it was and faced so that caught the full, watery
brunt of his blind socket. "That guy's stealing my carrots."

The Ringstock man was not new to the show. He started a spiel.
"I wasn't stealin' 'em. Count Majestic needs 'em. He needs carrots
for his coat."

"*His* coat!" Brownie interrupted. "How 'bout Betty Lou's? Her
skin gets so dry. And the monkeys stop having children." Brownie
tossed the stake aside and very meekly went to the cop car. They
must have thought he was a gypsy, with his green pants and red
shirt. "Look, officer, I'll explain: We take care of the animals, this
boy and me and that woman over there." He pointed at Fiddler
and at the fat woman sitting out of hearing on the hay, and he
picked up the cub. "My wife and son, the three of us have a lot to
do. We have to take care of this little tyke, for instance. And he's
got to be the color of a tiger. He's got to have that orange color or
nobody will want to see him; so we have to give him carrots,
chopped up — you probably know more about this than I do — the
pigments? In the wild he'd get them for himself, or his mamma
would. The color of the carrots, you know, it enters the fur and
makes it the same color, in the right places, of course. And Betty
Lou, she's our hippopotamus. She's got to have carrots to help keep
moist all the time. They have to be moist. You put her in water
and it doesn't do any good unless she's had some carrots. You probably know more about nutrition than I do. It's nutrition. And
with the monkeys it's the same thing. They can't have children.
They love each other but they can't have children unless they get
some carrots. Oh, they want to, they love each other — they hug
each other; but they can't have children."

The squad car was in motion. "Okay. Don't fight anybody.
That's all we care." The cops didn't look at each other as they
drove away. They didn't know what to believe.

Brownie's bad eye watered like a faucet. He was laughing and laughing inside. His face was redder than it had been, but that was the only other sign. "Take five," he told the Ringstock man, who was not keeping a straight face.

"But they weren't looking for Chief, though, were they?" Fiddler couldn't help wondering.

"No, they don't know what they're looking for." Brownie locked the front of the wagon. "I bet that sonofabitch took more than five, the sonofabitch. — How many did you get?" he shouted after the Ringstock man.

"Five," the guy called back, holding up not less than ten.

"Sonofabitches, give 'em an inch and they'll take your wife."

Fiddler tied the cub to the wagon axle and lay down again by the hay. But he didn't feel like sleeping now. He itched. He wanted the water to come. He could have been washing his clothes all this time. He was thirsty, and Nigas was thirsty, and so was the baby tiger. The big top poles and canvas also were overdue. Most everything else was set up, the piddling things done, but the giant oval space in the center remained empty as a meadow. The town fire marshal in his uniform was standing out there with nothing to inspect. Hundreds of men were waiting, lying in the grass, who'd been loafing ever since dawn till the big top should come. The snub-nosed cats sat driverless, the chatterbox, pick-a-fight engines silent. At the Light Department all the bulky spools and coils of wiring were out, along with the tools for digging the trenches the wires were laid in, and the batteries of spots arranged in ordered rows — and everybody'd gone to sleep. The midway was a gaily bannered passageway to nothing. And the elephants looked much too big, with nothing to dwarf them.

The big top itself was much more of a home than the individual department tops or the railroad cars. Not to have it going up by this time in the morning made Fiddler uneasy. Already the townies were making the rounds a second time, and they always began to get snotty the second time they saw a thing. By the third it got really rough. They disliked anyone in a circus because they thought he was doing so much that was strange and wrong. He was riffraff to all of them, respectable rich or respectable poor. If they weren't

given something constantly to watch they might do anything —
throw stones, jail you. Without the full hugeness of the circus here,
a town like this might run you out for a pack of gypsies or a shanty-
town of tramps.

The water truck pumping sounded like castanets. Water swished
in the barrels. As soon as he got the water started the driver climbed
up to sit in his truck again, where he could feel like a big shot. The
truck was almost the size of 12 Wagon, and he probably liked that.

"The main down in town busted and my hydrant went dry." The
guy smiled an insolent, liar's smile. He was a typical hobo: Scaly
hair, lips sucked in by the loss of teeth, the flesh padding gone from
the bones of his face, and the hollowed-out, staring depth to his
eyes of a tramp. This one was strong. He wasn't a wino yet, but
he would be. Fiddler hated the type. Sure they'd been through
hell, but you didn't have to like them for it.

Fiddler poured water for Nigas and for the cub and drank a lot
himself and washed his face, arms, hands, took off his shirt and
washed his body, rolled up his pants above the knees, took off his
shoes and socks and *washed*. When you had to go thirteen or fourteen hours without any water you appreciated it, even when it
tasted froggy. He stuck his head in a bucket clear to his chin,
opened his eyes, blew bubbles. He dipped his hands in and washed
his neck. With his ears under water Fiddler could hear Brownie
swearing about the driver's lateness and telling the guy he'd go to
the silver wagon and get him canned. Brownie was too old to beat
the driver up and had never been able to have him fired. He'd
been to the silver wagon as often as he dared.

It had been seven weeks since Fiddler had taken a regular bath,
he realized, since he'd been in a tub or a shower. Seven weeks ago
he'd joined and started living like this — getting covered with last
night's deposit of coal dust every time he climbed on top of a wagon
and regular dirt no matter what he did because of living out of
doors, scrubbing a leg or an arm, like now, whenever he got the
chance. He'd had to sleep with somebody else all but the last few
nights of those weeks, four different winos who'd come and gone.
One dodderhead would roll into bed with a ten days' coating of
brown on his rump.

And Fiddler had gulped food for seven weeks because the men around him either had revolting eating habits or were suffering hunger so, they ate as if it was their first meal in a month, as if they were from Buchenwald. He'd been a "circus bum" to every townie — there were an awful lot of townies in the world when you stopped to think about it — and a "bum" to half the circus, the people on the second train. And he knew, he made himself admit, he *was* a bum, without clothes to go to a dance or ride a passenger train without being stared at. Townie women would peek through the flaps of the can, not imagining what it was, and giggle with shock and hurry off giggling. — Fiddler had gotten used to this sort of thing. He was so callous now he scarcely bothered to get out of sight in the Animal top if he wanted to change his pants. He was a bum, he knew.

Fiddler filled two pails with water for the cats and found the watering pans where Red or somebody had thrown them.

The circus was a magnet to peculiar people. Every queer and whore and misfit in a town would come out visiting the lot, hoping to meet cases like themselves there. And they all succeeded. In the circus you saw so many horrible things and lived with so many degenerate people you got used to anything and probably degenerate yourself. If Fiddler'd stopped drinking it was only because of the cats, being able to concentrate on taking care of them. Being in the circus, it was a wonder he hadn't gone back to the bottle as soon as he'd quit. The last drink he'd had was just before Detroit. He looked back on all the days since then — three in Detroit, five in Chicago, Milwaukee — two, Minneapolis — two, plus all the different one-day stands — and was amazed. He wondered how he'd possibly done it. Seeing so many winos must have helped. And Chief had encouraged him once in a while, and Brownie. But the cats had done most of it. Fiddler would liked to have seen a wino take care of those cats.

He set out for the cages with the pails and the pans, a heavy load.

His LEGS were like spokes on a bicycle wheel spinning him down the street. All he watched were the walks on either side, to keep himself in the center. Someone was hot on his heels and the train pulling out and the houses hunched crablike and ominous. Then the streetlights stopped and the sidewalks stopped and he was stumbling in grass, over rocks, and then on the tracks practically spraining his ankles. He was dizzy from running and didn't much care if he broke a leg, felt sure the show had already hauled ass and left him. There were yard lights, small and glowing — no help for running — and boxcars big as lumber piles to get around, strings to cross, climbing over the couplings. Cars were being slammed around, switch engines working. It was a busy yard for this late. The circus trains showed up in the dark because they were white and silver, but Fiddler went for the wrong train first and by the time he hit on 127 car he was bursting his news. "I got the biggest chance, I'm not kidding you, I came so close — "

"What in hell's your buzz? You look like you just seen ghosts," Hopalong cut in. He was the only person Fiddler saw. The rest would be inside in bed, even Chief probably.

"I had to break out of there, that's how hard it was! I had to hurt her, I think, to get out. I could have left this show, left my stuff, I could have given it away, I could have dumped this job. You won't believe it; nobody will." Fiddler made piggy noises, trying to catch his breath. He was holding his side with a stitch and waving a key. Hopalong sat on the track next to the train, drinking beer, eating salami, and smiling up insultingly.

"I could have got rid of this crap life, period. I could be rich. I could be drinking bourbon right now, and taking baths and buying clothes — the biggest chance I'll ever have, I bet you."

"Hell, tell it, tell it," said Hopalong, less scornful.

"You know when I left you guys, you know how I went to the beer joint? Well, that was where — she came in there and I was in there like anybody else and she came in because that was where the circus would be — afterwards she said that — and she pointed at *me!* She hardly looked around. She pointed her finger, 'Follow me,' you know. I would have thought I was drunk if I'd had a chance. — I hadn't started. I said come on over and have a beer, naturally. I thought she was a whore and I could play along even if I didn't have any money. But she wouldn't; she seemed so impatient, she wouldn't let me stop a minute, and I couldn't keep from going; I wanted to, naturally." Fiddler still panted, and tried to talk fast, and couldn't do both. His hand sweated and hurt where he clenched the key.

"She was awfully strange. She chose me. Everybody was there, all the big winos and all the punks and why the hell she chose me — Nobody saw, she made me go so fast. So I went. I remember I forgot to cancel my beer, I'd just ordered it, and I was out on the street before I even took time to look at her. She tried to be ahead. She didn't walk beside me unless I went awfully fast, she stayed ahead if she could, and so I was afraid she was going to get me mugged from some door. So I stayed wide from the buildings. I was behind her. She wasn't sexy. She wasn't old, though. Her hair was gray, but that wasn't it. She was thin. Her ribs just about slit through her dress. Her dress was meant to be sexy, or else it was meant for somebody smaller. She was plenty small, though. She wouldn't tell where we were going. 'You come and you'll see,' she said. I could hardly understand her because she'd gotten in front of me again and she was trying to go so fast, as if I was chasing her or else that was the only way she could get me to her place before I chickened out or something. I couldn't even see her face. — Maybe that was it! Maybe she was afraid of me seeing her and not being interested any more. We covered whole streets of this town. I was afraid some cop would think I was after her, the way we went, her so fast and me after her."

Hopalong listened raptly, rubbing his stunted leg, all ears. Fiddler leaned against the circus train and was glad to be home.

"It wasn't late, so some of the houses had their lights on and some didn't. I was wondering which kind of place she was taking me to, one with the lights on or off. It wasn't such a tough district; it was just that we went so fast I never could see where we were. And her house we were in almost before I realized it. I was catching up with her — she was still trying to keep ahead, but I was faster and I was catching up and she grabbed a door open suddenly. I wanted to grab her because I wasn't going to chase after her much farther — I was catching up to find out a couple of things. She got in the door and naturally I was in the door too before I knew it. 'Darling, up here,' she said. She was almost up the stairs. The mailboxes were all broken, and the banister, and no light. I don't know why a rich woman like her was living there. When she got the door open she stood in it smiling at me. I didn't know what to do, so I went on up. She was like a little girl. I didn't know what to do. Nobody else was there, and she shut the door when I was in. . . ."

A train whistled, wailing high. The narrow sliding yellow blob of light seemed to be on Hopalong's track. He stood and limped up the first steps of 127 car. Fiddler went on telling. "I've never seen anybody so thin, even some of these guys who come on here who haven't eaten. She wasn't like a woman at all, and her dress was like a little girl's. Her hair was gray; it was in a little knot on the back of her head. She was like a little girl, even the gray hair. Her shoulders were so bony they stuck out and her knees were bony and she had buck teeth. She didn't know what to say to me. She was shy. And she was so excited. . . ."

The circus cars were all lit up by the other train. It was just on the next track, all right, a diesel coming fast. Light garishly bounded and slapped like a wind and shadows thrashed. "Hey get in here, Fiddler! Don't stand out there!" Hopalong shouted. Fiddler determined to stick it through. The train whistled again, much closer, and didn't let up. Engineers always did that, passing the circus train, knowing how many winos might be dead to the world on the tracks. The headlight sliced at Fiddler and the ties by his feet vibrated. So did his feet. Cinders hopped. Fiddler pressed against the circus train. The other one quick as a bobsled came. He was jouncing up and down like a ball of cotton. Hopalong was yelling under the thunder. The air blazed shaking brighter than noon with a ghastly blinding light. The banshee whistle steadily blasted a screech. Fiddler crammed his eyelids shut and skinned his fingers scratching bolts on the circus train. His scalding ears threatened to crack, and the jellying bones of his head. The whistle was froth. The stunning, mammoth wall of wind-roar smacked him sideways so he thought the train would hit his shoulder. His shoulder pained sharply. His ears were wet as if with blood. He lost the sense of where he was. It felt like he'd been killed.

Fiddler didn't see the engine, when his eyes would open. The rest of the train was rattling irascibly by two feet away. He was safe, stooped over shuddering and woozy, that roar still tearing his ears.

Hopalong pestered him, climbing down the steps from the car. "You crazy dope, you could have got up here! You could have killed yourself! Do you want to kill yourself?"

"I wasn't, so why don't you mind your own business?" Fiddler managed to answer.

"Okay," Hopalong agreed instantly. "Tell me more about this rich whore." He sat on the track again, kneading his leg and eager as a child hearing a Santa Claus story.

Fiddler spoke slowly. He could hardly make his shoulder believe it hadn't been hit, and his ears hurt, his nose was filled with diesel fumes. "She wasn't a whore, though, that's the thing. She was a rich woman." Fiddler prided himself on how quickly he recovered from frights. His head revolved like a merry-go-round. The key was almost embedded in his hand.

"Well, tell, tell."

"She's a rummy. She started pouring drinks. I tried to stop her because I'm trying to quit. I'd only gone to the beer joint to have one — I really needed one — I'd only brought a dime. But she'd poured bourbons and sodas, so I figured if I drank it really slow I wouldn't have time for another. I haven't been drunk since Saturday's town. And I did; I sipped. But you never saw anybody drink

more like a fish than her. She didn't know what to say to me, so she
drank. She'd look at me and take a couple of swallows and look at
me and take two or three more big swallows. She was nervous. She
had a whole kitchen full of expensive liquor. I've never seen such
a strange-looking woman. Gray hair and buck teeth. She wasn't
wrinkled or old in that way. But her eyes were red, around her
eyes, and bad buck teeth. She was so thin you wouldn't believe it.
No sleeves on her dress and those thin arms — arm *bones*, almost —
and knees like a little skinny child."

"Yeah, but how was she rich?"

"And I did what she wanted me to because I was drinking her
liquor; but it felt awfully bony. — She made me stick my head on
her knees, when she got up the nerve. It took her a long time. She
was such a nervous little woman, afraid, afraid, very shy. It was like
putting your head on a bunch of rocks. And she stuck her arm
right on my face — poked her elbow in my nose. 'Now I've got
him. I'm so happy.' She was always talking to herself about how
lonely she'd been, hardly ever said anything to me. And she was
saying how she'd been scared to come to the beer joint. I was going
to play along with her. She was a little off her rocker, and it might
be fun, that's what I thought. And I was drinking her stuff and I
was going to take a good bath before I left. But she started fooling
with my hair — it really wasn't comfortable with your head on her
knees because it was like a bunch of bones. She got drunker and
started kissing me. Have you ever had a woman with buck teeth kiss
you?"

Hopalong shook his head.

"It scrapes. It hurts. And she was yanking her drink around. I
didn't want to be under it. So I tried to get up, move my head. You
should have seen her then! She drops the drink on the carpet, and
she comes down on top of me so I couldn't get up, and she pushed
her fingers on my eyes to hold me down. She put my head where her
tits should have been — and there weren't any! Just ribs. I was so
surprised! I'd seen there weren't any, but you know how it is with
lots of girls, they don't show anything but when you get the chance
you find there's a little something there, like on anyone else. But

she didn't have a thing. She smiled this big smile, and suddenly she stopped and pulled her lips over her teeth and blushed like I'd hurt her feelings, when I'd never said anything about her teeth. I looked, I guess, but I couldn't help that. So she pushed down on me with her chest — *chest,* too — and put her hands up and took the pins out of her hair. She wanted to be romantic. — So it came down about as far as her ears and there wasn't much of it and it was ugly-ugly-gray; I hadn't realized before. And when she bent down her breath didn't smell bad exactly, but it smelled. She kept smiling and then stopping and trying to cover up her teeth as if I'd hurt her feelings. When she kissed me I thought I was never going to get rid of the tooth marks. Have I? Are they gone?"

"Yes," Hopalong laughed. "But you said she was rich."

"She was. And the trucks were hauling only one street away and making a hell of a noise and the cats on pavement sound like an army column. And the horses were clopping and snorting. I never knew we had so many horses. I heard the whole damn circus moving. I could have set a watch by it, if I had a watch. I knew what everything meant. And it really put the heat on, hearing the show leaving without me, while I was getting scraped by that nut's teeth. — So I said I had to go. I couldn't stay in her lap like that, getting chewed. I hit her chin, I'm afraid. When I was getting up my head bumped her chin. 'I've got to go,' I said, and I finished the drink, naturally. At first she didn't believe me, but when she did she went bats! I was scared somebody would hear. 'We can stay! We can stay!' She grabbed me around the neck and hung on to me. She didn't weight more than a little girl. And she opened her bureau and there was more money than I'd ever seen outside of a bank. You can't imagine — why there was a thousand bucks! You couldn't tell how much because it was all mixed in with her clothes and stuff. Dresses and skirts and handkerchiefs and twenty-dollar-bills all mixed together. I don't see how she can get dressed in the morning without losing her money all over the floor.

"A *t h o u s a n d* dollars?"

"It looked it. I couldn't believe it. And she had a bathroom there all to herself and a kitchen and a bedroom and a living room, rugs, curtains, towels, sofas, lamps. . . . But I kept thinking about the show. I didn't want to get to be a regular rumdum in one day, and sleep with a bunch of teeth and bones. And the damn show moving — I could hear everything — the elephants blowing off steam. I could even hear the different wagons — Commissary, stakedrivers, giraffes. She probably stole it anyway. She was so drunk she — "

"Where does she live?"

"And I'm on cats now and I won't be able to drink. They'll kill you if you drink. And that's a good job; they're fun to take care of. And nobody's better to work with than Chief. If you're around with Chief and those cats all the time how can you possibly drink?"

"Where does she live?" Hopalong persisted.

Fiddler stared at him defensively. "You think I'm crummy, don't you, to come back to this dump heap, that I don't want anything decent! Well, I don't want to be a wino! That's what I'd be! It would take about two hours and I'd be just like I was. That was unhealthy there. I'd be a wino and God knows what she'd have me doing with her. — You think I'm crummy, don't you?"

"No, if you're not going back there I want to, that's all. I want the thousand biscuits."

"Well I want it too. But I'd just drink. That's true, you know that's true. That doesn't mean I like this hole. — I don't want to be a wino!" Fiddler kept explaining, twisting the key in his hand.

"Is that her key?" Hopalong couldn't believe it. "How could you get it? Is it?"

"I couldn't get out of there, and it was late. The show was rolling. I didn't want to hurt the goddam skinny thing. She said she was so lonely, lonely, the loneliest thing in the world. You should have heard her say how lonely she was. She was crying. She was holding on to me so tight I couldn't get away without hurting her. It had taken her so long, see, to get up nerve to come and get somebody, come and bring somebody home with her — she'd been reading about the circus coming, and planning — she couldn't believe I was leaving. See what I mean, how lonely she was?"

"Yeah, yeah, but is that the key?"

"Yes, I told you I couldn't get out of there."

"Yeah, but how — "

"So I said, 'Give me the key! Give me the key!' I said. She didn't know what I meant. Christ, I couldn't get her off me. And she didn't know what I meant, so I had to think up a reason. So I figured out to say, 'Because I want to lock the door so we can drink in peace.' She was so happy! She got me the key, and I fussed with it till she let go of me, and then I ran out and slammed the door right in her face — I almost caught her arm in the door — and I locked it so she couldn't come after me; and that's all there was to it."

Hopalong leapt, took the key from Fiddler. "Where is it?"

"Where's what?"

"Where's *her place!*"

"I told you, it's along the haul, one street over from the haul, because I heard the whole show moving. I probably would have stayed otherwise. I would have gotten drunk and then I would have stayed."

"Sure, sure, but how do I *find* the place!"

"Take it easy, fella! — Go up the haul about a mile and then start looking. It hasn't any sign or anything, and I don't know the street. I didn't look to see the street. It's on the second floor and it's near a delicatessen or a grocery store, and the sidewalk's being repaired, I think. I don't remember more than that."

Hopalong stuck out his lower lip and beetled his brows. "Are you snowing me?" It looked funny because he wasn't suited to playing tough. He was a cripple. "If it was all that good, all that dough, you'd be there, buddy. Don't feed me snow."

"Listen, bastard! I'm no crum! I'm just as clean and decent as you! Don't tell me I should be staying with her. I know I should — *except I'd be a wino!* That's what I'd be!"

"He don't know what's coming off in his own head," muttered Hopalong, hobbling away very quickly across the tracks.

In a flood Fiddler desperately wanted to get back the key. Then he didn't. Then he didn't want to go climb in his bunk, either. He walked beside the train, very tired, beginning to feel the blisters from his running; and his ears still hurt. He saw an occasional light on — one or a couple of men sitting with coffee. They were usually middle-aged and had been with the show a good long time, or at least the off-again-on-again type. They looked at home and pretty nice. With most of these night-owls the sting of whatever it was that had first made them join was way back in the past — and then they'd gotten the habit of traveling, and maybe a record, and forgot how to stop.

Fiddler came to the flatcars soft and slow, letting his feet almost float and very excited. He hunted up his cages, his new cages, his and Chief's, in the mulligan stew of wagons and wagons of every department. The moon was enough. The cages were hooked one to another and didn't look very big, compared to the ticket or Ring-stock wagons or some of the trucks; but they were big enough, and there they were — there they were! they were Fiddler's! The very thought of it was like an animal, getting away from him and won-derful to catch again. Like jumping beans they were very still and then thump-thump! they jumped! and shivered as peppy as chip-munks. Fiddler wanted to check that the vents were open and the wheels chocked right; and he did. Each cage was numbered, but he couldn't remember who went with which number. He'd learn it tomorrow, he promised himself. Even being so tired, and after the train coming past, he didn't want a drink. He felt in his early teens. He made sure the tires had plenty of air, although there wasn't a chance in a thousand they wouldn't. He didn't dare open the cages because in the dark he wouldn't be able to see the paws if they reached through the bars. But, just touching those walls and feeling them shake, he pictured the cats. Giant, one-muscled, shat-tering, foreign. That could turn this town upside down. Leopards lithe as smoke in wind. Tigers glittering like cymbals. Fiddler bal-anced himself on the edge of the flatcars and crept along putting his hands on each of his cages. A gentle, meek breeze curled round his head and down his arms and fingers — round the cages. The cages were his. The moon hung thin on its back like a cradle.

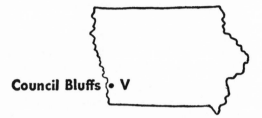

Council Bluffs • V

On his way to the cages Fiddler stopped at the Light Department and found that their Indian, the little Sioux who had helped in the diner, was gone also. And the Bulls' Chief must have disappeared with Chief, Fiddler already knew. He decided to stop at the blacksmith wagon, since that would be near the cookhouse, like the cages were today. The blacksmith, being an Indian, might know what the story was.

Fiddler found the wrong Indian at the blacksmith wagon, the one-eared Boss Chief, and he was as worried as Fiddler.

"I don't know where they are. They're all four of them gone, your guy, the Bull's guy, the Lights' guy and this guy. They must have beat it to see the guy in the hospital. I'm the only Chief here!" His laugh was explosive and somber.

Fiddler went on, the very weight of the water pails and pans he was lugging by himself taunting that Chief was gone.

"Listen!" the Boss Chief said, unnecessarily loud to be talking to Fiddler. "I don't want this boy touched! You can yak, but I don't want him touched!" Fiddler didn't have to look far. By the cages some of the Seat men were waiting. He was thankful for the Boss Chief.

Fiddler hated being stared at by anybody, townie or wino. That was what he minded most about having the Seat guys there. He wasn't afraid. The worst they might try to do — he reasoned carefully — would be upsetting his pails to make him carry water all over again. Once he got the first cage open there'd be no more danger because he'd keep the pails right in under the paws. Still, he'd rather have had the cages next to some friendly department like the Bulls.

Mousy and a few of the other wiseacres who'd been in the diner welcomed Fiddler with such remarks as — "When you tried something with us you did a bad thing, son" — and — "Some sonofabitch is goina be a very sorry boy." Broad daylight was not complimentary to their complexions. They looked sick, either too red or too gray. Something was wrong with each of them — a misshapen mouth, runny eyes. One man was an epileptic. Fiddler had seen several of his fits — once on a bridge, of all unlucky places; he'd nearly run over the side! Another had nosebleeds. His hands were the color of scabs and his pants where he wiped his hands crackled with dried blood. Fiddler opened a cage and put the pails safely close. Then he turned and made a short speech.

"Did you know Heavy has been fired? And did you know he isn't dying at all? He's going to be able to walk in about three or four days. Chief isn't here. He's visiting Little Chief at the hospital. So if you care so much about your friend Heavy why don't you go visit him? Instead of hanging around here like a bunch of townies."

Then he turned his back on them and immersed himself in his animals. Vaguely he could hear "We'll massacre your Chief!" and such malarkey. "He's brave! Look at the scars on his hands if you don't believe how brave he is," the Seat man jeered, more and more in the distance. Actually they were not like the townies, but could be trusted to keep back from the cages. Fiddler could forget about them.

The leopards were thirsty, and the friendly ones hoped for attention. They didn't want to be petted, exactly; they wanted Fiddler to try and pet them. They cut fast in different directions, so that one instant the middle of the cage was empty and the next, dazzlingly full. The tails tossed like puffy scarves. It was hard to keep the various bodies straight, but crucially important. The first paw leveled at Fiddler boxed his cheek soft like a muff, the claws withdrawn. Sweetheart's. Four seconds later he tipped his head and let one miss that was meant to kill, that scoured the air. Rita's. She fizzed. She hung behind the others, slow, not covering much ground, self-conscious. Rajah was the genius with his feet, much better than Rita. Rajah could take off your ear — whichever ear he wanted to. Once he'd nicked the tip of Fiddler's nose just for the fun of it, straight out and straight back and fast as a flash. Instead of lopping off the nose he'd left a half-inch scratch, now a bump of white scar tissue. It was good Rajah was friendly.

Fiddler put in the pans and filled them. The leopards let their energies run down as quickly as they could. It took a little time before they could get settled at the water. They'd be involved in pacing out some pattern and, like a child hopscotching, find it hard to break off. Even at the pans their feet fidgeted.

Rita squatted, awkward in her hate. She wasn't dainty like the other females. She was all business. She was a killer and drank staring at Fiddler whenever he moved. Rita wouldn't have brought *him* water if he'd been in a cage, and she drank at full speed, assuming he might take the pan away at any time for spite. Not till she was finished did she stop. Then she crept backward from the pan, wary that he might hit or splash her with it.

The other leopards dawdled and kept their tongues wet long after they were through, and when they'd gotten the edge off their thirst they'd sometimes take a breather. One would start pacing, thick-headedly going right over the pans, getting its feet wet and knocking the rest. Then just about the time this cat decided to stop and drink some more, one of its buddies would be on the move. There wasn't a moment's peace. Fiddler leaned his elbow on the bars, watching Rita. Rajah came over and sniffed him very noisily — practically snorted, as if Fiddler's scent enraged him. By Fiddler's shoulder Minny was complaining, letting her breath ruffle the trim lines of her lips and burble hoarsely in her throat. She'd finished her initial gulping and, instead of walking up and down, had remained at the pan because it was easier. Minny was so fat and lazy she always looked about to pop with kittens; whenever a new man predicted the blessed event you could tell he was starting to feel at home. But Minny was in everybody else's way.

She was getting pushed around and she didn't like it. The ruffle in her breath became a growl, rising and subsiding as she breathed. Rajah stepped on Minny's tail. She rOUrrrrred. Sweetheart roamed round and round gazing at the ceiling of the cage as if there were birds trapped up there and she was going to pull one down. Her blue-gray eyes got wider, wider; she seemed to be limping, going half into crouches. Sweetheart collided with Rajah and bammed into Minny and again Rajah stepped on Minny's tail. Minny thumped them both at once. She drove them both to the far side of the cage with two haymakers and the weight of her body in a charge. Taboo, the black panther, leapt for the side wall: as she hit, shoved off with her feet and plunged down on top of Minny. It was over almost before Fiddler could see the beginning. Taboo was in the corner with the other two and the fat, righteous Minny had everything under control.

Fiddler banged on the bars to make them finish drinking. Grudgingly they came, except Rita. Rita, the killer, did her drinking all at once. And Minny didn't want much. The exertion had been tiring.

As soon as a pan was free Fiddler put it in the lion cubs' cage. The cubs hadn't learned not to spill; they scrabbled for it, and not in play. They were just thirsty, and wanting the water very much didn't make them careful how they acted. This was one of the ways the cubs would change as they grew up — becoming aware of Fiddler's power. Deftly Fiddler kept from losing most of the water and was quick enough to shove the pan under the bars between the first grab, when they could reach only halfway up the pan, and the immediate second one, which hooked their claws around the handle — his fingers had to be away by that time. Once the cubs began drinking everything was different. They got very conscientious and looked wistful whenever Fiddler made a move, hoping he wouldn't tempt them to mischief. If they wasted time fooling it was his fault, not theirs. Even when they took a break between drinks the cubs tried to conduct themselves properly. All Fiddler had to do was touch the pan and they'd start drinking again, when they didn't really want any more — making every effort to seem sincere. Fiddler loved them for it. The cubs tried approaching the water from various angles, lapping at different parts of the pan, prolonging the godsend of having something to do and things to see besides blank cage walls.

Already the female looked very much like her mother Bessie — aloof, dark, great eyes strongly outlined, the haughty goatee-point of an adult lion plain on her chin. Her feet were better proportioned to the rest of her body than the male cubs' balloon paws. The males were less mature. They had fleshy faces, wrinkled on the foreheads from bewildered frowns. When they played they bumbled — snapped at the scraper, the broom or Fiddler's hands without the slightest attention to which was which. Fiddler had to punch them down sometimes; he could still do it. It was on the back of the neck that the male cubs came into their own. The tousled hair sprouted wild as weeds, oily with lion scent, forming a mane. A hedge of it grew to the top of their heads like an Indian scalp lock. Chief would grab them by that, shake them and tell them how great they'd be when they grew big, as if he were their father. They wouldn't stir; they'd listen.

When the leopards and cubs could no longer even pretend they wanted the water Fiddler took out the pans and prepared for the real fun — if only there weren't too many townies.

The Seat men were helping him out! whether they knew it or not, standing there where the townies would like to stand and passing their little curse words around, scratching their jock itch and having nosebleeds. Either afraid or disgusted, the townies were hanging back. The kids must have been with the Punk Boss; there were very few kids. Fiddler thought he could take the chance. He'd have to put on a show — keep the townies so involved in the risks he seemed to be taking that they wouldn't have time to want to be heroes themselves or decide "lions aren't dangerous."

He opened all the rest of the cages and sauntered between them, happy and bouncing. Four tigers, two lions, the jaguar and the cheetah — "Cheet! Cheet!" he chirped at her. Needlessly he romped from cage to cage so rhythmical and lightfooted, even bowing, he seemed caught up in some square dance. *Swing* your partners! His partners couldn't come out and do any swinging, so he danced to them. The townies and Seat men would have had to get themselves killed to have entered his head. Fiddler was a carefree kid.

The jaguar circumspectly put his paws around the pan and launched into his usual marathon drink. You'd think he ate nothing but salt, the way he drank.

The cheetah lapped like a nervous terrier, trying to make up for a small tongue with speed. She purred while she lapped, looked at Fiddler, and her ears seemed to tremble; the white eyelids tensed. Faster she lapped and then stopped, lifting her mouth. Fiddler reached and wiped the wet from her whiskers, the back of her lips and, with his fingers moistened, cleaned the quivery corners of her eyes.

Wise, lazy cats like Joe the lion lay down while they waited. But the nimble lady tigers couldn't be still. They had to be pacing. Snippy was making a half-circuit of her cage, back and forth, back and forth. Every time her eyes lighted on Fiddler her lips drew up in a silent snarl. Fiddler raised his own in return — that was something Chief liked to do. Snippy wouldn't stand for it. When she saw him "snarling" she uncovered all her teeth and her mouth slipped open. Fiddler dropped his jaw as far as he could, conscious how puny his teeth must seem. Snippy actually roared — halted in her tracks and banged him with a roar. Fiddler had to shake the shivers out of his spine before he went close to soothe her.

"Hey, did you think I was serious, Snippy?" Snippy's lips lowered unevenly as if she were forgetting to hold them up. She watched Fiddler suspiciously. Then he saw her eyes change, become pensive and indirect, and he stepped to the bars. She looked at him as if he were a tree, started moving again, going by Fiddler peaceably. He swayed from foot to foot in time with her padding. Four times she passed within a few inches of him, her thigh at the level of his head. As she came the fifth, glancing his way — the same eyes, celluloid pupils a shading of blue, green and opaque gray — caught by some rhythm he stepped back. The scooping paw big as a chair seat pendulumed up barely too late. Snippy snarled aloud at having missed.

Fiddler brought water. Snippy was just settling herself with her paws enclosing the place where she wanted the pan when the male rose up from the other side of the cage and took over her spot — even when Fiddler put the pan between her paws — shoved her aside. Snippy hissed scorchingly. This time Fiddler couldn't come close and quiet her. He didn't even try.

Fiddler went to Joe, rapped the bars and told him to get up and not to be so lazy. Joe was glum. Joe pulled in his feet and pushed them out at Fiddler, clearly motioning him to "Go away. Go away, please."

"Listen, listen, Joe, maybe you're sick, maybe you've got a limp. I've got to see about things like that."

Joe groaned and pushed his feet outward again and poked the cage floor with his claws. He shook his mane and ears, groaning mildly, and he yawned a slow, resilient yawn, fitting his teeth together when he closed his mouth as carefully as if membranes grew between them. Joe was the gruffest, biggest, best lion Fiddler had ever seen. The forehead extended far back from his eyes; his face was long, gaunt and fine. The dots which constantly swirled in his eyes might have been shaped like arrowheads without making his gaze any wilder. When he looked at you you couldn't keep from hopping, you'd swallowed hornets, you wanted to bite on a knife and run hog-wild. Kids would dream of straddling Joe's back like Jungle Boys and going anywhere, snuggling themselves in his mane if the weather got bad. As well as a boys' lion Joe was a lions' lion, a patriarch with an anger-roar that could knock out your knees and sprinkle your face with tears. Fiddler was cautious with Joe. He was afraid of provoking that roar.

Joe got up for Fiddler and slouched like a bear. Joe wasn't neat or graceful or "catlike." The fur tufts on his elbows and toes looked sloppy; his mane was tangled. He had the unkempt-hairy appearance of a bear. There was so much mane that of course it could not flow and be controlled, but piled upon itself in heaps massive as the shoulder hump of a grizzly. The parts of his body were so big they had to be rangy and loose, bearish, and not in the compact cat form. Joe slouched because he felt like slouching. He'd outgrown the rules. And he could surely trounce the daylights out of any gliding, namby-pamby, catlike lion.

As Fiddler thought about it, bears seemed to be the only ani-

mals whose way of walking didn't change as they grew oversized.
The biggest of the act bears, like any cub, slouched half the time
and the other half used that lazy-rolling bear-shuffle which Joe
or a huge tiger or dog, much as they resembled bears, never had.

"Joe, Joe, what would you do if I let you out? Would you
bother me? Huh? You old bastard, what would you do? You'd
go out and catch a cow and chase the farmer's daughter and ramble
all around, and they'd shoot you. You wouldn't be easy to shoot,
but they'd have to shoot you. I'd like to see you charge. Maybe
their aim might not be so good on you as on a pheasant or whatever they have here. They'd be talking about you for the rest of
their lives around here. They'd tell all their grandchildren. I'd
like to see you make that charge." Fiddler pushed his face against
the bars. Joe listened to him — Fiddler could tell he was listening
— not to individual words but to the stream and the tones. Fiddler
could stand as close as he liked and Joe took him for granted,
which was the best Fiddler could hope for. Joe was no pet and
no lady in heat. He had no affection for people at any time.

When Fiddler brought it, Joe slapped his tongue in the water
with a calm, irregular beat, taking up the space of three leopards
drinking.

Without any dillydallying around the jaguar turned from his
water when Fiddler came. Fiddler, pulling the pan, glimpsed the
jaguar's hind legs stiffen — tried to drop! The yellow jet at body
temperature splurted on his ear. "Better late than never," Fiddler
laughed, on his hands and knees watching the rest arc overhead.
Then the dislodged pan splashed down and drenched him. The
Seat men thought it was a riot.

Snippy the tiger's mate had rudely pushed her aside because
he was thirsty. In the other tiger wagon it was a very different
story. Mabel got to drink first and she took her time, fastidious
about keeping her whiskers dry. They were milk-white and a
cloudy light shone through them; they were curved and extrava-
gantly long. Mabel's poor mate languished at her side. He had
crouched so low he could lick her elbow, an orange elbow, plump
and cutely tufted. His body blocked up a fourth of the cage, he

was such a giant; but now he licked her elbow — softly, not to make her mad.

Among the cats the lady, when she came in heat, was boss. With the monkeys the situation was reversed. When the male wanted to screw, he screwed. He hauled a lady over by the ear and put it to her and then might keep her pinched there absentmindedly by the ear five minutes before letting go.

Mabel lorded it. Her tail flipped up and down and she bopped her lover under the chin with the paw he was licking. All he did was sidle back and lick her flank, stroking the fur to a gorgeous gloss. When Mabel finally got through at the pan she went to a corner and rubbed against the walls voluptuously. The poor mate, thirsty as he was, couldn't concentrate on drinking, had to twist his head away every time he began. Coolly Mabel glanced and made the fluffing sound which meant "Supper's on." But when he bounded, stumbling clumsy as a little cub, she changed her mind. She let him lick her tail, though. She let him kiss her rump.

The lions started grunting. Out of the blue Bessie produced half a grunt. Joe was caught by surprise and also half-grunted, not having time to prepare a full one. He was used to taking the lead. Then he got himself ready and came out with a fair one — an emergency grunt without the usual sliding prologue-groan. Joe got himself ready again, squinting, pondering, and did better. He pushed out a high gradual groan which deepened and powered into a loud, resonant grunt. Bessie let him get things going and then she joined in companionably. Her "a a a a a a a a ar-UH!" was less nasal at the higher tones, less prolonged and not so loud. Joe strained, pushed, sounded like an engine whining as he began. Then his mouth rounded and the grunt funneled out. First it was a throat sound. Gradually, as he pushed more and more force into those warm-up groans, the final UH grunt reached back to his lungs, losing the nasal quality, and at last gained the entire diaphragm as a sounding board. It was a process of opening the whole length of the passageway from lungs to lips, making it round and wide like a megaphone so that the grunt would swell and swell as it came and boom like a great bass drum. Once the

passageway had been fully opened Joe didn't have to wind up with
the a a a a a a a every time he made the deep gut grunt — he
could drop extra ones, as many as he liked, until the muscles around
the megaphone got tired from holding it open. A a a a a a a a
a a a a ar-UH–UH–UH–UH–UH–UH–UH–UH — sometimes he
couldn't decide when to stop; "afterthoughts" would come out —
UH! He was going at full steam and didn't have to purse his lips so
much, and the rib casing of the sounding board pistoned back and
forth with almost mechanical ease.

Grunting was usually a social thing with lions. Joe and Bessie
each got started on a series, answering grunt for grunt. The act
lions soon were adding their utmost from far across the lot. There
were many of them, but they all sounded younger than the patriarch
Joe, with shallower grunts. It was like jungle tomtomming. When
the tempos happened to jibe, four or five grunts at a time, the
townies couldn't hear themselves talk. Joe and Bessie seemed to
be trying to match all eleven lions in the lion act. Fiddler leaned
as close to Joe as he dared. The gruff, booming UH–UH–UH
–UH was not frightening. It was not a roar. The lions did it
when they felt wide-awake and full of energy, whether happy or
sad, but not when they were angry. Mostly the grunting was for
no one's benefit but their own, and they ignored any people who
happened to be around. Still, everybody was having it dinned in
their ears that *lions* were here. The fish in the river a thousand
yards away couldn't help but listen. Fiddler's ear was six inches
from Joe's mouth and Joe, gazing over Fiddler's head with eyes
a swirl of swimming dots, didn't mind.

Outwardly the tigers seemed disinterested. But they were waaah-
ring softly in spite of themselves. They wouldn't grunt. The tigers
couldn't see the lions — maybe had never seen them! — because
the cages were always in a line. Fiddler wondered how they pictured each other. Aside from cagemates, all any of the cats saw
was humans. Fiddler and Chief presumably were their favorite
humans. They had to hate practically the whole world to hate
Chief and Fiddler.

The jaguar broke into the lions' tomtomming with his own dis-
cordant grunts, longer and lower in pitch even than Joe's, deep

and rasping, as if the taste of blood was in them and he was hunting a trail. Fiddler didn't go down to his cage because the jaguar got self-conscious. He wouldn't grunt if people were watching him. — He stopped soon because of the townies. At night, in a town where they stayed overnight, Fiddler and the jaguar had their fling. Fiddler bedded down under the cage and lay all night flooded with waves of the sound that could crunch a raucous jungle into silence.

The bigger cats were done with their meat. Some of it hadn't been tasted after the initial licking. Fiddler thought he should put the better chunks in cages where they'd be appreciated, where at least the juice would be gotten out. The lion cubs chewed everything thoroughly that came within their grasp. So did the cheetah sometimes and the leopards.

The rhythm of the pacing was what you watched when you took meat away from a lion or a tiger. You waited till the cat was going away from the meat and you were quick without acting hasty. The rhythm of its walk was the important thing, not where its eyes went. If it was lying down the eyes were the thing to watch — or the front paws would do just as well or even the mouth. But when the cat was up and around you put yourself inside its skin and bound your hands to the rhythm of its motions, almost carelessly slipping the meat from between the hind feet.

Vociferous lot lice had been drawn in such numbers and so impressed by seeing Fiddler hand meat from the paws of tigers to the jaws of panthers that he shut the cages. He took the pails and pans back to Number 12 Wagon and didn't remember the Seat men till he'd gotten there. They hadn't even succeeded in making themselves a nuisance. If anything, they'd helped him, scaring back the townies for so long.

Brownie had hidden the baby tiger in its box again and stuck the box in the shade under the wagon. He was reading the paper while a lady explained how she believed the circus formed a small but vital part of the culture of the country and was making an inestimable contribution to the pleasures of growing up and Brownie should be proud of being a part of it. Fiddler didn't hang around.

The kids who worked on Wardrobe were lugging the leaden

costume trunks from wagons into the various dressing-room tops. They had a tough job. Fiddler's was comparatively easy, he had to admit, and certainly much more exciting. Yet those Wardrobe kids, helter-skelter and impetuous, were about as happy a bunch as any on the first train. They were younger than Fiddler — could revel in wine without being winos and erase with a plunge in some local stream the results of weeks of going dirty, climb out white as Sunday school valedictorians. They'd just left home.

"Hell's-bells, it's about time!" the most mopheaded of the kids exclaimed. He scrubbed the hair up from his eyes. A column of trucks was flying along the road, two ten-ton canvas trucks in the lead. Scarcely slowing, the first swerved onto the lot, beelined through the peripheral tents and the stakeline and swung once around the great vacant oval space triumphantly. At the proper place it stopped and a cat ripsnorted in behind it. The second truck zoomed halfway around the oval in the opposite direction, taking a position on the far side. A cat got behind it also. The trucks were late. Lost time had to be made up. The Big Top crew of jigs hurried dragging chains and harnessed them to the cats and hooked them on to bundles of canvas in the trucks. Then the trucks pulled away and the cats backed, the jigs jumped clear and the canvas bundles, one from each truck, thudded out on the ground. Everybody moved ahead and the process was repeated. Simultaneously the pole trucks made the rounds. The small ones, staying about forty feet inside the stakeline, moved along in first while jigs slid the ends of the sidepoles out the back and left them to fall at ten-foot intervals. Larger trucks carried the quarterpoles, which were taken off on the shoulders of jigs and placed much more exactly. There were two lines of quarterpoles, paralleling the sidepoles and, ultimately, the stakeline as ovals within ovals. The four centerpoles rode on a giant trailer and were handled like glass. The jigs spent a lot of time with them and never just laid them on the ground. Tripods supported the tops. The bases slanted snugly into the little squares of stakes the Boss Chief in his jeep had driven long ago.

The townies were perked up and saucer-eyed again. They had

plenty of things to watch. The guy in the cab that towed the centerpole trailer *really* knew how to wheel a rig. He could maneuver. The jigs were doing gymnastics up on those canvas trucks. The bundles teetered on piles of bundles at the ends of the chains, crashed this way or that unpredictably, bundles as big as elephants, that could squash a man. But the jigs took care of themselves. And they hefted the quarterpoles like old-time troupers, knew where to put them without being told. They did it all like play. The poles were light as straw and everything was easy and there was a rhythm to everything.

Magee, the boss of the show until lunchtime, had taken off his sharpie sport jacket and monogrammed shirt and galoshes since Fiddler had seen him at Number 12. He was in his undershirt now, the only white man out there except the drivers. The Boss Chief was Magee's assistant and stayed as far from him as possible because the two of them were overseeing the whole job, all of it at once. Magee had a faculty of looking sideways when he seemed to be looking straight ahead. You never knew when his eyes were on you. The Boss Chief wasn't as clever at catching loafers, but half the hairs of anyone he caught turned gray. The jigs hadn't been working long enough to be tired or careless. The jigs were minding their p's and q's and feeling lively. What shouting Fiddler heard was them kidding each other, not Magee or the Boss Chief blowing up.

"Dat pole yo' wife, Jamey? How you hug dat pole! You sure pick heavy wives. Don' you let her lan' on yo' toe, Jame!"

The shouting, the racketing motors, flamboyant-busy jigs were wonderful to Fiddler, apple pie, what he loved. The rhythmic poles dropped into place of their own accord, it seemed. The canvas ponderously bumpety-bumped from the trucks. No holdups. The circus was rolling again. Nothing would interfere. Fiddler swelled and nearly yipped, he was so happy. He would have answered questions. He could relax and *ride*.

Iggy the gnu had nice big bull's horns which he clattered on the bars, scenting Fiddler. Fiddler always came to Iggy fresh and

reeking from the cats to test if he could overcome Iggy's hatred of
the smell. Iggy snorted, shook his head, shuffled his hooves. Fiddler
waited till Iggy had calmed down a little before putting his hand
in. Iggy wagged his head with outrage and hooked the bars face-
level to Fiddler. Fiddler kept his hand in front of Iggy, midway
between the hooves and the teeth and open and steady so Iggy
could see it. Gradually the shaggy shoebox nose stopped wagging,
barely nodded toward Fiddler's hand instead. He began scratching
the gnu high on the nose, where the very motion to bite would
throw his hand free. The collapsible nostrils flared and sucked
shut. Poor Iggy shivered in fearful loathing. His head wagged,
protested — slowly enough so Fiddler's hand would shake off. Iggy
refused to turn sideways and let Fiddler touch his flanks. The
muddy consternation wouldn't dull in Iggy's eyes. He stood head-
on to Fiddler, whipping the back of his legs with his tail. But
Fiddler, reeking with the stench of lions and leopards, could pet
a gnu's nose. That was a victory.

Fiddler was surprised when Iggy came nearer and licked the bars,
a foam appearing on his lips. "The guy's thirsty! Where is that
Coca Cola bastard?" he said out loud. He looked under the cage.
No Coca Cola. He went hunting.

Red was at the monkey wagons showing some townie housewife
how he gave the monkeys their milk. Fiddler was going to ask Red,
but the giraffe wagons were a little ways beyond and there was Coca
Cola, asleep under one of them.

"Hey," Fiddler said. "Did your animals have anything to drink?"
Coca Cola squirmed in his sleep.

"Hey!" Fiddler repeated.

Coca Cola's mouth struggled slow as putty forming words. His
face was a red, cooked color. "I brought the hay" — moaning — "I
brought the hay." His eyes were closed. A matting of hay outside the
wagon doors indicated he was telling the truth. At least part of a
bale had reached the giraffes.

"I said water." Fiddler caught hold of his arm, squeezed it, and,
when the guy wouldn't get up, dragged him out from under the
wagon.

"They have to have water, Coke," Red explained. He nudged the townie woman in the ribs to make sure she was suitably amused by Coca Cola. She gasped first for breath and then again with surprise.

"I'm goina die," groaned Coca Cola. In the heat of the morning he was wearing a coat, very fumy, which must have been discarded by three or four previous owners already. Several holes had enlarged when Fiddler dragged him. "You don't know how sick a person can be." His tongue was partly hanging out as if from nausea. Fiddler balanced Coca Cola on his feet. He was precariously tall, had a long way to fall. He pressed Fiddler's hand against his filthy shirt. There was gaseous activity of some kind going on inside, all right. But Coca Cola was "sick" every day and you had to ignore it.

"I'm goina die today, I'm so sick. Oooooowow! Please! You've never been so sick."

"If you'd quit doping yourself you might get better," Fiddler told him. "Go to the doctor; but don't take it out on your animals. Water them." Spaghetti-legged, Coca Cola leaned on Fiddler's shoulder, shutting his eyes in a spasm of pain. He stunk powerfully when you got close.

"Go on, go on," Fiddler insisted and pushed him on his way.

"You see we got some pretty dumb guys," Red said to his housewife, smiling at her affectionately. She edged away. When Red tried to take her hand she left immediately.

"What's the matter with you? Crazy?" was all she said.

Red looked disappointed only a moment. "I'm goin' to quit this show. That's what I'm goin' to do. You can't get nowhere with a broad when she knows you're in the circus. I'm goin' down the road. I'm goin' to Hollywood. Ever hear of place called Beverly Hills? That's where I'm goin'. You never heard of there, did you, I bet? Movie stars live there. That's where they live when they're rich. I'm goin' to get a job there. An' watch me make out then! Sure, I'll be a gardner or somethin' — but not for long! Them women'ill like me. They'll want to fool around. I'll take care of their horse for a while an' then they'll want me takin' care of them."

Red made a sly, tongue-in-cheek face and drew his fist up to his mouth and crooned at it as if it were a microphone —

> "Night and day, you are the one,
> Only you beneath the moon and under the sun —

Did I ever tell about when I worked at that broads' boarding school in Virginia, taking care of their horses? Rich, lonely broads?" Red grinned smugly. He had bloused his pants with rubber bands so that the cuffs were turned in and bound tightly to his boots and the bottoms of his pants puffed out snazzily.

"You better look around here some more before you do anything rash."

Red dreamed up the wildest plans. He thought them up as he talked along. Fiddler got sick of Red. When he'd joined he'd brought his clothes in a shopping bag. From what Red said, he'd been living off the charity of cafeteria clean-up girls who would slip him uneaten rolls and desserts. That was the way Red would be when he quit this job in a day or a week, and ten years from now, until he grew too old and crummy to wangle girls' pity. Then he'd starve.

Fiddler wandered in the direction of the dog and gorilla wagons. He might pay a call on Bible, the dog man, and the gorilla lady, who was Bible's sweetheart. They were good people to see when your regular friends disappeared or acted foolish.

A dumpy little man twitched Fiddler's sleeve.

"Chief must help me, you know. I pay him to help me." The voice sounded mellow and reasonable, but the man was as quibbly and higgly a guy as you could find. Julius was one of the concession men. Chief unloaded his stuff for him regularly in the morning.

"I'm going to hire his friend who takes care of the elephants. I can't trust Chief any more. I've paid Chief for this week and I'm going to have to hire his friend too now."

Fiddler laughed. "They're together. They've both gone."

"Well then I'll get the one who takes care of the horses."

Fiddler laughed harder. "They all went together, even the Lights' Chief. You'll have to get a white man, I guess."

"Well I will," Julius countered in all seriousness, his voice smoothly modulated like a radio announcer's.

"You'll get a wino then, who won't be here as much as Chief and won't be able to work when he is here because he can't work when he's drunk." Fiddler laughed and laughed at Julius. — "All right, if I help you will you save Chief's job for him?"

"Yes, I'll save it, unless this happens again. I have to trust the people who work for me. You can understand that. They have to be fair to me, and I have to trust them."

Brownie rented Julius the use of the orangutang cage during the night, when Buddy was kept in the sleeping box which only took up one corner. Julius's stuff consisted of several aluminum barrels, a very heavy chest, a beach chair, some painted boards and sawhorses and a hand cart. He couldn't load or unload the things by himself. He was too small. He was not particularly weak for his size; he was just too small — not small enough to be in the show, though — and didn't belong in a circus at all except in a talking or haggling position.

Julius opened the wagon door and waited complacently for Fiddler to get inside, do the work. He had taken off his suitcoat, as if he might possibly be planning to help. Links gleamed in his shirtcuffs. He wore suspenders of white satin bordered with black. Sweat had spread in dark bands through the shirt alongside the suspenders and in circles down from his armpits. The shirtfront was speckled with sweat. A couple of shaving cuts on Julius's cheeks glistened where sweat had collected. He was pink, pudgy, soft and very hot. Why did he wear a suit on an August day? To show off? From all reports, Julius cleared two hundred dollars a week at least. Fiddler would have believed it — from the links, suspenders, thirty-dollar hats, ruby ring, two-tone shoes. Julius didn't need to prove it with a suit as well. Fourteen bucks a week Fiddler earned.

As he climbed in the wagon Fiddler was relieved to see an empty milk carton by the wheel. He wouldn't have to worry about Buddy being thirsty. Inside the wagon it was warm but not oppressively hot. Fiddler's height gave him leverage with the heavy, padlocked chest. Julius's lips pouted enviously. Wearing a hat, Julius didn't come up to Fiddler's breastbone.

Buddy's arms flailed from the window of his box. His fists bang-bang-banged. Then he stretched out his fingers plaintively. The sides were creased lengthwise like the fingers of an old baseball mitt and had an oiled, glove color. Buddy was sucking a straw wisp, looking like an Irishman somehow, an Irishman trying not to smile. The humorous lines around his nostrils made him look that way. For all the begging motions of his hands, he must be enjoying some joke, not too unhappy in the box. Maybe he was laughing at Julius, behind that Irish straight face.

Fiddler got all the things out the door of the wagon. Julius helped a little in easing the chest to the ground, and the two of them — mostly Fiddler — set the chest on the hand cart.

"There you go, Julius. That's the only thing hard and you can handle it by yourself now."

Julius smiled ingratiatingly. "Chief will settle with you. I paid him a dollar for this week, which includes today, and he knows it. I should never have paid him except for each day as it came. But he owes you money now. — And I keep an agreement. If he's here tomorrow he can have his job back."

The pleasant, radio-announcer voice was always startling, no matter how often Fiddler heard it. He wanted to see if there wasn't a ventriloquist hiding under the wagon throwing that silver tongue (which could sell a townie Brooklyn Bridge) into such a higgling toad as Julius.

Fiddler went on toward the dog and gorilla wagons, leaving Julius steeling himself for the labor of getting his stuff to the big top some time in the next hour or two before he'd be able to set up his stand inside. This was one job he'd never hire anybody for, since, by pulling ligaments and popping arteries, he could do it himself. Fiddler hoped the sun burned real hot. — And then again he didn't, because it seemed as though it *might* in the course of the day, and everyone would sweat, animals, people, not just Julius. All morning the temperature had been rising from the dawn chill faster than usual. The sun was nearing the crown of the sky and kept getting hotter and kept getting hotter.

Taylor did the work of two men. Brownie had given him the hardest cages to make up for the nuisance he caused by being a madman. Taylor was shoveling out the hippopotamus's water tank. It had been drained, but the bottom was clogged with dung and waterlogged hay. Taylor stood in the tank and the hippo Betty Lou loomed above on the platform supervising with gaped jaws. Betty Lou's jaws opened a distance of three feet. She was exercising her jaw muscles and it took a lot of yawning, tusk-chomping and head tossing to do that. Also she was trying to bluff Taylor into giving her more apples. Every once in a while he took one from a bag and lobbed it down her gullet. Masticating one apple, she used strength to chop a man in half. Taylor's head didn't look much bigger than an apple with that mouth so close, the upper jaw like the lifted hood of a car.

Fiddler couldn't resist stopping. "Hey you Betty Lou!" The shovel head swung around, the bulged frog eyes surveyed him. Then the whole behemoth body struggled to turn and waddle — the round peglegs very inadequate.

With a whoosh of froggy breath Betty Lou rested her jaw on the bars above Fiddler's head. This was not the position he wanted her in. He had to punch and slap her throat before she'd move. Her head pitched up and down, tusks gnashing in fun, ending yawned wide apart at Fiddler's fingertips. Fiddler put his hand in her mouth, but had to pull it right out again. The hippo took a while to grasp the fact that apple-feeding time was over. Fiddler poked in her ear, a ludicrously tiny ear hardly fitting around his finger, not much wider than a tablespoon. She continued munching imaginary apples. He couldn't stick his fingers in her nostrils because she shut the flaps on them so fast. Her eyes flattened when they blinked and, opening, bulged like bubblegum. The eyes perched on the very brink of the sides of her face and stared off bulbously in different directions. What a funny animal — a hayburner with monstrous, fighting walrus tusks five times bigger than any lion's!

Taylor talked, rattled on in a headlong half-whisper about how
"the cons'ud beat on thir plates. They'd spit up the food and beat
on thir plates, and the woman in the kitchen, she'd smile. Ya c'uld
see hir through the door; she liked it, she'd smile. The cons'ud use
the knives. They didn't let us 'uve knives after that." Taylor
bonged his shovel on the metal water tank. "We'd use ur knives.
We c'uld make hir smile. She was the only woman we had. We
made it loud. We beat and we beat. Nobody liked it; the guys with
the guns, they were on the balcony and they c'uldn't stop it, but they
didn't like it. They had the guns on us. And this woman, she'd
smile; every time somebody opened the door we c'uld see hir smilin'
in the kitchen. She was the only woman we had."

At last Betty Lou caught on. Blinking with anticipation, she
propped her upper jaws on the bars and let the lower hang down
loose. Fiddler rubbed the gums in front of her teeth, the flabby
lips and the corrugated roof and cheesegrater sides of her mouth.
Blissfully her eyelids drooped. He ran his arm way down and up
her tongue and tugged the blunt front teeth. Betty Lou's mouth
would have kept a blind man busy for a month, feeling things. Her
tusks crammed Fiddler's hands, the points and edges sword-sharp.
He picked hay strands from the pockets and nooks behind her
teeth, under her tongue, and Betty Lou breathed noisily with
pleasure.

"Chief'ull be there. That's where they'll send 'um — the pen.
He'll beat the best of anybody 'cause he's strong. That's what we'd
do. She'd smile. She'll like 'um 'cause he'll be loudest. She used
ta like the loudest. We'd spit up ur food and beat on ur plates like
anything."

Fiddler couldn't stand that. He had to leave. The Chief stuff
gave him the jitters. He couldn't get the picture of Chief there out
of his mind.

The dog man, Bible, being sane as anyone on the first train, ought
to be a good person to see right now. Fiddler wanted to hurry, to
run, and he did run, sprinting as he and Red had at dawn after
meeting Taylor on the road. But then he tumbled down in the
open grass joyously like a kid when he saw what was being done
with the big top. The centerpoles were going up!

It was ticklish and beautiful. It didn't take long. The four poles were bolstered on tripods at a slight angle from the ground and pointed along a line one after another toward the horizon. Two-hundred-foot cables had been rigged to each and guyed way to knots of stakes beyond the stakeline. In addition, each pole had a cable loose in the grass for the cat to hitch on to. The boss driver, driving the biggest cat, raised the first pole with infinite, offhand care. The base was set in a wedge of stakes, and the cable ran from the top end back the length of the pole and out to the cat. Twisted around in his seat, the boss driver watched only behind him. The cable drew taut, the cat pulled steadily. For a moment the force was backward against the wedge of stakes — the driver kept it steady, steady — and then the centerpole upped and rose with progress as smooth as a clock's second hand slanting steeper and steeper until it lofted perpendicular and glorious. The radiating cables held it stock still, a tree limbless and towering.

Fiddler hardly knew he was smiling. The townies were spell-bound. From a distance the cables were thin as strings; the pole, going up, looked ponderously big and on the verge of toppling back or to the side. The cat's straight, *steady* pull was vital. A jerk would break the lines.

The Boss Chief checked the next pole's rigging. Magee was out by the stakeline watching for trouble. The King jig sat enthroned on a canvas bundle, his crew loafing around, since they weren't needed, enjoying themselves, matching pennies. Some of them swung on the centerpole's cables. The pole was a Maypole, the cables were ribbons, and they were the dancers as teeny as flies. The cables seemed of respectable size where the men held them — until you saw them threading up and piddling when they met the centerpole.

The cat was backing. The Boss Chief waited with the cable and attached it, walked away. The motor idled. The driver dried his hands on his hair; it was thick enough and evidently not too oily. The motor grated into gear; the line snaked straight; a humming pressure built. Abruptly the pole started, stiffly rising an intermi-nable time — Fiddler kept expecting the pole to bend, the line to snap — finally resting at ease, swaying perceptibly with almost a breathing motion because the collaring cables were not so tight.

The midget quarterpoles didn't matter; but you wanted those last two big ones up in a hurry once you saw how they would look — tall above the flittering swallows. In a hurry you wanted them up.

2

FIDDLER was just coming to know Bible. He was a hard man to get close to. Bible lived like an island in the circus, slept in his own wagon, did what he felt like, took lip from practically nobody. He was the dog trainer's assistant, the next thing to being a performer, and the dog trainer only was around during shows. Fiddler envied Bible's independence and admired the skill he had with animals.

A low portable pen of screens tied to stakes extended from the dog wagon. Bible was sitting in it in a camp chair. The gorilla wagon was near by. Magee had the wagons placed together each day as a favor. The gorilla woman was squatted against her wagon's wheel, smoking and doing washing in a pail. The mournful guy who took care of the gorillas' air-conditioning machinery sat in his private compartment, with the machinery, as usual. All of his clothes were black. Fiddler had never seen him in anything but black. Bible smiled at Fiddler and the gorilla woman glanced up from her washing with interest. They made him feel welcome. Fiddler stepped over a screen into the pen.

"How's the cat man?" Bible said. He took hold of Fiddler's hand and traced the scars with his finger. "No new ones, I guess. That's good. They like you, I guess, or they'd kill you; they'd fool you. Something's wrong with the way you do things, if you have to get cut up."

The gorilla woman looked at Fiddler expressionlessly. She'd wrestled tigers in her early years with shows. She was scarred too, Fiddler imagined. He pulled his hand away and changed the subject.

"When are you going to let them out?"

"Not yet," said Bible. "Too many people." The dogs and gorillas were dangerous animals and could only be out at special times when the townies were swarmed somewhere else on the lot. Bible had already given his dogs a run early in the morning, so they weren't suffering.

The Big Top jigs, aided by forty or fifty local kids under the direction of the Punk Boss, were flapping the kinks out of the canvas, pulling from all sides and stretching the various sections flat as sheets on the ground. "Shake it! Shake it! Shake it!" Magee bellowed over the lot, growing savage, until the jigs and boys were "shaking" in a frenzy. Elephant Department men dodged here and there hooking hauling chains on to the quarterpoles before they got covered up. — There was plenty going on; but the magical moment hadn't arrived when all the thousand townies would have eyes for nothing but the big top.

The man in black wasn't saying anything. He would answer yes or no. He could speak. But he never volunteered anything. If you needed help working he was willing and strong; but he wouldn't talk.

Bible was not much more of a talker, when you came right down to it. Bible yawned. And the gorilla woman silently washed her clothes, blinking because of the smoke from her cigarette. Her legs, bunched close under her, must be elastic as a child's. She was washing a pair of coveralls. Coveralls were what she wore all the time and she kept them as clean as a wardrobe of dresses. The gorilla woman had funny, round eyes and a bottle-cork nose and dense short hair encircling her head like a fur cap. Like Bible she was very good with animals. Bible wore combat boots, army pants and shirts and a mustache and dark-rimmed glasses. He smiled a lot, showing how good his teeth were — rare teeth for the circus, where nobody had any. He slept a lot and yawned frequently and was the fastest person conceivable when there was something to be done; faster than Chief, though not as strong, of course. — Here Fiddler was thinking about Chief again, when it would do any good, kicking himself for letting Chief out of his sight. Anything might be happening to him now.

Bible looked at Fiddler and frowned. "Chief takes care of himself. You can't do nothing. But you don't need to worry. He'll take good care of himself." Bible could read expressions. He didn't say any more for a while. He yawned. Then Bible laughed. "I used to be a kid like that." — He was watching the townie kids slaving with the canvas. "I used to screw around circuses and do that stuff. I remember I had a wolf I'd caught and I'd trained him as well as any of these dogs and I tried to get in shows with him. But nobody believed he was a wolf. He looked like a shepherd dog. It wasn't easy to tell if you didn't know dogs."

Bible grinned, bent forward as if he couldn't think which part to tell next and the words were jamming up in him. He spurted them out — "I went out there with this wolf on a rope, and they wouldn't take me on, the show wouldn't, and I found myself working out there like the rest of the kids for a pass. Oh, what a comedown! — with this wolf, he was with me out there putting up canvas. I couldn't tie him anywhere because he'd bite somebody. Friends of mine knew he was a wolf, but the showpeople wouldn't believe me. I guess it wouldn't have made a difference if they had, because he wasn't worth no more than a dog because you had to know a lot to tell him from a dog. But they might have taken me on. So I earned a dinky old pass like anybody else. That was a comedown. Oh, I was a stuck-up kid!

"And then we shot marbles — yeah, that was what we did — and I cheated because I was mad. I had a hole in the bottom of my shoe. Half of us didn't have shoes in the summer, and I had a hole in mine, so I started stealing marbles with my shoe. Can you believe that? I'd step on a marble so it went in the hole and then I'd get it out when nobody was looking and get another the same way. Nobody noticed where I had my feet. If you'd put your hands anywhere near those marbles they would have bitched to beat the band; but they didn't care where you put your feet. — But somebody caught me. Oh, did I get a pounding! They pounded the hell out of me. They didn't give a screw for the wolf. He bit some of them, too, and he was big; he was on my side. But they beat the hell out of that wolf and they pounded me so hard I couldn't see, I couldn't hear nothing but bells for a week." Bible laughed and laughed.

The gorilla lady's face creased into a smile. She was swarthy and suntanned like a man. She nodded as if reminded of experiences of her own, but wouldn't come out with them. Fiddler was sorry. She'd had some honeys. She'd been with all the old shows in the heyday of circuses and knew cats, apes, horses, bulls, bears, everything. The gorilla lady was the only woman on the first train. She was a neat one, no messy slut. Fiddler wished she were washing his clothes, she took such pains. The soap had curded above her elbows. Her hands foamed the suds like an eggbeater. She hadn't been able to touch her cigarette except to light it from the last because of soapy hands. Ashes were flaked down her front and you could see it bothered her sense of neatness. She'd offered to wash Bible's clothes, which could have stood it. But Bible had to "smell the same. Your animals don't use their nose so much as dogs; they mostly see." The excuse couldn't get along on crutches. Still, dirtiness didn't seem like such a vice with Bible.

"Good-looking day." Bible grinned around at the clouds and blowing trees, leaves white with the sun on their undersides. "Hot but good." The gorilla woman smiled agreement. You could see a long way. Above and beyond the river, or the scrub thickets hiding the river, a haze of light smoke showed Omaha. No buildings were visible. On the highway which came from the bridge a regular assemblyline of city buses was leaving off flocks of families just from church.

The gorilla woman rinsed two pairs of coveralls in a pail of clear water, wrung them and draped them on the pole of her wagon to dry. She emptied both the washing and rinsing pail and got new water from a large barrel she shared with Bible, mostly for their animals. After drying her hands and brushing the relics of five or six cigarettes off herself, she squatted down like a squaw and rolled two more from a Bull Durham sack and lit the first, saving the other to light from it, chainsmoker style. Then the gorilla woman started in on her socks and underwear.

"Some s. o. b. is going to try to move that wagon before they're dry," she predicted.

Fiddler lay down on his back. He wanted to sleep. It felt like the middle of the day now. He should have had lunch, by the way it felt — the sky and grass surging with sun grainy and chafing as sand to the skin, even through clothes, a sun that furred the wind with a crawling heat. The sky was an ocean blue — as rich a blue as that — and the clouds a salty ebullient sea-froth white you could taste. The feel of beach sand was on Fiddler's skin wherever the sun reached it, slightly itchy. He was happy. He wriggled from side to side, happy. He thought this must be about the peak of the summer, and if you weren't working, at least, it was fine; if you were lying down, just working to make yourself comfortable. But the way the day was jumping ahead of itself probably gave Magee the idea he'd fallen more behind schedule than he actually had. Magee would be putting the pressure on even the Animal Department when its time came.

Bible's boots were crossed a few inches to the left of Fiddler's head, one heel gouged into the ground; big clodhopper boots — you had to trust the owner, not to mind them being so near. Stubborn Chief would sit on a crum box when everybody else had sprawled out napping in the grass and stretch out his boots, crossed like that, and glare down disapprovingly. If you were a friend of his, Chief would openly sneer. Bible didn't disapprove. Most likely Bible was half asleep himself, having gotten the habit of sleeping in his chair instead of on the ground because the dogs made the ground a madhouse when they were in the pen.

But Chief would sneer, "What a buncha deadheads! Can'tcha stay awake, Fiddle? You're as bad as them winos. Here it is, broad daylight, an' every bird's awake except an old stupid owl, and you fellas can't keep your peepers open! You oughta go to a doctor, boy. Want me to carry you? I'll carry you, Fiddle!" Chief would be that way regardless how tempestuous and drunken a night he'd spent and how hung over he was.

Fiddler couldn't settle comfortably. He felt so silly! —If Chief *had* been here he would have razzed back some reply and scooted down a greased chute to sleep.

Wrapping his arms around his knees, Fiddler sat up. The ground was alive with dog prints, all sizes, thrust through the crushed grass in mad lopings. He wished Bible would let the dogs out again right now. Then there'd be some excitement.

"Since you ain't got better things to do, how'd you like to come over here and fix me a cigarette, Fiddler?" the gorilla lady said like an aunt with an errand.

"They're in there," she muttered, nodding her chin at the breast pocket of her coveralls. She was blushing — the telltale pink seeped under the ears and the hair-roots, everywhere the years of sun had not baked oak-brown. "I made one goddam one too few."

"Watch your fingers now. I'm jealous," Bible joked.

Fiddler blushed too. And he didn't have a scrap of technique at rolling cigarettes. He hardly knew the theory of it.

"Child, child, child!" exclaimed the gorilla woman, waving her hands, strewing soap bubbles. Bible's laughter was like clapping. Fiddler didn't get anywhere. The tobacco blew out of the cigarette paper; he tore the paper; he dropped the tobacco bag.

Several times he told the gorilla woman, "You better do this." But she just waved her hands and teasingly flipped soap in Fiddler's eyes.

The man in black rescued him. Jumping from his perch in the gorilla wagon, the man in black took the paper and tobacco from Fiddler with a self-effacing smile and proceeded to fashion as trim and nice a cigarette as anyone could hope for.

"Fix me another, huh, Bill? — Thanks," the gorilla lady said. She faked a scowl at Bible for not being gallant like "Bill." . . . . "You're green, green, green, Fiddler. You're a First o' May. But you're a good boy."

Fiddler hadn't been called a First o' May since New York state. The gorilla woman had trouped with circuses as long as Brownie or Bible or Magee, so he guessed she could call him that. She'd wrestled tigers and waltzed with bears, stumpy, wizened and weathered as she was (and must have always been). — Fiddler assuaged his pride.

The sun sneaked the sweat out of you, dried it off before you felt sticky or wet. Fiddler swigged and swigged from Bible's water jug and passed it to Bible and his lady and the man in black. A towel was tied around it, and he dipped the stoppered jug, towel and all, in the animals' big water barrel when everybody was through to keep it cool. The jug was stored behind a wheel of the dog wagon out of sight. Fiddler barely stuck it there in time.

"We're wondering where we could locate a drink of water. We're all thirsty." The man smiled apologetically. "Sorry to trouble you." Either most of the children were friends of his own kids, or else he had more than that one wife. She was pretty and winsome and sweet, for a mother of eight. Fiddler was left to answer. The others had dropped into a see-nothing-know-nothing-hear-nothing trance fast as turtles plopping off a rock. Bible stared at grass blades.

"If you're not used to it, I wouldn't advise you drinking that water." Fiddler thumbed toward the barrel, repeating Brownie's line when somebody wanted to guzzle up his department's day's supply of drinking water. "It's not too clean and you're not used to it."

The man peered in the barrel, astonished. "You're not saying you boys have to drink this, are you? That's terrible. Don't you have a union? That's worse than I'd ever believe." The pretty wife looked very sympathetic. "If I were you, Petey," the man said to one of the little kids, "I wouldn't really want to be in the circus so much. — But it's swell to see anyway. I'll agree with you there." He rubbed his hand through Petey's hair gravely.

Fiddler got inside the pen and went into the trance himself to speed the townies up in leaving.

The Ferris wheel went round and round across the highway. It was a stodgy, undecorated, small-town Ferris wheel. Early in the morning the amusement park there had seemed like something, Fiddler remembered. Now the only thing you would notice, over the circus tents and throngs, was the Ferris wheel. They must be doing a smashing business with people who'd gotten tired of not having to pay for being entertained. A fiftieth part of the circus crowd this afternoon would keep them happy.

The Big Top crew was lacing the sections of canvas together and gingerly creeping around checking the position of the quarterpoles underneath, mooring them to the big top. Magee and the Boss

Chief were out in the middle doing the crucial job of hooking the
canvas on to the centerpole bale rings. They wouldn't let anyone
else near that. A bungle there and down would come the top, ripping and flapping, and all the poles in the first strong wind. The
Punk Boss had collected his charges at the stakeline in preparation
for the larger work ahead. The boys stayed collected but not peaceful. The younger ones took on the older ones, and there were other
feuds — maybe the kids from Council Bluffs thought all Omaha
boys were schmoos. The Punk Boss had to jump rope. He was in
danger of losing his footing.

The Light men were moving the last of their hoops and coils into
position for quick unraveling when the big top would be up. Already cats had hitched on to some of the seat wagons, an hour before
they could be brought in. Julius was marking time at the stakeline,
fanning himself with a handkerchief, his suitcoat folded over his
arm. The bunch of them were there, the guys who made the money,
and the usual barrels, beach chairs, chests and dismantled stands.
The concession men didn't talk to each other any more than Bible
and the gorilla lady, but, instead of relaxing in comfort, they pa-
troled, lemon-faced, impatient with any delay, and kicked the
stakes and drummed ringed fingers on the barrels. Magee couldn't
run things well enough for them. They were stewing to set up their
stands and *sell*. The cheerfullest guy was the one with the pennants
and plastic planes and kewpie dolls. He didn't have to wait for the
big top to go up and ice and fresh peanuts to come or get out cups
and juice-mixing bowls. He could do his hawking now. "Hubba-
hubba, hey they dance! Say, they dance! Watch them dance!" The
dolls leaped prodigiously on elastics on the end of sticks. The rest
of the concession men prowled around him envious as sparrows.

Bible was yawning, picking his teeth. The persistence of a fly
which circled Bible's head, trying to land on his mouth, and still
circled when he slapped at it, drew Fiddler's suspicion. Bible
liked candy.

"Can I have a piece too?"

Sheepishly Bible threw him a caramel and one each to the gorilla
lady and the man in black, and ate another himself, slapping at the
fly.

The gorilla wagon's somnolent hum was trying to put Fiddler to sleep. The dry, restless sun streamed colors on his eyelids. Fiddler turned away from it and couldn't sleep.

Bible licked his mustache and brooded. The man in black smiled, thinking about something. His face was lumpy and gentle. The buttons on his shirt were gray instead of black, and he was playing with them. His belt buckle reflected silver like anybody else's belt buckle.

Fiddler could almost see the Punk Boss whew! above the melee of his forty kids when Magee and the Boss Chief made up their minds they were satisfied with everything and strode off the canvas shooing the jigs before them. Magee signaled Okay. The Punk Boss pointed. The kids burrowed, pushing the canvas up in furrows, like moles. "Get it up! Hurry up now! Lift it up!" — Fiddler could hear the Punk Boss across a hundred yards. Magee and the Boss Chief were sifting through the welter of guy lines, four to each sidepole — long ones, short ones, and the occasional extra-long emergency lines clear to the quarterpoles, which could be tied way out in X's and V's. The proper lines went to the proper stakes. The kids caught deep breaths and disappeared. It was a game to them. The littlest led and braced and lifted. The hulking bullies found themselves following, for once. Each boy made a small imprint in a small mound on the very edge of the canvas. The jigs gathered where the kids were struggling — enough of a hump had formed now to show that the littlest boys were standing up, supporting it on their heads, and the bigger boys were rising one by one, pushing it higher still — and the jigs began to wrench the sidepoles up. All the kids were under, the littlest in the front doing the hardest part and the wild and woolly jigs alongside rassling with the poles. The King and the Punk Boss supervised.

An ant under a pie crust — that was about the size of the mound the gang of them made; and it was at the big top's very fringe. They were going to have to work all the way around, put up every sidepole, before the quarterpoles could be touched or even seen. It would be a long job. But the townies were magnetized. Each townie.

The gorilla woman soused her socks and underwear in the pail of

clear water and hung them on the wagonpole. Then she went in
the wagon, immediately brought the two gorillas out on chains. —
They must have gotten the chains themselves and been impatiently
ready and waiting. She hadn't made a cigarette and, suddenly
wanting a smoke, she squatted squaw-fashion on her toes to roll
one. The gorillas saw and tiptoed so as not to jerk the chains, paying them out with both hands. The gorillas could have been tied to
a dandelion. They were like bellhops, good as gold, obsequious.
But, spying Fiddler, one sprang into the pen — balancing its chain
over its head, not to cause the slightest jerk — embraced him. It
wasn't half grown but already its arms were stronger than Fiddler's.
He sat powerless to break its grip around his shoulders. The gorilla
could have broken the shoulders. Its tongue licked and tasted his
adamsapple. The hairless part of the face was a sleek, colorless,
masklike black with beetling ridges tough as leather over the eyes.
Fiddler did the best he could. He stroked and "held" the gorilla in
his thin arms, acted parental, when really he was helpless. He didn't
know what to do. These gorillas weren't lean-armed and -legged
and pot-bellied at the same time like Buddy, the orang, who was
just as old. Squat black kegs of muscle, bodies boulders on thick
legs — they moved with such instant flattening confidence, if you
had only scuffled around with Buddy you were lost. These were
gorillas. These were tanks.

The gorilla woman was prissy as an old maid about her cigarette,
it seemed to Fiddler in the clutches of her pet. At last she put away
the tobacco sack, lighted up, and twitched the chains. Fiddler's
gorilla let go of him and went to play at her feet with the other.
They fooled together and could have torn up Chief. Like a grandmother the gorilla woman stooped to pick dirt from their hands,
scratch behind their ears with a tortoise-shell comb some townie
lady had given her. The gorillas kissed her as she'd trained them.

Bible was yawning and stretching in his chair with particular
emphasis, working at it. The gorilla woman took her babies off a
ways to prevent trouble. Fiddler opened the dog wagon door and
stood beside the ladder where he would be able to see everything.
The cages rustled. Blue looked up and panted with wide-open
mouth, a big smile. Blue lived free in the wagon.

Bible appeared beside Fiddler — the dogs except Blue barked like crazy, battered the cage doors. "Shut up," Bible told them, grinning, and they choked the joy mute in their throats.

Bible shouted "Oops!" rushed in. Lying on the floor, Blue flipped on his back to get his legs up in the air, out of the way. Bible stamped the floor at the foot of the cot. "Killed him. Good. That's the end of him." Blue wagged his tail. The puppies yapped in Zeena's cage and blindly treadmilled in her fur. Bible shoved the thing with his foot past Blue. Blue sniffed politely. It was a cockroach. "He's a big one, isn't he?" said Bible, almost proud, and he kicked it out the door. "That's the last one, I'm sure. I never had the goddam roaches before this year. It's embarrassing. I don't know why they — they don't go with shows much — I mean they'd rather stay home, have a home!"

Blue went outside, happy tail tip waving. He brushed Fiddler's legs amiably. He was the boss of the dogs and a valuable friend to have when you were in the pen.

The cages were stacked four high and extended the length of the wagon, facing Bible's cot and chest of drawers. The juice had been turned on. Feet pattered as if they were singeing. From behind the rattling wire doors trilled ribbony whines. The dogs' eyes were planted on Bible, on his hands and face, and the red tongues trembled between gleaming rows of teeth.

Bible went to the cages at the far end of the wagon — like a cowpuncher exploded "Ee*Yaaaaaaah!*" He tapped the latch on the bottom cage and stood up fast flicking latches on cages above. Doors popped open, dogs zipped out, little, big, brown, spotted, foxy. Dogs like comets streaked from the bottom cages. From the top tiers dogs sailed into Bible's arms and he hustled them onto the floor. His hands flew. He ran and snatched at the cages and a cornucopia of dogs poured past Fiddler out the door. Bible set his knees, formed a basket of his arms at his side. The dogs aimed for that and launched themselves with unsquelchable squeaks of joy, hit with a grunt, sometimes two side by side. They slid down his arms while he bent for the next bottom cage. Split-second timing did it. Little, sailing dogs hit perfectly, one instantly after another, and he dropped them so they fell between the larger dogs dashing from the cages on the floor. The middle of the wagon was full of dogs, from floor to ceiling — Bible seemed to comb them out of the air with his arms — and they rollercoasted through the narrow door in file.

Zeena was last. She was as eager as the rest. She frolicked out of her first-story cage, trying to be puppyish, with milk for nine puppies swinging between her knees. Bible made Zeena stop in the doorway while he poked amongst the balled-up, tiny figures she'd just left and gave each one of them his finger to suck on. "Eyes going to open pretty soon," he said, maybe to Fiddler, maybe to Zeena.

The runt was hungry, Bible decided. He told Zeena to "lay down."

The runt (a regular butterball) feasted like an emperor's child alone at a banquet table. He looked enraptured, eyes closed, yanking on the teat and alternately pumping with all four feet as if he were playing a very rhythmic and moving hymn in front of a congregation. Bible was with the other puppies at the cage, looking them over. He tested their bones for rickets and inspected under their tails to see if Zeena was cleaning everywhere properly. Zeena resigned herself and relaxed at full length but kept an eye on Bible, watching for her release.

The freed dogs swept round the pen like a scudding whirl of feathers. They knew better than to leap the fence, but they hurdled Bible's chair and the sloping wagon ladder next to Fiddler, and when Bible got in the spirit and lay on the floor of the wagon kicking his legs out the door as if he were practising swimming the dogs vaulted over his legs. Blue called the plays. Blue was much larger than the rest of the dogs, and big-jawed like a wolf. They raced in front of Blue like football blockers. Every so often he shifted his field — dropped one set and picked up another. Blue was having a great time. He was a marvelous bluish gray and he had the best sense of humor Fiddler had ever seen in a dog. When he came near Fiddler sometimes he feinted as if to bring the whole careening team upon him and snapped malevolently and then, swiveling, left Fiddler safe and sound. The dogs were really getting rough now. They jostled each other, fought with the weight they could throw with their shoulders. Bumptious yearling pups used their paws as weapons — and got pushed all over by the big bluff adult males who knew better how to handle themselves. Round and round the pen swept the pack. Quick, maneuverable dogs outstripped their buddies but could never get the last laugh, because once they'd lapped them there was that gauntlet to pass of burly, jarring shoulders. The husky shoulder-fighters won the pen from both the speedsters and the young pups who lacked the confidence and weight to do more than punch long-distance with their paws. They could not afford to be pompous about it, though, since Blue bossed everybody, and besides, there were several dexterous, slim-necked little bitches who could snap the legs from under the most braggadocious heavyweight of dogs.

Fiddler had never seen such silent dogs. The softest yip sounded loud because it was the only sound except the pell-mell feet and bumping bodies. Bible didn't want the dogs attracting attention — if the townies happened to *see* them roiling like a rabid pack of wolves, he couldn't help it — and during the act they'd been strictly trained not to peep.

The most acrobatic was the smallest. She seemed to think it quite a challenge to jump over Blue, but half the time she couldn't make it and landed on his back, rode him awhile as the next best thing. She rode Blue in earnest whenever the other dogs got bully-ish. She was brown and white with curly hair and weighed an eighth as much as he. One of her stunts in the show was standing on just her front feet on Blue while he galloped. Now she didn't bother with the fancy two-feet part, of course. Blue gave her a rodeo ride; he made her hang on with her teeth on his collar. Everything went fine until Blue, loping along, tried scaring the dog in front of him. He took its tail in his mouth. The dog did a cartwheel of fright right in his path and Blue tripped and spilled. The little passenger went sailing out and on and on — no Bible crouched at the cages to catch her this time — adjusting herself to hit loose, not be hurt. She fumphed on the ground like a pillow and got up, okay.

"See that?" Bible laughed. "She's good."

Fiddler went out in the midst of the traffic and knelt down low. The noiseless pack stormed so close the lolling tongues slapped him wet as washclothes — the serrate teeth like pellets slingshotted by — and then the follow-up tails swiped off the slop. Fiddler gagged with the dust, scarcely could hold his eyes open. He was off-balance, trying to dodge oncoming dogs. His eyes stung hazily; he groped. Swift as hawks the dogs wheeled round the pen, drove at him. He didn't get more than a roughing-up, but not because of anything he could do. He didn't see the pack come, much less grab time to brace for individual, plummeting dogs.

.... And Bible could dive and out of the pack fling any dog that needed a lesson. If it tried to bite, Lord save it.

Inevitably the dogs dizzied from circling and slowed down, reeling and weaving, rubbing their eyes on their paws and sitting down. Bible was filling a washtub from the water barrel.

"It's pretty tough for them to live in a cage," he said. "Can't smell nothing but their own selves in the straw. All they do is chew fleas and lick their feet." He laughed. "They lick their feet — that's the one place they can smell anything — they lick them till you'd think they'd go lame, peel the skin right off. You can't find no dirt."

Bible brought the washtub and let the dogs bury his hands in fur. They were in such a hurry, some of them put their feet in the water and, flustered, had to pull them out. Short dogs crept under tall ones; short-necks monopolized the edges of the tub, leaving the center to the long-necks. Soon the water was out of sight under the heaving crazy quilt of dogs. The excited lapping sounded like plywood cracking. Acrobatics didn't seem to help the little brown and white rider. She ran up and down Blue's back expectantly. Nobody made room. She got so angry she did it on *two* legs, twisting her mouth as if she were going to yap, but Bible's training kept her silent.

"See that? Oh, she's good, she's good!" With his hands Bible fixed a space for her to reach the water.

The runt had finished nursing, and Zeena was appreciative when Bible took it away. He stuck it in the cage, came back and sat down in the door of the wagon, dangling his legs. Zeena didn't struggle for a drink. Instead she plumped herself beside him and sniffed up the front of his shirt. Bible's fingers skimmed on her side, turning the fur deliciously like a breeze. He could pet a dog in a hundred ways. Closer and closer Zeena poked to his neck and face. She bit his collar, then darted her muzzle into his cheek, then curled a soaking red expanse of tongue over his lips and nose. That was enough for Bible. He wiped himself off.

"A hussy! That's what my mother'd have called you!"

Zeena wagged her tail, tried to poke him again with her nose. Bible made another space for Zeena.

The men and boys putting up the big top were opposite the dog wagon now. The boys were very hot, some pale, some red, licking their mouths from thirst. The canvas had scraped dirt on the faces indiscriminately. Where heavy dirt wasn't smeared they shone clean with sweat, hair pasted to the foreheads by the salt of dried sweat. — These were the faces of boys on the outside. Just the legs could be seen of a lot of the boys, who worked completely under the canvas, not getting *anything* but the raised dust and the crumpling heat and weight on their heads, shoulders, backs if they bent. They must be fish-faced, glass-eyed. Fiddler had never done that job. He was thankful. He'd quit the show if it ever assigned him there. The jigs' skin didn't show dirt but glistened with sweat. The jigs' work was easier, on the poles and ropes; they didn't have to be actually under the canvas yet, stifling like the boys. The hardest part of all — getting the canvas the first yard off the ground — was done by the smallest kids, since the smallest kids stood nearest the ground. They were wobbling like old, old men, from what Fiddler saw of them. He felt the hot canvas on his own hands.

"Hurry up, boys!" urged the Punk Boss. "Lift it up now!"

Magee bellowed, "Get it up! Get it up!" as if they were straw, not even glancing at them.

"Gititup!" sang the one-eared Boss Chief, staccato and bloodcurdling. And the jig crew flouncing along beside the boys with its rhythms and yammer helped keep things moving.

"Up goes de lady, up she goes!" crooned the King as if to a baby girl in his lap.

Townies cut off Fiddler's view and started giving the gorilla lady a hard time. All she could do was warn that when they had you by the neck the "monkeys" didn't feel as cute as they might look. Nothing she said impressed the parents, and certainly not the kids. Clowning innocent as two sprites, the gorillas trotted to the ends of the chains, made foolish, flopping leaps to catch the children. A vague instinct pulled the children back and lasted long enough for the gorilla woman to lock her babies up without them killing anybody.

Bible told the townies, "I don't care if you get bitten, but if you get your fingers in this cage you'll get bitten sure." He motioned his dogs to be still and dropped into a yogi trance. The gorilla woman came out of her wagon and sat on her ladder deaf as a statue. Two more impervious people were never seen. The dogs were lifeless. The townies went away as they had come — following the action on the big top.

"Hell," said Bible, "I was a chicken-sexer for two years, but I wouldn't be able to tell you if 'that little girl' was a little boy or 'that little boy' was a little girl. Did you see how they fixed its hair? You couldn't tell what it was. That's an awful thing to do to a kid!" Bible was vehement, and the gorilla lady agreed with a peculiarly affectionate smile. "They don't treat a kid like a person. Little dolls they fool around with, that's how they treat 'em. That's not the way." — Bible winked at the gorilla lady. In the midst of his anger he winked! Maybe they were going to have a kid of their own, for all Fiddler knew! They might be up to anything. Alone in their wagons on the flatcars every night, except for the man in black. They might have a baby in a crib inside her wagon right now being brought up with the gorillas! The man in black would stay mum naturally. . . . Fiddler reined in his thoughts before they got silly.

— But Bible was lucky as hell! The only man on the first train with a woman around: living with her instead of crowded with winos in the sleeping cars and department tents. The one solitary woman on the first train and she was Bible's! Maybe you could be better off by quitting the circus; no other way.

● *Rockford, Illinois*

RED LAUGHED, "Sure, 'Treat a queen like a whore and a whore like a queen.' You get your woman. I know. — But who the hell would *want* to treat a whore like a queen!"

"Listen now, I'm going to marry her!" Dry Wash shouted, sinking the tip of his finger in his ear and rubbing. "Listen now!" He was excitable.

Red heckled him. "You can't marry a *whore!*"

"I'll marry anybody I feel like it! You bums'll never see a woman. We'll be fine. She's going to marry me and we'll be fine; and you bums'll never see a woman — "

"But she's a *whore!* We was all in her. Even Taylor! Taylor, Chief, me, and then you — you was fourth on that ol' pig! Number Four with a dollar whore an' you want to marry her! What did she do to you, Dry, hex you?"

Dry Wash swung at Red. A haymaker. Red ducked and waited for Dry Wash to recover his balance and bring his fists up into fighting position. Then Red knocked Dry Wash's arms apart so hard they nearly flew off. He didn't want to bring them together again. He rubbed around his armpits, lips pursed in pain. Red quit teasing him.

Rose had gone to the ladies room of a gas station near the lot to fix herself up for the wedding. Dry Wash had told her he'd meet her at Number 12 Wagon, so he had to stay and wait there with all the Department hanging around. But nobody teased him any more, Fiddler was glad to see. Dry Wash sat on a crum box and wiped his long, spaniel face, cleaned his ears nervously and tied his shoes over and over again. They needed to be tied tight in front because the heel stitching was coming out. The heels flapped like slippers when he walked. Brownie had given him a pair of polka-dot socks for the ceremony, saying on second thought he might as well just keep them since they'd have to be burned anyway when he took them off. Dry Wash's pants were his own — blue jeans which had been worked in for quite a while. The shirt was loud and Hawaiian and ripped in the back. It had belonged to Red. And there was a blue uniform tie in perfect condition which somebody must have snitched from the ushers' and bandmen's top.

Fiddler was curious to see the bride-to-be. Three nights ago in Chicago Chief and Red had picked her up, and Dry Wash and Taylor had joined the party. — Dry Wash had been worthless to the Department ever since, off smooching with his love. When the show had pulled out of Chicago last night he'd brought her along inside one of the trucks on the flatcars and announced he was leaving the show to be married. Evidently he was serious. He'd gotten his pink slip and what little money was coming to him and packed two or three pieces of clothing in a box that had held the monkeys' plums. Dry Wash was all set.

Red was almost as eager. "Wait till you see her! Jeez — Marry a whore! Whoever heard o' that!" he whispered to Fiddler. And Chief was "snoring" in the grass, with his hat partly hiding his face and his eyes open.

Chief sat up, pointing.

"That's your dolly, Dry," said Red.

There was no mistaking who they meant. No one else on that whole lot, out of the hundreds of townies, looked like Rose. After all, nobody else was headed for their own wedding. Rose was brimming happiness, chortling like a parrot, rouged a feverish pink. The thin, pink skirt could hardly contain her hips; nice, nice hips. She carried a pint-sized suitcase, almost a toy. She waggled her arms behind her as if to keep the wedding guests in line. Maybe Rose thought there were some. Every townie gazed and gave her the right of way. She might have had a motorcycle escort.

Dry Wash cracked a giant smile and without thinking picked Chief's hat off his head and put it on; which was an awfully drastic thing to do.

"Are you ready, Gilbert?" Rose asked, long-distance. "Did you get your money?"

Dry Wash nodded, his upper lip folded over the lower in a big smile. Like any other wino he was toothless.

Chief took back his hat amazingly gently.

"Who's Gilbert?" Fiddler said.

Brownie answered dryly from the wagon. "It's his name. Gilbert Drinkle. It was on the payroll." Brownie's expression when he saw Rose was the one he usually saved for Mayors and mounted police-men — his best.

Dry Wash scrubbed an ear like mad. He was entranced. He twined his fingers. He scratched one shin with his other foot, bal-ancing awkwardly. Fiddler hoped nobody would make fun of him.

Red did keep quiet. So did Brownie, even.

"They gave your money to you, Gilbert, okay, didn't they? Are my shoes all right for church? Does a church want white shoes? A lady said no. I only asked one, but she was very rich, a rich lady who knows. She goes to church. Any nice shoes, she said." Rose had a strong voice. She was thirty yards away still.

Dry Wash pranced like a horse without a tail. The very air itched him.

Rose was pale except for the rouge and big-bodied, with the rub-bery, durable arms of a whore. The V in her blouse was the largest such V Fiddler had ever seen. She was missing some buttons. "The gas station man said you are a lucky man. His wife is a pain. He said my stockings are nice, but he didn't know about the shoes being all right. He's done so many bad things he wouldn't dare go to a church. 'Just think of me!' I said. — *Then* I was sorry! I could have bit my tongue off." Her voice at high pitch squawked like a parrot's; low, it ground along like a washing machine at "Wash."

"Do we get to kiss the bride?" Chief said, taking hold of Rose. Chief kissed her chin and ears, the insides of her lips, and with his hands he had her dancing up and down.

Red was moving in when she gasped, "No!" Fiddler stopped Red. "Listen now, you think you're Hitler! Get away! You think so, you think you're Hitler!" Dry Wash clamored, pulling at Chief.

Fiddler stepped in and helped Dry Wash. Chief sometimes was cruel. — "Cut it out, Chief." The struggle didn't last long. Chief almost apologized. He put his hat on Dry Wash, since the guy had wanted it.

"I'll letcha use it for a while." Then to Fiddler with a grin — "Okay, boy. Okay."

Dry Wash and Rose clasped hands and chastely kissed. Then they collected their possessions — her child's-size suitcase and his cardboard box — and set out to find a church. Without planning to do so, Fiddler started following, along with Red and Chief. Fiddler felt a little sheepish.

"What's the idea?" Dry Wash demanded. He was really standing up for his rights.

"You gotta have witnesses, don'tcha? We're witnesses," Chief explained. "We're your witnesses."

And Red chimed in, "Hey, we won't fool around none, Dry. We wish you many happy returns. We won't kid you."

Red sounded sincere, and Dry Wash probably would need witnesses and was exceedingly happy at the moment anyway — he began to stick his finger in his ear and rub, as if he were going to argue, but then thought better of it. He shrugged and lost himself to everything but Rose.

"You guys be back to work," Brownie warned.

The wedding party started toward the road, easily slicing a swath in the ranks of the townies, a regular aisle. People made way. People *moved*. Partly it was Chief. He got out in front and scowled. Maybe Red looked unusually rakish and dangerous for daughters. Or the aroma from Dry Wash, since the wind was at his back, might have had something to do with it. Fiddler walked behind Dry Wash and Rose to avoid Dry Wash's smell. Fiddler guessed that to the townies he was the most normal-seeming "bum" of the five. The townies didn't glance twice at Fiddler. Fiddler was dusty from having to live out of doors. Dry Wash's skin was encrusted with filth and, underneath, as dirt-soaked and permeated as an earthworm's. No doubt his mother had given him "wet" baths — so it couldn't have been over twenty-five or thirty years he'd gone without one.

Rose was comparatively clean. You could say that for her. She was a whore plainly enough — still wearing her hair to her shoulders, although it had turned a dingy gray. Her nose was broken out of shape, too, Fiddler had noticed. He watched the calves of her legs above the lavender shoes and white bobby sox. The muscles were flabby — and she limped, he saw now. She was an old whore. There were plenty of them in the world. But they didn't get married. Who would marry an old, worn-out whore? — Here was who! Fiddler was getting a demonstration!

Rose didn't have eyes in the back of her head, and Fiddler could look her up and down without feeling embarrassed. He made out a scar on her neck under the hair, an old, big, shapeless scar lined like dried meat. Maybe that was another reason she wore her hair long, besides it being the natural style — hair a gritty, dishrag gray. Rose didn't have much left to attract. She lacked the playful pertness of a good young whore. She'd lost her looks. She must have been running out of business when Dry Wash happened along. The one thing she'd retained was those hips. What she had was a walk — a *walk.* A rollicking, come-on walk with a bump and a grind and a virtual red light slung on each melon hip like a pistol. Watching the hips, you forgot her hair and broken nose and sagging calves. The limp was confined below her knees. Rose could walk with the best.

The big top canvas and pole trucks had just arrived, so the lot itself was still quite open and roomy. But the lot was at a curve in the road and the road was not wide. Chief for all his fierceness could scarcely wedge a passage. Cars had been parked on both sides, sometimes carelessly, allowing very little space for the traffic and pedestrians, who had to walk in the road because this was a residential neighborhood with fences and hedges. A cop was doing what he could to speed up things, and Rose went to him. Dry Wash's finger was in his ear again. He was getting upset. "No, no!" he hissed at Rose.

"Is there a church that wouldn't be busy now?" Rose asked the cop. She waited, smoothing her tight pink skirt, which was split to the knee and resembled a slip in its thinness.

The cop smiled at Rose with an easy air he might use good-naturedly making an arrest. "You go up to the stoplight, miss, and turn left and walk a ways and you'll see several down the street." He added, "You know, we can't let you run around town very long like that with your blouse open. You'll need to sew on some buttons before I see you again; and put on a different skirt."

Rose didn't push her luck any further. She guided the group away, taking Dry Wash's finger out of his ear and wrapping his arm around her waist. "You weren't scared I was going to ask him about the jewelry store, were you, Gilbert? I'd even invite him," she went on. "I always hate cops, but even him I'd invite 'cause we're going to have a bing-bang time. — Do you have a safety pin?" Nobody did. Rose looked round and round. "Ah," she said at last and she slipped between the cars and families so fast Fiddler almost lost track of her. On the other side of the road she intercepted a baby carriage and bent over it, apparently praising and cuddling the baby, because the mother beamed proudly. Then Rose left, nodding and cooing over her shoulder at the mother, who seemed a little puzzled at the shortness of the visit.

Rose had acquired a safety pin. She closed the gap in her blouse.

"We heard about the church," Dry Wash said. "We have to find out about a jewelry store somewhere, a jewelry place."

"I am," Rose rasped. "I couldn't ask the cop, could I? A jewelry store, I am asking."

Fiddler wondered if they hadn't forgotten about the license, and whether they could afford both a license and a ring. "How about your license?"

Rose questioned a lady sitting in a snappy gray-green sport car: "Is there a jewelry store that my husband could get his watch fixed at?"

The lady was startled at being addressed. Her suit and purse and gloves and shoes were the same chic gray-green as the car. The dashboard, steering wheel and upholstery were all that color. The lady had plenty of jewelry but looked like the kind of woman Fiddler would have walked half a mile to avoid asking a question of. Her earrings were the same gray-green. No one but Rose would have chosen her with so many other people around. "I don't know a thing about the town," snooted the woman. "I don't live here."

Rose was undaunted. "She had nice rings. I could tell she knows nice places, but probably she goes to Chicago." Rose sashayed along in her tight skirt, limp and all, searching the crowd. She and Dry Wash were holding hands. Not just anybody could direct her to a store. Rose let perhaps a hundred pass. They were getting to the light the cop had mentioned.

"Have you bought your license, though?" Fiddler asked again.

Rose squeezed Dry Wash's hand. "There's a tony lady!" This one was driving a gleaming Buick and didn't seem to be going to the circus, but just hugging the wheel and trying to get past without running into anyone. When Rose cried out, "Missus! Missus, stop, Missus!" she stopped horror-struck, screeching brakes, gasping. Rose's strident voice must have made her think she'd hit a child.

"Is there a jewelry store that would fix my husband's watch?"

"*What?*"

"Is there a jewelry store that would fix my husband's watch?"

"Don'tyoueverdothatagain! No. Don'tyou ever! Don't you ever do that to me again. You could have had me a heart attack, with my nerves. You shouldn't be   allowed to   do that. In   my condition, in the state I'm in,   and you do   that — " The woman wept.

"Come on," said Chief, leading the wedding party on.

"She can pick 'em!" Red grinned to Fiddler.

It was better having Chief in front because when anyone else led he'd get impatient if something held them up and tread on their heels and shove — "Come on, Come on!" Nobody but a new man would put himself before Chief trying to work through a crowd.

They turned left on the road where the churches were supposed to be. It was wider. The townies going to the lot could spread out and take it easy and use their eyes more. People's faces brightened, seeing Dry Wash and Rose.

"Yessiree, we're gettin' there, we're gettin' there. There's some o' them showpeople." — The man smirked. His wife answered something stupid with a flat false ring to her voice like a boy mimicking a woman.

"But did you get your license yet, Dry Wash?" Fiddler insisted on asking.

"Yeah, in Chicago."

"You could have gotten married right there, couldn't you, in the courthouse?"

"Aw, those jokers were making cracks, those jokers hangin' around. Bunch of smart Hitlers. — 'When's your case due, Rosey?' Smart guys."

"Chicago's a wicked, dirty city," Rose said, her eyes peeled for another likely lady.

Kids were posted out in the road coaxing cars to park in some of the driveways at a quarter apiece, while baby brothers and sisters sat with dogs on the curb wishing they could be dodging around in the traffic too. The kids were having a wonderful time and getting in everybody's way, rapping on windows and kneeling down in the road, not watching at all where they were going. Chief frowned at them, but they didn't deign to notice him or anybody else not in a car. Chief waited till he had a chance to grab one —

"Why ain't you at the circus!"

" 'Cause I'm makin' money," said the kid testily as he turned around to look at whoever was grasping his shoulder. His eyes popped. Chief's lips were drawn back from his teeth like two rolls of muscle and his high hair was tangled as snakes, above the fist cheekbones, eyes black as the hole in a gun.

"Why ain't you at the circus? I'm surprised at you not being there! You don't wanna hang around home!"

"Oh," said the kid, weak as a rag. "Is it going to start?"

"Yeah." Chief gentled his voice.

"Oh." The kid stood under Chief's hand quiet and straight without trying to move, losing his fear. "I will. Heck with this." Chief started after Rose and Dry Wash, who had gone ahead, and the kid came right beside him, wordless.

"No," Chief said. "I ain't going there. You go to the circus. And take all them kids with you. You shouldn't be around here. You should be at the circus."

The kid stopped and stayed, watching Chief walk away. Then he ran back to his nearest friend. "See that guy? See him? See him? That guy's an Indian!"

Rose's next woman was friendly as well as rich in appearance, and she had children with her. The minute she saw Rose she smiled — smiled still more, hearing Rose's question about a jeweler to fix her husband's watch.

"Which is your husband?"

At first Rose was uncertain who to point out, but, since Fiddler, Red and Chief were no closer to having watches than Dry Wash, she acknowledged him. Dry Wash put his finger in his ear, and Rose pulled it away, laying his arm around her hips.

The lady was unable to control her mouth. It broadened and broadened, bursting giggles. She had pretty teeth. She struggled to bend her eyes away from Rose and Dry Wash. "Yes, yes, the funniest thing happened to me yesterday. Whenever I think of it I have to — to laugh," she choked merrily, eyes glistening, she was laughing so hard, and she bit on her lip. "That was so funny yesterday." She wove her fingers together, squinted, bit her lip, looked way down the street and still couldn't stop.

Red nudged Fiddler. "What'd I tell you? She can pick 'em, all right. Trust a whore!"

Eventually the lady got the directions out, and Rose thanked her. "He's just the man for you to see," the lady concluded, with a giggle.

The jewelry shop was part of a block of stores not far from a couple of churches. Rose peeked in the window. She breathed relief. "It's a man." She undid the pin that was holding her blouse together. Her instructions were, "Spread out, everybody."

A customer was leaving as they entered. The jeweler smiled behind his hand and coughed to make him turn around and look at what had just come in.

"Can we see your rings?" Rose asked, grandly bowing. The jeweler sniffed nervously because he saw deep down her blouse, or else because of Dry Wash. Rose and Dry Wash and Red, who of course played along, and even Chief spaced themselves along the display case. Fiddler stuck beside Chief, wondering what Rose was trying to pull off.

"Do you *all* want to see them?"

"It's my wedding and I need a ring and we want to buy the best we can, we're looking for a real dinger one and we all want to see them, sure."

The jeweler nodded indulgently, then caught his breath as Rose bent over the case and again he saw into the gap in her blouse.

The stones glowed and glittered under a wreath of brilliant little bulbs. The rings were contained in open white tiny boxes couched on a spotless bed of cotton.

"You're not married, are you?" Rose said — clearly by his how-did-you? expression he wasn't — "And you don't know how good it feels to get a ring. You can help me choose if you like. We all want to choose. It lasts your whole life, so it's important. — Can I see some, please?" She raised her voice to snap him out of his reverie, gazing into her bosom.

"Yes." He slid aside the glass on the back of the case. "What price range do you think you would be interested in?" He fingered amongst the sparkling boxes nestled in the antiseptic cotton. He was dainty and adept. Fiddler's hand would have looked indecent there, like a bedbug or a wad of chewing gum. The jeweler's clean nails shone.

"Not over a thousand," Rose said.

The jeweler suppressed a sigh. "Yes, that's quite a range. That includes a lot of rings." He began to bring out a few of the boxes. "The price is on the box. Could you tell me the minimum price you are interested in? That would be a help."

"You see, they may kick in if they like it, so I don't know how much. It may be a pile if we all pay. I can't estimate." Rose bent again and sinuously wiggled her hips and put all the rings he had given her on at once, not favoring any particular finger.

"Just a minute. Don't mix up which ring goes with which box," the jeweler warned, fighting with his eyes. . . . "Or I'll have to go to a lot of trouble straightening it out," he went on absently. "I'll have to straighten it out."

Rose motioned for more rings and, as they were somewhat regretfully brought, passed the old batch down to Dry Wash, who kept several and distributed the rest among Chief and Fiddler and Red.

"Wait a minute. Hadn't we better keep them together?" suggested the jeweler.

Rose leaned lower still, and wiggled. "Maybe we're all going to kick in, honey, so we all need to look. That's why. Don't worry. — And we may want some nickernackers to go with it."

Rose got him to show her sets of bracelets, brooches and necklaces which matched some of the rings, and more single rings, and she duly passed everything along for her friends to inspect. The jeweler found himself trying to keep track of rings in five pairs of hands, and answer questions — it must have been very confusing.

"Lemme see this fella," Chief spoke up, thumping the glass over a fine emerald.

"Why that's a little above your price range, I'm afraid. That's my pet, that's my prize." The jeweler's nostrils wrinkled as he moved past Dry Wash to explain. He sneezed. There was more than a whiff of the smell in the room. Chief grunted unco-operatively.

Rose took the jeweler's side. "No, Chief, he's right. We couldn't get it. We don't want to waste our time."

Chief glowered at the guy. "You won't show it to me?"

"Can I see these rings?" Rose pointed at the last group in the case, giving the jeweler a chance to get away from Chief. The jeweler's eyebrows lifted roguishly as he brought them to her and she bent. — But these too she scattered among her friends. And then suddenly the jeweler's face knitted in suspicion. Without being conspicuous about it, he began to gather all the little boxes and slide them under his arm; and, when he wasn't distracted by some switch of Rose's hips or her bending down, he appeared to be counting the dents in the cotton in the display case and then counting the boxes he now guarded behind his arm.

"Here's a dinger!" Rose rasped, shifting rings from finger to finger.

Red crowed, "I got a peach!" He showed one off on his thumb. Chief was trying to put a fingernail scratch on a diamond.

Fiddler had never been in an enclosed space this small with Dry Wash before. That was the thing about the circus: if you lived with Dry Washes, you were almost always out of doors. It was getting hard to breathe. Fiddler was afraid his clothes would permanently absorb the smell. The jeweler was sneezing and glancing about in bewilderment, probably not believing such a stink could come from a human being. Rose was up to something big; otherwise Fiddler would have left. She looked like a gypsy mindreader, stooped over the display case, an old hag from the shoulders up and the knees down. She was shuffling her collection of rings from hand to hand like a carnival sharp. She had something cooking, that was for sure. The jeweler sighed, sighed, as if he were panting, then sneezed. His hand brushed over the desolate bed of cotton. The poor guy was going cockeyed from trying to guard his boxes and watch all the rings in all the hands at once; and if Rose had taken off her clothes completely she couldn't have been more distracting. Fiddler didn't know what to do with the rings that were passed to him, so after he'd seen them he gave them back to Rose. In this way she soon got most of them again in a hoard in her hands.

"Come here, boys," she said. "It's time to choose." The corners of the jeweler's mouth had drooped with melancholy, but this announcement cheered him up. Everybody assembled around Rose and gave her the last few rings — the jeweler wanted to take some back, and she let him have the bracelets and brooches as a compromise. "Now we have to make our minds up."

She began slowly, hands crawling like crabs, tricky fingers out at odd angles, sifting the rings. There was a rhythm to it and the rhythm speeded. Rings spun on the tips of her fingers and her hands glided palms down close over the case. Wherever the hands went the rings were whisked from sight as if they'd been sucked away by a vacuum cleaner — except for the twirling ones on her fingers — and then taptap-tap–tap they'd reappear, dropped from the heel of her hand. It was very hard to follow; you had to work your eyes. She was flipping the rings up into her hands from the ends of her fingers and

jabbing down for other rings on the case. Quicker and quicker
darted the fingers, to the tap-tap dribbling from the cupped palms.
The jeweler opened his mouth several times but wasn't able to say
anything — the poor jeweler rubbing his nose because of Dry Wash
and skittish with Chief's tough puss leaned next to him.

Then the tapping ceased and the hands bulged fuller and fuller
with rings, the fingers slim pistons chucking them up, until the last
had gone with a click against the others, and Rose turned her
hands.

"Do we know which yet?" The stones twinkled with a thousand
pricks of light. She rubbed her hands together, mixing the rings,
and laid them out in a mass.

"Here's the sixtyfive bucker, right?" She poked one and looked
at Dry Wash.

"Don't ask me."

"And here's the eighty." She winked.

"Yeah, yeah."

"No, hold it, it's the thirty, isn't it?" — winking again.

"Might be."

They talked back and forth: "I remember the bluest was the hun-
nert-and-seventy." . . . "Yeah, but here's the bluest an' it's fortynine-
ninetyfive, I know." . . . "The reds are for the big dough; three hun-
nert smackers this was!" . . . And Red and Chief joined in: "Only a
sawbuck for this fella." . . . "Soon as I seen that ring I could tell it
was the peach; seventynine, though; that's plenty." . . .

The jeweler put out his hands and opened his mouth, spurring
himself —

"Isn't this a shame!" Rose interrupted. "We've hashed 'em up.
You were right. You told us not to and we've done it."

"J-Just a minute. How much money *have* you got?"

"That's a good question." Rose set her little suitcase on the case
between the jeweler and the rings. Mostly it contained brassieres;
but from the single pair of socks she did extract three dollars with
some change. And Dry Wash showed the contents of his box —
soiled pictures out of magazines, a soup-stained shirt, cigarette butts
long enough to salvage, crusty underwear. He got three pennies

from the box, fished in his pockets and, amongst a pile of crumbs, brought forth four dollars and a half, his pay when he quit.

Red pulled his pockets inside out — "I ain't got nothing." Chief shook his head at Rose, meaning she needn't ask because he was keeping whatever he had. Fiddler included himself with Chief by giving no answer when she turned to him.

Rose put the proposition to the jeweler: "If we gave you this money, eight dollars and twenty-one cents, would you let us have the ten-dollar ring so's we can be married like nice people?"

"Yes! Fine, yes, certainly, fine!"

"Do you remember which it was, Gilbert?" she said slowly. The jeweler's face fell. The rings were in a jumble. Rose started sorting through. She watched the jeweler. He reached to help her but the suitcase was in the way; Rose didn't want it shut or moved. Having his hands above her brassieres seemed to embarrass the guy. Rose bent very, very low and hula-ed with her hips. Her fingers nibbled at the rings. Again began the sleight of hand. Chief hulked on one side of Rose; Dry Wash was on the other. The jeweler sneezed and held his nose. Fiddler opened the door and stood in it. The shop stunk like an airless outhouse.

Rose's rippling fingers snared the rings and spun them up in the air. "Which is it? You were right! We shouldn't have hashed 'em up. Which is it? Oh, how awful! Which is it!" Her eyes were glued to the jeweler. Rings popped out of her juggling hands — "Is this it? Is it this?" She speared them on a finger as they fell. The jeweler was exhausted, the rings dipped in and out of view so fast. Rose bent toward him as if she were about to eat him — Rose read his face.

Gradually, ring by ring, the most expensive were weeded out, handed back, and a few of the boxes filled. The jeweler sweated blood for each of them. By the time it seemed to Fiddler all the rings worth over eighty or a hundred dollars were in the case again the jeweler was panting as if he were digging a ditch. He sounded frantic, voice feeble and high. "I know how many there are, remember! I've got the boxes. You can't sneak off with any!"

Rose reached her decision.

"Here it is! A dinger! Here all along!"

"Let me see," said the jeweler. Rose slipped it on her finger and flourished it.

"Fits and everything. A dinger! I knew it would work out. Oh, I'm so happy!"

"Let me look at it," the jeweler insisted, until Rose made as if to grab up all the other rings. Then he was glad to have her let him take them back and to begin matching them with the boxes — not agreeing yet that hers was the ten-dollar one, though.

It was hard, putting the proper ring in the proper box. He'd recognized the expensive rings, of course, but these weren't so easy. Rose helped. Her hands moved very swiftly and everything seemed to come out right. He could make very few switches, and, if he found it hard to picture the ring on her finger in the ten-dollar box, he wasn't able to substitute any other. Rose was patient. Rose smoothed things over, gave him good long looks down her blouse. He was rubbing his eyes now as well as his nose because of Dry Wash, and Red and Chief had been driven by the stench to stand with Fiddler at the door.

"Come on. Come on," Chief groused.

Rose nodded and turned to the jeweler with the patience of a good mother. "Okay, honey?"

He sneezed, rocking his head in his hands, shrugged. "Leave the door open."

"Am I tired!" Rose puffed, outside.

"Which was it?" everybody wanted to hear.

"The sixtyfiver!" Her sudden grin exposed a lot of rotten teeth she'd been hiding; but it was a grin of the most complete contentment.

One of the two churches in the neighborhood was white, the other stone. Rose decided on the stone one and they walked to it. She pinned her blouse together. Her feet caused her a great deal of trouble — she *was* tired — and she wheezed softly. But the sweet, swelled rolling of her hips went on unchanged. Nothing of the painful limp showed above her knees.

The front door of the church was locked, and Dry Wash knocked on it.

Chief snorted, "Stupid, you don't do that to a church! You go round to the back! Don't you know that? I'll find the fella for you."

The rectory was a wing attached to the back of the church and set amongst trees and shrubs and flowerbeds. Rose made Dry Wash take off Chief's hat, and she fussed with her safety pin. Chief knocked on the door. Rose was nervous, blushing, watching the knob fixedly. "I hope he lets us do it in the church," she whispered. In view of what Dry Wash wrought on a small room Fiddler thought that might be a good idea too.

"How did you learn that" — he tried to demonstrate — "that stuff with your hands?"

She whispered, "I was in carnies." She licked her lips. Dry Wash was rubbing his ear. The door opened and Rose pulled Dry Wash's finger out of his ear, caught her breath and couldn't speak a word.

"They want to get married," Chief told the minister.

Fiddler helped out. "Are you pretty busy right now? — Because, if it's convenient, these two people would like to be married, and we just came along."

The minister smiled like a nice enough guy. "You're circus people?"

"Yes," Fiddler said.

"Well, it will be an honor. I'll be glad to do it right away. Come in. You have to get back for a show, I imagine. I'm happy you chose us."

"Thank you. Do you use the church itself for a thing this small? They would rather have the service in the church, if that's possible."

"We can have it there, yes." He asked Rose, "Do you have a hat?" Rose blushed, started to shake her head and then reach for Chief's, and Fiddler was going to find out if there wasn't one they might borrow. But the minister didn't give him a chance. "Wait, my wife has several — more than she should, I'm sure." He laughed at his joke and left them in the hall a minute. Rose stowed her suitcase and Dry Wash's box behind a table in the corner. Anxiously she fluttered her hands over her blouse and skirt.

The minister came back with a flowered hat, which Rose put on as if it were made of glass, and he took them all through a side door into an anteroom and into the church. Dry Wash and

Rose went hand in hand. Chief, Red and Fiddler trooped after, as well-behaved as choir boys. For one terrible second it seemed that Rose and her groom might be stuck by the hips in the narrow door, but "Ladies first!" she whispered, forging through ahead. Fiddler wondered how the minister would react when it was done and they told him they had nothing to pay him. At least he wouldn't call the cops.

Council Bluffs • VI

BETTY LOU knew the peculiar metal-rattling sound a water truck made. She went all in a tizzy; she tried to get up — she was lying on her side like a downed blimp and she struggled mightily to put her nubbin feet on the floor of the cage. The left feet made it, but not the right. They were stranded wiggling high above a ton of fat. The hippo cage was a good distance from where Fiddler sat, and Betty Lou looked small — a pig in a piano crate, except that her head was out of proportion to a pig's. When she didn't get excited, she could manipulate much better, but now she was about as skillful as an awkward turtle.

The truck drew up at Betty Lou's wagon. Taylor uncoiled the hose from a rack over the fender and directed the nozzle through the bars at the empty water tank. The driver started the pump. *That* noise sent Betty Lou into paroxysms. She *got* on her hooves and hastened toward the tank, already chomping her jaws. Her body traveled in sea-deck lurches, each foot for a moment foundering under the crush. Betty Lou liked to catch the stream of water in her mouth. And she wanted the tank full so she could rest in it — the water would buoy her weight. It was a considerable physical strain on her to be out of the water for long. Also she got hot and thirsty very fast.

Betty Lou spectacularly spread her jaws. She trapped the stream of water and Fiddler saw the bottom of her throat gagging to swallow. The pressure being fairly high, soon water was fountaining all over the cage, and Betty Lou was having a marvelous time. She partly closed her jaws, shook the writhing, splatting water like a rat and then chomp-chomped. Taylor was sympathetic. He opened his mouth and bobbed his head. Not too much of the water was getting into the tank, however. That was the trouble with letting her play. Taylor himself was splashed. So he had to move down the cage, beyond the platform, where she couldn't reach the stream.

The top of the tank was at the level of the platform. In the tank, Betty Lou would be total mistress of the situation. — How to get into the tank?

There was a stair; but she seemed to have forgotten about that. She was up on the tips of her hooves on the brink of the tank, stretching, s t r e t c h i n g, eyes closed, tongue tentatively out. — "Use the stair, stupid!" Fiddler heard himself saying. The water torrent hammered in the tank. Betty Lou's blubbery, whitish tongue poked out and reached and reached — and then she threw discretion to the winds. She pounced. — Her front feet, that is, jerkily pounced down. Her belly oofed against the platform and remained there, aslant; and Betty Lou was beached, half in the tank, half out.

Still she couldn't taste the water. What humiliation! And how her feet must ache! Taylor seemed to be glad of a chance to do his job without her interference, and telling her so. His madman mouth was running. Betty Lou's legs labored bravely — Fiddler could only see the hind ones; they weren't made for such work. Her neck was bent as if she were prodding the floor with her nose. Step by step she got herself free. She came to almost a handstand position before she managed to slide her hind end down the wall and into the tank.

Now Betty Lou was boss. Taylor couldn't aim the hose anywhere she couldn't reach. The young gangling bears when they were being hosed down would lope in one place like rocking horses. Betty Lou tried her own version of this. The floor of the tank rang out like a gong. And she chomped and chomped that water column. She took it all apart. She yawned her cavernous mouth and splattered water far and wide. Taylor had to give up the idea of keeping dry. He was a good sport. He sprayed her where she wanted to be sprayed, washed off her backside. And Betty Lou had terrific fun.

She gargled and snuffled and slurped, burst open the valves of her nose and sucked them closed and rinsed her bulbous eyes. As the tank filled higher and higher she would settle into the water, voluptuous as a sultan, take the load off her feet, and submerge, chewing gallons and wallowing waves, slosh out long sheets — farther than she gave you time to jump. You had to be always on your guard with Betty Lou. No one slept in the shade of the hippo cage or near the cage at night.

Brownie came up to Betty Lou's cage, patted Taylor on the back and wryly listened to the gabble, looking around all the while, particularly behind him, as if he thought he were being tailed. Then he went over in front of the cookhouse and talked with some of the old bums who had already gathered for lunch and after a minute came on toward the dog wagon, glancing behind once or twice, not scared or anything like that — from his expression, irritated. It was rare for Brownie to leave Number 12 Wagon before the big top was set up. Fiddler was going to say something about it to Bible, but Bible had already seen.

Brownie walked with the hardened step of a fit old man. He was twenty years older than Bible and he dressed as though he were twenty years younger, in those green pants and the flashy red shirt. He and the man in black were a real contrast.

"I don't suppose Chief's shown his nose around here?" Brownie said to Fiddler.

"No."

"What's he going to do, walk-away on me?" Walk-aways, who didn't formally quit, were never rehired.

"Get away from here, Brownie, you ol' half-ass. You know he wants him back here as much as you — more than you." The gorilla lady told him off.

"He's at the hospital," Fiddler argued. "For Christ sake, he'll be back!"

Brownie didn't come in the pen with Bible and Fiddler. He sat in the shade with his back to the wheel of the gorilla wagon beside the man in black's compartment. He had to get the man in black to move his feet a little. "A guy like Chief leaves here drunk like he did and he usually doesn't come back even if he wants to. They leave the lot an' they're gone."

Fiddler was going to sneer. He looked to Bible and his lady for support — but they had turned their heads away as if they agreed with Brownie! Fiddler began to feel lousy again. After dark it was different; you could get away with plenty of things after dark. But he had to admit Chief had never been gone as long as this, drunk, during the day.

Two or three trucks went by, raising dust. Now in the heat of the day they stayed on a regular roadway as much as possible to avoid chewing up the ground. Even so, there was plenty of dust. Fiddler stretched out with his head between the paws of a dog with tapering, shivery jaws like a pair of pliers and ragged fur a motley brown and black. She was one of the wildest dogs, bought from some gypsies. She bent and chewed in his hair, and he got a pleasant sense of being guarded.

The gorillas angled down the wagon, the light chains dragging almost soundless, and rushed Brownie, long arms bendable crutches propelling them. Brownie tumbled out of reach. "Keep'm away from me! I don't want to be strangled." The man in black smiled from the wagon. The gorillas clasped his shoes like children shaking hands. The gorilla woman called them back to her, had them sit down and *sssssst* at them so that they slid their eyes away in shame and finally hid their heads. She didn't punish them more because she thought what they'd done was kind of funny.

Brownie looked out toward the cookhouse, muttering.

"What?" snapped the gorilla lady.

"I wasn't talking to you." — He realized she was angry at his language. There were certain words she wouldn't listen to. "I'm sorry." Brownie continued looking out at the cookhouse. "You know what that Red's doing?" (Fiddler couldn't see Red anywhere Brownie was looking.) "He's giving kittens away. Yeah. Giving kittens away! This woman walks up with a feed bag in her arms; I knew it was something bad, and she was the kind that'll talk and talk and talk; you have to get 'em out before they start. I said, 'Get out!' And she started to. 'It's only some harmless kittens' " — Brownie piped like a woman — " 'who need a home. Poor harmless kittens.' She was *going*, and that Red says he'll do it! 'He'll do it.' God, I could have fell over. So he's got 'em. He's finding homes. 'Best way to catch a girl there is.' He'll be locked up too, before Frisco. — If he sticks with us, I mean."

The gorilla woman had her pets playing toesy-wosy, and she was combing her hair. A scampy young dog was fooling with Fiddler. Lying playing on his back, Fiddler felt like a puppy. Bible said, "Here." The dog leapt over Fiddler straight into the air in an arc which landed him in Bible's lap. "Go back." He plumped on Fiddler's stomach.

Brownie's mouth twisted as he looked toward the cookhouse. All Fiddler could see was the usual townies and a few circus men sprawled asleep where the trucks and cats wouldn't run over them and one or two standing up not doing anything. "Now my best man's gone, my only good man except Fiddler here" — Brownie motioned impersonally. "Best man I've had all season. You people have it easy."

The gorilla woman laughed. "You don't *have* to be a boss!"

"Hell, I won't be, if guys like that stupid bonghead out there are all I can get." He nodded.

"Who?" Bible sat up straight.

"That hamhead that wants a job. Damn circus is going to pot. It was different a few years ago — ten years ago — you remember."

"I wasn't here," Bible said. "I was with Beatty."

"Well his show was different too. They all were. They'd stay. If you hired somebody by God he'd stay awhile; maybe half a season! It's better in a carnie. You don't give 'em any more money than they can eat on, an' they don't run away."

"Chief didn't run away," Fiddler protested.

"Jesus, the guys I've got working for me. — Like this nut, Taylor. He'll work good, but you have to watch him all the time and keep him out of trouble. He'll be locked up pretty soon too. He's been lucky. I thought he'd have us all, that time he told a bunch o' cops he was getting shot at. 'Nine times.' 'Nine times,' he said. You remember, Fiddler. I never talked so fast in my whole life. When I'd got rid of them we took him in the wagon, Chief and me, with a chain, a little length of chain, and by God *he* had to do some fast beggin' then. But it doesn't do any good with a guy like that, because he's off his rocker an' you can't change him. . . . And this Fiddler kid's always fooling around trying to get himself killed with the cats. I tell him and tell him. I have to worry about him."

"You stay with a show too long. Shift around; you get some soft deals," Bible told him. "Stick with a show and you get in a rut and they give you a lot of responsibility."

Brownie's mouth twisted. He was staring at whoever this guy was who wanted Chief's job. "Hey stupid! Come here!" Fiddler still didn't know exactly who it was, except that everybody clear to the cookhouse but one guy had turned to look at Brownie, neither coming nor getting mad. That guy must be the one, deaf or in a dream. "Bugbrain! Come here! Hey, I want to see you!"

"Maybe he's deaf," the gorilla woman suggested.

"He isn't deaf." Brownie was on his feet, shouting with a stored-up anger, "Come here, you goddam bonghead! Look at that guy just stand there! He isn't deaf; I tested him. He was following me before, and now when I want him he won't come!" Brownie stopped a Ringstock man who was passing and pointed out the guy. "Send the sonofabitching bastard, will you?"

"Don't blow your stack," the gorilla woman muttered, mad at his language.

"If you were about three men short to start with and your one single real man left — "

"Thanks," Fiddler said.

— "And the only thing that showed up looking for a job was *that* — Yeah! Yeah," he shouted, "That's him. That's bonghead. Yeah, that's right, bonghead, I want you! Come here! Come here!" The guy raised his head and headed for Brownie at a moderate, mechanical sort of a shuffle, not seeming a bit disturbed. "Now you look at that guy. He can't take care of himself. If I get rid of him out in Wyoming or Idaho somewhere, why they'll lock him up for the rest of his life. He wouldn't last twenty minutes in a strange town; they'd pick him up right away. That Taylor too. It's a responsibility, having those guys."

The man was under thirty. His workclothes were clean and his face had been recently washed. As he came closer he grew timid and hesitant, slowing down more and more until finally he stopped, almost ten yards away. Yet he didn't fidget. His feet stopped moving; he stood like a sack. He was a funny-looking bozo. One half of his collar jutted above the other because the shirt buttons had been buttoned into the wrong holes. His head was bony and large, especially the jaw and nose. His hair hung into his eyes, eyes blankbrown as the shucks of nuts. After a while his eyes dropped, slowly, as if they were falling asleep, his shoulders softly slumped like a bird just lighted relaxing, and he gazed at the ground, dreamy, at ease more and more.

The gorilla woman concentrated on her babies. "Don't hire him," she said. Bible and Fiddler scratched the dogs. Brownie's mouth twisted as if he were going to shout again, but he looked away too. The man in black was the only one who didn't.

— "And you hire a nice, healthy, well-fed, bright, honest kid from a decent family, and you're lucky to get out of town with him, and you're just as lucky to clear the next town with him. I've seen parents come *in person* four or five hundred miles after this show to get their kid away. 'We've found a job, Johnnie, in old Umpletumple's mill,' and that's the end o' that kid. So all you get's the wino tramp kids, or else kids that have just knocked up some broad. — You come into a town that's doing well and all you can find to hire is winos. And when it's really a prosperous town you lose half the men you've already got, and God save you if you go through some place at harvest time; you're liable to lose everybody!"

Bible winked at Fiddler. "It's a tough life." Brownie spat into the dog pen at him, causing the whole pack to spring snarling up, about to fly at Brownie. Bible had the dogs "lay down."

"All right, watch," said Brownie. — "What's your name?"

The guy standing out in the roadway didn't hear, apparently.

Brownie whispered, "What's your name?"

The guy looked up, slow as a tortoise waking.

"See, he isn't deaf. — What's your name?"

The guy opened his mouth, and held it open, as if surprised that wasn't all he had to do.

"I'm going to call you Tombstone."

"Ahummmm-my naaaa — "

"Your name's Tombstone. — How'd you like to have to hire him?"

"Brownie, I know it's hell. What I'm sayin' is, you should switch shows once in a while and you wouldn't have to."

"You can't hire him," the gorilla lady interrupted. "Something'll happen to him."

"He can help Fiddler on the cats," Brownie joked — Fiddler *hoped* he was joking! "See how his shirt's buttoned? He must have done that himself when his brother wasn't looking, 'cause the guy had tried to fix him up so nice. And when he saw it — hah, hah, hah, hah! he tried to turn him around so I wouldn't. 'Leave him be! Leave him be! I can see!' " Brownie crowed, imitating himself.

"His brother seemed all right. His brother brought him. — That's the clincher. When somebody comes out with the guy, then you *know* something's wrong. For sure. If somebody's own family wants to run him out of town that bad there must be something pretty wrong. The only guy I ever hired like that who almost seemed okay got amnesia after a couple of weeks and he did something or other; they locked him up. Whole family came out with him, but I bet he never remembered who they were to write for help."

The gorilla lady didn't like the story. She was displeased at even having Tombstone around. She looked at Brownie sourly. And Fiddler felt bad because of Chief. Brownie seemed to take it for granted that Chief was gone for good!

Brownie came into the dog pen after a drink of water, and the dogs got up and surrounded him instantly. His spitting rankled in them still, and they fitted their teeth on his legs as he walked, measuring for bites, swarming around him, warm eyes intent and pitiless. Bible didn't intervene.

"Sonofabitch," Brownie said, more at Bible than the dogs. Brownie was not a real animal man and didn't quite know what to do. He got mad. He kicked —

Which would have been the end of Brownie if Bible hadn't yelled

"Lay down!" Bible laughed and jumped out of his chair and gave Brownie the water jug without rubbing his joke in. He clapped several dogs on the ribs, jouncing them, telling them they were okay. The dogs could barely control themselves. When Fiddler touched his gypsy bitch she smelled his hand abruptly, smelled again, and doublechecked again, making *damn* sure the hand was his.

The man in black was smiling.

Brownie stepped out of the pen. He was angry and you couldn't blame him.

"Want a drink, Tombstone?"

Tombstone didn't hear.

"*Tombstone!*"

Violently he flinched and stared up, slack-mouthed.

"The man's a nitwit; we can see it; you don't have to make fun of him to show us," the gorilla lady said.

"Yeah," Fiddler agreed, though Brownie was his boss.

"He usually isn't listening," Brownie answered sweetly and waved the jug at Tombstone. He carried it out to him, pointing down his own throat and gurgling, "Water? Water?" Tombstone fumbled slowly with the jug. Brownie helped him hold it. Tombstone drank without haste. He had to be reminded to tilt his head back and even then he spilled a good deal out the corners of his mouth. When he was through Brownie disentangled the jug from his hands and started back, but stopped. "Come on, will you? Don't stand out there. You'll be in somebody's way. What's the matter with you! No hat, standing out in the sun. We won't bite!"

Tombstone's shoulders made that womanly birdlike slumping motion and he drifted stationary in a dream, eyes on the ground. Brownie offered the gorilla lady a drink and then he sat in his old spot and handed up the jug to the man in black. He watched Tombstone wryly. No one else said anything. Brownie was not the silent type like Bible.

"At least I'll be able to find him. He won't hide. So he'll be better than that Invisible Man. 'Member him?" Fiddler, having had to sleep with the guy, did. "He was never around! Never! You could never find him! I know where to look for almost any kind of hide-out guy like that. Almost anybody I can find. But this guy! — he wasn't anywhere! Drinking, no; after girls, no; under a wagon sleeping, in the bushes, no; spouting off to townies, fooling around some other department, no, no. — He wouldn't be *anywhere!* He really was invisible, I claim. I got rid of him in the crummiest, hickiest, deadest little dump of a broke mining town I could find. They even had a strike. I saved him up for it. Soon as we pulled in, four in the morning, I woke him up. 'You're fired.' Just like that. He didn't have no money coming to him, either."

Bible was about to go to sleep. It took him about a minute if he set himself to do it, and he had closed his eyes. Fiddler was counting the seconds, planning to test Bible in some way at the end of sixty.

One of the larger cats rumbled down the makeshift roadway toward Tombstone. "Look out, stupid," Brownie said, half smiling. Tombstone didn't lift his eyes. Brownie quit smiling. The cat driver cocked his head at Tombstone, who with a few steps could have gotten out of the way. Brownie flared into a fury, popping to his feet, "Hey look out you stupid sonofabitch! Look out!" Tombstone gazed bewildered-slow at Brownie.

The cat bore down. "Wise guy," the driver shouted. Tombstone hunched his shoulders, looked in the sky, moved his head from side to side as if he were hearing planes. And Bible was hurdling the pen in a ravening wedge of dogs; Brownie and Fiddler ran and the man in black and stumpy lady racing the longarmflailing gorillas. The driver realized then this wasn't a wise guy and, spinning his cat on a dime, missed Tombstone. A truck could not have turned in time. Bible ordered "Stop!" and the frenzied dogs yapping-snapping froze. He sent them back to the pen. The gorilla woman held her babies close by the wrists to keep them out of trouble.

"All right, now do you see you can't have him working around here?" she panted.

Brownie spoke gruffly. "Go on home, Tombstone. Tell your brother I don't want you." Tombstone's hands were drawn up to his mouth. He was sucking his thumb and watching the gorillas in torpid fascination, not paying any attention. — "Go on home! Go 'way! Go home!" Tombstone stood with his thumb in his mouth, sucking his thumb.

"Don't yell at him!" the gorilla lady shouted. And with the man in black she went up and talked very quietly in Tombstone's ear, squeezing her gorillas' wrists to keep them behaved. The man in black put his hand on Tombstone's shoulder.

"I think he don't know where his home is," she said.

"Well, Jesus," Brownie complained, "What am I supposed to do with the poor guy?"

Then right away he and Bible chanted in unison, "Take him to a cop." The never-fail solution.

Brownie paused. "Why don't you do it, Fiddler?"

The gorilla woman smiled teasingly. "He didn't bring him here." Brownie made a face.

"I don't want to hang around here anyhow," he said. He took Tombstone by the hand, and, holding him at arm's length, led him off toward a cop directing traffic. "You rake your bones, Fiddler," he added, having to show he was boss.

Fiddler made a point of leaving the bones in the cages as long as possible in the morning so the cats could play. He'd wait a while longer despite Brownie, he decided.

Sinking back in his chair, Bible yawned and closed his eyes again to go to sleep. Fiddler began to count the seconds, but he couldn't just relax and fool. He broke off to ask, "*Don't* you think Chief's going to come back?"

Bible opened his eyes. He could get to sleep so quickly that he wasn't annoyed.

"There's no place like a circus," the gorilla lady said, her voice creaky as leather. "You get in a show and you forget what it's like in the rest of the world."

"We stay around the show, most of us," Bible said.

"He just went to a hospital for Christ sake. He didn't go to rob a bank."

"He may come back. You can't do anything, Fiddler. Brownie always thinks things'll turn out bad." Bible frowned.

"I'll tell you what I think," said the gorilla lady. "I think he's coming back. He's got a lot of luck and most of the time he's pretty sensible when he's drunk."

Bible chuckled, "As long as he doesn't stop at the cars and finish off what's-his-name, Heavy."

"If Bible Smarty-pants there was the one, I'd send the dogs after him, I'd go myself. I'd get everybody on his trail. But Chief has a little more sense."

"I'll send the goddam dogs after *you*, young lady!" Bible thumbed his nose at her. Joking or not, that wasn't such a funny threat.

Bible shut his eyes. He opened them once more, as if just thinking of something. "Lots of guys who 'vanish' like they do are just leaving, that's all; that's their way of doing it. It's confusing because you get to think that every guy that doesn't come back has got hit on the head or something, when actually lots of them are takin' off. And Chief would have told you if he was doing that. So that makes the chances better." Then he went to sleep.

The big, piled, custard clouds floated substantial-looking, and Fiddler thought how good it would be to be up there, scanning all Omaha and Council Bluffs, and spot Chief some place, on some street. He thought about going after Chief right now, but that seemed impractical — where would he go? — and also a little silly and unnecessary. In his heart he wouldn't admit much chance of Chief not returning. He couldn't see anything outside of a whole police force stopping Chief if Chief wanted to come back; or the Indians with him, for that matter. When Fiddler remembered the moley, sniveling, numberless winos who'd joined and disappeared or been thrown off the train in querulous fights in the night or left passed-out in the weeds on a lot, then he found himself in a fever and planned hard where to go look. But once the picture of Chief came into his mind he knew it would be silly. If Chief wasn't back for set-up he could worry. He'd go after him then, skip set-up himself, and if Brownie fired them both for missing the work it would be better than staying on in the show alone.

The Elephant Department's tents were down the stakeline from the dog wagon, not too far, about even with the middle of the big top. They were easy to pick out because in front of them were heaped the great work harnesses, large enough for a school of whales. A man came out of one of the tents, strolled into the other and led out a horse, mounting. The gait of the horse was suavely unhurried; this was a fearless horse that never shied. The man carried a coiled black twenty-five-foot whip and, hanging from the crook of his arm which was holding the reins, a bull hook shaped like a very thick cane with a curved steel prod sticking off from the end like a second handle. This was the Elephant Boss. He rode past the dog wagon to fetch his bulls.

Since before breakfast the bulls had been lazing and diddling around, amusing themselves — it must be their favorite period of the day. The men had watered and fed them and then had lain down in the grass in a loose ring around the bulls to stop townies from getting too close. The men had been snoozing and playing cards, seeing from time to time if the bulls were staying in a row; which was all the bulls had to do — keep in a row, so friends would always be with friends and enemies apart.

The men lay like logs in the grass, and the elephants ceaselessly moved, the row undulant, the trunk ends balled-up boisterously striking, bounding back from the ground like miniature tires, or scything the grass, or bashfully feeling the knee of a neighbor. The bulls swayed easy, graceful, bulking left to right to left to right, ears waving, heads in motion in the rhythm, like swaying, swaying boats in a bay. The bulls were fat and crinkle-skinned and dowdy — playful, well-padded old women leisurely dandling grass and caressing each other, trunks high, and kissing mouth to mouth. Dust-laden, aimlessly fidgety, great ship bulls big enough to pull over trees or carry around a nation of monkeys. The eyes were small and obscure on the sober heads, but the eyelashes long as a flirt's; the wide ears were frayed. Between the crate feet snooped the trunks like an anteater's nose.

Now it was the Bull Department's turn to work. Of all the bosses theirs had the loudest, harshest, hoarsest, most gigantic voice, a voice like an opened furnace, a voice to shout and buffet a plane. He could be heard in a hurricane.

"LET'S GO. LET'S GO," he told his men.

"HEY! WHAT'CHUR DOIN' THERE! HEY! LET'S GO! HEY! PUT A MOVE ON! WHAT'S GOIN' ON? LET'S GO! LET'S GO!" He bullyragged the bulls. They didn't look at him or seem to notice the commands, but out of the hundreds of motions of trunks rockaby swinging and stocky legs and ears flapping, stringy, whiskered tails and nodding heads they all appeared to be turning and in the same direction. "HEY! LET'S GO! WHAT SAY! LET'S GO! HEY, WHAT'CHUR SAY?" Trunks in an arc dropping and lifting, old docile great wrinkled heads wagging, porch size. The men were on their feet and reaching with the hooks, barking like sergeants, and the bulls humped this way and that, reluctantly straightening the line. Each bull had a man under her ear who knocked on her trunk until she curled the tip around the tail of the bull in front. The column started away like a row of houses bumping along in a landslide, and the bulls lengthened their stride until they were swinging by smooth as a breeze. The handlers almost had to run to keep up. The boss rode at the head of the line on his swashbuckling horse. Townie children flushed like quail from under its nose without it batting an eye. Ruth the lead bull's trunk was free. She arched it S-shaped, trumpet-blared, and could have been carrying kings.

At the harnesses the column stopped, the elephants' heads bowed halfheartedly to a height where the contraptions could be thrown on. The men dragged them to the bulls, and the bulls turned away, restive, vainly stretching their trunks and muffling squeals in hard whushes of breath. The boss was riding in to discipline them, when two started a fight.

At the same moment, as if at a signal, they reached around two intervening bulls and banged each other's eyes. Shrieking angrily they squeezed aside the neutral bulls, who bawled alarm. The shrieks plunged rumbling into awesome growls deep as a cliff cracking. The growls dragged up the scale to a booming OOOU-AWWWWW!

Every man laid hold of his hook. The boss on his horse went for the bulls nearest the fight — "HEY YOU MODACH GET OVER OVER GET BACK!" — bulls about to join in, poking trunks and crowding. The horse lurched next to them stiff-legged, jolting, jagged-eared, teeth bared. c-rAACK! the boss's whip was in the grass looping like a bursting hose; his hook clubbed left and right, aimed at the tender trunk tips curved behind the higher, broader parts of tough rubber. "HEY YOU GO BACK, BACK YOU GO DAISY! MODACH!" Modach and Daisy gave ground, and the rest of the neutrals. The boss browbeat them back. Bingo, with those others of the men who knew what to do, culled away the few the boss couldn't get to and, prodding behind their ears with the hooks, led them around on the run to where his group was milling.

"Troubles, troubles," the gorilla lady said. "It's one of those days."

The two bulls fighting battered broadside, trunks pythoned around each other's heads, trying to wrench them off. The boss ignored the fight. He was with the neutrals. He coiled his whip — "EASY, EASY" — rode back and forth, wheedling them into a row. The elephants shoved each other, anxiously waved their trunks and faced sideways, afraid they were going to be punished. Ruth was in the center. She was a heavy-built bull with the dome of her head as big as her chest. The boss himself handled Ruth in the show and she was dependable; nobody pushed her around. She kept the bulls in one place and helped calm them down.

The men supposed to break up the fight got nowhere. The elephants shivered the air with their roars — their trunks like boat booms wild in a storm — and the dull, bomb thud of their bodies. The peewee men were scared. The elephants crashed, sagged spraddle-legged against each other, drew apart as slow as locomotives starting, and woodenly they crashed. It was kind of funny — something in slow motion — if you partly shut your eyes and didn't watch the trunks. The force of each elephant exactly matched the force of its opponent. The site of the battle didn't shift more than a few yards in any direction. There they stayed, two ponderous mammoths who could have laid waste the circus, nullifying each other. Every week or two a fight like this occurred, and nothing ever came of it; it was always stopped.

But these bull men were new. They screwed up every scrap of

guts they had, and then they ran in, shouting high-pitched shouts that shattered, dug their hooks into the skin behind the ears and yanked frantically, even swinging on the hooks, until they lost their grip and let the hooks go out of reach, still stuck in the skin.

The boss had his twenty-odd bulls lined up tame as Pekinese, heads bowed and humble. He turned round in his saddle. "WHERE'S THAT GODDAM INDIAN? . . . . WELL BINGO THEN?"

Tiny-cheeked Bingo brandished his hook— weasel-faced and narrow as a weasel, a three-legged weasel; Bingo was missing an arm. The boss dismounted. "LET'S GO." They went to the fight. The horse stayed put. The men were gasping for breath, hands exhaustedly flopped at their sides. The boss lectured them. "YOU GUYS WATCH. I'LL HAVE TO SHOW YOU." He threw his whip aside. "YOU JUST HAVE A HOOK. — LOOK, YOU WERE MESSING WITH THE EARS. THAT'S OKAY FOR ORDINARY. BUT THIS AIN'T ORDINARY. GET THE MOUTH." He and Bingo laid into the bulls, placing their blows under the lifted trunks, on the mouths and lips. The elephants thundered, heaving and driving, and, when the blows hurt, took it out on each other. "JENNY COME DOWN, JENNY, HEY JENNY DOWN!" The boss jumped and hooked into his elephant's mouth, hauling down on his weapon. Bingo did the same, except his bull's head wouldn't come down and he chinned himself with his single arm, corkscrewing up and devilishly twisting the hook in her mouth. The bulls bawled like housefuls of furniture scraping a floor; and the bawls became ear-ringing shrieks, the low heads wriggling massively. The shrieks thinned shrill to whistles. The trunks threshed above the boss and Bingo, and the bulls leaned apart. The fight was over.

Very quickly and with little patience harnesses were strapped on all the bulls to be used, and they were led out to their places, having to hump along faster than usual and getting tweaked back of the ears by the hooks. But they didn't really need to exert themselves, since the bulls could walk faster than their keepers anyway.

The sidepoles were all up now. The townie boys were through. The rest of the job would be done by the bulls.

Before the quarterpoles had been covered by the canvas, long chains had been attached to the bases of some and stretched beyond the stakeline. The tops of the poles were tied to the canvas and the poles lay pointing outward, so that they had to go up when the chains were pulled. Similar chains went to pulleys on the centerpoles fastened to the canvas. The chains snuck out unobtrusively from under the pieplate rim of canvas raised on the sidepoles, the great sixteen-foot curtain running all the way around and hiding everything clear to the towering centerpoles.

A jig was assigned to each of the bulls and he waited behind her holding the end of the harness. The bull man stood under her ear. The bulls were stationed at wide intervals, but they swayed and swayed, calmly frisking their trunks, as if they were still close-packed in a row. They grubbed up the grass under their trunks and ate it, inhaled the dirt they'd loosened and blew it up on their backs to keep off flies. At a distance the bulls appeared to have five legs, unless you thought of the trunk as a tail. They were very, very fat, and also long-legged — too long-legged to be fat. They looked too big to be alive. Nothing else in the circus, nothing else in Iowa, even vaguely resembled the bulls. Old, placid, inscrutable, little-eyed bulls swaying as patient as trees.

Magee was in front of the Elephant Department's tents with the Bull Boss, who would shout his orders for him since the bull man's voice was slightly louder. The Boss Chief had been posted as a lookout on the far side of the big top.

"Number Eight," said Magee, loud enough for Fiddler to hear at sixty yards.

"NUMBER EIGHT," the Bull Boss repeated, and the elephant nearest the chain to the number eight pole was hitched to it by her jig. The keeper prodded her ear and she pressed forward in the traces, walking, showing no special effort except that her trunk didn't swing as much as before. A certain area of canvas toward the middle poked above the level of the sidepoles and irresistibly by jerks went up and up — "NUMBER THIRTEEN" — and up some more, and in another spot the canvas shuddered into view, rising like a second pointed top on a very daring, choppy wave. "WHOA EIGHT." — The first bull stopped. "NUMBER EIGHTEEN."

The bulls went straight out as they pulled, the huge chains tautly quivering behind them, and everybody in the way had to move. In his first weeks Fiddler sometimes had tested his nerve by lying beside the path of Bingo's bull and steeling himself as the tree-stump feet marched toward and past him by a hair.

"WHOA THIRTEEN. — NUMBER TWENTY–THREE." Now the few poles poked up awkward and conspicuous, forming a cone of canvas, but soon there would be so many poles, pushing such an ocean of canvas in the air, that new ones would rise as naturally and rhythmically as a swell in the sea. "WHOA EIGHT–EEN. — NUMBER TWENTY–EIGHT." Not only the canvas' rocking sweep would look like the sea, but also the color. The big top had been a sprightly bird's-egg bluish green when the season started. Lying on the ground every day, on mud, sand, soil, dirt, being rained on and baked, had stained it a wonderful weathered, grayed blue-green which even on a stormy day, when wet and darkened, looked exactly like a stretch of sea.

"WHOA TWENTY–THREE. — NUMBER THIRTY–THREE." Soon Magee would start on another round of numbers, and the bulls would be shifted to other chains, and the chains to other poles, the jigs hopping to unhitch and hitch; more and more poles would go up, and the bulls would haul the middle belt of canvas up the centerpoles, in stages, not to cause a strain.

"Whoa on twenty-eight," hallooed the Boss Chief, who was in a nicer position to see it than Magee.

"NUMBER THIRTY–EIGHT." Magee and the Bull Boss went under the canvas. Space had been made to stand and they would be able to keep track of the poles much better.

Out of nowhere the numbers continued to toll, and the canvas rose in segments, of its own accord, if you didn't watch the bulls. Fiddler tried not to watch anything. Once the big top was up he was going hunting for Chief. The time was nearing, nearing — he couldn't shut out the Bull Boss's voice. The waiting got on his nerves. The dogs weren't much fun. Like Bible they were asleep, but unlike him they twitched and whimpered, and, when Fiddler petted them, they opened and rolled their eyes, still dreaming, prob- ably sticking him into their dreams. One gorilla lay on its belly beside the gorilla lady. The other was sprawled in spanking position across her lap. She was picking through its fur for fleas while it performed the same chore for its brother.

The man in black smiled at Fiddler — he couldn't imagine why. "There's your papa Chief," the gorilla lady said.

And there Chief was! — with the rest of them, the red little bright-shirted Sioux, the dark deep-brown Cherokee blacksmith and the tall bull man from Alaska with a Roman nose you could see half a mile. Whooping it up, tossing a bottle, howling at dogs, the big-nosed bull man with a tireless plunge of a stride like a moose and the dogged, slight Sioux keeping up, Chief and the Cherokee two wide-bodied bears unstoppably tearing along. They came in a boiling knot off the road and trampled a trail in the grass. Past the white wardrobe tents of the ballet girls, the ushers' top, the outhouse top for performers and the outhouse top for jigs, right under the half-raised big top, dervishes whirling and whooping they dashed.

Fiddler skimmed over the pen, longlegged ate up the ground. Three townie kids also were running, and he passed them as if they had washtubs for shoes. The guy ropes crisscrossed in his path. He didn't see how he was going to get past; he couldn't stop; no time to dodge. He leapt as high as he'd ever leaped and kicked himself in the ass, maneuvered his arms, and neat as a bird he dropped through. First thing he knew he was under the top in the dark and dust groping and blinking, afraid of hitting a hauling chain an elephant was on or tripping in one of the ruts the poles going up had gouged. The far edge gleamed whitely luminous like the end of a cave, the light hazy with dust but almost a silvery bright. The quarterpoles slanted at crazy, irregular angles — he made them out before anything else — and the canvas hung overhead so low and impending he crouched as he ran. The steel chains glinted. The ruts he saw last. Fiddler ran like a skittering bat, jumping the chains and ruts and weaving around the poles. He breathed through his teeth because of the dust and ran feeling trapped. He was catching up with the Indians. They were going fairly hard, but they might have just covered five or six miles at their pace. The marks of their feet were struck compact in digs in the ground like the tracks of a single creature. The men themselves were indistinguishable except for the bull man's tall head, which seemed to serve as the head for them all, they were so bunched.

"Get those guys settled down," Magee shouted at Fiddler. He didn't like people inside at this stage of the job.

Ahead of Fiddler they burst from the twilight into the sun and drove for the Boss Chief. The Boss Chief gazed at some distant peak of the big top. He knew very well who was coming, but he wouldn't grant them so much as a glance until they were almost upon him kiiiyipping. He loosened his knees and his arms at his sides and got his lips back from the edge of his teeth. They would have bowled him into the dirt if they hadn't caught him as they hit, by the hair. The Boss Chief shut his eyes, grit his teeth, and they shook him, grabbing his arms, legs and handfuls of his belly, and threatening to rip off his single ear. Into his teeth they thrust a bottle the whiskey color of his own skin.

Somehow Fiddler never slowed down. He barreled into Chief at twenty miles an hour. He nearly broke his jaw against Chief's back. His ears buzzed. He'd lost his breath and he clung weakly to the shoulders, unable to stand.

"Whoever it is I'm gonna kill 'im," Chief grunted, reaching for Fiddler. Fiddler was dragged like a sack into the middle of the powwow. "It's Fiddle!" Chief said, practically having to hold him up. The Sioux flashed a knife with a snubbed-up point like the snout of a shark.

Chief's cheeks and chin were streaked with·red, and the big grin put zigzags in the streaks. He got the bottle from the Boss Chief. "This'll grow hairs on your tongue!" Fiddler took a gulp fit for a dragon. His head cleared. "No more? Okay, give it here." Chief's voice rang flat and drunk. On his forehead were more streaks, short ones loud vermilion in the sun. Fiddler figured they must be lipstick. They didn't look like lipstick. A butterfly was pinned to Chief's cap.

"Thought you said you'd kill him?" The Sioux thumbed his knife. He was drunk too now; in the diner he'd been sober.

"Not Fiddle. No."

Fiddler said, "I'll fight the guy."

"Oh you will, huh?" laughed the Sioux. He was over thirty, leaving his prime, and a head shorter than Fiddler. But he shrank Fiddler down to two feet tall with those eyes. They settled tingling on him fire-clean and blue and chill.

"He hasn't got a knife," the Boss Chief pointed out. The Sioux gave Fiddler his.

"If you c'n throw: that isn't fair."

Fiddler couldn't look at the eyes. Even the shirt dazzled him, showy and brilliant, banded gay like a flag. He concentrated on the jeans. The other four Indians, all much bigger and darker than the Sioux, watchfully ranged round them. The Sioux wolfed in for Fiddler and Fiddler made the stab prematurely. The Sioux got his knife hand, twisted the knife away, and, as he did, Fiddler socked him in the nose. Chief and the Boss Chief grabbed the Sioux as he clutched the knife. — "That's okay. I'm not mad," he shouted, wiping blood off his nose. "So, I could have killed you, kid, if we were alone. And if I was sober you couldn't have got my nose."

The Boss Chief had his job to do, and they left him. And the blacksmith said he'd better be heading back to his wagon. He shook Chief's hand solemnly and Fiddler's. Fiddler winced at the grip — which caused it to tighten even more; he felt it clear up in his shoulderblade. The blacksmith peered at him with humorous curiosity. Not until he got the point and smoothed his face of any sign of pain was Fiddler's hand released.

"Them fingers is gone," Chief said, not looking at Fiddler, who was trying to work some life back into his hand. "That's what the doctor said. He's through with them fingers. The muscles was cut."

"Oh" — Fiddler realized who he was talking about. "What's Little Chief going to do?"

"What d'ya think he's gonna do!"

"I don't know!"

"Well neither do I!"

Chief-on-Bulls went to his Daisy, stood under her head and patted her cheeks. "I'm home to darlin'. Here I am. I'm home." He pinched the bottoms of her ears.

"See you round," said the Sioux. He smiled, still wiping blood off his nose, and jogged away toward his department's wagon. His stiff hair rose and fell with each stride and the banded colors of the shirt glared gaudy on his back, as if he were wrapped in a flag. Chief and Fiddler walked toward Number 12 alone.

"Didn't you tell the Boss Chief about his hand?" Fiddler asked.

"He knew."

Something seemed to kick inside Chief's shirt. — Or did it? Maybe Fiddler was the drunk one!

"How?"

"What d'ya mean, 'How?' 'Cause he knew, that's all, Fiddle."

Fiddler closely watched the shirt. "Okay, Chiefy."

"Chiefy! What's this Chiefy!"

"You call me Fiddle, I call you Chiefy." The shirt quivered. Again something kicked. "What have you got?"

"A rabbit."

"A rabbit? No. A *rabbit?* How did you get him? Let's see him."

"I ain't gonna take him out till I have a place to put him. And I don't want him getting scared." Chief spoke painstakingly. He was drunk and he wouldn't say anything foolish. "He's a regular rabbit. He ain't special. He's for the snakes."

"Oh-ho! For the snake *woman*, you mean."

Chief grinned, glittery-eyed. Half his teeth were gone, but those he had were in such good condition it showed the others had been knocked out, instead of rotting out like the winos'.

Nigas trotted from the Animal top to meet Chief, wagging his tail, and smelled Chief's pants leg, smiling up at his face a couple of times. When Nigas scented the rabbit he threw his head way up and barked and walked backward, barking steadily and regularly like a baying hound; his head was pointed up as far as it would go and his eye cocked brazenly. Chief put the rabbit, a scroungy cottontail, in an apple crate in the front of the wagon.

"Old Brownpuss is probably gonna keep me busy, so you may have to give it to her. You tell her *I* got him. And I wanta see the big fella eat him. And I want to be there with her when he eats it."

"How did you catch him?"

"We all got him. We ran 'im-down, by the river, but I needed him most."

Chief took Nigas in his arms and squeezed him until he behaved himself, then stroked him. Nigas didn't stir or even loll his tongue.

— "Where's your boss man? I ain't got all day!" The guy leaned out of the circus ice truck just asking for an argument. Chief would have given him one if Brownie hadn't been rustling around in the rear of the wagon.

"I said, where's your boss man! I got a ton o' melting ice in back that won't wait in this hot and I can't screw around!"

Chief snorted. Nigas was going to bark, but Chief squeezed him.

"*You* can't screw around!" — Brownie stomped into it — "Neither can I, and I've been waiting on this goddam Indian hours! Now we got to wait till we've set up to go after the horses. We haven't got time to go now. — This sonofabitching horseass Indian!" Chief grinned. He pointed at Chief and the gaudy daubs of paint above his eyes, the cheek streaks like razor slashes.

"Buster, I got things to do. I'm busy. I can't come back, you know."

"I know! I know! I know!" Brownie rocked up on his toes and down on his heels in his anger and spat. "I want three hundred and fifty pounds. We'll have to cover it over good or we'll lose the whole damned pile."

The ice man, whistling, hopped out of his truck. A key ring jingled on a chain from his belt, the jaunty way he walked bouncing it up and down on his butt. At the tailgate of the truck he stopped and, flourishing the ring, riffled through the keys and chose the proper one for the padlock. There was no necessity for all this lock-and-key business; most of the keys probably had no locks anyway. The guy who'd had the job before didn't use keys to show off. He'd been an ex-wrestler and he'd literally broken his back trying to prove he was still strong.

Brownie spread canvas over the ice blocks as they were brought.

Chief put Nigas on the ground. The dog wagged his tail, smiled up and trotted out of reach. Only favorites of his, like Chief, could hold him even for a minute, drunk.

"Well, you going to pull your bones? Or what are you going to do?" Brownie demanded.

Loud as he could, "Gonna get them goddam bones out!" Chief whooped, and he grinned and the paint zigzagged on his cheeks. "Come on, you, boy!" Chief stripped off his shirt, grabbed up a scraper as if to throw it, spear-style, and they jogged side by side.

2

THE CIRCUS BUS, a silver livened with somersaulting red and yellow clowns, rolled up to the sideshow from the road. Chief watched between the cages earnestly. It was too far for Fiddler to distinguish the different people getting off, except the giant and the jiggly, toddling midgets, but Chief was able to. He smiled suddenly and leaned forward until one particular figure vanished in the tent and then seemed satisfied. That had been his snake lady.

The two tigers, big as bears, surveyed Chief.

"What'cha gonna do?" He pushed his fist to the bars. The tigers twitched their noses like sedate rabbits, sniffing. He stroked his finger down their noses. Ajax's was a good deal broader than Chief's finger was long.

"What'cha got? What'cha got up there?" Chief pointed at the ceiling. Both tigers looked up and snuffled in soft snatches. Ajax lay in a corner of the cage with his paws crossed grandly. Snippy faced Chief head-on, her white downy chin turned up. Finally she stood and stretched up on her hind feet, pawing the ceiling and smelling it, and snuffled as if communicating what she found to Ajax. Then she dropped back down, sat on her haunches and licked her snowy chest with neck and tongue contortions and stood up, still trying to lick but not doing as good a job. Ajax drew his tongue across his nose.

Instead of using the scraper Chief reached after the meat with his arm. It showed he was drunk. He never did that kind of thing when he was sober. The tigers acted so unconcerned, it was easy to see he could be doing it every day unless they happened to be riled up for some reason.

Chief turned to Fiddler sternly, hardening his lips and trying to force his thoughts to words. "I see you all the time screwing with the cages. And you don't do it right. That's what I tell you. That's what I don't like." His voice was flat and drunk-sounding and unnecessarily loud. He reached in again, this time very close to Ajax' paws. Ajax was not a cat that Fiddler fooled with. He'd torn off three guys' arms in the last two years.

"See, you wouldn't do that, Fiddler, wouldja?"

Fiddler started to nerve himself up.

"No. No. No. I'm not daring you. I don't want you to unless you really *would*. I *know* I can do it. You never *know*. You can't trust them cats! — you trust; all you do is trust, shutchur eyes and trust! You never know. I do. I *know* I can do it!"

Snippy stopped grooming herself and stretched her dainty paws and claws and paced in a U, ending at Ajax' tail along one wall and at his forepaws along the bars. She was very considerate. She didn't step on him. Ajax looked at her with unaffectionate, rodent eyes. His head was too big for his eyes; the fur puffed crowdingly around them. Ajax became restless, snuffled once or twice and got up to walk too. In the middle of the cage they met. Snippy lightly half rose on her hind feet as if to go over him somehow. With hardly a tremor of effort he smacked her flat on her back.

Bessie, the lion, heard the rumpus and stood up tall and straight-legged like a Great Dane. Her Joe didn't treat her that way. But then, she was almost his size. Her jaws hung open, doglike rough-and-ready, but soon they closed to a cat expression bland as cream. Chief and Fiddler came for the meat, and her face crinkled up like a peachstone.

"I could put my hand in there. She won't jump for your hand if it's very far, because — because she don't think a hand's worth the trouble. You know that and I know that." Chief carefully chose his words, not to let his drunkness foul him up. "But you *would*. You'd put your hand in there. And I don't. She don't want it in there and I won't put it in unless I have to. — I can.

I can now. But I'm not in-interested in having my hand in there when she don't want it, unless I have to. Understand, Fiddle? That's how we're different; and you gotta change." He used the scraper. Bessie's packed growl buzzsawed through her teeth. When he was finished her face all smoothed out again, the lips precise in a *w*, the broad, mature nose serene.

The bones in the second tiger wagon were way back. Chief brought them forward with the scraper. Then, instead of just pulling them out, he put the scraper down and reached in, both shoulders pressed to the bars, to take them out that way. It made Fiddler nervous, seeing him do it with the tigers. They were much moodier and harder to judge than the lions.

"Watch, boy." — Chief thought he was up in front of a class. Fiddler was glad he didn't get drunk and demonstrate things often. Mabel and her mate didn't try for Chief, of course. They just looked at him, lying alert side by side — not only at his eyes, but all over him, at his arms and his chest and his hair. Chief left his arms in front of them a very long time, and he didn't talk or use any tricks. Fiddler wasn't surprised the tigers didn't hurt him. But that they kept looking and looking at Chief, not taking away their eyes, Fiddler grudgingly had to admit was amazing. Fiddler couldn't have held their interest more than five seconds; their eyes would have turned past him or swum out of focus; and, unless to kill the guy, they wouldn't have glanced at a townie. But Chief kept up the spell at least a minute — except for Mabel's being in heat, they wouldn't have paid attention to *each other* that long! — then flashily grabbed out the bones like a showman and confronted Fiddler. "See? See, Fiddle?" — struggling for words to explain what he'd done. Fiddler nodded, and Chief was relieved. "I'm somebody to them cats. You're nobody. They don't even think aboutcha! You're a leaf." He patted Fiddler on the back, not to hurt his feelings. "See, you gotta change, Fiddler."

"Nobody seemed to think you were coming back," Fiddler said, changing the subject.

"They don't know their ass from a hole in the ground, those guys."

Chief had opened all the cages at once and was leaving them open so the cats could have the breeze. He went from cage to cage in no particular order.

"Bring me the meat," he told the cub lions, as if he thought they understood him. They knew he was speaking to them, but that's all they knew. He went on to the jaguar.

Immediately the jaguar sauntered to his bone and picked it up, clamping it at a cocky angle in his mouth, although the quaver in his hind legs showed he had his doubts. He was usually so lazy and accepting you could trust him not to stick his paws outside the bars no matter how close you were — and now on an impulse he wanted to rebel. This was one cat, *the* one cat, whose reactions Fiddler never claimed he could predict. Chief piled the scraper into the bulky, bullseye-spotted legs, first high and then low, and rammed it for the throat. The jaguar danced around a little and gave up the bone. He licked his chops inscrutably. He hadn't been hungry.

Chief pointed at the cubs and from them to the meat halfway down the cage. "Bring me that meat!" The cubs flustered and grew self-conscious under his gaze and trotted to the bars, snuck to the back of the wagon, ran to the bars, bumping and batting each other and not knowing what to do. Chief left them to get the cheetah's cage.

Poor Cheet couldn't make up her mind where to stand. The scraper upset her any time, like a cobra coming in the cage. She stalked stiff-legged as a stork and hissed with horror. There was no place she could go. She ended up leaned and flattened against the bars themselves — Chief poking the scraper between her legs — staring down at it, eyes wide in shock and outrage. Her fur was coarse and dry as the average dog's. Fiddler scratched until his fingers came away black with the skin resin. While he petted Cheet she purred pleasurably and ignored the scraper, except for moments when it moved. The purr was throatier and gentler than the leopards'.

"Nice, don't you think?" he said to Chief.

"You get a puma to love you, boy, and she'll — " Chief cooed and burbled like a pigeon, and grinned. "You should take care of a puma."

Chief went back to the cubs. They were up and flexing their toes the instant he opened his mouth, but naturally they didn't know what he meant — "Bring me that meat." He didn't frighten them, but he got them all excited, tripping over each other, bumbling around. They swatted each other and scooted from side to side in the cage and once in a while stopped cold and straightened to stare Chief full in the face, then maybe loped toward him aggressively before veering off. They were hitting each other, having a free-for-all, when one stumbled over the meat. The meat didn't hit back. That started them whamming the meat up and down like a ball; they were strong. Pretty soon it got near enough for Chief to reach, and he pulled it away. "Good cats. They do whatcha tell 'em!" Chief winked.

"See," he went on, "they'll look in your eye, them cubs. But a wildcat — full-grown wildcats just as big as them — they'll look under your eye. They look at the bottom of your eye. That's the difference between lions and wildcats." Chief took the best cub's paws in his hands. — "What'cha got to say, young fella?" Again Fiddler was impressed. If he'd done that the cub would have dug out with its nails automatically. "Can'tcha speak up?" Chief laughed and spread apart its lips and tapped on its teeth. — "Those'ill getcha along."

The leopard gang took cage work of any kind in their stride like sophisticates. Rita stewed, of course, tilting her head as she snarled. Rajah marched, huffy and brusque, always hearing things that Fiddler couldn't. He got very irritated when Fiddler came in his line of vision. Sweetheart sat on the panther, Taboo, next to the bars. Taboo growled and grumped, and Sweetheart lazed on top of her as though on a cushion and licked Taboo's ear and poked an elbow into her neck. Rita crept beside them with a secretive, sidling motion, fixing her round blue eyes on Fiddler, head aslant. Sweetheart put her paw on Taboo's head and leaned on it. Taboo looked into space and laid back her ears and hissed with mouth stretched like a yowling monkey. Then she changed her face so nothing was wrong. Then she hissed again, toward the empty air. Sweetheart rested her chin on the paw on Taboo's head. Sweetheart's nose was long for a cat and her pink tongue showed, frothed with saliva because of the heat; her lower jaw receded slightly, like a dog's. Fiddler stood nearer. Sweetheart clambered still higher and more comfortably on Taboo, who hissed as vague as the wind in the trees. Rita's head twisted still farther around, shifting the weight of her body by slow degrees until one paw lashed out like a spring let loose. It might have got Fiddler, but Sweetheart struck Rita right in the face and ruined her aim. — Fiddler hardly believed it, but there it had happened!

"Did you see that? — Saved me!"

Chief burped. "Didja ever hear a turtle burp?"

Taboo sprang out from under Sweetheart, up to the vent at the top of the wall and clung, her claws in the screening, watching a child. Rita growled in fat sputts like an old car idling. She opened her mouth so the teeth just met and the growl got plenty of room. Taboo thumped down, rolled on her side next to Fiddler. He scratched her chest and fingered her chin. She put her paws up on his arm where he'd rolled up his sleeve and pulled and pushed as if she were scrubbing, holding her claws withdrawn. Then she started licking his hand. Her tongue was so rough it almost hurt. Chief was very disapproving.

"Do they burp?" Fiddler asked.

"Yeah!" Chief brought Fiddler's hand away from the cage. "Cut that stuff out!"

Fiddler didn't answer. He'd learned not to get mad. He could be by himself with the cats often enough.

"Listen! Listen, you know how you pick up ice?" Chief made his arms like a pair of tongs and caught Fiddler's arm. "You know? That's what they do! To a man; that's what they do! You can't get away! They got you *better and better!* You never get away unless your arm's off! I've seen." He gripped Fiddler painfully hard, glared at him in a blaze of frustration, trying to make out if he'd put across what he meant. And he thought a minute. Then he exhibited Fiddler's hand beside his own. "I ain't got those cuts! I ain't got a single cut!" — It was true. The back of Fiddler's hand looked like a map. The back of Chief's was unmarked. But cuts

weren't going to kill, Fiddler decided. Chief's face fogged drunk-
enly. He couldn't seem to say any more.

The bones were scattered on the ground where Chief had dropped
them. The act lion man would stop by for them. He had been
raking his own cats' bones. Chief waved the scraper high in the
air and got a faint "Okay." The guy was coming. Chief swung
to face the cages, suddenly fighting himself, towering crouched
savage and ignited.

"*Now* I want some noise! *Now!* NOW! *NOW* I want some *noise!*"

Rajah coughed a growl and Rita sizzled hotly. Big old Joe, the
lion, humphed and Bessie wadded up her lips and power-sawed.
The cheetah hissed. All the tigers except Snippy snuffled. Snippy
cannoned out a roar. Sweetheart purred as blissfully as if she were
singing, and right in harmony with Chief, getting loud when he
said "*Now!*" and "*noise!*" Even the jaguar stuck in a grunt. It was
like all the cats were a family and Chief was the father, the way
they did what he told them.

But Chief didn't smile about it or look pleased.

"You couldn't do that, Fiddler, see? I mean never. You never
could." He struggled not to blunder with his words. "You never
could do that. — You-*you* gotta be boss! *You*, not them!"

The act lion man was a wino, fairly intact still. Each day he
seemed to be a little thinner, though. Fiddler saw him every
day. His co-ordination was okay so far, which was the most important thing for somebody around cats, but day after day he got
a little thinner, a little thinner. Already he was what you'd call a
really skinny man. Except the first day, when he'd talked in a burst
to Fiddler for an hour, he usually didn't say much. He'd been a
teacher; he'd found out his wife was sleeping with her father; and
now he was in the circus. That was the story. With his cats, he
did his job and nothing more. Fiddler always liked to pretend
this would be the last day he'd have to see the guy. But here he
was again, thinner than ever — brittle-looking as a dead limb —
and all lushed up. God, he'd be a walking skeleton in a few
more weeks!

"It'sh the bonesh man. Got shome bonesh?"

Fiddler and Chief gathered theirs and threw them in the wheelbarrow on top of his.

"Much oblidged! All for one and one for all! The white man and the Indian!" — When he said that, Chief glanced at him for the first time. To Chief he was a worm, like any other wino. The guy sucked in some dribble and, smiling, drew imaginary paint streaks on his own wan face. "Blood brothersh under the shkin. That'sh how it should be. That'sh what I told the kidsh, and they won't forget it. I gave them that much!" He bowed goodby. There was a messy blackened scab on his lip, and he was trying to hide it with his hand. — "I have to let it heal."

Side by side lay Mabel and her tiger mate, groaning a snuffle, answering back and forth abrupt and eager as two horses whinnying. They rubbed their bodies together and the ruffs of fur on their cheeks and jaws, and each took a turn at stroking an eye on the bulge of the other's ear. Every touch they savored. Every time their haunches grazed the tails whish-whished with the thrill.

Chief grinned appreciatively. "You go get that rabbit, Fiddler — and my shirt, my good shirt, in my box. I can't go back there. Brownpuss'ill give me somethin' to do."

At the wagon Nigas was asleep and snoring, in a violent dream. Brownie was doing paperwork. Fiddler gave the baby tiger some meat to chew and a drink of water. Chief's crum box was full of magazine pictures of Indian wars and movie queens, and he had a collection of newspaper clippings of him and his cats — he'd be cleaning a cage, or something. The shirt was a snap to find. There was no other halfway good one.

Chief had closed the cages and gone. Fiddler strolled on across the lot toward the midway and sideshow. He felt sure of himself and strong, owned the show, and Magee was a punk. — This sun would do as much as that for almost anybody. It nipped and bristled with energy. You couldn't look at the clouds, they were so sharp a white. It was hard to look at the grass because of the charged rich brightness and color, but once you'd toughened your eyes it was that very color and brightness which set you on top of the world. — If you couldn't look at the sky, so what? Here on the ground you were king.

The last quarterpole had been pulled up and the big top was high and vastly spacious, but empty as a shell. You could see right through it, end to end. The sidewall was not on yet and without it the top looked sort of indecent, like a woman with a blouse but no skirt. The lot was as noisy as if they were running an auto race. With great racket the cats were being started up. The bigger cats were hooking on to the seat wagons, storming and jerking — the drivers didn't care. Then the boss's great square one came up, which finished the fooling around. Like a squad of tanks the cats ranged out in line and started hauling. The top would not be empty long.

Chief was waiting behind a stand across the midway from the sideshow. He put on the shirt and tucked the rabbit in it as before. "Good thing he don't bite."

On the midway things were beginning to hum. Streamers of bunting blew and the colorful canvas was clean and eye-catchy. Popcorn churned in machines, cotton candy wisped, frozen custard oozed out of tubes from vats. The townies, in better than straggler numbers, were jingling their change. They hadn't started spending yet, but their faces had loosened up as if they were just about ready. Concession men leaned over the counters calling out to likely customers in conversational singsongs blending with the midway chatter. Or, when they weren't doing that, they stared vacantly and dropped their adamsapples for the barking deadpan spiels which cut through the general buzz almost like the chugging of a bunch of frogs. They seemed so complacently unconscious they were making any sound at all, Fiddler laughed. — They *were* like frogs along a stream.

Wing Ding promenaded up and down. A multicolored bulbous palm tree of balloons — enough to shade him from the sun — floated above his head. The strings were tied around his shoulder; the arm was gone, and he could easily slip them loose. Any child in reach he'd give a balloon. The parents had to take it away from the kid if they didn't want to buy it, and tie it again to Wing

Ding's shoulder, since he'd say he couldn't; and all the time he'd stand there shaking his head at such stingy heartlessness. He sold a lot. If Wing Ding saw a pretty lady, "I've got a big one!" he'd shout and point to the balloons, his tongue in his cheek, and leer. Chief thought that was a riot.

Chief and Fiddler peered in the entrance to the sideshow.

"Pinito's dressing, hey," said the calliope man. One end of the tent was partitioned off as a dressing room and Chief and Fiddler walked along behind the billboards to that.

"Pull your skirts down!" Chief warned, lifting the sidewall and barging under. Pinito was brushing her hair. She gave Chief a cool look.

"Hi," he said, his confidence dampening.

"Hello." The inside of the lid of her snake trunk was all mirror so that the townies could see the snakes from the moment she opened it. In this mirror she was brushing her hair. It fell below her shoulders and curled luxuriously black. She sat on a suitcase and brushed with a lovely wand-waving motion.

"I broughtcha a rabbit."

"Good." She smiled a nice smile.

"Yeah, I wanta see Lester eat him."

"Can I fix my hair?"

"Yeah, I got a little time."

"Sweet as jam," Pinito said. She was from the Caribbean and lighter-skinned than Chief. Around her hips and torso were wrapped two flimsy squares of cloth a sinuous mottling of colors. Obviously she wore nothing underneath. The squares were small and between them they revealed a satin, muffled-gold midriff of skin which narrowed or expanded every time she moved. Pinito was in no hurry. She knew people enjoyed watching her. The hair shone and rippled as she brushed.

A snake's head as large as a trowel rested on the rim of the trunk. Its tongue flickered occasionally, but otherwise the snake was still; the hair was more lifelike. In the trunk were three or four boa constrictors and pythons, although you seldom saw more than one at a time. She kept them in layers with blankets and hot

water bottles between for the cold nights, and they were so sluggish they usually stayed as she stowed them. The blankets were
cloud-gray and set off the black and green linked-oblong pattern
of this snake beautifully. The pattern on Pinito's strips of cloth was
almost the same, Fiddler realized. Maybe it looked even better on
her, with those black S's curved around her own curves, blunt like
placards.

Smooth as grass bending the snake flowed.

"Lester, be good boy," Pinito said, taking and stroking him with
her free hand and then, still with the one hand, coiling the three
or four feet of his body which had left the trunk back inside. He
was supposed to be twenty feet long — "strawng enuff to crush the
life! outuva horse! oranox!" — and from what Fiddler had seen of
him he probably was. Except to raise his head again to rest on the
rim, Lester remained as she'd put him.

At last Pinito finished brushing her hair and scented it and
began to coil it tightly on her head in a bun, having to use both
hands and take more care than with the snake. She slipped on an
intricate bracelet of pink seashells, none larger than half an inch,
and cuddled a gauzy red shawl about her neck, and she was ready.

"Want to help me with the box?" Pinito stuck Lester's head
inside and shut the trunk. She was going to have Chief handle one
end and carry the other herself. That was the kind of woman she
was. Fiddler got her end — the trunk weighed almost three hundred pounds — and Pinito lifted the canvas partition and Fiddler
and Chief brought the trunk to her platform.

Each attraction had its own small stage, one of ten or twelve
spaced in a square. The armless-legless man's was on one side of
Pinito and the midget family's on the other. — The barker called
them a family, anyway, two old people and two around Fiddler's
age. Fiddler hoped they weren't a family, as a matter of fact, because the boy seemed awfully sweet on the girl.

"Let's see the bunny," Pinito said.

"Bunny, bunny, who's got the bunny?" babbled the armless-
legless man loud as a goose. He laughed and laughed. Chief took
it out from his shirt, swinging it up like a sacrifice. When he'd

first shown Fiddler the rabbit he'd been concerned about not scaring it. Now he wasn't. That was Chief: one time kind, the next almost cruel. Pinito looked cruel too, with her upturned, snake nose, but she had just the right amount of flesh on her face and the lines were smooth and handsome.

The midget boy and girl stood on tiptoes — he was feeling for her hand — and the fat lady listed over in her chair to see and the sword-swallower left his platform and came, the magician strutting with him. The magician was only twice as big as the midgets, about four feet tall. The girl smiled invitingly and he picked her off her platform and held her in his arms. The boy glowered with jealousy.

"He's freshly caught. He's wild as sin. He'd be hard to use for tricks." The glib magician rattled off his words.

"He's okay," Chief said.

"I wish I had a pet," said the midget girl, who should have been a pet herself. Fiddler would have loved to have her. She was normal-shaped and pretty; except her face was wrinkled like a wet cloth doll's — and you didn't have to notice that.

Pinito passed close to Chief and Fiddler. "Bring the bunny." She was perfumed so alluringly it made you ache. They followed, and behind them the magician with the girl clinging to his neck. — Nobody Fiddler's size could even boost her over a puddle, but let him be as small as the magician and she'd act like a slut.

Printed oilcloth hung from the platform to the ground everywhere except in back. The platform stood on four legs, and Pinito had tacked chickenwire around it underneath to make a pen. Inside she already had several rabbits, white ones, black ones, and a few guinea pigs, all nibbling lettuce leaves she'd scattered and the grass. Most of the rabbits came from townie boys. She'd show them her snakes in exchange.

As soon as the cottontail was in the pen the old inmates hopped boldly toward it to give it a rough time, an initiation. They stamped their hind feet in excitement. But then something seemed to scare them into leaving it alone.

"Hah, there's how wild he is," said the magician. "The hares

are afraid of him. You call domestic rabbits hares. They know
when to look sharp."

The armless-legless man laughed and laughed. Fiddler had no
idea why. The guy was not in a position to have seen what had
happened.

Pinito stooped and filled a little dish of water for the rabbits
from a pitcher. Every movement she made exposed some area
around her waist of satin skin like dark honey and hid another
that she'd just exposed. Fiddler would have watched a quarter
of an hour to have her bend in certain ways again.

She stood up coldly, told Chief, "Thank you very much." She
paused as if expecting him to go. When he didn't, all of a sudden
she laughed, clear and bright like a brook, sunk her hand in his
hair and kissed him on the lips. The midget girl giggled, clinging
to her man. Chief was bringing his arms around Pinito, hard as
posts, but she imped away, raising her hands to slap him down if
necessary, and tripped up the ladder steps to her platform. The
clustered shells on her bracelet clicked mockingly. There on the
trunk she sat, smug as a princess.

"Ain't fair, is it, Chief, to horn you up like that?" gasped the
sword-swallower. He always gasped; he couldn't use his vocal cords.

Chief almost left. He didn't like being made a fool of.

The round armless-legless man sat tipped back like a jar against
his chair and laughed and laughed and laughed.

"All right, we'll feed him," said Pinito. "Fill the tub for me,
Chief, please." Chief went out to the sideshow water barrel and
came back quickly with a washtub, slopping water on his legs.
Pinito opened the trunk. The snake's head set itself in its perennial spot on the rim.

"Aw, I wish I had a pet," the midget girl complained again.
Armless-legless laughed. In winter quarters but not on the road,
the older midgets started telling her, their voices high and cackly
like a record playing too fast.

The boy broke in, "If Sheila wants pets she oughta be let to have
'em!"

"Who asked you?" — The girl herself crushed him. The magician snickered, patting her bare legs, and kissed her. He covered her neck with his mouth. Then, making sure she didn't see, he mouthed *Shorty!* at the boy.

Pinito knelt in front of the head and stroked forward on it with her fingers, leading it out. Once she could touch the chin and throat the snake moved faster. It was like pulling on a line, except that Pinito's graceful hands could not have met around the snake and she could not have pulled him anywhere. Creeping sideways, keeping her fingers slowly tickling on the head, she got to the tub and guided the head to the water. The snake stopped to sniff and test the surface, then, wetting his eyes with a cautious shake, began to slide in, foot after foot, taking his time and coiling as he came, drooping down from the trunk, rasping slightly on the platform and, like a bridge truss, rising to the tub. Coil settled on coil — the head explored the tub, drinking, in the meantime — and the water threatened to spill over. He was such a thick, great, heavy snake Chief could hardly have carried him. Until the last few inches of tail were in, the head remained under water, leisurely drinking and nosing. Finally it lifted and rested, placid as ever, on the rim of the tub.

"O o o o oh–*ah!*" A loud thump of a sound startled Fiddler. At the other end of the tent the giant was yawning.

"Lester loves the ladies. Lester's sweet as jam, pretty Lester." Pinito rubbed the python with a rag. "Lester loves the ladies, sweety Lester, ootsie-tootsie boy." She made his markings shine. He took no notice of Pinito until she bent to kiss his nose. Then he moved aside and raised his head a few feet, staring straight at the midget girl as if he'd been watching her all along and Pinito had gotten in his way.

"Stop it," she whispered soothingly. "Hungry? Pretty Lester's hungry?" She drew his head down gently like capturing a fluttering bird and made him stop staring.

Chief hadn't said a thing for five minutes. He was quieter than if he'd been sober. He was too quiet. Next time they were alone Fiddler was going to tell him to talk more with Pinito.

Pinito began tickling Lester's chin again and coaxing him out of the tub. She held a towel in a loop for him to pass through and had Chief take the towel while she guided Lester's head to where she wanted him to coil. The python co-operated goodnaturedly. He seemed to travel without the slightest effort, although the platform creaked in protest at his weight, and he fitted himself into the space Pinito allowed him with offhand ease. Fiddler had never seen the snake's whole body straightened out. Pinito always had the front end coiling as the hind parts unwound.

"Get your little bunny," said Pinito. Chief did, and she took it by the loose skin above its hips and offered it to Lester. Lester had been gazing at the midget girl again. He turned; his head wavered and trembled and his wisp tongue flicked while he smelled the meal. Smooth as a crane his head glided near and examined the rabbit, then back, and then, direct as a dart, he seized the whole front half of his prey in his mouth, not even needing to unhinge his jaws. Pinito's seashells clicked as the rabbit kicked, and she let go.

"Most snakes are hard to feed. That's a good snake to go right at it like that," the magician said.

"Aw, poor rabbit," murmured the midget girl. She quit looking.

Lester pulled the headless, writhing blob of fur into the midst of his coils and out of habit tried to squeeze it. There was no use in doing that. There wasn't enough rabbit to get a grip on. Lester's jaws hitched forward alternately once or twice and all except the dangling hind legs disappeared from view.

"Bye-bye — hah, hah, hah, hah, hah, hah, hah! — bye-bye!" howled armless-legless, shaking his head, tears in his eyes. He started to splutter, as if he thought it was so funny plain laughter wouldn't do. He hissed, blew and spluttered, now almost as though he'd swallowed something hot. — He wasn't laughing any more. He was livid, squealing, wringing his head, bobbing around on the chair like a jar in a pot of boiling water.

"Lift me, lift me," said the midget girl. She reached up and flicked the armless-legless man's nose. Something flew away. He quieted down.

The rabbit was gone. Pinito stroked Lester over the vague bulge that showed. "Lester hungry still? Was it only half a bite, sweet? What a tummy!" The bulge moved farther down. Chief brought another rabbit.

Once was enough, Fiddler decided. "I've got to go and work, I think."

"Yeah," Chief agreed. "It's time for you. I got a little more."

"When I go, you aren't going to pull another try-and-find-me act, are you?"

"Say your prayers, Fiddle! Say your prayers!" Chief warned, insulted as hell.

"You'll come back this afternoon when your work's done and see me, won't you, Chief, please?" Pinito pleaded, in mock-fear that he wouldn't. He grinned and she smiled and mussed his hair. Chief had a lot of fun in the sideshow but Fiddler didn't enjoy it much. He came because Chief came and was always glad to leave.

Fiddler stepped out of the tent and the dazzling sun hurt his eyes. Right away he wanted a drink of water, he wanted to look for some uncrushed grass in a strip of shade and lie down. He went to the jigs' top, helped himself to a cup of their water and sucked on some of their ice. While he was dawdling and playing with the ice he heard the roar of a caterpillar and had a feeling that might be his guy. It was. The driver was cruising around at full speed, looking for him.

"Where in hell you been, youngster?" The cat veered and steamed in Fiddler's direction. He set himself like a bullfighter, his legs straight and his body curved slightly over them, but the driver wouldn't play along, he wouldn't come real close. Fiddler grasped the back of the driver's seat, jumped on the coupling behind and held on. They went on a tour, clacketing the length of the big top, the wind cool and the sandy and white and sea-colored tents sliding past, the guy lines tan as deer hide hung with washing. Behind them the dust swirled. The driver smelled of cloves. He liked to chew cloves. He must have been tinkering with the motor. Black oil was smudged on his neck, where he'd scratched, probably.

"Ain't like the fleet, is it, Fiddler?" He'd been a Seabee and

kidded Fiddler, one sailor to another. He had blond hair that
Fiddler looked down on, riding behind him, and arm tattoos, and
his jaws worked, the breeze carrying back a medicinal smell of
cloves.

"It is for you, I should think. A cat's a cat."

"They don't have so many raids here while you're working,
though."

The cookhouse, long and low, spread out before them, and
the little weed-green lean-to kitchen tents beside it with their
stovepipes smoking. Already lunch was in full swing. Beyond, to
the left, were the cages. They looked boxy and small, except for
the giraffe wagon monstrosities taller than they were long. The
driver pulled up at the hipp cage. Fiddler hopped off and raised
the wagonpole to a level with the coupling, having to support it
with his knee as well as his arms. The cat backed and Fiddler
dropped the pin through the pole ring and the coupling. Taylor
had remembered to board up the cage for the trip, so Fiddler
didn't have to do it. Nuts or not, the guy wasn't a bad cagehand.

Fiddler got up on the pole and coupling, one foot on each, and
the driver started away. It was fun riding like that — like standing
a galloping horse, when they went over rough ground. The water
in Betty Lou's tank swashed stupendously and streamed between
the boards. The route they took was behind the cookhouse and
the backyard, clear around to the other side of the big top, opposite the horse tents, where a break had been left for them in the
stakeline.

Brownie was waiting just under the big top, watching with his
one, shrewd eye. On either side of him stretching away was a solid
rank of backs of townies goggling at the goings-on inside. Brownie
stood out like a sunset because of his clothes, and he alone, among
the hundreds, was facing outward. When Brownie saw the cat he
moved out of the entryway to one of the sidepoles they would pass
between. Standing there, he made some indistinct gestures which
would have been meaningless to anyone who didn't know the cat
was coming. On purpose he kept them like that. The townies
glanced at him questioningly, shuddered at the pit in his face
where the eye should have been, and from his clothes and appear-

ance probably judged he was just another circus loony. Brownie
didn't say a word. He continued playing his game, gesturing
vaguely. The cat made plenty of noise, but there were three or
four big wheat-ranch-size cats maneuvering seat wagons inside,
even louder, and they had had to come in through a wider break
down by the backyard — the townies never dreamed anything
would barge through right where they were standing.

"Why does he crap around like that? Tell 'em to get the hell
out of the way. What's the matter with him?" said the driver.

The townies were somewhat like Tombstone, the way they
fidgeted and looked around while the cat roared closer and closer.
Then the smartest turned, saw, and started dragging his children
out of the path, shoving into six or eight other townies who after
a moment also caught on and fled in a dash. The road was cleared.
Brownie stayed by his sidepole, smiling snidely.

They spotted the hipp next to the men's outhouse wagon. When
the cage was in place Fiddler pulled out the pin and away they
went, parallel with the townies — all of whom for fifty yards were
now warned and prepared to jump for safety — until at the last
second, with a smoking, right-angle turn, they showed they were
going to leave the same place they'd come in. The driver wasn't
trying to scare the townies, like Brownie. But, having so much
power at his fingertips, he liked to demonstrate his skill.

The rhino cage they brought in next. The rhino clomped lurch-
ingly about as they sped along. The sun chafed Fiddler's skin but
the wind kept him cool. He was enjoying himself.

This time the townies were ready and stood out of the path
with expressions of worldly-wise self-satisfaction. Lots and lots of
things were going on inside. Three elephants were putting the
finishing touches on the quarterpoles, pulling them a few yards
here or there as Magee directed. The seat wagons were being
parked around the hippodrome. They left great tracks and the
rumbling cats made the ground vibrate and took up all the room
with their sweeping turns. Some places the dust in the air got
thick as moss. Fiddler's little cat had to make its way as best it
could.

The rhino went between the hipp and the ladies' donniker

wagon and completed the line of four outhouse and animal wagons that followed the edge of the big top around from the main, midway entrance to the beginning of where the elephants would stand in a row.

"Where's Chief?" Brownie wanted to know. He'd corralled Red and Taylor.

"He'll be here. He's around," Fiddler told him.

"Where's Coca Cola?"

"I don't know," Fiddler said, being carried away.

The giraffe wagons had the heaviest poles. The driver was careful to be as accurate as possible when he backed and not waste time. They were just going to haul the first one off when Fiddler saw Coca Cola — lying under it! — Coca Cola's feet, he saw.

"Get out of there, mister!"

Coca Cola woke with a groan. "Wh-whatsa matter?"

"You're going to get run over, stupid fudgehead! Another second and you would have been!" Coca Cola made no move to get up. "Well, what are you going to do! How do you want to be squished, across the back, or only the legs?"

"I need a doctor quick. . . . Have to see one. I ain't going to live past today."

"Son of a bitch, you ain't goin' to live a minute if you don't get out from under there!" the driver shouted, mad and revving his engine. Fiddler dragged Coca Cola.

"I have to stay out of the sun," he was mumbling. He was breathless, sick and green. "Can't stand the sun. — O-o-o-o-oh," he groaned, on his feet, clutching the door of the wagon and trying to cover his eyes. The cat started away and Coco Cola stumbled along still holding on, as if his hand was caught on something. Fiddler stopped the driver. Coca Cola panted, "Lemme get in. I have to lay down; I swear I'm going to die. Lemme get out of the sun and lay down."

Fiddler opened the door and Coca Cola flopped like a fish into the straw and lay with his body painfully twisted. Maybe he really was sick. Boston, the big giraffe, bent his head around to look. Coca Cola was lying beside the yellow and brown blotched hind legs as though beside a stepladder. Fiddler could think of plenty of times Coca Cola had neglected to feed or water the giraffes. By just stirring his feet a little Boston was going to be able to take a lot of revenge. In fact he could kill the guy, easy as pie.

"Jesus, I had a bad night too," the driver said, tapping his head. "But not that bad."

When they pulled the giraffe wagon into the big top they made two right-angle turns as if they were going to pull it right out again through another entryway, and that's what they did, stopping, however, when the back end came even with the sidepoles. The giraffe pen would be constructed just inside the top with its door meeting the wagon door.

Brownie, Red and Taylor were there, ready to begin the work. Brownie was about to bust a gut. "That goddam Chief! That — "

"There he is," Fiddler said. Chief strode from the Animal top, scaring the townies out of his way with a grunt. The sixteen-pound sledge sat like a rock on his shoulder; he wore no shirt, and the lurid paint on his cheeks gleamed fresh as blood. As usual, he was late enough to justify Brownie's worrying, but not quite late enough to fire.

The second giraffe wagon went next to the first. When they brought it Brownie proudly greeted Fidder: "I found the other sonofabitch! I always find 'em." He had Coca Cola strung up by the collar from his fist.

"I'm going to quit," moaned Coca Cola.

"Be sure and write," Brownie said. Then he bellowed, "Until you *do* quit you're going to work!"

The Sidewall gang of half-grown kids came jack-in-the-boxing along. They carried slender ladders which they leaned against the sidepoles and scooted up, carrying a rope from the strip of sidewall on the ground. Slipping the rope through a ring at the top of the pole and holding on, they'd jump into space and swoop down like parachutists as the sidewall rose. These were the youngest working kids in the circus. They slept three to a bunk. Some of their voices hadn't even changed. The ballet girls made pets of them and used them for errands, and they got away with murder with the winos,

running circles around whole departments. They were like animals,
shaggy, all impulse, hardly talking — hardly able to talk, some
of them — but seeing everything that was done. The grubbiest
townie kids were fops next to them. A townie kid with a smudged
T-shirt, a patch on his baseball jacket and holes in his socks and
sneakers, who'd gone five weeks since his last haircut — a typical
townie boy who had ducked out of the house early enough this
morning to escape his mother and was not too nice or clean or
goody-goody — this kid was an archbishop's son, next to the Sidewall kid with foot-long hair, whose man-size shirt looked like a rag
for cleaning carburetors, the sleeves rolled up thicker than his
shoulders and the shirttail in shreds. — He *never* washed behind
his ears, and hadn't seen a schoolbook after ten, and the closest he
came to having a mother was when a bevy of gorgeous showgirls
might catch him naked in swimming and, homesick for brothers,
soap him a little and shear off a chunk of his hair.

That was one of the things the Sidewall kid really knew about —
girls. He'd spy some eight-grade queen who half a school wor-
shipped from afar and give her a look that would either have her
creeping out her bedroom window that night or shuddering under
the covers with her mother.

The Sidewall boss was a gaunt man, short, old, bald and as dirt-
black as if he'd gone through a fire. He walked as stiff as a man on
stilts and was kind to the kids. They needed a little kindness. They
had some rough days ahead, between the cops and the big-city
fairies, both waiting to gobble them up when they left the show.

Once the giraffe wagons were spotted there was a lull for Fiddler
and the driver. Chief and the others were working like mad on
the pen; Fiddler was lucky to get out of that. The cat moseyed back
to the rest of the cages and Fiddler coupled them into two lines
as the driver, steering by Fiddler's directions, pushed or pulled.
The little danger of being caught and crushed between the wagons
made Fiddler enjoy the job. Any job with a spicing of danger he
liked.

The act lions began grunting like a whole tribe of tomtoms. Poor
Joe and Bessie were aching to join in, but, with the cage being

jerked around, it was hard. And the closed-up wagon didn't let the sound out very well. It must have been awfully loud in their ears. The grunts penetrated through to Fiddler, plaintive, nasal and trapped. Joe and Bessie soon stopped even trying.

When the wagon strings were made, Fiddler climbed up on the tread of the cat beside the driver, who took out a pipe and propped up his feet. — "How much time have we got, do you say?"

"I don't know. But not that much." Fiddler nodded at the pipe.

"Hell, that's okay." The driver went ahead and filled and lit it. He still had a twang of a hillbilly accent, after all this knocking around, and he went about doing things with a sudden, homey, finicky, independent kind of way which reminded Fiddler of other hillbillies he'd seen.

"Where did you say you came from?"

"Tennessee."

Yes, he was the Tennessee type, more than the hayseed Arkie.

"You expectin' to get in on the killin'?"

"Where?" Fiddler said.

"If you ain't heard, maybe I'm a fool to tell you. Maybe you'll snitch my share." The driver laughed. He looked away. "No, I wouldn't touch it. I don't want a bit of it."

"What?" Fiddler got ready to punch the guy.

"Okay, okay," the driver laughed. "Yesterday a guy joined up with the Cookhouse who's a millionaire, I guess. He's passin' out twenties. Every once in a while. They didn't know he had it till this mornin'. They'da got it in the night if they had. What you have to do is tell him a hard luck story, and he hands over the twenty. I bet it's goin' to screw up lunch. There's a big crowd around him, they say, all the time. — I bet there is! And his relatives were dancin' around here like they had the itch. They couldn't get him away and they couldn't get him to quit passin' it out. Now they say they're tryin' to get a court to declare him bughouse. I don't blame 'em. But it's Sunday an' all. . . . The Cookhouse boys are tryin' to keep it to theirselves, but I don't care who I tell. I don't want a penny of it. You don't take money from bugs any more than you take it from drunks. I'm not the kind of guy that takes it

from drunks." He squeezed the gear levers of the cat emphatically.
"You'z a Democrat here. Thissiz the *Nawth!* In the Nawth you'z
got to be Democrat! You'z got to change!"

— A rollicking posturing mass of jigs swarmed down the stakeline. They were guying out — tugging in unison on the loose line
that went to each sidepole and taking in on the lines to the stakes
whatever they gained. The dense wall of townies turned around
from watching inside to gawk at the jigs, and the jigs responded to
the audience. They goose-stepped and bunny-hopped, laughing at
their shadows, gleeful as kittens in a fishcart. "R-e-a-a-a-r b-a-a-a-a-g-g
— Joomp!–joomp!–joomp!–joomp!–joomp! — wawgalong." The
magnificent King shouted the beat. He clenched his fists like
handles pumping out the words, and his voice went dropping down
so deep it gargled.

The jigs had tied their shirttails across their stomachs, pirate
style, and their flashy handkerchiefs in bands across their foreheads.
They were hollering what they were going to do when all this work
was through. Some were walnut-brown and bushy-haired and
sprouting Turk mustaches and some a slick shiny black all over,
skin and hair, and one jig was a pale drained gray. You had the
feeling you didn't want to be in front of them. Their arms whizzed
and they all packed razors. Blackbeard's gang would have seemed
tame. The King could handle the other jigs because he was larger
and he thought the same, but nobody else could possibly understand
them. They'd been born squirming next to furnaces and they loved
it to be hot. Like every white man who joined was a wino, any jig in
the circus was a wild man fresh out of jail. The reason they leaped
around so much was probably that they'd just been in chains. You
could see whip cuts on their bodies and actual burned spots where
they'd been tortured. These were jigs that had never learned their
place.

One left the mass and, waving goodby, grabbed on to a guy line
and started climbing. He had reddish-brown hair caked on his head
like unraveled rope and he pulled himself up like a squirrel, using
both arms, then both legs, then both arms. Three-quarters of the
way he tired and went much slower. When he got himself on to the

canvas right away from the waist down he was lost from sight, as if he were wading. The springy canvas joggled him around and almost threw him over backwards several times. Climbing, he followed one of the central strands of the big top's ribbing. He went on all fours, or sometimes spread his arms for balance. Breezes snagged in his clothes and hair. He was awkward and slow, like a crawling moth fighting the wind, his arms like splinters of wings. He reached the first line of quarterpoles, struggled over the ridge and, higher and littler, higher and littler, on toward the second. Finally he rested, hugging a quarterpole horn. Fiddler envied the guy. He was much smaller than a moth now. The wind rocked him up and down.

"Kind of fun." The driver smiled. He was watching too. "I used to take my wife up on the mountains at home. That guy rigs for one of the Kraut acts."

In the big top, where the Sidewall crew hadn't gotten around to block the view yet, the seat wagons were parked with their backs to the stakeline, and the huge flaps on the sides were rising to meet the flaps of adjacent wagons and then be tilted down, together with the tops of the wagons, to form the solid ramp that would seat the thousands of townies. The wagons each were as big as the herd of elephants, and the flaps went up grand and slow and not like mechanisms, but majestically. There was no sound except the townies' talk. The wagons each were big as a grandstand, but there was no sound.

Suddenly and violently the townie tourist line was broken. People staggered back. Brownie emerged in all his green and scarlet glory. He stood puffed proud like a cock and made a single sharp sweep of his arm, turned and parted the townies again. Under Fiddler the cat roared to life. He jumped off the tread and up in his old spot and, towing the monkey string, they rolled for the top.

The entryway had been left open, but a fold of sidewall hanging from one of the poles had to be pulled aside. Fiddler leapt between the moving cat and wagons, ran ahead and did it. Things were shaping up. The menagerie would be located behind the bleachers at the front door end of the hippodrome, so that the townies could see the animals on the way to their seats. The cat line was going to go along the back of the bleacher seat wagons, the peanut-and-drink stands on one side and the monkey line along the other.

Fiddler ran between the caterpillars, seat wagons and elephants to catch up with his driver. The ground was plowed and trampled and the air clogged with the ruckus of motors. He had to look out for himself and zig and zag like a water bug. The six-man jig gangs were toenailing the quarterpoles — driving a couple of stakes at the base of each for anchors. They'd group around a stake, all six of them, every height and shape, and one would take a swing, and the next, the next, the next, next, next — sometimes one-handed and always easy and limber, jerking the hammers out of the way with a wrist twist, not worrying if somebody missed a turn once in a while or didn't hit his strongest. They got going and the hammers fell in sequence like piston rods on a train and were tossed high again, round and round and round fast as you could follow. The stake went down in one continuous plunge. And the jigs lavished a sort of gentleness on it, never seeming to bang too hard and almost reluctant to leave the stake, giving it last licks just for enjoyment.

The cat ripped past and Fiddler was sucked into place as if by a whirlwind. The driver was feeling good and even when he had to slow down he kept his engine popping.

Bringing in the line of six wagons took the skill. The driver headed for the wide-open spaces, the trees with their moiling leaves, the river glinting the sun, as though on a pleasure trip, puffing his pipe. He made a huge circle until he was going toward the big top again and the cages were sailing behind him straight as a file of soldiers. The top looked small like a Quonset hut and the townies like skinny bees and the entryway gap in the sidewall dark and the size of an eye. The climbing jig was a speck up by the centerpole flags. The top grew bigger and bigger, its contours rounding and deepened, the quarterpole horns sticking through and the broad sleek gliding canvas swooping between them green like the sea, over the sand-colored sidewall. The jig was in an upright position now and walking along the crest. He was small as a dime, but his body proportions were just right, his arms as he balanced as graceful as wings. Fiddler had never seen a man look any finer.

The canvas stirred through all its expanse with the wind, settling and adjusting slightly, the guy ropes like ligaments. In one corner the shivering was a little more rhythmic, although it didn't extend much farther than the first line of quarterpoles. That was where the guying-out crew was working. Rag snips tied on a string was how they seemed. The King was bulkier, like a spring peeper. The top soared buoyant and poised — the tune-up they were giving it would set it perfectly. It has home and a glorious home, wavy and resilient as the sea, day to day almost as magically changing. The sidewall swept coquettishly against the poles like a lady's skirt, outlining them, and the edge of fringing on the big top canvas ruffled like a duck's down. Who would have wanted to live in a house!

The top got as big as a stadium, and Fiddler sprang off the coupling and outraced the wagons, which would have crushed him if he'd fallen. A middle-aged townie already had hold of the sidewall and didn't want Fiddler to take it; the guy was getting the thrill of a kid. Fiddler crouched by the pole to wrench it over if the gap should need widening all of a sudden. Behind him a soft-fleshed, fastidious man and his wife were getting the giggles. Fiddler wondered if they were laughing at him for being dirty or something. A lot of townies were pushing to see through the entryway, since the sidewall had cut off their view everywhere else. Legs pressed against Fiddler. Everybody seemed determined not to give him enough room.

The treads of the cat clanked like a prehistoric monster and the engine had its own tremendous stutter. The cat came by, and the first wagon, and the second as straight as can be and the third almost as straight, then the fourth, not quite in line — the fifth was not quite going to follow — The driver had to make his turn with the fifth and sixth wagons still to pass Fiddler. Fiddler's townie helper raised his arms and pulled on the sidewall and Fiddler jerked the pole and jerked — the fifth cage was barely missing it; and here came the sixth! The driver could do nothing now; he was parallel with the stakeline. Fiddler yanked the stubborn weighted pole as if he were trying to upend it, backing and cursing into the townie gigglers. The wagon looked sure to hit the pole. He lifted, pulled, and his rib muscles started to tear. The wagon ticked but got by.

The driver made another turn so the cages behind him were going in a **⌐** and, as they straightened into an **L**, turned once more, then led the string nicely between the quarterpole row and the back of the bleachers. Fiddler unhooked.

"Sorry, kid, I'll do better tomorrow," the driver said. He went off to another job.

Brownie opened the orang wagon and gave Fiddler a hammer. Coca Cola laid out the first few stakes, moaning in pain. Red and Taylor were unrolling the guard nets, one along each line of cages. Everybody except Fiddler was already dripping with sweat from putting up the giraffe pen. The giraffes were out and licking the wire like ghouls to get the salt.

Fiddler and Chief started in front of the gnu's cage. Fiddler squatted down and held the stake straight and steady and Chief drove it the first foot and then they both drove, alternating blows, Chief making about three-fourths of the progress. Chief hammered with a fury and intensity of rhythm utterly unlike the jigs. He was a shade slower, but he put much more of what he had into his blows. His mouth opened at each one, the teeth and the red tongue in back showing, and he lunged up on his toes and his whirling arms zeroed in the hammer to hit square on the head of the stake. He breathed deeply but not hard and only had eyes for that stake. If Fiddler didn't set it straight he'd yank it over — "Hold it right!"

Taylor and Red began opening the metal flaps which covered the bars, and the yakating, chippering monkeys caught at their sleeves. The leader dropped his jaw in astonishment when Red and Taylor didn't stop to pay attention and tightened it in a flare of anger, screeching like a trolley. A baby hung from its mother's tail, watching the leader. Everything the leader did the baby tried to imitate. It hadn't learned how to be mad yet, though, and its teeth were most unthreatening. Fiddler couldn't look at the cage except in glances. The next thing he saw was the baby climbing the tail hand over hand and the mother's fingers lifting it under the arms to her breast. The baby nursed on both teats at the same time, stretching one into each corner of its mouth.

Taylor was talking to a quarterpole. Now and then he did that.

It was too bad he hadn't felt the urge with the monkeys, who would have appreciated his conversation more. Red was accustomed to working with Taylor. Moments like these he'd spend on the lookout for girls.

Fiddler was getting unpleasantly hot. His neck and the small of his back were wet. Across the way the Elephant men were pounding stakes too and the jig toenailers hadn't gotten very far. It sounded like a horseshoe-pitching tournament. Brownie had stolen the Animal Department's stakes from the City of Chicago. They were thinner than ordinary circus stakes, not as good targets, but light and strong. Fiddler didn't actually do much hammering, Chief was so fast. Most of the time he was holding for Chief, his head about on a level with the head of the stake.

The monkeys did trapeze acts and one tried backflips off the wall. A flock of them zipped to the top of the cage and piled into the straw like children cannonballing. The mother with the baby hugged into her belly fur chattered fit to kill. She came off the swing she'd been rocking on and let herself down along the bars, going slow enough for the baby to hang on. She snatched another baby out of the straw from where it had been burrowing and held it by the waist, *rrikittikittikittikittikitting* like a locust while she bit the yellow flakes away from its fur. The baby wasn't hurt. It grabbed its brother by the ear and twisted until he gave up one of the nipples and moved over.

The sideshow had started operations. . . . "Say, all you good people are going to have an awfully long, long wait. You can't even get into the circus tent until one o'clock! What are you going to do with yourself? — Why not come in here and enjoy yourself? We've got the strangest people in all the world to entertain you, right in here. We've got the *tallest,* the *smallest,* the *fattest* people alive; we've got the lady with the big snakes; we've got the pet of all the circus, our little man born without arms or legs, hands or feet — you'll be curious about him. Come in now and see the strange people. Come in; they're all alive. . . . " Unless he went swimming Fiddler wouldn't be really out of hearing until after teardown tonight. But the voice would dissolve into a formless murmur he never noticed unless he wanted a laugh. Like the loud somnolent drone of the generator wagons and the queer calliope toodeling, it would serve as reassurance that the show was all around and even the cops of Council Bluffs were suckers for today.

It was hot! Fiddler's eyes filmed over with sweat that dripped from his forehead. He couldn't see properly and was afraid Chief would miss the stake and crunch his hands. The chance had been just as great before, but it hadn't bothered him while he could see. How could it be so hot in the shade! He was sopping with sweat that was gritted with dirt and warmer than blood. His feet had begun to burn and his soaked socks felt even grimier than they were. Red and Taylor were tying up the guard net already, which made Chief work faster. Fiddler went up and down, up and down, standing to slam the stake a few times, then quickly squatting to steady the next. Chief's face was iron and his shoulders bunched in round ridges and the sledge of dull-glinting iron fell bucking and clanging the stake viciously in Fiddler's hands. Sweat pulled the lashes into Fiddler's eyes. When he wiped it his hand got slick as a fish and dried sticky and hot, with the dirt of the sweat left, as itchy as ants. Remembering how easy the jigs had worked, he couldn't believe it. He pounded with Chief, hitting as Chief's hammer rose and having to get his own out of the way as Chief's came down. He worried a little about his aim. He was afraid of hitting the stake with the handle, breaking the handle and hurting his hands. Worrying weakened his blows. Chief always said that was what would make him miss — flinching, afraid of missing.

Chief didn't even take an extra breath before he started on the cat line. Sweat ran on his face and he angrily blew at his hair and blinked, hitting all the harder.

Some of the bulls were being brought in; their place was ready. They were noiseless and well-heeled like high-class bouncers. A loop had been raised in the sidewall, and the bulls ducked their heads under that and carefully lifted, so that the canvas slid down their backs without ripping or being torn off the poles. Going into a tearoom, they wouldn't have broken a cup.

Outside, the sun looked a withering white-hot now. Really it was no worse, but, with sweat like tears in your eyes, things seemed different. The monkeys chitting in the dark of their cages weren't sweating. They were lucky.

" . . . . Say, it's *air-cooled* in here! Why not come in?" the side-show loudspeakers were saying. Fiddler got a certain pleasure from knowing it wasn't. He didn't have to envy anybody except for not being at work.

The townies were giving Brownie a bad time. The break the cages came through had been closed. The townies couldn't see through the sidewall and so they had pushed it up, and then they'd gotten tired of holding it up, so they'd stepped inside, and now the inevitable process had begun of standing a little farther in and a little farther, until eventually they would be squeezed against the net as if it was showtime and they'd paid to get in; or, if the net wasn't up yet, they'd kill themselves against the bars. Brownie had his hands full. Brownie shriveled the townies. He let them have the benefit of his advice.

"You half-asses are getting out of here if I have to goose the jizz out of every one of you. Egg-eyes! We own this lot today! You're trespassers! Run, you lop-tailed lilies!"

The townies were shocked at Brownie's language and disgusted by him. They moved wherever they could to avoid him, but did their best to stay inside the sidewall. Now, of all the times in the day, Fiddler hated their watching. His shoulders quivered and ached, and the back of his legs; his eyes itched; his ears were sore from the clang of the sledge, his hands jarred numb; his clothes clung water-logged with sweat; his mouth was dry as onion husks; his nose felt fiery with the dust and his crotch and armpits seemed to be cook-ing. — He hated them. This was how it was at night when you got by the crisply lighted houses and down to the cars, exhausted, smell-ing and filthy and hungry, with no prospect of a bath or a meal. There would be the townies to pass between, sucking on candies, in their starched, gay clothes for watching parades.

Fiddler stood up to hammer and he whaled the guts out of the stake. Chief and he began to work like a team. Coca Cola, stagger-ing ahead lugging stakes, could barely keep up. Chief hammered at the pitch of a giant and Fiddler felt so angry and bad he almost matched him. The stakes went down *whoom — whoom — whoom*

— *whoom,* firm and fast. If a stake hit a rock, they busted it right through the rock. Fiddler coasted along in a frenzy, hardly needing to breathe. It was like dreaming of walking on air, everything was so easy. There was too much blood in his head; otherwise he felt okay. The aching, the sweat and heat were distant like a wound under ether.

The cats heard the hammering and restlessly stirred around. They could probably distinguish Chief's tempo and style. Red and Taylor were opening the cat line wagons. When they got to the tigers Fiddler rushed over to help. The bottom flap swung down. Both cats struck out with their paws and balled up blistering roars like cars smashing, the male thunderous but no more fierce. Fiddler was small on his knees below them hanging to the flap and chilled to jelly. At both wagons it happened. It was a ritual. Chief scowled at Fiddler when he came back but didn't say anything. A tide of townies broke for the opened cages. Brownie met them, cussing parents, swatting kids, shouting in the faces of people asking questions so they couldn't even hear themselves.

Fiddler had trouble collecting himself. Chief's mouth had a resigned, contemptuous set, as though he'd known Fiddler's burst of strength wouldn't last. As before, Chief did most of the job. Fiddler just held for him. Fiddler's tongue felt like a stick, and all he could see in his mind was that river out there. He was going swimming. He could look forward to that.

Brownie was chasing some show-off brats and slipped on an elephant turd and went on his face in the dirt. The townies tittered and retreated. They were having their revenge. Brownie was an old man. He didn't get up fast. Fiddler found himself laughing too, but not in the same way. Yes, Brownie's falling was funny, and it would be funnier still to split you bastards' heads to bits with this hammer — that was how he felt. Chief worked methodically, blank-faced as a hangman.

"Hsst!" Mousy's head peeped between the tiger cages. He and the rest of the Seat Department lived behind the cat line, under the seat wagon flaps.

"Chief! C'me back here, son of a bitch; we want to straighten out things." The meager lips and pointed nibbly oatmeal features, eyes slits between the lids. The crouched tigers rose and planted themselves by him in the corners of their cages, not quite seeing Mousy but smelling him plenty. "C'me get your med'cine, Chief. Are you scared?" The pinched mouth smiled. The tigers raged at Mousy, plucked with their claws at the bars. "Chicken, Chief? C'me face the music."

Powerhouse Chief slammed the piss out of the stake, chipped sparks in the air. Once! twice! it was in; Fiddler was dizzily fuddling with the next. Chief grunted, whirling his arms, and the hammer sang light as a sword and fell true.

"Chief, chicken, c'me and meet the boys!"

The tiger wagons shook. The males blustered and Snippy and Mabel wildly slunk. Fiddler's hands pained as though his scars were hours old from trying to keep hold of the stakes. Chief wasn't going back there, at least. Brownie wouldn't have been much help in heading Chief off. Brownie was ranting and running. The more townies there were to start with, the more that were attracted.

Taylor and Red returned from opening the rest of the cages. Red's face lighted up.

"Hey, Mouse! How goes it?" Red kicked off his shoe, pulled off his sock and filled it with dirt in a jiffy. Laughing and hopping on one foot, he was ready to fight. Taylor like a scrawny turkey gobbled: "He'll kill ya too! Ya're done! I seen what they done. Ya'll scream, an' that won't stop 'um. *He* bled and screamed. . . ."

"Get out! *Get out!*" Brownie was shouting, almost sobbing. It was lucky he was old, or he might do somebody in when he got crazy-mad like this. Only the wise guys were giving the trouble now, but they were outdodging him. A group of bull men on the way to lunch stopped, waving their hooks.

Chief and Fiddler had gotten almost out of earshot of Mousy, Chief was working so fast. "Anywhere you are, Chief, we'll get you; you're dead. You go out on the flats and off you go. Sure they stop the train fast, but it don't help a broke neck." That was the last Fiddler heard. Red poured the dirt from his sock and put it on again. Mousy must have quit.

"I got to get in there till Doc comes," Coca Cola whimpered, stumbling past. His eyes were on Brownie and he looked half dead.

Fiddler didn't doubt that he was sick now. But Chief grabbed the guy.

"Got them last stakes out?" The breath was frightened out of Coca Cola. He couldn't breathe. Chief waited and didn't hurt him.

". . . . Yuh, I swear." He stiffened with a spasm of his belly pain and moved his mouth as if he'd bit his tongue. Chief let him go.

"Fiddler?" the guy whined timidly. "When the doc comes, maybe could you tell him I need him awful, awful bad, in my wagon?"

"Okay."

"I need him awful bad."

Coca Cola half ran the rest of the way, hardly daring to see if Brownie had spotted him.

— "Go on! Go on! To hell with you." Brownie had. Coca Cola snuck into the straw of one of his wagons and closed the door. He was lucky to be taking care of animals with wagons he could get in.

At the end of the cat line by the lion cage was Julius's stand. As they came within hearing Julius began his own variety of heckling.

"There's Chief" — mincing, pretending to be talking to himself — "who won't keep his bargains. The boy there had to help me this morning because Chief was off making trouble for somebody, wouldn't keep his bargains. He doesn't know what's right to do. He doesn't care. He'll get drunk and break his bargains as quick as he'll sneeze." Julius had tied a white apron on over his suit pants. It made him look like a white duck, his rounded body soft and plump. He was caressing his hips, smoothing the apron, and getting the barrels ready for mixing the drink he sold.

The lions yawned, and nothing was left of their heads but the terrific, grisly mouths. Then again they watched, slant-eyed and somber like two sphinxes.

Fiddler climbed on top of the lion wagon and knelt on the edge. Chief pushed the flap that covered the top half of the bars up on a pole to where he could reach it. "Lean, boy! Lean!" Chief shouted. Fiddler hooked the flap to the top of the wagon and was preparing to jump across to the next, when the wagon quivered. Somebody else was on it.

— The Sioux! He was hitching up the circuit of cage lights. Neither he nor Fiddler spoke but quick as shots they were racing —

in midair — pounding onto the next wagon. "Lean! Lean!" Chief bellowed, half smiling, and the Sioux got his lights and heckled Fiddler, trying to make him lean too far so he'd fall.

"Tied down? Poor kid; must've got him chained down! You might reach farther if you used your dong!"

The tops of the wagons were coated slippery with coal dust and any part of you that touched them turned black as a mine. Fiddler's arms to the elbows looked like a jig's. His pants could have been buried in coal. The Sioux maybe got the soles of his shoes dirty and his fingertips, but otherwise he kept as clean as a nurse. The dirt couldn't catch up with him. He moved so fast you thought he had a twin. When he plugged in the cords that put on the lights the electricity might have come right from him; his rainbow shirt crackled with color, his hair blazed black. In the air between cages he mocked Fiddler, "Can'tchou fly, kid? You ought to learn to fly!" — eyes wild as a plummeting hawk.

What with the cages being opened and Mousy snooping, the tigers had a case of nerves. "AaaarraaOw." They swayed the wagons gently with their prowling. Bessie and Joe, feeling the same, would have been grunting, and working off their jitters twice as fast. Chief was deliberate about his job, not at all like the Sioux. It took a lot of strength to push up the flaps — he couldn't have done it quickly — and he had to stand so near the cages that he had to go slow. But Chief enjoyed the Sioux's antics, in between some brooding spells.

The wagon tops were hot from having stood outside. They could burn your hands. Even the dirt was hot; mixed with sweat it felt like an acid. And the slope of the wagons was tricky for jumping. And the dust was enough to silt up your eyes. — Nothing bothered the Sioux, though. He was a comet.

"How's about it, kid?" He stretched way out and plucked the flap off Chief's pole as if he wore suction cups for shoes. "Anything I can do you can do better!" Chief was in one of his gloomy moods, but the jubilant Sioux more than made up for it.

When Fiddler got off the last wagon he was so thirsty he would have drank mud. He didn't run, but he walked as fast as he could without running. He was hungry too, but that was nothing to the thirst. Water was going to taste better than all the meals he'd ever eaten. He was going to fill his stomach and fill his chest and fill his throat and ears and nose, and when there wasn't room to cram in any more he'd wash out his mouth a dozen times and keep it full with only the coldest water.

The Animal Department's drinking water was in a snug old barrel which had a permanent flavor of whiskey charred into the wood. Fiddler took five cups in five swallows; and breathed; and drank nine more. He didn't taste the water, and it left his throat dry. He felt he would taste it if he kept drinking long enough, and that it would taste wonderful, but it didn't seem possible he'd ever get rid of his thirst. Brownie, Red and Taylor all wanted a drink, so he gave up the cup for a minute.

"Where's Chief?" Brownie burbled, water drooling down his chin. He bent his head again and drank to stop Red from taking the cup. . . . "We're going after that horse. He'll have to frig his lunch. Right away we're going. — Hey! He hasn't run off, has he, the son — "

Fiddler ran to the animals' big barrel, splashed water on himself, and ran toward the big top rubbing at the coal dust on his neck and arms. The water made it clammy but didn't wash it off.

"He's asking for trouble, that's all," said Julius as Fiddler rushed up. "I don't ask a man to be an angel, mind you. But a trouble-maker can't be depended on." Julius was concentrating on what he was doing and talked without looking at Fiddler.

"Where is he?"

"I've decided I'll have to find somebody else. I can't depend on a man like that to turn up every morning because he won't." Julius was tapping a brilliant orange powder onto his thumb, a very serious operation. Enough to cover half his thumbnail, plus a little canned milk and sugar and a whole lot of hydrant water, made a great barrel of his "orange" drink.

"Why, supposing they shoot him. What good — "

"Where is he!"

"*I'll tell you fellas somethin'! I'll tell you what'll fry your ears!*" Fiddler went for the voice.

"*You fellas think you're scary because there's a bunch o' you. But you're not scary. And you think you're mad. But you don't*

*know what it's like to be mad. I'm gonna show ya what it's like.
You'll hav'ta change your drawers!"*

Dramatically Chief paused, like an orator, his arms cocked stiff
for emphasis.

*"You say you're gonna do something to me. What couldja do?
What couldja do to me? You're sick. Winos. What couldja do to
me? You got guns, you say. But you know that wouldn't do no
good. They ain't machineguns! You'd need machineguns! You
know that."*

Chief stopped to muster himself. He'd picked the wrong day
to get drunk. The Seat men breathed a little more regularly while
he was silent. Evidently he'd surprised them lounging in their
chairs, but they hadn't gotten up. Some still had their feet stuck
on boxes — not because they felt comfy, but because they didn't
want to move a hair.

"This kid" — Chief grinned, seeing Fiddler — *"this kid could
pulverize you fellas!"* Fiddler didn't know whether he ought to
try and lead Chief away or stay with him and have the whole thing
settled once and for all, let the winos be squashed.

*"You've been blabbering all day. I've heard aboutcha. You've
been makin' like you're something to be scared of. Now I'm here.
And nobody's with me but this kid. And I don't wanta wait all day;
so — whatever you're gonna do! — do!"*

The Seat men furtively cast looks at Mousy: You brought him
on us. One guy suffered from asthma. He wheezed like a bag-of-
bones cow.

Mousy had a pal, a sallow zoot-suiter with a smirk like a curling
worm and a rattlesnake knife-throwing arm.

"Ssssst! Sam!" Mousy signaled and stood up to distract Chief.

Chief ignored Mousy and got to Sam before Sam could even
slip the sheeny out of his shoe. Sam huddled on the ground like
a squelched pup. Chief broke off the blade under his heel. Mousy
sat down.

Chief walked from man to man. *"Gimme your gun,"* he said to
Blotchy. Blotchy had a blazing red rash that circled one eye and
banded one side of his face to his chin.

"I ain't had no gun in this show."

"I'll kill you, Blotch!"

Blotchy gave him the gun.

— *"And you don't wanta have none, do you?"*

"No, I don't want no trouble from nobody."

"You don't wanta get hurt."

"No, I don't want to."

Quickly and simply he got several more. Somehow he knew who to go to. One guy didn't even wait to be asked for his. Chief dropped the guns in the Seat Department's water barrel.

Fiddler's mouth had a waking-up taste. He was thirsty again. He wished Chief would get finished. Chief was thinking. Old Blotch-face itched himself; the red strip seemed to have spread. One wino chewing tobacco didn't dare to spit. His cheeks bulged. The only Seat man Fiddler's age was a black-haired boy from one of the steel towns — he'd joined in one, anyway. Fiddler had drunk with him once before going on the wagon. The guy was the type who aged a year every month. He'd come on the show as healthy and husky as a butcher's son. Now he looked desperate, haggard, braced — and not because of Chief — jouncing all night on the battering rivets and boards of the flats, too drunk to get to his bed.

"I know what." — The wino faces limp as bacon raw. The bodies concentratedly inert. *"Mouse, I'm gonna use Mouse like an example. I'm gonna show you fellas some things!"*

A pudgy frightened man suddenly was very, very sorry he'd happened to sit next to Mousy. He threw his hand in front of his face and his mouth stuttered violently without producing any sound. The hand was all mangled. Years ago it had been done, the thumb and fingers cropped off at the first joint or closer. The guy was holding something short and brown — at first it looked like the rest of his thumb! A rabbit's foot it was.

"No don't move," Chief told Mousy. He extended his sledge-hammer over Mousy's head and just with his wrist he jogged it up and down. Mousy didn't move. The hammer lightly clunked him on the head, lifted and clunked again, hard enough to hurt, and brushed his nose. Mousy blinked and winced and trembled.

Chief let it drop a ways and then would catch it up — all with his wrist; nobody else's could have done it.

"Okay, Chief. Call it off, huh? Uncle."

Chief used the hammer delicately like a surgeon's tool and reddened Mousy's nose, made it tender and sore like a gash, and blackened his eyes and scraped at his ears.

"You fellas think you're somethin', but you're nothin'! You're nothin' worth lookin' at. You ain't got no salt. You know what I mean? I mean you ain't got no salt in you. You ain't worth nothin'."

Mousy's eyes were shut tight and he was glistening pale and sick. Rhythmically the hammer tapped him on the skull, harder now, so he could scarcely stand it. Several places he was cut. Chief was a little hoarse — that was the only sign he might be tired, and he certainly wasn't much tired. His voice was drunken — as powerful as ever, but flat, and the vibrant Indian accent was obscured.

"You're through now. You won't shoot your mouth off no more, you fellas. You'll keep your mouth shut; like I tell you" — the extra words fell heavily out like the tag-end grunts of a lion. *"You'll keep your mouth shut. And if I wanta see a dance, I'll come back here and I'll say, 'Dance!' And you'll dance, you fellas. You'll dance plenty!"*

Chief took Fiddler's arm and could have squeezed it in half.

"We'll go, Fiddle. We'll scram."

The eyes were prickled with tiny lights. The face paint-striped gaudy as a tiger's. Under the dust Chief's body glowed like a coal.

"You've got to have a shirt. A cop'll get us. They always watch for that." Brownie was in the pickup truck, all set to go.

Chief washed himself skimpily with a pail of water. In half an hour he'd be as bloody as the horse. He rinsed his mouth, permitting himself four big mouthfuls to actually swallow. Then he took off his belt, colorful like a beaded lizard, which he'd made himself, and gave it to Fiddler for safekeeping.

"I hired a guy," Brownie said. "And he's supposed to help you

now while Chief's with me. He's eating. I let him have a ticket.
I shouldn't have, 'cause now he'll never show; that's all he wanted.
But if he isn't here when you get back from lunch, you tell me
and I'll beat the living Christ out of him, playing me for a sucker
— if he's anywhere, I will."

The truck went.

The water had been heating in the sun. Only as you let the air
dry you did it cool. But even so, just bathing your arms was delicious. Fiddler's skin soaked up water like a frog's. He didn't want
to go to lunch. He took off his shoes and socks, rolled up his pants
and spilled water over his legs. This afternoon he was going to get
in that river and sit in it and have the current swing and swirl
around his waist and ribs. He'd be naked and he'd lie back and
there wouldn't be an inch of him that wasn't covered in the river.
He'd roll like a seal and he'd float and swim. He'd hold to the bottom by the water plants. Except for the soapsuds when he washed,
no one would know him from a fish.

● *Elmira, New York*

CHIEF WAS DRUNK too and making Fiddler sleep outside on top of the bear cage and watch the moon and the stars and the country go by. None of the comfortable floats were any good. This was the only spot on the train to get a decent view. Fiddler, being drunk as a lord, didn't argue. They climbed up there and found the hunchback whose cage it was already snug in the barrel that held the rain canvas and the catwalk running along the very top the only place left to lie, except on the naked bars. They tied themselves onto the narrow walk by their belts. Chief's feet were at Fiddler's head.

"Keep your hands on the wood," Chief warned. Fiddler was ready for sleep. He was dropping off — Chief's voice came out of a fog — when this stranger showed up.

"Watch out, you bears, or I'll wipe you out," he said as he climbed past the paws. His hair shone out red in the light of the quarter-moon. He carried a paper bag shaped like it had clothes in it and he didn't even look like he was with the show. But the catwalk was long enough for five or six people. The kid stretched out at Fiddler's end. Fiddler's mind felt like a spinning-school for spiders; the moon shrunk and grew; and goddam Chief started an argument.

"Ain't you got a belt? You ain't gonna stay on here without a belt! You're gonna bounce off! Ain't you got nothing you can use? Suspenders? You ain't drunk. You ain't got no business up here without being drunk!" He shouted across Fiddler.

"I like it. I like the looks of it, that's all."

"You're gonna roll right off here, an' them bears'll break your fall.

They'll have some fun. And when they're through you'll go under the wheels, without a belt."

The hunchback didn't need his, in the barrel, but he was the kind of guy who wouldn't have lent it to Abraham Lincoln. There was no use asking him.

"I heal fast," said the kid after a moment.

Chief and the train snorted in unison, and it got under way.

● *Williamsport, Pennsylvania*

> "Hey, girls!
> Primp your curls!
> I'm here!"

Somebody — who the hell? — was standing and waving at houses and cars.

"— Red Rooney's my name."

" 'Red!' You ain't red. *I'm* red! I'm a redskin. Ain't that right, Long Hair?" Chief shoved Fiddler with his foot to make sure he was awake. "Him, we don't know what to call him." Chief pointed. "Long Hair. Fiddler. — You shouldn't drink if you can't keep your hair cut, boy! You look like hell. And you didn't watch none of the scenery! What the hell didja think we came up here for? To watch the scenery! And you went to sleep! And you was even shivering in your sleep! You shouldn't drink if you get cold and go to sleep!"

The sky was pink and golden and everything was either very black or very green. Fiddler was fuzzy still, but a drink would clear that up. He wasn't trying to move yet, though. He didn't dare to try.

Chief got up and yawned and stamped to hear the bears and kicked the hunchback's barrel. "Wake up, Turtle. — We call him Snapping Turtle because he's like a turtle an' he snaps. But not at me, he don't. — Tcht-tcht-tcht-tcht," Chief went at the bears. They were up on their hind legs and clicking their claws on the bars, squeezing out their maneuverable tongues and lips. Willowy, snowy polar bears and Russian bears and Syrian bears and chummy bears from Vermont and Montana. One little cinnamon tyke the trainer had scooped into his car in Yellowstone Park last year. "Them bears didn't sleep," Chief said. "They smelled every mole in the ground."

Fiddler's muscles ached like after an injection. Ice grains sifted through them and prevented them from working. His bones ached also, and the back of his head was sore. The train was parked now, and he followed Chief and Red down to the flatcar. Every motion hurt like a blow from a stick.

"I feel good. — Wonder they stay so pretty." Chief nodded at a tinsely float a blood-smeared wino was crawling out of. "What's the town?" he shouted at a cop.

"LEMME SEE EVERY KID IN THIS TOWN!" he shouted more generally and in about ten seconds was looking at most of them.

"You know what a beer joint is?"

They did.

"I want a kid whose father runs a beer joint and who ain't afraid to get tanned."

There were two volunteers.

"Com'mere. I want the kid with guts, and he's gonna get to see the show today if I hav'ta bust him through the silver wagon and all the assholes in it."

When the two were under Chief, whooping he jumped from the train, grabbed each hard by an ear. One boy wilted.

"You ain't afraid of me?" he asked the other.

"Nope."

"Then you got guts. I want some beer."

Most everybody else seemed to want beer also — that is, ninety or a hundred kids. All sorts, rich ones, ragged ones, on bicycles and barefoot, they filled the road and followed as the boy with guts led the way.

"I ain't the circus! There's the circus." Chief pointed at the train. But they didn't take the hint. It was like being with Joe DiMaggio, or teaching school, except the kids were quiet. The traffic cop watched in blank astonishment. And more were joining the parade.

Chief didn't like it at all. He wasn't going to be trailed through

town by a hundred kids. "What the hell is that story?" He glared
at Fiddler. "You had an education. You musta read it." Then he
turned around.

"You ever read that story of that *Piper?* You know what happened to them kids? I don't remember; but I ain't no *Piper!* Beat
it!" He got a stick.

It took a little doing — they didn't go peaceably — but they went.
Chief ran 'em out. And still he wasn't satisfied. "An' you think
you're gonna tag along?" he said to Red.

"If it keeps lively."

"Lively! *I'*ll keep it *lively!* Livelier 'an you like, two bits. — Well,
you're all pale as milk, you three fellas, but you got some salt, huh?
You ain't scareda me yet, you town-boy?" The kid shook his head,
serious-faced. Chief jabbed Fiddler and Fiddler punched back.
"Even Big Hair here's got salt in him if he don't drink and if you
poke him enough."

The kid brought eight quarts of beer to split, and they sat drinking on the porch of some neighbors of his who'd gone to the crossing. Chief didn't talk much, so nobody else did. Chief drank fast
and seemed restless and dissatisfied. "You ain't any fun to drink
with," he told Fiddler and ignored Red completely. When the
townie boy had finished half his first bottle Chief took both away
to drink himself. "You'll get sick."

"Can you fight, kid?" he asked him after a while. "Can you work
hard? — Yeah? You go to school? — You stick at school. This
Long Hair was at school. It done him good, even if he looks like
hell now. This fella" (pointing at Red) "this fella hasn't had much
schooling. I can tell. You don't wanta be like that. — Can you
swim?"

"Sure."

"Where?"

"The river."

"Where?"

The kid said he'd lead them, but Chief made him tell the way,
and stood up disgustedly. "You ain't any fun to drink with, you
three. I never had so many kids." He looked them over. "Oh, I

got some kids around, but they don't know me. Their mothers hardly does — they *remember* me, but that's not the same. I was wild when I was the age of you fellas. Well, you done your job, town-boy. You gotta go home and rest up after it. You come around at showtime."

"I'm not tired."

"Get outa here! It's bad enough with one" — he thumbed at Fiddler — "and this other fella turned up, and that goddam Little Horse Indian Blackfoot. I ain't no *father!* Showtime you come."

They were three again. Fiddler would just as soon have had Chief get rid of Red now, but Chief didn't. Blackberries grew in the fields they crossed and they ate some. Chief turned over logs and found beetles as flashy as jewels. He caught a mouse and made it eat too.

The river looked slow and nice, its ripplings reflected on rocks. Mists were twined on the water. But Fiddler hoped he wouldn't have to swim. He was groggy from the beer. Red had taken his without showing it, just blinking and a little heavier in what he did. Chief was his usual self — busy. He threw stones that splashed far out insignificant on the water and sailed and skipped the flatter stones. He caught a frog and stroked its pulsing belly until the frog stopped squirming, stretched back its head and lay in a trance in his hand. Then he tossed it in to see if it would drown. It didn't. And Chief went on and threw handfuls of leaves and a whole birch branch into the current. Chief was quieter. He studied how things traveled in the air and how they floated, and dug to see how deep the mold and muck of leaves was before he came to clay.

"This ain't your country. You think it's yours, but it ain't. You fellas go to sleep," he told Fiddler, standing looking the river over — the bottom sloping sharply from the bank, the opposite shore with its stands of hardwood trees, and all along the layered toiling belts of current. Fiddler had a headache. He hoped Chief wasn't going to — he dreaded —

"Let's go swimming."

— That was it.

"Yeah," Red agreed.

Fiddler stripped with them and hid his clothes. Chief and he had swum together at Utica and Binghamton, so he couldn't say he didn't swim. The river was wide. He hoped they wouldn't try to go across.

The water was warmer than the air, but there were fingers of it plenty cold. It moved along faster than Fiddler'd expected, sometimes strongest under, sometimes on top. He tried to stay close to Chief in case of a cramp. His headache was worse. He wished he knew if Chief was going to have them swim across. Blackberries didn't mix with beer. This Red guy hardly knew how to dogpaddle, but he made out somehow without seeming awkward. It would be a long way for him too. It must be nearly half a mile.

The beer slopped around in Fiddler's stomach, brewing gas. He saw a bridge with bugs of cars each time he raised his face to breathe. The bridge was long. His stomach weighed fifty pounds and, out here, he had to try to keep himself from vomiting. They were so far now, obviously Chief was going across. The current was never impossibly hard, but, working against it, you gradually tired and tired like a fish on a line, and, swimming with Chief, you couldn't relax and land a little downstream from where you'd started — he made you swim straight. There was a small island a hundred yards from the shore they were heading for. Chief would stop, Fiddler was sure, and he set himself to last that far. It would be longer back to the shore they'd left than to that island.

The pains from the gas were getting worse. Fiddler was frightened. And the water wasn't water any more; it wasn't even wet. It was like heavy car grease. First the warmer currents lost their wetness. Finally even the cold ones got rubbery-dry as long balloons and as hard to swim in. Coming back, Fiddler was going to walk. This river must be over half a mile. He wondered what was saving him from cramps. His stomach bulged sore as a boil and he burped and burped. Chief didn't stop at the island. He went right on past it, way out in front of Fiddler and Red. Red was even a little behind Fiddler, but not having trouble. He just didn't know how to swim. Fiddler was mad, because *he* could swim fine! — but not with the middle of his body like he'd been kicked by a horse. Being mad took energy he couldn't spare. He settled himself to just surviving.

Aches and chills plowed through his body. Sure as hell he'd steal some clothes and take the bridge, coming back.

The bank was difficult. Fiddler was slow getting up it. He had trouble lifting his head. He was shuddering uncontrollably, fighting his stomach and on his hands and knees at Chief's feet.

"Can'tcha swim no better'n that? I don't wanta drink with you. This ain't a hard river! I seen you swim better'n that. You better quit drinkin' — wino. Goddam you better quit. Next year you're gonna drown!" Chief dived into the water again and groped under a log on the bottom. He pulled himself under it until just his feet and ankles showed, and then came up with a fat and angry muskrat by the neck.

"I'm gonna make me something from him." He felt for the knife in his pocket, and cursed because there wasn't any pocket. He laughed. "I'm gonna make me some britches."

"Let's not hang around here," Red said. He'd already gone several yards up a little trail through the grass. Fiddler wanted to lie down,, that's what he wanted to do; and he was cold.

"Some kid'll have a knife." Chief followed Red. — "What are you gonna do, puke?" Fiddler came along.

Red was poised like a setter next to a tree, motioning them up to him *quietly.*

A house was there, with a lawn and a barn and, near Red's tree, a flower garden. A couple of girls in the late teens were kneeling picking bouquets, maybe to go watch the circus with.

"What of it?" Chief demanded, hardly willing to whisper.

"We got ourselves some snatch!"

"You ain't got no clothes on, boy!" Chief was amazed.

"What d'ya want me to do, swim back and get 'em? They'll like it all the better." He tapped his palm. "They're in the glove." He stepped from behind the tree. The girls weren't facing Red, and he walked in one of the furrows; his feet made no noise.

Chief was scornful. "He's off his bean. They'll run."

Red lapped his lips and kneaded with his fingers meaningfully. Still the girls were unawares.

A dog was running at Chief and Fiddler, one of those confident, smart-aleck dogs that wouldn't stoop to barking, just ran, ran, and bit. Chief gave it the muskrat smack in the face. Dog and muskrat tangled with a *schree!-yee!-yee!* The girls turned, and there was Red a foot away and raw as a worm. They shrieked and tossed their scissors at him, shrieked again and ran.

"I'm not goin' to hurt, hey! I didn't have my clothes with me," Red pleaded, trotting after them. "Honest, I'm not goin' to hurt!"

A woman came to the door of the house with a coffeepot in her hands. She was calm, as if she thought the girls had maybe seen a caterpillar. But then the pot was in the air, awkward as a chicken flying. The woman was gone. Sooner than the pot had landed she was gone.

One girl raced straight for the house like a deer, but the other, since Red wasn't chasing too fast, peeked back and giggled — stopped to kick off her shoes. She headed more for the corner of the house, rubbing her sleeves.

A window smashed as an object was hurled through it. A new woman appeared in the doorway, with a stride of iron, and a man waddling (he was the woman of the two), and the first woman, behind, hopping up and down to see over them — the deer-footed girl trying to get past and inside. Somebody's shotgun took the gutter off the roof and made Red shy a little farther from the house. "Susan! Susan!" they were calling to the girl he was after.

"This town, we lay low," Chief said. He grinned.

Susan, reaching the end of the house, couldn't go on straight or she'd have gotten into some woods on the other side. And she didn't turn the corner and run around the house. She grabbed hold of a big shade tree and put herself on the far side of it. — Red immediately slowed up, as if he knew he mustn't frighten her now; it was crucial. Red flirted and skimmed like a dragonfly.

The people in the doorway couldn't see what was happening very well because of the angle of the house. The woman with the iron stride came out in the open, and the rest ran inside and were working at shutters and windows in places where they would be able to see. Not satisfied, again they rushed out, except for the terrified deer-footed girl.

Red had maneuvered his prize so that her back was to the house

— or maybe she'd done it — and had caught one of her hands around the tree and was pleading and coaxing while she smiled. The iron-footed woman started for Red, and Red began to prepare to scat. The other woman dragged a pail of water and splashed it wildly on the lawn. The man threw his gun to his shoulder and fired a barrel into the sky and had to reload. The juggernaut iron woman stomped towards the tree with nothing but her bare hands. Red kissed the girl's fingers and won a saucy wink. He slipped for the river. The deer-footed girl was covering her eyes at a window, and the muskrat was losing his fight. Chief and Fiddler didn't stick around.

There wasn't much question of walking back now. There'd be cops on that bridge. But the first, drooly touch of the water set Fiddler to shuddering. The mud sucked sickenly and the beer was like lead. An ache drilled back of his eyebrows, and he was more scared of the river than of the cops. Chief charged in like a brawling bear, high-flinging sparkles of water — for Fiddler a look that would have insulted a bug. Fiddler swam.

He didn't gradually tire. This time he was facing the sun every stroke when he lifted his head. It was a slam-bang chest-thumping sun, not far off the water, and hazzled his eyes. His mouth was filled with saliva, and he tried to push some out with his tongue. The water was just the same as the spit, though — the regular river water. He was swimming in drool. It was heavy and stuck to his arms. He knew he was going to drown. Brush floating knocked him. His head ached like his skull had shrunk, and teeth were biting and biting his stomach. Suddenly he had to take a leak so hard that it hurt and couldn't because he was swimming. He breathed half air and half water. His head ached viciously and felt soft, mushy-dissolvingly soft, as if it were seeping away in the water. Chief was letting him drown. His body was falling apart. He couldn't feel his legs at all, with the pain and the shuddering sick in his middle; only his arms were keeping him up. Even looking into the water flares were going off in his eyes and a black choking curtain blindingly thrashed in his head with a force to burst it apart. Now he was vomiting. Now he would drown.

Chief took Fiddler's hair and towed. It hurt wonderfully. Fiddler was glad it was long. It hurt in regular tugs, and he only wished it would hurt worse and bury the rest of the pain. He vomited, then not for a while, then again. His hair *really* hurt when he vomited, but not nearly as much as his stomach. Chief twisted his hair so his mouth would stay on the surface, and Fiddler struggled to keep himself high in the water. He hadn't many worries, though. He felt kind of good. He was coughing and fighting to breathe, but again and again and again he won.

When Chief let him go he could lean on the bank. Chief climbed out without helping any more, jumped up and down to dry and got dressed. Fiddler rested and then tried to haul himself out of the water. He couldn't. His hands slipped, and he floundered, swallowing scum. Plants pulled out by the roots, and he stepped on glass. The punishing sun glared in his eyes. The pain in his belly doubled him up and he took a leak and it felt like blood, and he wept now.

He might have been gorging on dung. "You're as good as dead, wino." Chief left.

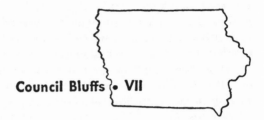

Council Bluffs • **VII**

THE COOKHOUSE smelled mostly of coffee, when it smelled of anything besides the constant breeze that blew under the tied-out sidewall loaded with the scent of miles and miles of prairie summer grass. Ham-hocks-and-sauerkraut and mac-and-cheese were the choice. The sauerkraut had a nippy odor and the cheese's was rich and sour, but you had to get close to the table to smell them, the wind was so lively. The coffee steamed in tall scalding tin pitchers. Coffee was all they gave you to drink. You couldn't even have water. And there wasn't any sugar spoon. Blood Bank used his slimy one just before Fiddler, and it made Fiddler feel a little sick. There weren't any napkins, either. And the oilcloth on the table was a dirt-smeared, white-of-eyeball white. Blood Bank coughed. Fiddler ate with an elbow on the table to protect his food.

On the other side of Fiddler was a fairly clean guy who, from his wary, mystified look, must have just joined, and wore a pair of *Ford* coveralls from his last job. Across the table were Flower, with the bobbypinned hair, and a couple of slobbery Train crew winos who maybe would wipe their mouths once during the meal if Fiddler was lucky. Fiddler ate steadily. He was hungry and the stuff wasn't bad — better than what the niggers got. If there'd been some water and dessert it would have been a good feed. He kept his eyes on his plate as much as he could, or on the waiters, since he didn't have to watch them eat. Both waiters were decent-looking. One was actually wearing a tie! A store-clerk bow tie and a white shirt, under the crummy, stained cookhouse jacket. Making believe he was living his old life. His partner made no pretenses about not being a bum, and was a sneaky stinker in a bar. But the guy had the remnant of what had been an intelligent face with quick, gray eyes, and now, sober, he was patient and soft-spoken with the men at the table, the deaf ones and the slow-wits.

Nobody was handing out twenty-dollar bills that Fiddler could see. He wouldn't have had the cat driver's scruples about not accepting the present, but he wouldn't have wanted to make up a phony story for it, either.

Some of the people at the table were so very foul-mouthed — every other word — if they'd been the last men on the whole earth they still couldn't have won themselves a girl. They'd felt what it was like to be starving. Why didn't they just eat?

Fiddler had been placed near the door, fortunately; he could look outside. Two water trucks were sprinkling the roadways, now that the big shots were about to arrive. A succession of townie sight-seeing parties peered in to find out whether circus people used knives and forks or ate with their fingers like cannibals. Fiddler busied himself eating, getting seconds, fourths, remembering to salt every-thing because of how he'd sweated. He made sandwiches of butter and jam. He was really hungry. Eating was going to take longer than he'd expected.

Blood Bank coughed and coughed. Fiddler hunched over his food.

"Can't you turn your head when you cough?"

Blood Bank, in the act of sucking in a mouthful, turned, all right. White grease was smeared on his chin and macaroni like a colony of maggots stuck to his lips as he began to chew. — His nose very nearly hit his chin! Munch! Munch! Fiddler was afraid Blood Bank's nose would be broken! No wonder he hadn't taken the ham hocks. Flower winked at Fiddler sympathetically. Wall-eyed Flower wasn't any joy to look at, though, himself. Fiddler was happy to see the buses coming. There'd be some girls on them to take his mind off everything.

The second-train people were brought directly from the crossing to have lunch. They ate in the Short End, behind a partition, off roomy plaid-covered tables ready to break down under a staggering array of sauce bottles and assorted jellies, coffee, milk and water pitchers, napkin boxes and desserts. Each day they arrived, self-absorbed, self-contained, in a whirl of joking and talking continued from the lounges of their railroad cars. Passing from the buses to the cookhouse, they wouldn't glance at anything. The lot was always just about the same as the one they'd left last night, except that now the sun was shining.

Clowns piled out first. They dressed like baseball bleacher fans — the clowns that weren't too fruity — and were almost as clean as townies, several shades lighter than anybody on the first train but Magee. Before twelve you could always tell if a man was with the circus in an instant by his skin, but after then sometimes you had to stop and see what his face was like. If he'd been kicked around a lot and obviously knew all the ropes, *all* the ropes, he was with the show. The clowns had been through every mill. Somewhere along the line they'd all been drunks, and missed being winos by a hair.

The dwarf clowns were much better able to take care of themselves than the sideshow midgets. They *did* take care of themselves; they swung out their stumpy legs in big strides. Everybody treated them as normal, and they didn't live off as freaks with other freaks. Seams in a dwarf clown's face had come from the same things as seams in anybody else's.

The performers looked European. A quality about their mouths and eyes seemed foreign. Hardly any of them spoke English. The boys and men grew their hair much longer than Fiddler's ever had been, and dressed like first-train people, instead of spending a dime. They only stayed a couple of years, and nobody got to know them — Fiddler couldn't have possibly, of course; but even bosses didn't get acquainted, and wouldn't have wanted to try. Most regular circus people, like Brownie, had no use for performers, said they were conceited nuisances. "Hooligans" was the show name for them. Fiddler didn't know what he thought. He admired the guts of some of those acts but couldn't recognize who was in them. A number of the guys getting off the bus had the foxy faces of daredevils, and just as many appeared cautious and grave. With performers the face wasn't a good indication. The daredevil killed time between shows bouncing across the fields at ninety on a motorcycle; that was the difference.

The stars were mainly in their twenties — straight-backed, healthy, buxom girls with rascally kid brothers they'd slap and tease and men with shoulders large as rolled-up mattresses and bulgy arms like giant-sausage strings. There'd be a mother, too, who'd come along from Europe to chaperon her daughters and supervise the family purse. Also a father, knotty and shrunk. And the stoic, ragamuffin youngest children tall as a table and already their bodies tough and fit like a champion's — the determination in their faces would have stumped a whole Gestapo. Seven or eight hours a day the family would train on some specialty, and a little of everything else: standing one-handed on stakes, walking wires or even a guy line, being flip-flopped off a springboard way up to perch, sisters on brothers, in a living totem pole. Whenever you happened to glance their way they'd be practising something, always together in a family and without mercy on themselves. The kids worked harder than anyone else, since they had everything to learn. Probably they worked harder than any grownup in the circus — certainly they took a greater beating. The twenty-to-thirty-year-olds seemed to go easier. They were at their glittering peak and anything they couldn't do most likely was impossible. The old people were stern like the ten-year-olds, being almost in the position of parents giving a spanking — "It hurts me worse than it does you." They were responsible for everything and could only live vicariously. But they were quite successful, after all. You looked at the girls, and every single one was pretty — *every single girl!* If the parents could do that so nicely, what couldn't they control?

The wiry well-groomed lion trainer, leashing himself with a struggle, stepped from the second bus guiding a long-stem bathrobed blonde by the lily hand and trailed by a chorus line of blonde, brunette and redhead beauties. Fiddler poked his fork into his lip. He quickly didn't want to watch — it made him feel as dead and seedy as a flophouse janitor — but he couldn't help himself.

The girls had polished nails and penciled eyes like movie stars.

They behaved like movie stars, except that movie stars, when you saw them, were usually trying to act the part of ordinary people. The ballet girls did anything but that. Some dyed their hair a preposterous flaxen and sported sunglasses like divorcees, looking about that rough. The lipsticked lips might be the only features you could fix on in the face, the rest being like a slightly rumpled napkin. And there were nice girls too. — At least from the faces you'd judge they were nice: from the bodies you'd judge they were dreams.

Most of the girls walked apart from each other and not as pals in a bunch like men. That was their job, walking, and naturally it was each babe for herself. In the whole bus Fiddler couldn't spot a dress. Sandals, slacks and pullovers or peasant blouses, or bathrobes and bathing suits and blush-pink sneakers were what they wore. No lace, no trimmings, just the tightly outlined curves. They had their hair in pony-tails and nets and teasing-cute in braids, and carefully they crossed one foot before the other as they walked to jut their hips. Their eyes went every way but Fiddler's, and yet they made him feel no better than a beggar jig; he tingled with shame. How clean they were. Petals were no cleaner than the girls' skin. It might have been glazed.

Every type of pretty girl he saw. Some were rowdy kick-'em-highs and some petite, demure as Goldilocks. Alongside callous icicles and man-haters, next-door good-sport chicks. Tumbly-breasted young things brazen in the first-flush triumph of being hired, and veterans with settled, well-grounded attractions, and still older, mask-faced charmers, heavily powdered, each itemized point of their looks chiseled into them deep as the grooves in a crocodile's hide. Mean-mouthed fun girls. Serene beautiful belles he'd remember aching months if they didn't cancel out each other. Tall, V-faced, high-strung strippers and lush, lame little bedroom broads. Molls with a dim, mad stare as if they were doped and money-money slum girls whose watchful features had been starved irretrievably sharp. Two or three fantastic-sashed exotic creatures who even wore high heels! High heels — in a circus! Every kind of girl, and each had her pocketbook crammed with compacts and brushes for keep-

ing nice and changed her clothing several times a day. A butterfly
grazing her arm would make her feel dirty. — And Fiddler! If
Fiddler'd touched one of the girls he'd have left a filthy smudge!
Seeing him must disgust them; that was why they never looked his
way — him and these other gray-skinned bums.

Really, girls were the more co-ordinated sex. Look at how they
walked! Every motion thought out and perfectly controlled, accomplishing a dozen things at once, the least of which was covering the
ground. It wasn't amusing to watch, no more than crack commandos
passing, or presidents of banks. The ballet girls were tops — so
flawlessly sex-supercharged it numbed; watching from the circus
bleachers would feel better. They pushed back their shoulders to
lift their breasts and shook out brooklets of gleaming hair. They
might have been hobbled — twelve-inch steps — and sexy anklets
tinkling, cute sandal straps, miracle legs contriving to show off
those contoured morsels of flesh and at the same time act as motors
for the pay-dirt hind ends' juicy, wobbly bubblings-out in twin and
slinky globes.

The only trouble was, if anything was in the way — a little stone,
even — that fouled them up. They were like four-year-olds, navi-
gating then.

Hands so small, delicate steps, ivory throats, porcelain skin, waists
a man's hands could meet around. — The circus had a rule that
anyone in Fiddler's section of it could be fired for trying to talk to
one of the girls. It wasn't a very necessary rule. Red wouldn't have
tried it. Fiddler wondered who was "human," bums like himself
and Blood Bank, or the ballet girls. They couldn't both belong to
the human race. Not at the same time.

Brisk behind the girls came the sourpuss short toughs in wide
Palm Beach suits who bossed something or other that started late
and chewed cigars and owned exclusive rights to at least one of the
girls. Then baby-blue-uniformed ushers with arrogant, I-know-my-
way-around expressions — schleazy bastards grafting twenty bucks
a day; they had their tarts too. And a fancy-plumed girl trapezist
who'd been a hungry dirty-neck thumbing into winter quarters not
so long ago. And a couple more European girls with gypsy knacks of

dressing which looked wholesome next to some of the ballet girls. And a paunched trick rider going under the title of "Brazilian," though he was really a jig, Brownie said. And the ringmaster, who wore his costume night and day and hadn't quite learned how to speak cultivated yet. More girls, in too tight T-shirts. More bosses, this time the lank type with hats almost as fine as a fireman's and the stature of Texans but who, even in Texas, could never be mistaken for a townie; they had CIRCUS stamped all over them. And a crowd of prosperous hangers-on, twitty and flitty and wearing panties underneath their pants. And, in the midst of all the sharpie-showgirl faces, two squirrely hooligan kids jabbering Italian like women on a phone.

One wino in the cookhouse wasn't toothless. He proved it. He took his choppers out and licked them clean before he left. Fiddler nearly lost his lunch. He'd stayed too long. He'd been hungry, but he should have eaten faster. Here Blood Bank too was almost finished, with all the problems he had eating. The townie kids cleaning up to earn a pass were getting close. They clattered the dishes, showing off, and practised how to swear.

Several sparrows were taking a bath in the dry dirt checkered by the cats. They acted as much at home as if they traveled with the circus regularly, puffing dust and twirping.

Boston and Edith had their heads under the fringe of the big top and were cradling them on the sidewall, rubbing their chins. They were wistful and cute, and could see Omaha.

The big top flags swirled with a long undulance like eels swimming. And a high bird glided lone and grand, with a lilt that proved it wasn't a plane.

Sharp-angled tops like the jigs' and the blacksmith Chief's looked rakish in the wind like Arab tents. It was appropriate to have a bunch of wild men living in them.

White was the right color for the horse tops. White canvas when it weathered never looked bad, and the horses were black, many of them, or roan or some brown or candy color which the white set off.

Ringstock didn't take their sidewalls very seriously. They didn't pull them very high and tied the bottoms out as far as they would go, so that the sidewalls slanted like sails and you could see everything inside.

The horses were lying down, the men asleep beside them, on the huge, abundant beds of straw. You practically had to *climb* into the horse tops, the boss was so free with his straw. It was a smug department — the fat horses proud of being fat and the trim ones proud to be trim, and the sidepoles whittled with sly nibble marks next to the ground as if there were beavers, in spite of the big shots' frowns. These circus horses lay down much more of the time than any townie horses Fiddler had seen. One reason was, their nights were not too restful on the train; but mostly they were just smart, that was all. Smart and smug. And if they weren't lying down the horses would be hazing visitors, threatening to kick — if a horse was standing on three legs, it was sure not to be the one it wasn't standing on it kicked with — and giving people the eye, or else a fishy stare. Their own Ringstock men weren't immune — nearly all were partly crippled. Whenever a guy healed up till he could move a little too fast and spoil the horses' fun, they'd kick him strategically just enough so he wouldn't want to move that much again. They'd play tricks, like all tossing their heads at once so it couldn't be stopped and watching it made everybody dizzy, and keeping it up until people were gradually stumbling, blinking and sitting down, and keeping it up until everybody was flat on his back covering his eyes (the Ringstock men were glad to lie down, their legs were so bruised). Then the horses would lie down themselves and go to sleep, after the exertion.

Even the men picked up the smugness, even the winos. When they strolled around only their arms below the elbows swung.

To see all that straw made Fiddler sleepy — corn-yellow where the sun tipped it and, back a ways, curved cool into shadowed hammocks — the top a complacent, halo white, almost as low as a bedcanopy, and the horses' heads snuggled down on their knobby knees and the men collapsed like sacks. He yawned enviously.

The horses didn't yawn. Maybe they stretched all the way out, so that the wrinkles went out of the skin on their backs and they rested their heads out of sight in the straw.

Why yawn?

No horse fretted so much as an ear when Fiddler's driver brought the act lions past.

The lions were different. The lions wheeled in boiling chesty charges at the bars. They jerked their paws and *uh*ed as if at a punch in the stomach. Over each other they leapt and rushed cage corners, shifting their feet like people trying to get by an obstacle in a doorway. The wagon was built on a different plan from the menagerie wagons. It had open bars on all sides. The lions liked it that way, throwing challenges in all directions. They did that now, in case there should be something else that planned to kill those horses, and turned with an erupting energy, so it was a wonder the floor didn't get trompled right out of the cage.

Through the lions' flexing legs Fiddler watched the horses — dozing.

Townies had been looking at the horses, and they got excited, like the lions, thronged for the cage, oohed and pointed from the horses to the lions to the horses. Old people clutched at relatives to keep from being pushed down. The townies were confused because the cage was moving and they didn't know whether they wanted to chase it or not. They'd run a few steps, stop, run a few more, arms paddling like chickens' wings, stop, run, stop. Or else they'd hurry and hurry and hurry, and find they'd misjudged how fast the wagon was going. Or, some — parent and such — would get self-conscious about being seen running and stop and try to make everybody else self-conscious.

Still, through the milling townies and the lions, the herd of horses slept.

A boy ran beside the cage trying to work up nerve to touch it. He didn't dare, so, instead, he got a rock and threw it at the lions. Fiddler got another rock and threw it at the boy. He scored just under the right hip. The kid could hardly walk. Some of the rest of the townies didn't like that, but the driver cut his motor quick and came busting off the cat with a monkeywrench as if he were back

in Tennessee and having a feud. What a temper he had! You could
see the air get out of his way! And the townies scrambled; they
went to look at the horses again. But one of the Ringstock boys sat
up on his elbow. He was a harelip and had to pause to pucker —
   "Why 'on't you gate outa heeah?"
   That whole mob of townies did.
   Fiddler found no sign around the Animal tent of this new guy
Brownie had hired. Taylor hadn't seen him.
   "I ain't seen nobody. I been watchin', I been watchin' thum cops
and dicks, all around; I seen one up a tree. Thir goina raid. I told
'um I don't know no Chief. Thir goina come in here an' none of us
is goina live! Don't shake ya'r billy at me! I ain't done nothin'! I
served my time. Don't know him! *Don't know him!*"
   "I wasn't asking about cops," Fiddler muttered, leaving.
   Red must have gotten a girl. He was sitting with somebody just
inside the big top sidewall, in back of the rhino cage. It was a nice,
secluded place; Fiddler only saw their feet. He recognized Red's
socks because of the nude pinups on them — Red's don't-let-your-
mind-wander-baby socks. The other feet were bare and sort of
special, looked like a girl's. The sidewall stirred enigmatically, and
Fiddler's curiosity was roused. He went to ask if Red had seen the
guy.
   " 'Fraid I haven't, Fid," Red said. The girl wasn't any peach;
Fiddler was relieved. She was the dark, large, homely kind that no
one ever dated in high school, the kind that would be very active in
the band. Putting her hand on Red's shoulder seemed to give her a
thrill. Red looked good, his best. He was smoking, and even the
way he lipped the cigarette was individual and sheik. But then —
below his head — the grubby clothes spoiled it all.
   For Fiddler's benefit, Red kissed the girl, casually, as if there
would be lots of time for passion later. He seemed to time his
breaths with hers, though, which maybe meant hers smelled bad.
   The sidewall let in a little sun, and pushed some of it out, and
let more in, cutting it off, and let more in, so that, once you got
used to the constant wavering of the light according to the breezes,
the ground took on a magic, dimly sunlit color, a mild yellow, as if

the light had sifted like water through sand. A tender green of early spring was in the grass. There wasn't a better place in the circus to bring a girl. Above the ground it was almost like twilight. The rhino was the only witness. — And here was this sad sack. The collar of her dress drooped like a skunk cabbage leaf. She had glasses, on a pointed nose like a radish. Red reached over and took off the glasses, but it didn't work any miracles. Poor Red — his face all lighted up with the pride of having finally caught a girl, and then to have her be a dull mushroom like that. He never looked at her if he could help it.

Fiddler stooped to go under the sidewall, but, hearing Red clear his throat, glanced back. Red's cigarette was tilted so that the bottom two-thirds lay on his tongue. After checking his audience, Red drew it into his mouth. Then he kissed the bag again, leaning back, luxuriously breathing smoke from his nose. Unhurriedly he straightened up and brought out the cigarette, still on his tongue.

Fiddler needed a helper mainly for carrying the bales of straw to bed down the cages with. Almost everything else he'd rather have done by himself. Since there wasn't time to waste he started alone, toting the hundred-pound bales on his shoulder one at a time. He went in by the giraffe pen, and friendly Edith and Boston bowed down their heads to sniff what he had. The monkeys cheeped and hung on the bars because it was time for Red to bring in their food: if Fiddler was coming maybe Red would be too.

By the time he got the second bale into the big top Fiddler was hot and tired. He set it down beside the pen, held up his hands and snapped his fingers. The giraffes were leery. They liked Fiddler, but even so it seemed he had to tame them all over again from scratch each time. He cupped his hands by his chest as if he had something.

Boston was the most daring. Boston's head meandered a couple of feet above Fiddler's, inspecting things from every angle with those sloppy-big, all-brown eyes. Automatically his ears laid back at each neck stretch. Then out stuck the purple tongue, reaching down. Boston licked Fiddler's cheek and nosed and nibbled his ear like a cracker. Pretty soon Edith was doing it too. She cleaned the other side of his face. They realized now he hadn't any food, but went ahead and licked. Coca Cola was no good. Two or three much better giraffe men had come and gone already, since Albany. The giraffes appeared to want to trust at least one person, so they were using Fiddler.

Being licked was one thing, but *doing* the touching was another. They were edgy any time their heads were low. The thought of being trapped down there frightened them. Also, the long face bones looked very fragile. When Fiddler raised his hands both heads were tossed up smartly. Boston let his swing partly down and flung it up again. Fiddler stuck his hands as high as he could and was patient; he had to be. It was like waiting for two limbs to blow a certain way. Boston and Edith drifted around, to the water, the manger, crossing their necks and eying the row of elephants snobbishly. Giraffes were very proper animals, always so high above the rest of the world; and they never made a sound to anybody. They'd sneeze, that was all, and turn their backs at the slightest excuse. Fiddler kept hoping maybe as they got to know him better things would change — they'd let slip a few "remarks" like any other creature and not get snooty if he had to spit.

Boston chewed with a scissory sidewise motion, like a man alternately talking out both corners of his mouth. He chewed on a mouthful of hay over Fiddler, being very careless about dripping and dropping, and, when he was through, considered going back to the manger — waved like a teetering pole — but, instead, curved his head down by stages until his moist breath tickled Fiddler on the arms and neck and his ears came level with Fiddler's fingers. Fiddler knew he mustn't touch the ears.

Nothing happened for so long Fiddler's arms were trembling with exhaustion. Boston's tongue tasted his elbow, turned aside like a worm burrowing and poked the air halfheartedly. Finally the bun-shaped mouth got down to business — nuzzled his palm, the hairs as short and tickly as fleas, while the tongue sopped after salt. But when Fiddler began to bring his fingers closer together the face withdrew disdainfully until again the incredible tongue was out as far as it would go, getting the last of the salt, before it, too, left him.

Somebody hoisted the sidewall, lurched under, thudding the ground with his feet, and let the canvas slam down behind him. Liquor reeked from the guy. Boston's head shot up. His legs kicked with a delayed, progressive, grasshopper action — his heels fairly snapped — and his round small belly floated high like a beachball. Long and purposeful like a flying duck's his neck stretched, and he went with a rocking gallop. Fiddler was dizzied holding a column of empty air, as if he'd been swinging on a branch and had it hurtle from his hands. Boston's head swam to and fro unhappily with Edith's fourteen feet up.

"Goddam, what the hell is that? What the hell is that!" thwacked a drunken voice. "Cold up there? Huh? Hah-hah-hah-hah-hah-hah! I'll feed you. I'll feed all you animals."

"What the hell are you, you stupid bastard! Where the hell do you work?"

"Are you the man with the straw? The man with the straw? Yes, there she is. Why, the crazy man said you wanted me. Jesus, he is crazy, isn't he? Huh? Hah-hah-hah-hah. You said it."

A wino! A goddam wino Brownie had hired, a wino!

"I don't want you." Fiddler picked up the straw and started for the cat line, when suddenly the bale tipped on his shoulder so he had all he could do to keep it from falling forward and the straw stubs scratched against his cheek. The wino was trying to carry the back half, pushing it above his head because he was shorter than Fiddler. Fiddler threw the whole thing on the ground.

"What in the hell is the matter with you? I don't want you! Can't you hear?"

"Nope, I was told to help you. I do my work. Anything you say I'll do. I do my work. But you're not the boss, you can't fire me, I do my work."

"Look," Fiddler said. "You can do this. You can get the water and the watering pans and the scraper, if you want to do something. The 'crazy man' will show you. And then you'll have done your share, and I won't want you any more, but nobody'll fire you." Fiddler turned away.

"I'm sorry," quacked the wino. "I don't ask crazy people any questions. Any questions. *You* show me what you want and I'll get them. I do my work. You're a nice, innocent boy and I'm glad to work with you, and I'll do what you tell me. I'll do. But crazy people I stay way, way away from."

It was enough to make you blow your stack. Fiddler burst out, "You take this! and put it behind that far cage! and I'll get them! and then I won't want you!"

Shakily the wino caught his hand.

"Okay. Steven L. Diamond's my name. That's how I sign checks. What's yours?"

"David." Fiddler wouldn't be stopped again.

"I sent the guy," Taylor said, out at the tent. He was cutting his animals' vegetables and his words were punctuated by the plunkings of carrot disks and beets into the pail. "He's straight. He ain't just out. I looked at his stuff and his shoes. They can get a tan, but they give ya ya'r stuff; ya can't change ya'r stuff, when ya leave. Mine were small. I told the guy, and he tuk that whip and give it ta me like I'd hit a screw. — 'Ya think ya're out?' Right at the gate; they tied me ta the gate. . . . " Taylor craned his neck to watch Fiddler through the door and continue talking at him. He didn't lift his voice, of course, so Fiddler didn't have to listen. Lots of people in the circus talked to themselves, and told hair-raisers, but most of them would be embarrassed when you caught them at it. They pretended to be humming.

Point was all Fiddler did and Nigas trotted from under the wagon, wagging his tail extra strongly to show his thanks. Fiddler set down the great, cat watering pan and Nigas approached it with the dignity of Joe. He brushed Fiddler's legs affectionately and straddled his shoes, drinking, to prove his trust. On a two-day stand when everybody else got tanked up Fiddler was the one he'd come to. Just like any townie dog, Nigas could feel lonely.

" . . . . You ast him! You ast that trainer where he gets his whips. The pen! Second-hand. That's where. . . . " Taylor was a gauntlet to be run.

The straw lay exactly where Fiddler had left it. Diamond was over conferring with Julius. He'd been given a cup of juice and was

peering at it as though something had fallen in, a bug, or a dime —
finders keepers — one beer; no, one wine, for a wino.

"Put somepin in it? Please? Have you got a pint? It'd be so
good with somepin in it, somepin added special." Diamond's tongue
peeped pleadingly between his lips.

Julius was trying to arrange the usual deal. "The boys generally
bring me a few cups after the show, cups people leave around. When
they finish drinking they leave the cup, because it isn't any use to
them, and the boys bring me the cups which haven't been crushed.
And of course when I give anybody a drink he gives me back the cup
when he gets through. It helps out. I wipe them off so that they
look the same as new; they *are* the same as new."

Fiddler with an elaborate, simmering calm explained: "Julius
means, the only way they have of checking up on how much he
sells is by the cups. That's what the boss goes by, the number of
cups. So he likes it if you bring him cups he can use over again. The
boss doesn't know, and he doesn't have to give him any share."

Diamond spat in the drink and shook it up, watching the saliva
disappear. Julius was agonized, half grasping for the cup. Suddenly
he wasn't sure if Diamond would co-operate. Fiddler wished he
could say something crushing, make fun of them both, but neither
one seemed capable of laughing at the other, and Fiddler couldn't
think of much. He didn't blow up. He went back to where he'd
left the stuff. It was all right. It would be better doing everything
himself. Diamond would only be a lot of trouble.

"Be a sport. Come on, please put somepin in it for me tasty."

The cup was enclosed in Diamond's hands and Julius couldn't
get it. He glanced at Fiddler bitterly. He jerked his head, formed
"Drunks!" with his lips. Fiddler was supposed to sympathize.

When Diamond saw Fiddler carrying the bale, "Wait! Wait!" he
cried, and crumpled the cup, spurting the liquid onto Julius. Heed-
lessly Julius snatched, but only got a worthless wad. Diamond hurried to Fiddler.

"No! Don't mess me up. You get the water if you want to do
something."

"I'm on the job, Dave. I'm no loafer."

Fiddler wanted to throw the whole hundred pounds right on the guy. "See where I left the water? Go get it. — Go get it!"

The day's heat was getting Fiddler down again; and this wino would have to go. There was lcts to be done before Doors. Fiddler would have to work right along.

Opening the rear of the lion cage socked him onto another planet. He didn't move for a while, and it hurt to breathe. His mind went woozy; he couldn't have smiled. The nerves up his back were ready to squeal. To the quicks of his nails he was scared.

They weren't doing anything, Bessie and Joe. They weren't goofy over a bunch of horses or striding around like upset tigers. They weren't even on their feet, in fact. But the pungent, lion, head-swimming scent came through the overlying smell of the bulls like a storm, the bars melted away like streaks of rain, and Fiddler was face to face with a pair of lions as silent as mountains, as plains. They gave him only the most cursory part of their attention. He couldn't crack a joke with them; they wouldn't laugh, like a dog. They weren't curious about him, as even the most formidable ape would have been. They wouldn't have sneezed to have him dead. He didn't bore them — they were scarcely conscious he existed. What they *were* thinking about he couldn't imagine. He never could, with the lions. They weren't half so active as the tigers, half so shifting-moody, and yet opening the tiger cage didn't carry half the shock.

You got used to the tigers: sometimes almost sloe-eyed, sometimes their pupils flinty specks of triangles, when they were mad and in the light. But basically they looked the same: the weaving hierogly-phic markings on their heads, the white eyebrows and fluffs of black and yellow, the body stripes, always with a curve, starting from the backbone thin and black and ending on the belly wide and gray. They couldn't change their stripes.

The leopards were classic cats, more unchanging than the tigers. They were like displays. Set, perfect heads, ears the right size, the down-sling of the underlip the perfect curve.

— But the lions! God knows how they'd be. Joe looked slab-sided and ascetic as a saint now; and in the morning he'd been untidy,

with a bay window. His spacious face was more complex than any
human's — the scoured brow ridge series, the lines down the cheeks
and nose, and the brown dot where every whisker grew. On the
rear of his lip he had the same frilled edging as the big top! The
higher you looked on Joe the more there was to see, from the toe
tufts up the starkly tendoned legs to the tousled uncountable strands
of his mane. Bessie was more business — an athlete, or, right now,
with that flat, chunked, lioness head, a thug. Sometimes her body
seemed longer than at others. When it was really short she looked
mean; if it got very long she'd almost seem like a lady. — The
prissy tigresses were always ladies. That was another difference.
Bessie would slurp when she drank. They never did. And she'd
make up her mind whether she wanted water and stick to her decision either way, instead of switching back and forth like a fickle
female. And she didn't fly off the handle if Joe bumped her, as
though her makeup had been mussed.

Being in a cage constricted the lions more than the other cats.
They didn't move much or find ways to enjoy themselves. And yet
you were seldom able to feel sorry for them. They didn't pine. Just
lying there and not trying, they packed the power to make you
never in your life forget what lions were. Loose-open mouths hot
as steam.

"No! Them?" Diamond goggled. "I'm seein' stars. That isn't
what we do! *Them!*"

Fiddler put armfuls of straw up to the cage and pushed with his
elbows and fists. The trill of laughter-feeling in his chest from the
danger he enjoyed. Once it was free from the bale the straw was
light and carrying it was fun — he pretended he was "tucking the
lions in" for a nap. The straw itself was some protection, covering
his hands, and Bessie and Joe were glad to have it, although they
weren't going to move to help him out.

Joe rested his paws on their sides and, as the straw got between
them, lifted his chin like a man with a tight collar. Every time
Fiddler touched him he stirred slightly in the opposite direction,
gazing out the front of the cage and pointedly ignoring Fiddler.
Fiddler prodded him, but that was no good. Joe growled and Fid-

dler's hand jerked away of its own accord and then wouldn't function. The cage was like an organ — Joe didn't want to have to growl
again — the sound boomed, starting so fast you couldn't get ready,
like the prelude to a landslide. You couldn't listen to it with your
eyes open, or with your eyes closed, or with your fingers in your
ears — you couldn't get your fingers to your ears. Diamond had
fallen to the ground.

The growl died down.

There were tricks, though. Fiddler laid a mound of straw in the
corner where Joe could see it and stuck a little more under Joe's
tail and scratchy against his hind legs. This time Joe only groaned
at being touched, with an air of what's-the-use got up. He went to
the corner, backed and squatted and solemnly kicked and kicked
his hind feet, making a place to wet.

Tough Bessie glared hideously over Fiddler's head. Let one
finger get too close and bone would be showing down it. For all
their tearing around and stretching after you. Bessie was worse
than the lady tigers.

". . . . Creatures that'd freeze your blood! — that's what this job
is!" Diamond mumbled. "I'm drunk, f'r God's sake! That's a lot
to expect of an old bum comin' in off the streets like me. They'd
love to kill me!"

"Swell. Go away. I told you I don't want you."

"No. No, I'm sticking. I've lost my last job" — Diamond began
to climb to his feet — "my last one. I mean by that I'm not going
to lose any more; I've lost the last one I'm going to lose. I'll stick it
out. You can't go on losing jobs and losing jobs. — Ain't you afraid
of those things?"

"If they were out maybe I'd be scared, yes."

"If you're not afraid of those things you're crazy, after what
they've done to your hands. Those would sell for hamburger. Hamburger! Huh? Hah-hah-hah-hah-hah." Diamond followed Fiddler
to the next cage.

Pasha and Mabel were at the exhibition side because the fresh
air was there, but when Fiddler opened the back they came, looking
to see what he had.

"Straw for my honeys."

"Huh?" Diamond had run several yards away.

"Shut up!"

Scuffing his feet, Pasha lay down. Mabel was nervous, being exposed on both sides, and Fiddler was the cause of it and she was mad. She seemed kind of small, though — well able to pull off a head, but not colossal like Pasha. Her face was rather hesitant, the way she peered every which way and, washing her nose on her paw, stopped again and again to check what Fiddler was doing. Her nose was too long for her face to seem invulnerable. Somebody walked by the front of the cage, and Mabel did a pirouette, whirling and sidling to stand in the straw by Fiddler's hands, forgetting he was there. He pinched her ankle, and wow! was she mad! He might have bit her foot off, she stumbled so, and snapped as if his fingers were still pinching. And then she sssssssssssed, until her hatred choked it into an almost inaudible *Hing!*

Pasha's form was like a drowsy bull; his shoulder bones humped out. His close-set eyes gave him the nearsighted look of a bookkeeper and he bent, poring over something on his folded paws. — Mabel stirred him up. She scratched his behind. Pasha rose like a warrior, so that anyone but Mabel would have quailed. — She cared not a hoot. Pasha soon remembered why; he settled himself in his old position, but watching her as if she were a little nuts — *he* hadn't pinched her, after all — and snarling when his stung part brushed the wall.

"Those guys have fun. They've got a bottle and everything." Diamond pointed into the dark under the bleachers at the Seat men.

"You stay away from them, now," Fiddler laughed. Birds of a feather. Diamond wasn't quite as bad, though. He couldn't be pushed around, and there was a certain independence in the way he stood, as if he were sort of getting up his nerve. But why hadn't he bought himself a shirt that fitted, and shoes that weren't about to crumble off his feet, and underpants, and pants that didn't have strategic holes? He was a drunk, skin a winy battered red, eyelids drooping like with sleeping sickness. His voice sounded like boards hitting together, and his face was chopped up from shaving probably with nothing but the water at outdoor drinking fountains. He couldn't even keep his head from tilting to one side. He must have gotten liquor in his ear.

Diamond turned back toward Fiddler and winced at the tigers.

"I was going to see my boy, but, hell, he wouldn't want to see me. The way I am. He's near here. Boys' Town, Nebraska, that's where he is. He's one of their leading citizens. I was going, but he'd be better off not seeing me."

"Don't tell me your story."

"No. I won't. So I'm throwing in with you instead. And I'll make good. And then next year when we come to Nebraska I can see him and he won't be ashamed."

"Nobody lasts a year. Chief and Brownie, that's all. Most people last a week, and better ones than you. Now will you not bother me, please? You've done your share."

"No. No. You can't fire me and I don't quit. I'm an honorable man. I can stick. I'll stick this one out. But this ain't dishwashing you know. I've had tough jobs before; but these're killers! So goddam dangerous it'd freeze your blood!"

"Shut up. Go away! I don't want you!"

Mabel took a leak and Pasha sniffed with relish where she'd left her blood-smell. That's what he'd been waiting for. His lips might have been burned, they lifted so high. The whole red curve of his gums showed. His teeth didn't chatter, like a dog's would have. He just held up his lips in a caricature of a grin, as though his gums, too, were smelling organs. And the enormous, bristling head hovered and bobbed to catch the rising tendrils of the scent. Chief liked to do the same when he thought about Pinito.

Mabel sat before Fiddler, their differences forgotten. She shook herself as a baby would, for the fun of it, and fixed her eyes on places, twisting her head till everything was upside down. When she got tired of that, she looked steadily at Fiddler and began shifting her weight on her forepaws, sliding them down until they were flat, then working forward on her elbows until her paws extended through the bars and she was lying looking at him — past him, thoughtfully.

Mabel drank with her feet drawn under her, turning her eyes here and there on the water like any other placid cat. When her mind wandered her lapping slowed, and then would speed up, as she glanced to see if Fiddler had moved to take the pan away. Specks in the water made her curious. She was gentle, happy, and the little tongue harmless as milk — Fiddler wanted to hug her. Crouched, her body rounded into a nicer shape for hugging even than a woman's.

Fiddler brought the pail to put more water in the pan. Mabel watched the splashing quietly enough, eying him appraisingly to see if he'd be smart and try and get her wet. She didn't want another whole panful, though. He kept pouring and pouring so Pasha could have some after her. Mabel didn't think about Pasha and she didn't trust Fiddler enough to drink while he poured. — She got impatient, made an ugly face, part hissing, part snarling. But something in his hair or on his forehead caught her interest and she stopped, like lemon juice the creases draining from her lips. Then they were back. Her eyes rolled like a plane dipping, snapped back an instant to his forehead and, finding nothing now, plunged reveling at Fiddler's. She rapped the pail, snarled. That's all. No clawing attempt, no roar. But she didn't take her paw off the pail. Fiddler could hardly keep the water from spilling and *really* getting her mad. He couldn't move the pail at all. Her claws were stronger than his arms. He tried to hold it as a shield, but he couldn't even move it. And the water was still pouring.

Mabel looked him up and down like a cop with a robber and squiggled her claws. Periodically she gave the pail a jolt to remind him who was boss.

"What shall I do, Dave?" breathed Diamond, sounding almost sober. He'd fallen on all fours again. "Shall I run for the boss?"

"She does this a lot," Fiddler said, and Mabel grimaced silently. Her claws eeched almost to his fingers on the metal; but with the momentary letup in the pressure he was able at least to stop the water pouring. It was a good thing. The pan was on the point of overflowing on her feet.

Mabel did a double take. No water pouring? She removed her paw.

Diamond was slumped over much as if he were weeping. "I've been in fires. I've had tough jobs. But these're killers! These will eat you! Eat you! This ain't dishwashing. It's an awful lot to expect of a bum. You're crazy, you're crazy if you're not scared! But I've had tough jobs. I want you to know. I want you to know. I can stick."

Between Diamond's pants and the end of his shirt was a sizable belt of skin, not clean. He must have gone a couple of weeks. "Why don't you take a bath?" Fiddler suggested. "Brownie's away, and I'll say you were helping me."

"I'm *sticking!* There ain't anything worse than fires, ain't anything, and I've been in them. So I can stick. I want you to know, because if we're going to work together I want you to know. I was out of work and it was on the radio to sign up and. . . ."

Fiddler decided to be a good boy and play it safe at Snippy's cage. He'd take the pan out before refilling it. — And he started to. Snippy lapped at the last few drops faster and faster with a worried frown. She thought he was taking the pan permanently. And when he was so blockheaded as to keep on pulling it when he could see plainly she was still thirsty, she caught on with her teeth until the filthy rust flaked off in her mouth and raked the pan with her claws, shaking it up and down as if she were trying to flip flapjacks. Fiddler won because of the taste of the rust.

When he brought the pan back she drew it in like a kitten with a ball of twine — watchfully expecting it to have some diabolic motion of its own — and then resumed her usual drinking stance, one paw stretched before her, head fixed and high, as if she'd paused a moment, stalking. She wouldn't deign to look at anything not straight ahead.

". . . . He took us out right soon as enough had signed up for a crew. We were a crew. 'Pile in.' 'Pile in.' And we piled in that old stakeside and rode. And we rode. Believe it? — He was out there under the hood hangin' on fixing the motor. At sixty we were going. Downhill. Downhill. He was out there. He shut off the motor when we were going downhill so he could fix it! The smoke was miles, oh what a smoke! Black as hell, coming so fast like a train. You'd see, you'd see the flames go right up there into the smoke

just as black and just as red. At the same time. The same time.
And each red as big as a, as big as a, hotel. That's rough country.
We climbed hills, poor old motor whining away — she didn't want
to go to that fire. The boss pushed her as hard, as he could. And
she whined up those hills. We didn't really want to, once we saw
that smoke, either. And it sounded like trains. We couldn't have
drove faster than that smoke was coming. Just as black. Black means
it's heavy brush. And the flames right in it. They burned on *the
smoke!* But we couldn't whine about it. *We* couldn't." Diamond
paused for a hiccup or two like a chicken clucking.

Snippy rested as weightlessly on her feet as a plane on its wheels,
and the paw out in front was the pose of a queen. How had she
picked that up, Fiddler wondered? When she was little did she
decide, "I want to look like a queen"?

". . . . All there was was us and these convicts — "

"Hey, don't tell me your story. I've heard dozens. I don't want
to hear about you."

Diamond's expression was hurt! The wino crumped out on the
ground — his feelings were hurt! Fiddler shrugged as if he hadn't
meant it.

"All there was was us and these convicts. Their reg'lar crew was
up fighting one up near L.A. And the fire, that fire; that fire, it was
going up that mountain lickety-split and coming down towards
us too. Down too, only not so fast, because of the wind, was from
us to the fire. And we were going up the mountain and get that,
head that fire off. Fire off. — I mean the fire going *up*. Hell with
the fire going down, the boss said. He was a crazy man. And we
went. We *went* up. Goddam, goddam it, I thought I was going to
die. Die. What a slope! What a, what a, slope! He was a crazy
man. . . ."

Snippy ever so casually hooked the claws of the paw she was resting on over the edge of the pan, leaving the other outstretched. She
tongued the water, dribbling back what she got, and still not a
glance at Fiddler. He took hold of the handle, and Snippy lowered
her face to the water as she'd never done while drinking and
watched him obliquely from that position. The pinkish, oilish,

pearly tinge he hadn't seen since early morning reflected from her
eyes. Her tailtip curled like a jack-in-the-pulpit. Stretched sideways
to him, Snippy extended from one corner of his vision to the other.
All he could see was gaudy tiger, tiger. You had to come within
their range to water them.

Fiddler pulled, smoothly tying each movement to the next. Snippy
was unimpressed. She waited till he was pulling as hard as he could
before she let the pan slip under her claws. As he went backward,
almost reeling, she walloped through the bars across the space where
he'd been standing and hit the pan so hard it nearly broke his
wrists. He got soaked. Snippy stood and curved one paw around
a bar and watched him.

Diamond had been wet a little and was shivering and covering
his eyes from the cage. He knelt on the ground there, sobered with
fright, and quavered on about him and his "tough job," trying to
lose himself in his tale.

". . . . That's rough country. Cliffs and cliffs. Obstacle courses?
What do they call them? Fire on both sides and under your feet
and breathing in fire, and you have to run through it? And the
birds falling out of the sky and the jackrabbits burning. You
couldn't see, you couldn't see; you couldn't breathe unless you were
a foot from the ground. And the bugs leaping on you to die. Burn,
right on your hands. Kneel to breathe. And, my boots! And my
boots were burning! A — like a stove. I had, maybe I had the
wrong kind of boots, but they were — oh! I hated to put my feet
down!" Diamond slapped his feet in agony. "So I, what I did was
pour a little of my water in my boots. Pour it in my boots. Then it
wasn't just the bottom of my shoes, it was my ankles even, in boiling water! It boiled! Didn't matter whether I had my feet up or
down. And, and God save you if, if you took your shoes off. And
you couldn't stop anyway because the fire burned right across where
we were right behind us. No-nobody could help. And I ran out of
water, and I had to eat my oranges, I was so thirsty. Running up
the mountain all the time. Heart hurts. And they're not any good
for, for thirst. Makes it worse. And what that smoke does to your
thirst, oh Jesus! your mouth, your mouth! Your eyes! You had to
kneel to even goddam breathe. Every time to breathe!

"And that fire hated everything, the way it burned. Get into a clump of trees and wow!" — he whirled his arms like drunken lassoes spinning — "it'd just burn every which way, yellow and red, scorch the tears right out of your eyes, raining sparks, burn up your legs in the grass. Everything was dying. The boss, the boss would hit 'em with the shovel, poor creatures, deers even, hit 'em with the shovel. And we cut line. And we cut line — did we cut line! We cut miles of line. I never worked like that and I never will. I never — But we did it. We were, we were good men, for just a bunch of bums that signed up. We caught her at the top. We caught, we stopped her at the top. They don't burn as well downhill and the wind didn't help as much. We stopped it at the top there. Convicts and bums, that's what we were. And we got down to the road, and there was that beautiful nurse tanker there. They have a faucet at the back. A reg'lar faucet. We didn't bother putting any in the canteens. Not us. We just all got between the faucet and the ground. Some boys lying down, and boys on top of them, and boys on top of them, and boys at the sides with their hands — you know, steer a little their way. Everybody helping everybody else. And I'm telling you we hadn't never known each other before. Everybody holding everybody else up. And, and we opened it up, and I'm telling you not a drop hit the ground. Not a drop. What one boy didn't get, another, another did. Off one boy's face onto the next's. — Black by the time it got to the boys on the bottom. And that, that driver. What a fatass! He hadn't done a thing. He laughed like he thought we were fools."

Diamond laughed mournfully into his hands, sitting lumped on the ground.

The monkeys fussed and fought with shrieks and thumpings on the floor. Red hadn't fed them yet, that was the cause of it. They jabbered rups that rose hysterically in pitch until you were imagining monkeys turning somersaults in apoplectic fits. The screening between cages rattled fiercely as the monkeys pounced against it, making faces through it. The males yawned to show their teeth and glowered at each other, glancing at their females for approval after each especially dramatic yawn.

The leopards slanted topsy-turvy like a flock of gulls. And they rolled on their backs on the floor — the bigger cats would have been too prim — took off. Fast as a squirrel in a whirligig, back and forth in front of Fiddler, Sweetheart almost loped. Her legs blurred like propeller blades and her body supple as rubber whipped in a pattern so perfect it didn't seem she was touching the ground. She drove down with her pivot foot much harder than necessary every time she turned, as in part of a dance. And her body bent like a bow and sizzled out, her paws in a dog-digging motion, her head weaving circles dodging the bars. When Fiddler touched her his hand got flung off like egg from a beater. She carried the jolt of a third rail.

Then Sweetheart jumped up on her hind feet and hopped like that, clasping at the bars, and wiggled down to sit on her haunches higher than Fiddler and hugging the bars, her paws assured and careless as a gorgeous woman's arms. She cocked her head with a girlish, imperious, birdlike glance at nothing in particular. Fiddler laid one of his arms up her back and one up her stomach and rubbed and rubbed. Sweetheart shivered and stroked the bars. She was a marvel, all her parts. The udder undercarriage was soft and loose, but beneath that she felt tougher than a punching bag. Her paws hurt like granite if you knocked against them. Her jawbone was fun to trace and the throat soft to poke, like a bladder. Like anyone else she had a bellybutton, and her knees were cute, sticking up round and thin like a dog's. In places where it didn't matter she was kind of tubby — in places where it didn't matter. Sweetheart was made for leaping trees, vying with birds, with her big hind legs, the skin loose around them, and her long, long balancing tail and narrowing body streamlined to the slender head that held those wonderful ears and eyes and even the cylinder mouth that did the killing.

Sweetheart kept one paw on the bars to hold herself up and hung the other into the crook of Fiddler's arm to vibrate when she got excited. He played with her whiskers and explored around for tickly places under her arms, found her pulse, and the tiny pouches on her elbows, and rubbed the velvety blanket of shoulder skin up and down the solid body underneath. What a body she had! Everything so well attached. Put a leopard on the rack and you'd break your rack. On the back of her neck the hair was stiff like a crewcut boy's but much denser. Fingers wouldn't slide through it; they had to be pushed. It wasn't oil that resisted, or electricity, either. It was Leopard, Essence of Leopard, and the feel was a thrill.

Sweetheart pricked her ears and poked out her tongue to be touched, her mouth in a little triangle, like a rabbit's. It was the only frivolous thing on her face, that tongue, the only place a slap from another cat might have drawn blood. There wasn't an overlong hair, a hint of a wrinkle or sag. Down between her legs the fur was pillowy lush and long as grass and on her ribs her coat was a tapestry. If sheer glossy beauty could have killed her meals, Sweetheart would have been the plumpest leopard alive.

She couldn't yet keep still, drawing doodles upwards with her nose, squeezing Fiddler's wrist into the hollow between her arms. He pulled her flat against the bars, and she liked that. She ran her paw against his chest sweet as a feather.

"Hey, Leopard-boy, you can't do this!" It was the bulls' Chief, across the runway from the cages. He was reclining, his hands behind his head, against the foot of one of the bulls. She'd stuck it out so that it made a comfortable backrest. And she wasn't drooling on him, or anything. In fact she'd fan him from time to time with her trunk. It was a mother-son scene, she looming above him, solicitously flapping her ears. Her trunk dipsydoodled back and forth, and he was cool.

"So I can't. So what?"

"Fresh kids get a learnin'!"

"Hey, leave that kid alone! Nobody picks on kids around this show that don't hear from me!" Bingo poked his fanatical, small face between two other bulls and shortened his grip on his hook. He knew the Chief had been kidding, but he liked to throw his weight around. "Kids are kids; you leave 'em alone. Besides, he craps around too much with the cats as it is. We don't want him trying anything new."

"You're a tough potato, Bingo. Sure I'll leave the kid alone." The

Chief grinned, friendly like a demon — he could have beaten Bingo into dog meat — and began carving his bull's toenails with his knife.

A third bull man was with them. He was the bug. He corresponded to Taylor in their department, except he was more carefree and more violent. The boss had him working all the time. The other bull men weren't too scared of him because they'd taught him that to hit a buddy would set the whole department on him. So the coot restrained himself. And he wasn't too hard on the bulls. It was funny — they'd rough him up and he'd bat 'em back moderate-hard, and both him and the bulls enjoyed it. What made the guy dangerous was how he went after townies. He thought they were just like bulls: you could hit them without doing damage. And he'd use his hook. When he'd cracked a jig for kicking at Nigas, it was one thing. But usually he didn't have a good excuse.

"These are better, Dave, huh? These animals? Want some help? — Look out! Look out for me." The wino had crawled to the leopard cage, and Fiddler had almost tromped on him.

Rita evidently had a cold. There was a mucus bubble in her nose. Fiddler wished he could have wiped it for her. It was too bad she never got any sun. Rita was trying to growl while swallowing and not succeeding with either effort very well. She remained hunched over the pan when she was finished, but not to trap him, like Snippy; just from stubbornness. Oh, she'd get him, all right, if he were to stumble — he'd lose his eyes — but she didn't expect the chance.

Rita squidged and flattened into the shape of a box — no fighting position — as Fiddler came close. Then she backed up on her haunches and ducked and scrunched her head and backed off with almost a waddle; her rear end swung from side to side. That was how she'd acted even as a kitten, Chief said. He'd never gotten a rise when he tried to fool with her, like with the other kittens. People weren't playmates. Uneasy and sullen, she'd sat, for the moment overawed.

"Isn't this exciting? Some man will catch us, I know. Maybe he'll be nice." Two townie ladies were blundering along. It was dark behind the cages, and every so often one of the steel doors to the seat wagons would clash open or closed and startle them. They'd make believe to "hide" from whoever it was.

"We have so much more fun than our children, it isn't fair. They haven't learned to enjoy life."

Diamond laughed and laughed about the ladies, got up. His face was redder than it had been.

A Seat man surprised the pair, and they "gave up" with a great show of disappointment and asked him something.

"Right down there, ma'am. Ask that boy. He loves to talk." The bastard pointed at Fiddler. The women thanked him with the glad, exaggerated courtesy townies sometimes felt it wise to use to bums.

Diamond laughed and laughed and clomped around as if his feet were in a sack, reeling right and left — against the cage, so Fiddler had to pull him back. Blood bulged Diamond's face when he laughed. He wasn't pleasant to see.

"Oh!" said one lady, her hand at her throat, at the leopards.

"I'm scared of them myself," Diamond confided, his voice like shingles clacking.

Speaking even to Fiddler with obvious distaste, the lady whispered, where could she get a glass of water?

Immediately, way down at the lion cage — beyond it — Julius's bald head wrenched round in his deck chair and he tumbled out and up on his feet, shouting, "I'm sorry, miss, no, the circus doesn't furnish water, but, if you'd care for some orangeade, that's what we have instead; only fifteen cents a cup."

Forty yards! What a pair of ears he had!

Diamond was thirsty too. He wandered over to the Seat men and was offered a swig.

Fiddler kicked straw to the tigers and started stuffing it in. His chest and arms were hot from holding the bundles and itchy because straw had glued to his sweat. He wished he could shut the monkeys up. One or two were being picked on. The sounds were different from when they just fought. If Red had only fed them — if Red *would* feed them, it would stop. Fiddler wondered where Red was, whether he could hear. Monkeys were like people, cruel deliberately.

They'd bite another monkey just to hear it scream. Not many animals were like that, certainly not to their own kind. Except for feeding them a lot there was nothing you could do, and everybody decent in the circus looked at you, thinking just because you worked in the menagerie you must be responsible.

If Red was still with the girl he could hear. Red had always been hard. Red's second night, Fiddler remembered, he'd been assigned to sleep with a man who'd that very day broken his leg. Fiddler had lain awake, with the whimpering and moaning, but Red right in the same bunk slept like a log, as if the guy were snoring.

Pasha stooped with his nose at Mabel's tail. She was licking her claws one by one expertly as a manicurist, curving them out to her tongue. First she was sitting, then lay down on her belly to do it more comfortably and at her leisure, relaxing her body so that the hind legs loosened out and gave a womanly breadth to her lips. Her tail stretched down almost to Pasha's ribs and was driving him wild, whether she knew it or not, as she smugly twitched the tip every time a claw seemed perfect. Pasha had plunked a paw on either side of her and was humping around as if he had cramps. He smelled and he smelled and drew up his nose like a connoisseur and he smelled — oh, delicious! — and smelled, smelled, and stopped and squirmed as if he were trying to get out a belch. His paws made grating noises on the floor. He humped and heaved like an inchworm, more and more excited, until he couldn't help but do something. Imploringly he placed his head on Mabel's hips and flinched, expecting to be scratched. She turned in exasperation but let him have his silly way. She didn't want to dirty up her claws.

Pasha groaned in bliss. He didn't rest any weight on Mabel, just touched the side of his face to her back and contemplated Fiddler — not seeing him, of course. A funny-looking tiger Pasha was, humble and kiddish, one ear down listening for the Lost Chord.

Pasha lifted his head with a gaze to shrivel an army. — Fiddler peeped like a robin. Pasha stared right through him and, not seeing anyone to fight, cuddled his head on Mabel again. In another day or so she'd be responsive, and they'd be having sex, sex, sex, sex like a couple of machines. And then in about two months, if Fiddler stuck it out with the show all that time, he'd get the thrill of his life: cling to the rungs up the front of the wagon and watch through the vent — Chief had told him about it — how wet and black the kittens would be, trying to crawl, bawling like teeny lambs or any other baby things; Mabel licking them so that they stood on their heads like little wriggling wheelbarrows and carrying them from spot to spot, her jaws aquiver with the strain of being exact, and, when she'd bundled them together, settling her body around them snug as the walls of a crib. Mabel wouldn't be so prissy then. She'd change. And what a roar! If Fiddler blinked, she'd blast him sailing off the wagon. The little kittens in her paws, the roar would be a lullaby to them.

"Dave, come over and have one," Diamond invited. He had a quart of wine. ".... You've got the wrong man, I told that cop. 'Do you deny you're drunk?' — Now I couldn't deny that. I'm always drunk. You catch me sober and I'll buy the round, I'll buy the round."

"If I were you I'd steer away from those guys, wino," Fiddler said.

Diamond talked right back. "You'll be the same as other people when you're our age. How will you be different? What's going to stop you? Huh? What's going to stop you? If you're in a circus now, where'll you be then? Huh? But I'll be through. I work. I'll be through."

Almost all of the Seat men, including Mousy, kept quiet. What did they think, Fiddler would run and tell Chief anything they said like a little teacher's pet?

Sterno, or whatever his name was, probably hadn't been around. — "Ol' Fiddler hits you and there's a bone broke."

Nobody laughed except Sterno.

Fiddler to have fun backed up against the tiger cage. "Come and get me," he said, smiling, since nobody but him or Chief would have dared come halfway near that close.

A couple of them shook their heads disgustedly. "He's crazy." They were not in fighting moods.

"He is crazy! You said it," Diamond exclaimed. "I didn't know you boys didn't get along. I'm coming to work, Dave. I'll stick with

you, Dave." He walked unsteadily toward the tiger cage, still carrying the bottle, which they seemed glad to let him have. They knew
the trouble it would cause. Bastard, measly winos — fireplug noses
and sucked-in mouths and "prominent" chins filthy with inch-long
bristles, since they never shaved. Blotchy and Sterno and even
worse ones with a dead unvarying zombie gaze and a creak to their
voices like coffins.

— Fiddler turned and took hold of a certain movable section of
bars and started sliding it up from the floor as if he were letting the
tigers out.

Pasha's head came off Mabel's back like a thunderclap and he
roared and he roared again, so Fiddler almost blacked out, standing
an orange mountain hulk, not interested a bit in getting out but
ready to make damn sure nothing else climbed in. Mabel quit preen-
ing and crept toward the hole, her face like a blowtorch. *She* wanted
out. The winos were scrambling out of their chairs for the darkest
recesses under the seat wagon flaps. Diamond had tripped with a
choked sob and was pitifully writhing.

Fiddler closed down the bars. They hadn't actually been high
enough for even Mabel to have squeezed through.

Mabel shivered as if in a bad dream. She put out a paw on a
line for Fiddler, just holding it there without lunging to reach him,
as though she were aiming a gun. Pasha roared once more, then
crashed a last one like a tree and moved to straddle Mabel guard-
ingly.

She was startled. She'd forgotten he existed. She let him have it
right across the chin. Getting away, bumbling Pasha stepped on
her, which made her madder yet. Mabel started at him again, but
remembered the real cause and rocked forward at Fiddler, roared
brief and gasping, tapering the remnant growl into the top of her
throat and flanks. Then she rocked back to a normal crouch. The
growl still rumbled visibly in her throat, although so soft Fiddler
couldn't hear it. Her eyes slid down and sideways — seemed to, anyway, but with a certain veiled, unfocused quality and in the air a
singing tension. Her body seemed relaxed, except the flutter in the
throat.

Fiddler started to unclasp his fingers on the bars, and stopped: the pupils of her eyes had tightened. Mabel waited. And Fiddler waited. And all the time the throat fur shivered and pulsed like a tiny motor and the veiled eyes hung imponderable. Fiddler loosened and steadied his body so that he felt he couldn't have moved, any more than a post, and his hands weren't part of him, really. Then he began to slip the hands from the bars.

Mabel's eyes rolled with a wallowing relish to pinpoint on his and the roar hot-highballing smashed him like an elevator falling — cut off abrupt, as her lips made a silent, retching motion and the wrath washed over him quiet as foam. Her claws spiked in and out of her paw on its side. She bounded up, sat in the front corner, viciously twitching her tail and glaring at the elephants. Soon even the tail, with a snap, curled pouting beside her.

The winos were panting that Fiddler was "Crazy!" and "Nuts!" while they dragged themselves into the light. They were funny, smeared like minstrel players with the dirt.

"We pulled out of Denver last year and they was three bodies left on the lot, under the strawpile," Sterno was saying. "Colorado cops were trailing this show clear up to Spokane. Denver's only acrost Nebraska from here — then Cheyenne, then Denver."

Nobody answered Sterno. The winos seemed scared of Fiddler himself. Not just of Chief, but of Fiddler. They came out of their holes. It was a fitting place for them to be — holes. The entire scene was fitting. Above, the bleacher seat wagon flaps made a roof of prison-like steel, with naked lights here and there for the winos to see to play cards. And down where the great flaps sloped to the ground it got black as a molding skid row bar and as rambling — the winos could feel at home. The shadows slunk to pitch-black areas where you never knew what you'd stumble on, a man passed out, a cache of bottles. On a long stand a man might crawl back there and die and never be discovered till he stunk enough to penetrate the piss and liquor-vomit smells.

The cubs were especially fun to play with because of the uncertainty: they were growing up. The things you did would have to

be stopped eventually, and the cubs could surprise you with a fast
and accurate snap, or follow through on a swipe that had thrown
you off your guard. When they roared they sounded less and less
like toilets flushing, more like lions. The occasional awkward bumpi-
ness of their walk could be like a swagger. Fiddler's favorite scratching place was low on the soft-furred front of the neck, where it was
most dangerous. Sometimes they enjoyed being petted there; but
usually they felt it was unseemly, or else the actual sensation was
annoying — they'd bite and bite. Every day improved the timing
and co-ordination. Soon Fiddler was going to have to find another
spot, or lose his hand. He'd have to judge; that was the fun.

He caught a cub's tail, pulled the cub close enough to grab its
hind legs and twisted sharply until it was in sitting position. Then
the claws came swatting back and Fiddler yanked his hands away.
The cub in its haste to regain its feet turned its head toward the far
side of the wagon, and Fiddler grabbed the scruff of its neck and got
it tight against the bars where the paws weren't much good. The
cub wuffed like a baffled dog and wrenched and snarled gustily. It
was angry, a little scared, and plenty strong enough to make life
hotter and hotter for Fiddler. The other two were trying to figure
how to join the game. Fiddler let go.

They ranged themselves before him, the one lowering and feeling wronged and its two buddies rather friendly-seeming but rough,
like pirates on a picnic. The trace of buccaneering crossedness in
the great dark pupils made the cubs' eyes wild; and the yellow
wolfish stringers in the brown, the crooked edges to it. These were
lions, all right — they drew themselves up staunchly — but why so
small? What was this, a midget race? — Fiddler couldn't resist.
He poked at the cub he'd played with. It didn't quite manage to
bite him, but the claws reached farther than the mouth. The scratch
hurt moderately, dripped on his shoe. Diamond would see, and that
would be embarrassing. It was down his forearm instead of just on
his hand. He'd been foolish. Catching the cub was okay, but not
jabbing at it like a stupid townie.

All three of them got on the straw in what could easily have been
mistaken for a conspiracy, did their damnedest to keep it from being

pushed to the front of the cage. Wherever he put the scraper they sat and leeched on to the bars. Straight force didn't work; he had to syncopate his shoves. One little section of the scratch was nicked pretty deep. It bled and bled. Fiddler was always slow to form a scab. Chief's voice from once before echoed in his mind — "Them are *lions,* not Siam kittens!" He was glad Chief wasn't here.

One of the monkeys shrieked and screamed. The rest had probably put tears in her worse than Fiddler's little scratch, and pulled off the scabs from the last time. Days like this, Fiddler hated monkeys.

Jaggy had nestled himself beside the cheetah like a lover and slowly was shaking his head from side to side. She licked and rubbed the screening by him tenderly and purred like popcorn putting, breathed in tiny pants. Once she lifted her head in a haughty stare over her shoulder down the length of her body at Fiddler and then went back to licking the partition. The jaguar licked too, with his broad, dragging tongue, and shook his head as though there were gnats, nuzzled himself as Cheet should have been doing. It was pathetic.

"I don't feel so good, you know?" Diamond came to Fiddler. He opened his mouth to say something more, but his tongue sunk and grew fixed and he bent over, carefully holding the bottle to keep it from spilling. Up came his lunch.

Fiddler reached in to scratch the tails. The cheetah's jerked away but soon twitched back. Jaggy pawed straw clear out of the cage. He was powerful.

"Hey!"

He rose, turned quick as a fielder ready to throw. Fiddler stuck his arm way in and Jaggy, emotionless again, plodded toward it and, when he found the arm gone, lazily tried the impossible task of squeezing his head between the bars, enjoying the rubbing it gave him.

The cheetah ran in one place. Her legs were long as the sleeves of a shirt, and that was how they looked — shirtsleeves madly whipping on a line. If Fiddler'd let her out she would have been a lightning streak. They were the fastest animals in the world, Chief said. In

a cage four by nine! Wide- and spindly-legged as a spider she ran
and ran, making sobs, and dropped down exhausted. Fiddler felt
like crying, he felt so bad. Cheet sprawled gasping, after only a short
exercise — her muscles were clotted. She gazed backward at Fiddler
with that grand, gracious curve to her neck, gasping and crazy and
hot.

Then she struggled up and walked swaying to him. Her mouth
was stretched like a snake's, the jaws about to dislocate and the hisses
rattling hate. In spasms she wrung her head. Fiddler reached to
the slavering lips of that outraged mouth and got her nearer,
stroked her throat and shoulders, wedging his arm between the
bars, and pulled her nearer still. She looked to be about to devour
his elbow; but her jaws slipped loose and closed, her eyes soft-
squinted with anticipation. If she could have knelt she would have
— Cheet lay and leaned against the bars. Fiddler caught her round
the neck and fingered down her spine, while she sputtered deliciously with pleasure.

Poor Jaggy sat like a mourning dog, the top of his head pressed to
the partition screening. Fiddler petted his shoulder. Jaggy nodded,
dreaming. He dreamed more than any human.

But the broad, businesslike ears turned and there was a snapping
sound like a dog makes after a fly.

Fiddler's fingers tingled. They almost were gone.

"You think I can stick, Dave don't you?" Diamond wanted to
know. He was setting himself to order, wrinkling his nose because
of the puke in it.

"I think you'll stick through supper. That should be a comfort
to you."

"All I'm looking for's a chance. A gentleman can live on what
they pay us. If I — " His belly was bothering him again, and he
was trying to be so dignified. "If I had a chance — " He was vomiting, more painfully now. Fiddler had to jump aside and pull him
out of the jaguar's range by the seat of his pants. Diamond was revolting. He must have missed a week's meals, the way he'd eaten.
— Jesus, Fiddler might have to sleep with the guy! In a bunk so
small one of you had to keep his hands above his head — sleep with
him, in those clothes, and probably still puking!

"Goddam it! God*dam* it!" Fiddler spat and kicked the tire on the cage and went to shut the goddam monkeys up.

"You've rid more bulls than me, but you ain't rid no bears, I bet. I used to ride 'em for kicks," the bulls' Chief was telling Bingo in the hoarse steamboat voice which marked bull men out from all other circus people.

Bingo smiled at Fiddler with disdainful disbelief.

"I'm speakin' the blessed truth, Bingo. I've rid bears — not no pesky little grizzly, either; *real* bears, kind you don't see even in Canada. The kid believes me, don't you, kid?"

"Yes, I guess I do," Fiddler admitted. And he did.

"You should bet Bing-gy there and make some money. I'm goin' to prove it."

Bingo's eyes were challenging-bright as a bird's or a weasel's. They always were. He was always up to something.

"You prove it and I'll kiss your keester."

"Okay." The Chief grinned satanically. "See, we used to hunt 'em in the winter by diggin' them out if we knew where to dig. I tagged this old lady before her tracks snowed in and I saved her up for when I felt like it. But I couldn't wait very long, and she wasn't in too well. It wasn't as cold as it should have been, maybe. Anyway, I was diggin' and she was kickin' around some under there because she'd woke up. I was wondering what the hell to do because it wasn't too good a situation. And then the sonofabitch of a thing fell through — me, I fell through like I was lead, right on old big bear. And I hung on where I landed because that was the only thing to do. I couldn't be under her. And I rid her right out uv that hole. She thought I was It. She gave me a hell uv a ride. She was goin' to have her cubs pretty soon an' she was mean. We had a tussle. She was as tall as these bulls when she was up on her two feet, and I'd lost my gun — "

"What's your proof?" Bingo interrupted.

"What?"

"What's your proof you've rode her?"

The bulls' Chief grinned. He grasped the trunk of his Daisy and had her pull him up from where he was sitting. And then he spread his shirt wide-open to the waist. Strung on a dried-gut cord down from his neck were the claws and teeth of a large, large bear. They would have looked the size of horns, except that he himself was tall and strapping. Setting his hands on his hips, he stood with a grin long as a salmon, under the huge, hawk nose.

"But where's your proof?" Bingo still wanted to know.

"Where! *HERE!*" Exultantly he thumped his chest so that the claws and teeth danced and rattled.

"That ain't no proof you've *rode* a bear!"

The Chief was thunderstruck. He couldn't think of anything to say. He thumped his chest again. He tried to think up what to say.

— "I rid her, for Christ sake, I rid her right out uv the hole all over the place!"

Bingo rolled a cigarette. He was the only one-armed man in the show who could do that.

The Chief was staring at Bingo, so Bingo offered him the weed. The Chief's response was not polite.

"Prove it," said Bingo.

The monkeys were scared by Fiddler's banging the bars, but just redoubled the tumbling speed with which they tore after each other. Pounding harder made them race faster. Pounding harder and harder and harder, Fiddler stopped them because they reached a point where they couldn't go any faster and he really frightened them then.

It was simple to put them at their ease. Being monkeys, they understood about temper tantrums — they thought that was why he'd been doing it — and were quick to forgive and forget. By clicking his tongue and showing how quiet his hands were, Fiddler soon had most of them gathered beside the bars. A cool breeze came up, and they liked that and even the individualists who'd been hanging back relented. The monkey they'd all been picking on was the only one who stayed away. She was the newest female, a skeleton with blood and fur. Off and on for days they'd chased and bled her until she could scarcely open her eyes — she only tried to out of fear. Her blood was in the straw and on the walls and even the ceiling in frantic trails and her beautiful smoky fur in places was matted with it.

Some of the little fiends were wanting Fiddler to pet them now. But when he stuck his finger through the wire one or two young males jumped back and forth insultedly, so conceited they thought he cared enough about them to try and tease. The ruling male looked at the finger with the benign expression he reserved for people. He was strict with monkeys but he'd let people get away with things. The healthy females, after searching Fiddler's face for mischief, crawled toward him soberly to have him stroke their stringy legs and nubbin heads and raisin titties. They were gentle and peaceful as doves, almost affectionate. They'd move wherever they could to be helpful to Fiddler, showed him a respect very special. And yet in a minute or two they'd be after the hurt one again — the poor thing already asleep, huddled bleeding and gashed.

Red had to feed the monkeys on time; that was all. It was that simple, and the sonofabitch hadn't done it. Fiddler went to find him, or do the feeding himself.

Red had ditched the girl. He was alone near 12 Wagon watching another girl in a flowery, full, summery skirt, who already had two well-dressed college-boy escorts.

"She wouldn't spread, and I can get better. — Wait'll we get to Salt Lake, huh, Fid? Two to one in that town. The prettiest chicks beg you there; you can't hardly walk into a soda joint. — Hey, listen, Fid, this'll kill you. You should have been here — " Red was hopping.

"Did you hear the monkeys? Did you? What kind of a guy — "

"Yeah I will feed 'em, Fid, take it easy." Red slapped his shoulder, too zapped up to get mad. "I just want to tell you about this guy. Brownie got back and he wanted to hire somebody 'cause the guy you've got's a bad wino, he says, and he wants to fire Coke too — I told him Coke ought to take an aspirin. Pretty good? So, anyway, he's keeping an eye out and this guy turns up after a job. Good build and everything. Only his shirt was wet; that's what we figured out afterwards. Not like sweat, 'cause it was so clean and wet the same all over and the guy wasn't sweating on his skin. Wet like he

hadn't had one and h'd just taken it off somebody's line. Can you
see a guy doing that; wet? — Wait!" Red shouted, laughing, as
Fiddler tried to leave. " — Listen. So Brownie gave him a dime
to bring him a cup o' coffee. He likes to see 'em walk before he
hires 'em, he says; see if they *can* walk. What a card! He's right,
though. He's always right. So when this guy-o got over on the midway, soon'z he gets there, these two detectives grab him. They just
put him in a cop car and away they went. You should have seen
Taylor! They knew him, Brownie says; they grabbed him like they
knew him. And it wasn't for no shirt, either, 'cause these weren't
regular cops. He was a good build, too. We could have used him.
And Brownie never got his dime. Never a dull moment around
this show! Don't get bored here!" Red sauntered away in the right
general direction, at least.

Straw had fallen into Fiddler's shirt and was itching and itching. He sweated hard now in the sun, and the sweat wasn't dried
away by the heat but held to the straw and got hotter and hotter.
He rubbed his neck and his arms and under his shirt and got rid
of the larger bits, but they weren't the ones that gave the most
trouble. It was like having ants.

He'd forgotten about Coca Cola till Red's mention of him. Going
inside again, Fiddler passed the giraffe wagon and wondered if he
shouldn't stop to see if the guy was alive. — No; he'd bring the
doctor as soon as he had a chance and until then one wino was
enough to handle. Coca Cola would cry out if he was in pain.

But Fiddler felt a little guilty about not remembering Coca Cola.
And a water truck was loudly room-rooming up and down, wetting
the dust. The monkeys couldn't be heard, so neither would a cry.
He listened on tiptoe at the crack of the door.

No sound whatever.

Coca Cola was either extremely comfortable or just plain dead.
He could wait until the cats were taken care of.

Somebody also was going to have to bring the giraffes and the
gnu their water and vegetables. They'd been neglected ever since
the second train had come in. Water was more important. Fiddler
sneaked a pailful out of the Light Department's water barrel and

hung it high up on a hook on the pen and made sure the bucket left in Iggy's cage wasn't empty.

The cats behaved as if they were under a siege. They hated the droplets flying and the arrogant, rancorous truck. During the whole day they never felt more helpless. The elephants didn't like the truck much, but they didn't mind the water. Any hay they'd saved they put behind their feet and then enjoyed the sprinkling, twiddling and twirling their trunks.

The bull men got among the bulls to keep dry. The Chief simply sat against the back of Daisy's foot instead of against the front and was protected like hay or a valuable purse. She was trying to soothe him, also. He was still mad. She tickled his chin. Bingo got even better treatment. The bulls made way for him as much as their chains would allow and blocked the spray of water from him when it passed. They courted Bingo — stood on their chains to prevent annoying clinks and were careful not to brush him in their rockings unless he showed he didn't care.

"Quit," said Bingo. And they quit everything — breathing.

Bingo darted his gay and furious glance at Fiddler. "How's it going, kid?" He stooped, tightened and tied his shoes, proud that he could do it, and stood up and let the elephants breathe again. "Hey!" he yelled at the guy in the truck. "Watch how the hell you drive with that water!" — All because the stream had come near enough to Fiddler to almost wet his shoes a little.

The bulls on either side of Bingo wound their trunks into compact shapes and placed them conveniently for petting — bearing in mind, of course, he only had the one arm. The bull on that lucky side of him bowed her head to a level he could easily reach. Bulls a longer way from Bingo stood attentive and discreet.

The coot, in contrast, was almost literally getting the pants kidded off him. The elephants goosed and bumped him like strong ladies at a sale, and they patted over his clothes smooth as pickpockets and pushed their feet against his so he couldn't help but worry for the safety of his toes. One bull edged very close, holding her trunk cleverly at her side like a sharpie palming a payoff, and wobbled up the tip to the buckle of his belt and tried to snap it off. Another joker caught a little water and snuffled the messy nozzle of her trunk down the coot's back. The coot jumped like a puppet on his craw-fish legs and let 'em have it with the hook. He didn't put any wrist action into it, just his long arm swinging, so it wasn't lethal. The bulls mooed partly in fun, curving out their trunks like scythe blades to receive the blows. The bat went boneless-goofy-wild and laughed and jitterbugged, all arms and legs, kicking his hands like a punter. He didn't look where he swung the hook — Fiddler was afraid he'd let fly. A jig doing the same thing would have run on and on and on, but once the bug had reached a fever pitch he slackened off. That was when the elephants did their piece. They'd found where they could stand and not be hit, and so they gave him pokes to wind him up again.

Bessie always liked to watch a scrap. She got up, her nostrils with a rather cruel, snipped-in profile. But nobody was getting hurt. It wasn't really a fight; it was dull. She slid her hind legs sideways to sit down, but instead straightened a little and slouched to Fiddler. Didn't look at him. Didn't bother. Eyes half-lidded, waited curt.

"Water?" Fiddler asked.

Bessie sneezed slightly and her flank twitched Her paws stirred with terse impatience. Fiddler hurried and brought it.

She only took a sip — she'd had a lot before — and lay down on the spot even though the pan was under her — jerked her head as if Fiddler had his nerve sticking it there. He pulled it out quick.

The elephants tossed hay furls up to their mouths, caught them and dropped them to toss again. They took their chains and tinked briskly in a rhythm and rested their feet on the stakes they were chained to and gave them a massage. Secretly they glanced from side to side out of their dusty eyes, swaying to get a better view of something as if only normally swaying, while the tattered, kite ears wagged tranquilly. The "rubber cows," some people called them, and that was what they were — rubber and like fat and very brilliant cows. No townie ever sneaked in through the elephants without the bull men knowing. The bulls tipped everybody off.

Diamond and another wino were admiring Ajax. Fiddler shoved them from behind and shot their hearts up their throats so high they nearly spit them out. They had to go kill a couple of bottles to recover.

If they were like the usual winos they'd been saying "boo" to Ajax, trying to stir him up. It was what every new guy tried to do. Ajax was a hard cat to excite. He didn't snarl or roar except for stated moments in the day, like when the fronts of the cages were opened, or else at poor Snippy. He was quieter than even the jaguar. And in the last two years he'd torn off three guys' arms. Fiddler was fascinated by him. No other cat had done that well.

What made Ajax dangerous was, he *didn't* hate people, like Rita, or despise them, like Bessie, or even peacefully dislike them, like the lazy leopard, Minny. Put him with a lion and a man and he'd kill the lion first — maybe never touch the man. In the cage Snippy was the frightening one. Usually Ajax's eyes were modestly cast down. If somebody petted him the chances were he wouldn't budge. He didn't seem to enjoy petting. He just ignored it, as ducks ignore dew.

Fiddler understood why Ajax had caught those three men (and goodness knows how many more before somebody had started keeping track). Fiddler would have made the next if Chief and Brownie hadn't warned him. Ajax was the biggest cat, bigger than Joe. Eleven feet, five hundred pounds; crammed in the cage like a ship in a bottle. And when the sign said ROYAL BENGAL TIGER, "Royal" was a whopping understatement. Ajax was as massive and as stately as a Caesar — the kind of buffalo-sized tiger that made elephants afraid.

And yet the face was nothing to run from — appallingly large, that was all. There wasn't the lions' hot ferocity around the mouth, Bessie's bitterness. Unless you stopped to imagine what Ajax with his strength could do, he wasn't awesome. His eyes were masked by slanting, oriental lids, so that you didn't watch the ruthless, machine-like functionings of the parts, as with the other cats. It was sometimes hard to even picture him angry. He was above squabbling, this great regal cat who never growled or wrinkled up his face, who co-operated when you worked and seemed gentle as Sweetheart toward people. After her, Ajax was the first one a new man would touch —

a new wino scared pee-less of all the cats but beginning to feel a
little ashamed of it and wanting to show off to townie women once
in a while — not caring a great deal about his life, anyway, and
wanting to be friends with this most magnificent of all the cats
when it seemed so safe and easy. The guy who had worked with
Chief while Fiddler was still assigned to the gnu had been typical,
always laying his arms across the paws and nervously tapping the
monstrous chin. Chief would tell him and tell him. A bouncer in
a clip joint had fixed the guy up before the tiger did, but it had
been only a question of time.

— That was the thing. Once a week, or once a month, if somebody's arm was laid across his paws Ajax would tear it off. He'd
happen not to want to be touched. Nobody could save the man,
nothing could be done. Off would come the arm like a twig. Chief
could spot these moods, and so could Snippy, of course — she stayed
in a corner — but nobody else, not even Fiddler. Fiddler knew
enough to watch how Snippy was acting; but that wasn't a sure
sign because Ajax might not be gunning for her, or sometimes he
was angry with Snippy but normally neutral toward people at the
same time. He was harder on other animals than on people. He
was a complex cat. Not really mystifying, though, not like the
dreamer jaguar. Ajax simply didn't care one way or another about
you, whether you lived, died, didn't give a damn about you.

Chief wouldn't tell how he knew if Ajax felt good or bad. "If I
toldja you'd make a mistake," he said. So Fiddler was having
to figure it out by himself. In the meantime he fooled with all the
rest of the cats, unlike the kind of winos who'd got their arms ripped
off: *they'd* been too scared.

Once Fiddle had seen Ajax kindle. It was the time the wise-assed
punk on Wardrobe had swaggered down the lines of cages showing
how tough a mug he was. Snippy'd slapped her claws in his shoulder
and bammed him into the bars. He'd ducked and managed to spin
free, luckily for him. She was about to peel his face off. As it was,
he'd only needed ten or fifteen shoulder stitches. — But Ajax had
opened up his eyes — that had been the most exciting part — and
he'd watched the punk whimpering and gagging on the ground.

Fiddler had stepped to the bars to see what the tigers would do. Snippy with flesh on her claws had tried to frighten him, storming away, sucking short, hrrock snarls, until by not flinching he proved he was *Fiddler* and had a right to stand so near. Ajax didn't do a thing but watch the punk, not gloating, just lying alert — but putting coals in Fiddler's back. And yet he'd felt he knew somehow that Ajax wouldn't hurt him. He'd put his hand between the paws. And sickened, giddied as his hand was trapped with a careless shuffle of them.

Snippy'd come and roared huskily but didn't dare to interfere. Ajax looked through Fiddler like a Greenland wind, the lax claws pointed pegs against his skin.

The gaze didn't shift. It merely enlarged. More and more and more, more, more and more was included, until, although Ajax was looking at Fiddler, Fiddler must have been scarcely a speck. The hand was hidden underneath the paws. Circulation in the hand had stopped because of the weight. Ajax had forgotten about Fiddler.

Fiddler began to try to work his hand loose. He'd wriggled for a while. Then Ajax shrugged his paw. Fiddler had been lucky, being human. No chimp would have been let free.

And little Snippy'd glared — "You get fresh with *me*, buster! and. . . . "

"*Snippy,*" he'd coaxed. And she'd softened, licking the blood on her claws, righteous and proud of herself. But Fiddler couldn't touch her, no matter how he begged. She'd have ate him up if she'd had him.

Well, well, here was Red with the food, now that his cage was as bloody as a torture chamber. Since Fiddler had spoken to him he'd taken twice as long as he'd needed. And now he had the nerve to be eating one of the monkeys' bananas — screwing up his face so he'd look like a monk and Fiddler would laugh and not see he was doing wrong. Red climbed over the guard net to talk front-to-back through the cage.

"Wait'll you hear, Fid — "

"What kind of a guy are you, for Christ sake! I told you they were screaming! I told you they were tearing her to bits! What a hell of a thing, to wait so long!"

"Oh, snookey-Fiddlecums, Brownie says you ought to be finished; you're slow too. Here's your guy's uniform. He's supposed to stand watch, 'cause you've got to help Chief when you're through."

Red rolled up the coveralls, wound up and heaved them clear over the cage, joyfully hopping around like a shot-putter. If the cage hadn't been between them there would have been a fight, Fiddler was so mad. The selfish bastard! Snippy nearly clawed him; he'd forgotten all about her. She was lunging back and forth with her fanny curved almost into sitting position — for some unfathomable, tigress reason she'd gotten the idea they wanted to poke her, and poke her there!

"Listen," Red rattled on, exuberant as a little kid. "I'm tellin' you 'cause we're friends. Wait'll you hear; you won't be mad at me." He chuckled. "This woman wanted to join, a wino, a pig, you know, just off a freight; only they don't have no place for her, of course, on the show. Only some of the Prop men told her, yes, they'd hire her if she'd give them some fun first, or no hire. I made peace with them. 'Forget about this morning!' I said. 'Cause she did. She spread. I was too late, but lots of guys got in on it, until she got wise. And then — listen to this — she *still* had to give it away! A *sandwich* she charged! She was so hungry. A sandwich from the cookhouse. I was out and saw. She's tired but otherwise she's okay — 'cept for how she puts her lipstick on — like she'd cut her throat! ear to ear! — she must be a little off. They're getting her boozy now so she'll keep on, an' they took her clothes away. I wanted to tell you 'cause we're friends an' I didn't want you missin' out. By the river; there's a crowd, circus guys."

"Feed your monks." — It was Magee himself, in the lighted doorway of his seat wagon. Like a performer, he lived in one of them.

Red made tracks.

Magee had on his good clothes again and was holding a boxing magazine he'd been reading.

"Good cats this year. Don't let them grab you." He disappeared inside, shutting the door. That was where he'd stay during the

show, with the bleachers full of idiot townies over his head stomp-
ing their feet, whistling, breaking bottles, crying because they'd
gotten candy in their hair, and the clowns exploding firecrackers,
and the band blaring savage as sirens: that was where he'd stay.

Fiddler opened the leopard cage, to finish up.

Sweetheart would drink from politeness, it sometimes seemed.
She'd always lap a little. And even while she drank she helped
Fiddler with the straw, pawing clumps under the bars for him when
they got jammed. She used his hand for a napkin and made what
sounded like the first part of a mew, a series of them with an edge of
growl stuck in like a jagged piece of metal.

Minny muttered crossly to herself because with Fiddler around
there were sure to be disturbances. Rajah posed for everybody,
contriving to stand very tall and at the same time get great length
to his body, arch his tail grandly. His shoulders had a touchy-toughie
bunchedness like a pool hall shark's. — Chief would have pushed
him or screwed him up some way. Chief wanted Rajah fierce like
leopards should be, and not puffing himself up as if he weren't
tame.

Sweetheart purred like water filling a glass. With the hand she
wasn't wiping her whiskers on, Fiddler tapped the bottom of the
shelf to rouse Taboo, who was sleeping there and hadn't drank since
the middle of the morning, and tugged Taboo's feet and tail. Taboo
tried to get them all the way up on the shelf but didn't have room and
only could jerk them with sleepy insistence away from his hand.
Sweetheart began to lick, like coarse sandpaper. Minny grouched,
and Rajah posed as if for a portrait, flexing his intricate, rough-
furred roundings of muscle. Taboo kaplunked down tardily like
a wakened child. Sweetheart licked with great determination, and
Taboo sulked, looked at the water as if at a chore, made starts of
licks at her chest but never touched it — like Rajah she was vain —
and Sweetheart all of a sudden caught Fiddler's hand in her teeth,
applying a slowly mounting pressure. She-she drew his arm into the
cage and tightened her teeth in a vise! The tendons and bones of
his hand seemed either to slide aside or begin to squish! He couldn't
grit his teeth. — Suppose Sweetheart gritted hers!

Doggedly he told himself it was better Diamond wasn't here because of the embarrassment; but if he shouted who would come? The Seat men, and jeer. Rita could reach him now. Rita knew, pedaling back and forth misty-colored like a wraith. — At the opposite side of the cage. The other leopards formed a sort of barrier: indolent Minny, Rajah putting on a show, Taboo watching the water with repugnance. Sweetheart herself made a part, a very pretty part, silken and fawning, sweet as a lamb.

He shut his eyes a moment with the pain. Lessened a little. Couldn't have spoken now, only screamed. Bingo. Should have called Bingo while he could. The bars were hard against his face. Shoulder wedged so it hurt. Rita was afraid of bumping the larger leopards. He couldn't have gotten his other arm in as far as the trapped one; kept that to shield his head. Deep, ragged breaths. Rita shuttled to and fro, picking her opening. Softly Fiddler moaned. It was candy to Rita. She looked at the ceiling, lifted her paw. She could get to him over the other cats.

But Rita lagged — lingeringly gazed around the cage as if she'd been dropped on the moon. Her snarls at Fiddler were perfunctory.

Sweetheart put the pressure on and belly-twisted like a dancer trying very hard to please. Minny growled. Fiddler's arm went right beneath her chin, and she was not a friendly cat. Rita looked as if she knew something nobody else knew anything about and wouldn't tell it for the world. She looked happy and light as a leaf — her blue eyes settled on Fiddler and she looked happier still, more knowing, and her wizard feet tilted her into that shuttling, quicker and quicker deadly back and forth, a clanging exultation in her eyes.

Sweetheart turned him loose, turned Fiddler loose, and was licking his hand again industriously almost before he realized it. The skin was scarcely broken — she'd been careful — and the worst of the pain let up soon. She was cute and beautiful. He petted her throat until she faked another grab.

Fiddler felt like his old self as far as Rita was concerned. She couldn't move faster than his hand. Taboo was drinking. Fiddler to tease squeezed her lustrous paws. Taboo shook them pettishly as if she'd stepped on wet ground; the sulky nails peeped out. Sweet-

heart streaked low-long piling at the wall, went up it with no per-
ceptible leap, her body the same perpendicular to the floor as when
she'd been on it. Through the gap Rita charged, claws high before
her wadded body, braked herself like a skater, throwing back her
weight, and roundhoused futile blows at Fiddler. Minny snorted.
She'd known this kind of thing would happen. Sweetheart pushed
out and downward from the ceiling, floated turning in the air and
landed motionless and nonchalant and calm.

Fiddler lifted the door to shut the cage. Rita clawed it in a
frenzy. Only the thump-thump-thumping could be heard, like from
a tomb.

The next thing was Diamond, getting him in uniform and stationed in front of the cages. Fiddler looked to see if the Seat men
had him. No. And he wasn't under any of the cages.

He'd gone to sleep, that was it. His eyes were open, but he was
asleep, on a bed of townie broken glass. He was in a bad way,
vomit drying around his mouth, cuts on the back of his neck and
head from the glass. It was dangerous to handle him because of the
glass prickled through his clothes.

"What'sa matter? What'sa matter? Leggo here! Leggo! I ain't
got money. — Dave! Dave!" Diamond called, as if he thought Fiddler was over at the cat line and would come protect him.

"It *is* me. Get up. You've got to do something."

With his hand Diamond tested how strong the buttons were sewed
on Fiddler's shirt. Fiddler yanked him to his feet. There wasn't
just glass in his clothes, there was mushed macaroni and decomposed
cheese. He was disgusting. He smelled of stomach acid. Fiddler
pushed the coveralls against his knees for him to step into.

"It's funny, isn't it, Dave, havin' to dress me like a baby? Huh?
Hah-hah-hah-hah! You said it. You'll be too. Don't be hoity-toity.
You'll be just like me."

Fiddler got the coveralls half on, when Diamond started hiccuping
and couldn't stop. Diamond was laughing too. He thought it was
funny — Fiddler having to hold him up, and all. But he stopped
laughing. Pain and fear came into his face as the hiccups grew to

pukings, violent ones, on and on until it seemed his chest and frame
must break. Fiddler tried to use only the tips of his fingers to hold
him, but he was like a little bucking pony now. The two halves of
his body were hinged and trying to spring together. His feet kicked
backward hard. Blood pressed into his head so that the glass cuts
poured red and the flesh between his cheeks and eyes got purple-
green. Still he retched and puked, to break in half. Nothing would
come up. Blood squeezed and squeezed into his face, shrinking his
eyes. He was suffocating. Then at last he drooled a sort of blackish,
final slime and quieted to sobbing, trembling.

Fiddler found a stick and scraped the coveralls and Diamond's
head. He was fed up. He wanted to be outside with Chief.

Steering Diamond was like steering an ungreased mechanical man.

Next problem: How to get a wino over a guard net? Fiddler
finally had to just lift him over.

Diamond teetered to fold to the ground.

"No, you've got to stand up, you can't lie down. Taylor will be
in front of his cage and Red will — no, Red'll be at the river, I
guess — and Coca Cola won't make it either, I guess, and Chief and
I'll be working; so it's just you and Taylor to watch all the cages, all
the cats, all the monkeys, all his, the giraffes, Iggy, everything." —
It was funny. You had to laugh at the situation.

"And your first job is to protect the animals from the people. And
your next job is to protect the people from the animals. — You're
not listening, Diamond!" Diamond was asleep, but he was standing
up, at least. Fiddler wound the weak, sweaty fingers among the
strands of the net. "Just hold on. Don't lie down. And shout 'Get
back! Get back!' once in a while so if somebody gets hurt it'll be
his responsibility instead of the show's. And when they ask you a
question say 'Yes ma'am,' if they're a man, and 'No sir,' if they're
a woman, and sometimes they'll go away. Or, better yet, don't say a
thing. There'll be so many people in here you can't breathe. And
the important thing is to keep your hands on the net because if you
step back just two steps the cats'll have you and tear your insides
right through your back."

— Diamond's eyes opened at that. He grasped the net feebly
tighter. Fiddler felt a little sorry for him.

"It's true. But as long as you've got hold of the net you'll know they can't reach you; and don't be scared if they roar, and don't be scared with all the people because things generally work out, and stand up, but don't bother answering anybody."

Diamond held to the net for dear life.

Already townies were massed at the door. The kids who'd earned passes this morning and skipped breakfast and lunch and the other, captive children with their parents; littler kids warbling their cries like the inmates of the birdhouse in a zoo; old ladies with sprigs of catnip for the cats — the whole town. The cats were simmering down, settling to go to sleep. In a way they were probably kind of fond of the townies. That hum-mum-mum of myriad talk put lots of circus guys, as well, pleasantly to sleep.

But *Diamond* hadn't better fall asleep. Diamond hadn't better even hiccup. Fiddler and Chief were the only ones who could stand in front of those cages without welding themselves to that net.

You couldn't worry about things around the circus. Winos were bound to die pretty soon, from the cold and the rain, or falls, or fights, or no food. You had to try and toughen yourself and not worry about them. Fiddler got the tools, to go.

2

THE LION MAN ought to be out working with Chief now, because it looked as though the people wouldn't be let in for a while — the shavings weren't even down on the rings and the hippodrome track — and after that it would be at least an hour before the show started and the trainer would need him. Sometimes the guy tried to get out of his share of the butchering work. Fiddler was making sure he'd have no excuse.

But Fiddler himself was strongly tempted to go in and sit on one of the cushioned seats and forget everything. Being in there was better than drinking, and no bad effects. The entrance between the bleachers and grandstand, where Fiddler stood, was like the thres-

hold to a storybook castle. The only source of light, besides the
entrance gaps, was pinpoint holes high and star-blue-white in the
rope-webbed canvas and the ventilation flaps which ran along the
topmost reach to catch the wind. The centerpoles towered straight
up like cathedral pillars. The silver quarterpoles pointed, rocket-
like, at angles. The rigging also shone aluminum-silver — bits off a
transcontinental train strung in a fabulous, interlocked maze. Crow's-
nest platforms, bars, wires, hoops and globes, bicycles and balancing
poles. And everywhere a welter of cables, ropes and ladders dense
as organ pipes hung down. There wasn't any color — just the dark
and silver-glitter — or maybe, high, high up, a granular, mustied
brown trickling through the canvas. Noise from outside didn't penetrate. It was quiet like a church was quiet; it was cool. The hippodrome had space enough for five acts on the ground and five more
in the air and a grand great rum-tee-tum parade of spangled girls,
all to go on at once. And banked around were seats and seats for
ten thousand people, section upon section upon section, so that
even Brownie couldn't find you — rows long as the big top — so
many, many seats and so much height and breadth and space you
got lost the moment you'd sat down. You forgot what you were
supposed to be doing, where you worked, the kind of life you had
to lead, and, instead, remembered way in the past, planned far for
the future. No one could see you, and you were the size of a mouse
in a world of fanciful clean and hush. When you walked out again
your life would start new as a child's. Bums like Fiddler weren't
allowed in here when there were any townies, but otherwise you'd
always see at least a few guys, lolling on four-dollar seats, playing
the tycoon, or looking up at the expanse of canvas and the intricate
rigging shining, or daydreaming, eyes on their shoes. People got
addicted to it. They always wanted to be sitting in the big top.

Various departments put the canvas up, pulled in the seat wagons,
set up the seats, laid out the rings, hung the rigging, and left. After
they'd left and the dust had sifted down — here was this creation,
magical as a cave of ice or a castle. No one had made it like that.
Most of the people who'd done the work couldn't even set foot in
the place after Doors, they were so drunk and so crummy. And

there weren't any middle stages. You couldn't peek in at eleven-
thirty and see how wonderful it was going to be. Everybody left —
staggered out — and the festooned rigging started glittering, and
the quarterpoles creaked, getting comfortable, and the candy-cane
stripes on the ring curbing looked like the shadows of trees.

Fiddler drew himself away.

Rita, rambling, arrested herself like a sentry with that peculiarly
constant preparedness of hers. Any position she was passing through,
she could stop and be ready to spring.

Joe took Bessie's ear between his lips and then between his teeth,
and then both ears, and then her whole, creasing-up nose. And
Bessie loved it. She opened her gruesome jaws like a steamshovel,
loving it. Joe considered whether to grunt. He put his face to the
corner, the best place, where it would all come right back past his
ears, and formed his lips like a person blowing; but decided no.

Outside, a scoutmaster was checking his troop, nicely in file. Two
of the Sidewall kids, bringing ginger ale in glasses for the ballet
girls, stopped politely to assist him. They pointed and counted the
members aloud. "One . . . Two . . . Three . . . Four . . . " — in
nothing but shorts, camouflaged green, and torn, and round their
heads lavender garters they were wearing as crowns.

It was a good day for using your eyes; Fiddler could enjoy himself.
The sky was a piercing blue, the clouds airy and thin, and the
dynamo sun still going strong. The big top big as the sky rose with
a sleek unruffled surface quality like water but with ridges and
crests hiding much of it so that he saw mostly the peaks. It wasn't
quite symmetrical at every point, and above the sidewall there were
droopings which needed to be guyed tight. The big top was so big
even Magee couldn't have the outside always looking perfect. He
just did the best he could with it.

But the Animal top *was* perfect — slim and light enough to fly,
the flaps tied way out and the wind filling it, waste straw fluffed like
fall leaves and the tool and bucket and food crate crap strewn
around like home; next to it old, indestructible ten-season 12 Wagon
that Fiddler had got kind of fond of too.

Brownie was so used to taking baths out of a pail he made all the normal splashing sounds and yet he wouldn't get the wagon wet a bit.

"Hey, not very many guys going to be standing watch," Fiddler said through the door.

"If anybody don't like it I'll tell 'em to go hire me some more. This hick town — I should have kept that Tombstone!"

Brownie was in the back compartment of the wagon. Chief was working around at the front. Fiddler stopped in the tent for a long drink and took off his shirt. Not that it was especially clean, but if he wanted a red shirt he might as well buy one.

"You got lead in your ass, boy?" Chief said. The blade of the axe lay on his shoulder next to his head, and he turned and rocked it into the meat one-handed, so that it practically shaved off his ear. "I been waiting on you!" There was a great stack of cut meat on the butchering table because the lion man wasn't helping after all and nobody had put it into the barrels.

"I wasn't doing anything. I was just fooling around," Fiddler told him.

Fiddler got the pick and tongs and hauled a block of ice up on the wagon pole and into the front of the wagon and, stabbing like a sewing machine, sent the ice in glittering splinters and silvery snowdrops into the first of the barrels. Then he took more care and split it into shiny, baseball chunks. Chief threw in some of the meat and Fiddler put another layer of ice in and Chief came with more meat. He didn't give Fiddler time to have the ice right. Chief was almost sober now but not much more reasonable than when he'd been drunk. He got impatient, climbed in the wagon. — "You bring the meat and I'll chop the goddam ice."

Of course, with their positions reversed, Fiddler still couldn't keep up with him.

"I'll get the lion man, Chief. We need three."

Chief grunted, "He ain't even worth what you are. Stay here." Chief was both carrying meat and chopping the ice now. He was like a man cleaning rags off a table; he threw the meat around as easy as that. He piled pieces on his shoulders and balanced chunks all up his arms so that they didn't fall.

After the table was cleared, "Now you got plenty time," he warned, meaning that Fiddler had better keep up from then on.

The horses lay on the ground where they'd been dumped, wrapped in a rain-stained scrap of last year's big top. Several hundred bugs were mobbing the canvas — gnats, mosquitoes braving the sun, little, thumbtack flies, rangy long deerflies and fast bluebottle flies like tough bullyboys. Bugs and Animal Department men were the only creatures Nigas allowed around the horses. He'd posted himself nearby. Nigas ate probably one-fivehundredth of the meat but acted as if it all was his. With Chief to help he figured he could fight off anything.

As Chief laid back the canvas fierce flies loud as wasps plunged into the blood. They plopped and waded. The horses had been skinned and quartered but still looked very much like horses, with ribs and rumps and jelly eyes. The blood was stiff and tangled with tissue — hadn't covered everything. Bones and fat stood out the same obscene, stark white in lines and zones. The canvas had gotten very warm from the sun, but, underneath, the meat was *hot!* These horses had hardly stopped running.

Chief slashed handholds for himself and Fiddler in one of the quarters with his knife. Fiddler got the lighter, leg end but even so barely could lift it. Meat was the hardest thing to carry. It did anything not to be lifted. The weight concentrated in the worst place. The blood slipped like grease. The shape was awkward. Unless the slit for the hand was well cut it might rip loose.

"The circus mensy-wens is working, sugar, see? Upseedoo on Daddy's shoulder, sweetie. See the circus menses?"

Chief flung his end on the table so hard Fiddler almost went with it. Chief gripped the axe and pounded it down handle-first so that the blade would stay on for a while. He looked wild and gory enough to be cutting up orphaned babes for a feast. His hands were washed in blood. Speckles of meat were plastered onto his chest and throat and blood was scoured into his skin. He would have felt slippery to touch. The sweat couldn't find room to run, and when he wiped it he smeared on more blood. A new butterfly was pinned to his hat, much bigger than the one before. And he'd taken out the mess of quills he'd gotten off a porcupine in Minnesota. They were stuck in the hat like trophies of war, bristling around the slaughtered butterfly. Blood and meat were in Chief's hair wherever it showed, and his ears might have been clipped by the axe, they were so bloody.

The butchering table was just in front of the wagon pole. Chief stood with his back to the pole and went to work in a swarm of flies, the knife and axe blades flashing sun and the meat appearing to hop around on the table of its own accord, parts of it sailing over his shoulder at Fiddler. He'd hardly touch the meat with the knife before it spread apart and the axe fantastically on the ends of his fingers was rising and chopping again. Chief handled a horse with a marvelous ease — like, taking a bath, his own body. Which part was which, where bones met other bones — he could have done it blindfold, probably just as fast. He flipped the meat under the axe on the point of the knife, wielding both at once like a hearty eater, and, with what fingers he could spare, slung the pieces into the wagon or into the barrels directly, not looking to see them land, knowing that it would be right. And the saw edges of the chopped bones never cut Chief, any more than the cats did when he took their paws in his arms. But Fiddler had to be cautious as hell, with the cats and the bones.

"What have they got there? I'll ask the man. What have you got there?"

"Meat? See meat? Meeeeeat? See the meat? See meat, honey?"

"Let me look. I want to look. Let me look. I want to look. Let me look. I want to look. Let me look. I want. . . . "

The axe head needed to be pounded onto the helve about every ten blows. Several times in the past Chief had forgotten and it had flown off, but no one had been in the way to get killed. Ten of Chief's chops took as long as ten blinks when he got going, and he'd be impatient with the damn axe head and, if he didn't forget to pound it unfailingly, at least he'd do less and less of a job. Fiddler tried to stay on one side of the doorway so that even if the blade came into the wagon he wouldn't be hit. Poor Nigas had no place to hide.

Wherever the flies found blood they were in it, swimming, until it appeared to boil. The flies gleamed a hot, malignant green. Everything the sun had touched was hot. It was no fun working. The heat was a weight.

There was the thw*ock!* of the axe on bone and the schluck in meat and the hiss of the knife and thumping refrain of the head being wedged on the helve and the bone chips' clitter. The split ice knocked and tinkled and heavy meat slabs whispered sailing at Fiddler, rang loud against the barrels. He had an awful time trying to concentrate on the ice with that meat coming at him — and maybe the axe — pieces having to be gotten out of the way of the pieces to follow. Thick and fast they were coming when Fiddler had to go after another block of ice — and piled up chunk on chunk until, just as he was getting back, one fell over out of the wagon into the dirt.

Chief could tell by the sound what had happened.

"I oughta make you lick it clean, Fiddle-diddle!"

"What do you think you are, you bastard! You can do it all your pissing self if you don't think I'm fast enough!"

Chief spun, clenching the axe. "I ain't gonna fool with you, boy! I ain't no nurse! I'm gonna take the sniveling goddam snot out of you! — "

"Indians!" Brownie shouted. "Fight! Brag ! Fight!"

Chief couldn't help but smile, and it was then Fiddler realized he'd been joking.

"Bastard."

"I'll 'bastard' *you* in *two*, Fiddle!" He scowled in make-believe and socked the axe into a bone that spat up chips like shrapnel.

Chief swung into his chopping again as if he were beating a drum. He switched the axe from hand to hand to get a better angle. Flies whizzed and spiraled at his head, eating up the air around him but scared to land. They'd land on Fiddler, though. They bit.

"That's not a nice dog. He growls. Growl, growl, bad dog."

"What is that meat, what an'mal?"

"I said to him, I said . . . so I said . . . I told him . . . Listen, I said. . . . "

With every blow Chief set the meat in place for the next. Now he didn't use the knife at all except for fat. It was like working against a machine that worked faster and faster and faster. The more Chief worked the soberer he got, and the soberer he got the harder he worked. Fiddler was sweating like before lunch — the hot blood spattered didn't help — and he couldn't stop to rub himself with ice. Straw from the cages had gotten clear into his pants. It itched and itched. He was thirsty again. And his fingers ached. You had to pick up meat with your fingers, not so much with your whole hand. He shouldn't have let Chief hurry him; he should have drank a lot more.

It seemed like maybe Chief was forgetting about the blade. — There, finally, he remembered. Fiddler hated to think how fast that meat would be coming if Chief didn't have to stop every half minute. The damn lion man!

Little Nigas had jumped right up on the horses and was about to go off his rocker — the bugs on him like fiends, and now he was almost an island in townies. Chief was an island, too, except for the wagon pole, which gave him an alley of breathing space, but the people were scareder of Chief than of Nigas. Luckily a dog his size could disappear until tomorrow if he bit somebody.

"Of high estate or low, we need God's message in our daily lives," a black-clad man was saying. He had a bunch of booklets. Fiddler shook his head. The man turned to go to Chief. Circus people seemed to be his mark. But Chief frightened him — that impossible grace and the arms wide apart, the arc of the axe, the blood-covered back. And the horse came to pieces easy as cheese. Black-suit placed his palms together and muttered to himself. He went a little to one side of Chief and he began, "Of high estate — "

"Put it down!" Chief interrupted, waving his knife at the table. "Can'tcha see my hands full? I alluz read those books. Maybe they're right. But you fellas" — the man was edging away — "You! — You fellas ain't any better than me. You think you're better. Don'tcha? You alluz think you're better. But you're not. You may be goin' downstairs too. You're no better. Maybe I'm better. Maybe we're all the same."

The pick slipped in the blood globs on Fiddler's hand, and the ice block slipped on the top of the barrel, nearly went on his toes. His arms ached from supporting it and his wrists ached from stabbing and his shoulders ached from hunching over. A fly went into his mouth, which was dry as paste, and he spit it out. But a wing had come off; he spit and spit. Mosquitoes hummed sadistically. He tasted fly. Everything was red, the goo on his arms and his beat-up shoes, the sheet-iron floor. Even the paint on the barrels was red. The ugly slabs of bone and meat flew out of a roiled red haze of sun. Fiddler had to remind himself how accurate Chief was — sometimes couldn't see them. The axe he saw — tricky snap-flickers of glare as if the blade already had darted loose. His hands ached and throbbed from all his scars and stung as if with new cuts from the bones. Blood, blood hid the skin; he couldn't tell if it was really all the horse's. Once a barrel was full it was as heavy as a house to move, and there didn't seem to be room for everything — ice, loose meat on the floor, empty barrels, full ones, boxes of fruit, crates of vegetables, not to mention Fiddler himself. Brownie was having a real leisurely bath in the other compartment, and Fiddler was bitter about it. Guys like Brownie might be good for emergencies, but some bosses worked, too.

The axe blade whirred and snicked and whistled down so hard it would have flown off spinning at two hundred miles an hour, cut through townies three deep. And it would have come backwards almost as hard. Fiddler did everything he possibly could to stay out of the doorway. Dynamite Chief practically worked himself off the ground like a helicopter. It took a great and visible effort for him to stop and fix the axe.

"You look out, you Council Bluff! You look out, you Bluebird-in-your-hat! This is gonna kill ya!"

". . . . Undoubtedly the rudest men I've ever encountered in my life."

A couple of busloads of institution inmates passed. They were usually kept locked in their buses except for the show itself, which was lucky. There were as many townies as flies. You couldn't really see them — only a swarming — there were so many. And Chief in their midst leaned into his chops, arms unbending, rising up on his toes. SZZZZZZchl*uck!* The axe sung. Chief was angry. He worked even harder. The bones were rocks. He worked even harder.

Banging the handle, Chief pointed in the most likely line the head would follow if it flew off. "This thing's gonna hit you!" Parents herded their children to the side, but new people arriving filled in the space almost immediately.

Without the lion man, Fiddler began to doubt that he would be able to last. His fingernails hurt from digging into the meat. Flies were next to his eyes and climbing into his nostrils. All over his body they burrowed and bit. Still he tasted the other one and, dirty as the ice was, put some in his mouth. The townies buzzed and the flies buzzed in such unholy numbers it seemed that Chief fifteen feet away couldn't be talked to — yelled to. The ice in Fiddler's mouth was gone already. Goddam, this day was hot! He was seeing red steam. Wearily he wondered if maybe in the evening there mightn't be a little rain, with thunder and a cool, white sky. Snug in his bunk after tear-down he'd lie, sniffing and listening to it. That was what he'd do.

The sailing meat bashed the barrels. Only the meat was preventing townies from climbing right into the wagon. They ducked their heads in at any pause and shouted questions. One guy tried to climb over the wagon pole and got hit by a chunk. He was going to start telling Chief off, but Chief didn't give him a chance.

"That piece is dirty. I gotta have another piece!" One wrench: the guy was on his knees, head twisted back by the hair. Whirling high, Chief's axe like a tomahawk plunged, jerked up just touching the collarbone. The blade wobbled with the force.

"Now I want you people to get back," Chief said deliberately, not even out of breath. They got back.

"More." More. Many left.

"More." More. Nigas was in the open again. Staunch little Nigas had held his own. Goodness knows what would have been done to the horses if he hadn't been there. Brownie's truck had kids climbing in it. The people Chief had scared away were tittering in the tent, prying like monkeys in the boxes, or fooling around at Brownie's end of the wagon. New townies coming couldn't see why everyone was standing so far back. The inevitable forward march began.

Chief brought another whole quarter to the table by himself, one of the heads sitting up on it grotesquely. After this, five more quarters would be left. The head had to be cracked in half to fit under the bars. It sounded as though Chief were trying to crack another axe. Heads went to Joe and Bessie. They didn't get much meat off them, but they got exercise. — And some of the townies were going to get exercise, too, dodging that snicketing, snap-flashing blade.

Fiddler brought more ice. The meat was clobbering the barrels again — faster now, with a new quarter. Sweat crawled on Fiddler like the flies, and the thickening blood on him itched. If the ice wasn't right the meat would spoil and his cats would all get sick — and Fiddler was gradually falling behind. He quit worrying about being conked by the meat or killed by the axe. He just worked. Red shapes — lizards — galloped in front of his eyes. Hunks of meat seemed to BONG on the barrels even when none had been thrown. He worked, and his arms and his fingers and shoulders ached, and still he was falling behind. Chief was a windmill. Meat endlessly flew.

— "Goddam you, yes, I'm bare! I'm washing my joint, if you want to know." Fiddler heard the door slammed, but Brownie kicked it open, his voice becoming very clear again. "No, don't shut it. It's all part of the show. You come to see the show and you want to see everything. You can see a man's joint, or anything you want to. We're entertainers. We're here for you. It all goes with the show." The ladder clanged dully with his footsteps. Fiddler hoped he was still naked. — No, he had a towel.

"Let's get 'em out of here," Brownie said. Arrowy Nigas rushed at people, leaping to nip like a sheepdog.

"If you were showing your son around you'd want him to see things."

"My son's in jail, ma'am. He raped a woman just about like you. — Take it easy on the kid. You work him too hard," Brownie told Chief.

Chief stopped in amazement. "Work him too hard! That's how

you get a good kid! You don't have a good kid if you don't work him hard!"

Fiddler jumped out of the wagon at that.

"I'm going after the lion man!"

"See what you done?" Chief grinned at Brownie, and started again, blood scoured into his cheeks and splashed on his lips and the quills and butterfly in his hat, his face grave with the teeth showing when the face contorted when the axe sung down.

Fiddler trotted into the big top. His head was very clear — too clear. He was tired. Betty Lou reared up like a menacing whale, streaming gallons, and opened her mouth to fit in a car and chomped her tusks at Fiddler. Besides Betty Lou, only Coca Cola's poor animals were moving around. Fiddler would feed them as soon as the meat work was through.

The well-heeled Front Door Boss was looking to see how soon he could let the suckers in. He was supposed to be raking in money hand over fist, convincing even the silver wagon people the show had several hundred seats less than it did. Fiddler felt like Jack-the-Ripper, passing him. Flies were still on Fiddler and following hard, and he was as soggy as if he'd climbed out of a mudhole, but red. The grandstands were empty, but, like in a nightmare, he felt watched by a crowd. Soundless, he jogged on the sawdust new underfoot. Way high at the top of his mind Chief's chopping tinked in a tiny, hot haze. The magical centerpoles soared and soared like stalks of stars, and that was how high the tinks sounded from. Fiddler was lightheaded — and dripping blood. He felt like a monster, hounded by flies.

The jigs were shoveling shavings in the center ring. They were the only people Fiddler saw right away at the act lion wagon. The wagon was parked beside the ring, low, dark and small. The niggers were throwing the shavings around, pouring it out of sacks into piles and swatting the piles, pretending their shovels were golf sticks. They started singing how they'd spent their pay last night, their twelve bucks. They cakewalked, loose as rag dolls, and spun themselves round-round to voodoo fits, eyes rolling red and streaming tears. "EeeeeeeeeOW!" They folded like accordions and shot erect. "And then, man, I *bit!* You ever stepped on a cat? You ever stuck a pig? Man, that's what that girl did. She went to town!" Showering each other with shavings, bending their bodies supple as snakes, hooting in a storm of sawdust and hurling the full bags at one another. Fiddler couldn't see under the lion wagon because of the clouds of sawdust and the vague light, but he began to see the animals — humorless and bored, their paws lounging out between the bars. The lion man might be sleeping under the wagon. That was where Fiddler would have been, with the paws dangling overhead, crawled in and out without being caught.

The jigs threw sawdust like confetti at a wedding and they hollered wild to beat the band. One guy had no cheekbones. In fact his face sunk in under his eyes just the opposite from cheekbones. It was a mottled black and gray. "Hey, *clear* the road!" he was shouting at another jig whose ass was bigger than his shoulders, who looked like a tenpin. "I'm gonna dust you down. I'm gonna bury you."

Tenpin didn't want to move. "Look out there! Don't you be throwin' them shavin's aroun'! You know what this shovel's good for? It's good for somethin' besides shovelin'."

"Sonofabitch, you come inside of a foot of me with that shovel — wave it around all you want — but you come inside o' one bitchin' foot of me and I'll feed you to them lions. I'll take you right up to that cage and feed you to them lions."

"Them lines wouldn't eat him. They'd rather eat sawdust. They'd rather eat sawdust than that whoozimibob," laughed another jig.

"Listen, I'm luscious. I'd make a meal." Tenpin smacked his fat lips, wet them with spit. "Those lions would love me. I'm their dish. They don't want sawdust." He threw a shovelful at the cats, into their faces. Several sneezed. One brushed at its eyes with its paws. Fiddler couldn't say anything. Words clogged in his throat; but he was getting close enough to stop it with his hands. That was how he wanted to do it, with his hands. The clunkheaded jigs!

The lions fumed. They were youngsters, smaller than Joe and Bessie. They didn't pack the punch.

Another jigaboo banged a shovel on the bars in front of the cat

who'd gotten sawdust in its eyes. "He didn't like that, man. *Now*
he wants to eat you. *Now* you'd taste good." The two of them, the
meal and the shovel-banger, hunched over, horse-laughing, slapping
their knees, dancing a jig. And another snuck behind them, hands
outstretched to goose them both. And another went around the
cage and chanted through it:

> "Hey you out there,
> I'se in this jail an' you is free,
> But don't you make such fun o' me,
> 'Cause I'll get out an' you'll get in
> An' I'll make you wish you'd never been
> So funny."

The lions yearned. Their bodies clenched till not a wrinkle
showed in the hides, tight, trembling with longing. Their pricked
ears were knives. They whetted their claws and butted the bars, not
seeing them. With their *elbows* they could have sprung twenty feet.

If the gooser had reached his two buddies first he would have
sent them jumping right into the bars. But Fiddler's words tumbled
up his throat — "Friggin sonofabitches!" They all three leapt sideways with the warning, raced past the cage. Fiddler began the
chase.

The lions were pitifully eager, quivering like dogs at a screen
door watching rabbits running in the garden. And Fiddler felt like
a dog — no, like a big-chested cat. Their tails switched urgently,
and Fiddler would have done the same, with a tail. He sprinted
next to the cage. Eleven faces flicked around, wide-eyed, pitifully
intent. Men fight with squinted eyes, but Fiddler's opened full like
a cat's. The lions' fierceness hummed in the air and he gulped it in,
sizzling and electric. He was free, and so they sighted on *him* their
yearning, and gave him the wind-speed and tawny bowling leap to
crumple the jigs as they would. He grew, grew. He and the lions
merged to crumple the jigs. At the corner of the cage he swerved,
shortcutting close.

A paw stuck out. He saw it drifting in the air. The sandy hairs between the black toe pads, the yellowed claws emerging. Never trust a strange cat. Two lungfuls of breath burped out. His ribs crunched. He couldn't breathe. There were eleven lions. The waist and midsection was the target. He was tall, with lots of waist. He tried to keep his arms around his face but couldn't make them stay. They went out wrestling at paws, and he poured the energy of his toes into it for a flash — the energy was gone then and the paws stronger and stronger, sanded girders to his spongy hands; it hurt even more to fight than not. Grunts chugged, cranked rapid into strings of dazing firecracker growls. A lot of paws were on him. Lions fight in gangs, tigers alone, and lions beat tigers. He was on fire. Cats kill with their teeth, Chief? Alleycats kill mice with teeth. He couldn't breathe. The elephants blared and rumbled and bawled. The breaths burned, moisture blown on him burned. Young lions — this trainer needed every advantage — fumbling, jostling each other, one even still watching the jigs; they'd never had a man before. Claws clutched him by muscles and ligaments, cords in his body, and furnaces roared in his ears. Cords snapped, and new cords. He lost three fingers on the bars. He couldn't seem to keep them safe. Another finger. They kept going there. They didn't matter. He was on fire. Chief, cats kill with teeth? The eyes wandered moodily, mustard-yellow — he was brought closer and closer — the eyes pointed back. Hot horrible-whiskered slabs of lips, grazed off his nose. They slurped for blood, pig-snuffling growls, they sucked the bars. Couldn't breathe. Couldn't breathe. Men were shrieking and running with stakes. The elephants blared and rumbled and bawled. Scarred on their faces from the whip, on their pug noses, and from fights among themselves, and the deep-dug snarling bulged the scars. They tugged, licked the blood as it came in the cage. The King was pulling tails. Scorching, on fire. The mustard eyes roamed dreamily. No breath, couldn't. A lion bounded and bounded and flipped on its back for a long reach and got Fiddler good. And one by one the goatee points on all the chins flattened until they looked no better than boxer snarling dogs, eyes buried in flame-yellow folds. Back of the wreck of the ribs they groped, tearing and hauling, wincing because of the clattering stakes on the bars. And the fire seared up and burned out his eyes. And strips of face and bone. The honey, fondling hands were gone. The elephants blared and rumbled and bawled. The elephants blared and rumbled

And Chief, Chief was a thickset man, a slow runner, and what could Chief do anyway?